TIME IS A DESERT WIND

Time Is a Desert Wind

by Jaime Gràcia

Ebook ISBN: 979-8-9884610-0-5
Paperback ISBN: 979-8-9884610-1-2
LCCN: 2023910904

Published by Eagle Ridge Group, LLC
Nashville, Tennessee

To Vlasta

Se souvenir des choses du passé n'est pas nécessairement se souvenir des choses telles qu'elles étaient.

[Remembrance of things past is not necessarily remembering things as they were.]

L'amour c'est l'espace et le temps rendus sensibles au cœur.

[Love is space and time rendered perceptible to the heart.]

Marcel Proust

PART I

Chapter 1

Loud knocking vibrated throughout my apartment on the morning of Good Friday. Someone hammered against the front door strongly enough to break it down. Were my neighbors alerting me to a fire? Did smoke and flames engulf our building as I wrapped my robe around myself and cinched the belt? Still confused by the remnants of a dream, I padded to the door.

"Hold on. I'm coming."

Hulking silhouettes flickered behind the blinds in the window.

"Open up. San Francisco PD."

Two detectives stepped in as I unlatched the door, shoving a written order in my hands.

"James Montez? This is a warrant to search your condo. Sit on the couch." A mute and lockjawed uniformed officer followed them and herded me to the sofa. I glanced over the warrant as the policeman stood over me, blocking my path as though I might sprint barefoot for the door and disappear into the mist.

Cold dread seized my guts. The document slipped from my hand to the floor as the room temperature dropped several degrees. I stared at the wall clock across the room, its second hand sweeping away my freedom with every turn.

Meanwhile, the two detectives plundered my condo, rummaging through drawers and cupboards. They collected every personal paper in sight, and a box of floppy disks, and tossed them into cardboard boxes labeled "SFPD" in bright red letters, unplugging my computer from its connecting wires.

No one spoke directly to me, nor did I voice the obscenities I conjured. The front door remained open as I shivered, exposed to the wintry air and my gawking neighbors.

"Time to go. Get dressed," a cop barked before he herded me into my bedroom.

Clothes littered the floor. From the closet, I pulled on the only suit still on a hanger and slipped on my favorite shoes. A detective shook his head as I considered a necktie.

Once I finished dressing, he said, "You're under arrest." He yanked my arms behind me, wrapped icy metal around my wrists, and cinched the cuffs tight.

Neighbors peeked out their windows as the cops dragged me from the building. Humiliated, I kept my head down, almost glad we would never meet again as they perp-walked me to a patrol car and shoved me in the backseat for the ride to the Seventh and Bryant precinct.

At the station, a cop escorted me into a vomit-green interrogation room, removed the cuffs, and left, slamming the door with a decisive click. Under the fluorescent lights, I waited at the table bolted to the scarred linoleum floor. The two-way mirror stared back at me as I struggled to penetrate its surface to examine the lurkers studying me behind the glass.

An inspector with glacial blue eyes entered and sat across from me, making a show of paper shuffling. "This won't take long, Mr. Montez, if you cooperate," he said as he flicked his blond hair out of his eyes. One loose sleeve button complemented his misshapen knotted tie.

"We received an extradition warrant against you for alleged offenses out of our jurisdiction. As a courtesy to the Feds, we picked you up."

The interrogator flipped through the documents.

"The Feds want you for bank fraud."

A lawyer had advised me never to speak to the police without counsel present. I sat quietly.

"Hmm. Nothing to say, Clyde? Where's Bonnie?"

I shrugged at his quip. "May I write something?"

"Sure." The cop tore a page from his notebook and slid the paper toward me with a pen.

I jotted down a name and a phone number. "Here's the info for my lawyer."

"So that's how it is? Are you making a formal request for counsel?"

Still poker-faced, I nodded, lightheaded and fidgeting while sweat rolled down my back.

The inspector gathered the file and exited without another word. The mirror occupied my attention as I kept my face emotionless. Whoever hid behind the glass would have to wait for a confession.

An hour later, a uniformed officer ushered in my attorney, dressed for court in his immaculate gray suit and tie.

"I spoke to the US Attorney's Office. The Feds will make a deal with you," he said.

"If you agree to extradition, the City will not drag your business partners or Ms. Sanchez down here since none are named in the warrant, nor are they under investigation at this time."

"Yes. All right," I said as I tapped my fingers on the arm of the chair, trying to dissipate my nervous energy.

"Fine. Let me pull the paperwork together for your signature. A friend from law school practices where you're going. I'll alert him to your arrival if you like."

"Yes, please do. Thank you for all your help."

"Best of luck to you. Sorry about all this, and I hope everything works out."

"We talked about this before. I'm relieved, in a way. The last several months have been hell, living with stress and uncertainty."

"I don't doubt that for a moment, Mr. Montez."

The attorney returned an hour later. My hand stiffened as I scrawled my signature across the extradition papers without reading them.

Another eleven hours passed in a holding cell until the US Marshals drove me to SFO and loaded me on a plane bound for my destination, a city surrounded by desert, five hundred miles from nowhere. I would not breathe free air again for some time.

Three of us were chained in the back of a dark-blue van. I stared through a tinted window as the vehicle negotiated empty streets before descending into the county jail's subterranean garage.

The sheriffs herded us into an intake room for mugshots and fingerprints. Belts, shoelaces, watches, and other traces of freedom and dignity sloughed off into plastic bags. My relief was palpable after prolonged sitting on the metal benches, which acted like medieval torture devices, precursors to a lifetime of hemorrhoids.

Dumped into a holding tank crowded with sweaty arrestees, I loitered against the wall and avoided eye contact. The faint scent of urine and vomit nauseated me as my restlessness and pounding heart compelled me to grab my chest to keep it from exploding into the room. I craved a shot of whiskey, perhaps a dram of Michter's, to counteract my mouth's sour taste and prevent me from fainting.

Nineteen hours had elapsed since my arrest in San Francisco and extradition to this desert city—an outsider in a room of outsiders. My skin crawled, and I craved a shower.

"You look lost," said a young guy next to me who appeared as distracted as I. Perhaps my Hugo Boss pinstriped suit, white dress shirt, and Bally loafers gave me away.

"I'm sure I'll make bail," I muttered, looking away.

"Sure. We all want to walk in the sun again. What did you do, rob a bank?"

"Sort of. I bounced some checks . . . " Didn't my lawyer tell me not to discuss my case?

"Cool. My little sister's old man beat the hell out of her, so I hurt him bad. It was the only way to stop him from killing her."

"Sorry." Claustrophobic, I stepped to the window to examine the hall and escape some flatulence.

After several hours, I stood before a white-haired sexagenarian night judge with thick-lensed glasses who set my *pro forma* bond at $135,000. A simple listing of my crimes and a booking number defined the totality of my identity.

A sheriff steered those of us who had not bonded out into a holding area and ordered us to remove our street clothes. Another officer conducted a cavity search.

"All right, men, assuming you still are—open your mouths wide. Lift your nut sacks, right and left. That's it. Now, turn around, bend over, and spread 'em."

I shivered and stared at the floor, clammy with cold sweat, as I followed instructions. After the search, the sheriffs powdered us with an anti-lice compound before hosing us down.

The stinging water left me trembling as much from shame as from cold. We donned jail garb—faded blue pajama-like clothes and plastic flip-flops. An elevator took us to a cellblock or pod where I would remain for an indeterminate time. The living nightmare that began that day became real and inescapable.

Don't worry, my love. I am with you, always.
I know, chérie. I'm sorry about everything.

Chapter 2

I remained interred in the county's concrete tomb as days, nights, and weeks elapsed without natural light. Eons passed—unknown, forgotten, unremarked—as my circadian rhythms adapted to unfamiliar patterns of incarcerated living.

Immured under the artificial lights, I slept whenever I could and laid awake at night, either reading or staring at the walls or ceiling until I mapped every crack and indentation, searching for a way out.

Hazy light shone through the glass slats in the cell door, bright enough to read but sufficiently weak to induce blurred vision in my dreams. Trapped in a personal wasteland, I recalled Eliot's verse: *I read, much of the night, and go south in the winter.* For me, wintertime never ended.

The reality of jail often interrupted my daydreams. The doors to our cells remained open for sixteen hours. The pod lights dimmed at ten p.m. and announced breakfast at six. Some of us lounged in the dayroom while others lingered in their cells, usually asleep. At lights-out, the TV powered off, and I endured the grinding of the ventilation system, the usual clinks and clanks, and the other prisoners' snoring, grunts, and farts until the cycle rebooted in the morning.

Poorly shielded against the overhead vent that blasted cold air, I shivered under a thin, woolly blanket. Once, a sheriff took pity when she spotted how I trembled and gave me a second cover, which I wrapped around me like a shroud. The next day, someone stole it. Anything coveted or of value, left unguarded, disappeared.

Meals in covered trays, loaded on a metal cart with unoiled wheels, rolled in three times a day. The fare arrived at room temperature, bland and uninspired, with enough nutritional content to keep our bodies alive but not much else.

Relief from eating dissipated as I picked at my food and ate only enough to suppress my hunger, giving the rest to my greedy compatriots, who acted as though each meal might be their last. A detainee beside me waited until I pushed my half-eaten meal away.

"Hey man, you gonna eat that?"

"Help yourself. I'm done."

Food provided a much-needed break from the monotony of listless and routine days. For me, the meal deliveries served as markers to pace off an otherwise long and uneventful journey to somewhere yet unknown. We received meatloaf on Tuesdays, Salisbury steak on Thursdays, and on Fridays, fish parts, all over-salted. Not with saltpeter, I hoped.

Sleep deprivation and anger fueled my rage, which found no outlets and inevitably turned to me as its focus. One day I lost the desire to eat. The capitulation did not come from measured thought, determination to make a point, or noble motivation. I didn't consider myself a political prisoner on a hunger strike. Perhaps the dull routine and hopelessness compelled an extreme response such as fasting.

On the fourth day, a guard realized I no longer picked up meals since one extra tray remained. He dropped by my cell to check on me. I lay on my bunk, too weak to sit up, with barely enough energy to open my eyes and answer his questions. Two sheriffs helped me to my feet, cuffed my hands in front, and escorted me to the infirmary, where a nurse performed a perfunctory physical.

"When did you last eat?" she asked, her forehead creased with concern.

"Several days ago."

"Are you ill?"

"Yes."

"Symptoms?

"Weakness, stomach cramps, fatigue, boredom, the usual." Speaking drained me.

The nurse sought to convince me to eat again, but I shook my head. Hunger became easier to bear the longer I resisted food. She gave me water in a plastic cup and left the room. The door lock clicked into place.

The small examination room tightened in on me as I glanced around, touched my face, squinted my eyes, and took a deep breath as though taking inventory would somehow confirm my existence. Not only hunger but fear gnawed at my insides, the kind of fear that overwhelmed the body, reducing it to the primordial.

The door opened; its movement yanked me back from the pit. A tall man wearing a white coat, with graying hair and a small goatee, entered and sat on a stool. Without introducing himself, he asked me a question.

"There's no point in eating," I said. "What I need are sunlight and unfiltered air."

The physician nodded while he took notes on a chart. He glanced up at me, his gaze unwavering, to ascertain my sincerity or expose me as a hustler.

"Are you depressed? Suicidal?"

"Suicide is for people who want to end their lives. I don't care either way."

"Is life so bad here?"

A joke, I thought, but no, he misunderstood or didn't care what happened beyond his safe little office. "Spend four months upstairs in a cage with a bunch of lunatics and ask me again."

His knitted eyebrows suggested he didn't like my answer. "If I temporarily transfer you to a unit where you can go outside daily, will you start eating again? Otherwise, we will strap you down and start feeding you intravenously. Neither of us wants that."

The doctor waited for my response as I mulled over his offer and heard myself answer.

"Good. Let me find you more water and some fresh fruit. Once you finish eating, I'll move you to a facility where you will recover in no time."

Too drained to speak, I nodded. The nurse brought in apple and orange slices, which I nibbled, the sweetness reminding me of days long ago by a creek at the base of a mountain, on a yellow cotton blanket, under the shade of oak trees, when life had meaning and I was happy.

True to his word, the doctor processed my transfer to the new Unit, the county jail's version of Bellevue. Restrained in the back of a police van heading southwest, I stared through the wire-meshed window at the sun, which floated on the horizon shrouded in red dust. We pulled into the psych ward—a desert satellite of single-story buildings that occupied several acres of desolation at the edge of town, miles from residential areas.

Chain-link fences rimmed with concertina wire shielded the complex, with a double-fenced front gate. Two sheriffs guarded the sally port armed with sidearms and shotguns. We entered and stopped in front of a nondescript brick structure. Random thoughts of gray PSYOP experiments perpetrated on unsuspecting prisoners crossed my mind.

The officers offloaded me from the van and removed the leg chains to allow me to walk instead of hobbling. No one spoke. We passed through massive glass doors into a spacious room littered with folding tables and chairs and an old television on a rollable stand. The enclosure supported high ceilings with long eave windows, blanketed with a dirty brown patina of dust.

Several offices or conference rooms encircled the interior. The place reminded me of a basement rec room suitable for AA meetings. Disheartened, I asked myself how staying here might improve my mental health. Despite my initial impressions, I appreciated the break from the claustrophobic central jail's hermetically sealed concrete and steel.

The transport guards ushered me through a double metal door with centered panes of reinforced glass, unlocked the handcuffs, and put me on a chair. The cells surrounded a dayroom lit by fluorescent lights and more high windows where sunlight filtered through. Dust particles danced in the beams.

A middle-aged woman dressed in a sheriff's uniform and carrying a clipboard greeted me. Forgetting where I was, I offered a hand.

"We don't shake hands here. I'm Mrs. Olivieri, the night nurse." She examined the sheet on her clipboard. "What medications are you taking?"

"None, ma'am."

"Really? Let's take the nickel tour before I show you to your bunk. Over there is the lavatory, and beyond that, the outside patio."

I followed her around the dayroom furnished with two couches covered with clear plastic.

"The dormitories wrap around this main room. There are some rules you must follow. Are you listening?"

Officer Olivieri caught me eying a bookshelf filled with paperbacks.

"Yes, ma'am. There are rules."

"Right. All meals are mandatory. After breakfast, you may not disappear into your cell. You must hang out here in the dayroom or on the patio. After lunch, you may return to your room for a nap if you wish."

"I understand."

"Good. Follow me."

She led me to a single-manned cell. For months, I had dreamed of a minute of solitude. Suddenly exhausted, I dropped to the hard bunk and fell into a dreamless sleep until an officer stuck his head in to alert me to dinner.

The same vendor prepared the fare for the ward and the central lockup. I picked at what might be Salisbury steak (Thursday) and a spoonful of boiled, tasteless corn, then returned to my cell. On the way back, I headed to the bookshelf and grabbed the thickest book available: *The Fountainhead* by Ayn Rand.

Daily life in the asylum unfolded in a controlled fashion, but was much less oppressive than in my previous billet. We received an obligatory breakfast at seven and mingled outside our cells for the next three hours, presumably to limit our social isolation.

A nurse dressed in a white uniform rolled the med cart into our sanctuary twice daily to dispense pharmaceuticals to my doped-up compatriots. The drugs left them near zombies. I appreciated sobriety and clear thinking for the first time in many years. If offered, I would refuse any antidepressant medications.

During the morning exiles, we loitered in the well-lit dayroom or out on the chairless patio, a twenty-by-twenty-foot-square of concrete bathed by the desert sunlight. I favored the deck in the mornings and early afternoons before the heat became unbearable.

Between two and four, with the desert sun overhead, the sunshine scorched our barren courtyard hot enough to melt rubber. The blue, shimmering sky stretched across us like a canvas tent. The walls disappeared from a particular position, and the uninterrupted, cloudless expanse invoked the illusion of freedom.

I craved the warmth of sunlight and fresh air and spent as much time outdoors as possible. The ubiquitous wind vibrated through breaks in the masonry somewhere in a serenading pattern only revealed after passive listening. As the self-appointed cataloger of wind-borne songs, I memorized each one, believing I might be called upon to testify someday.

At 3:00 p.m., we reported to our cells for the count, and by 3:30, I went back outside to follow the sun as it dipped below the high patio wall. Our minders enforced the 6 o'clock curfew and nudged us back into our monastic dormitories for a few hours of quiet meditation and prayer. *Just kidding.*

The cell doors remained unlocked because the compartments contained no toilet or sink. Without needing to seek permission, we crossed the dayroom to use the communal bathroom when needed. Ensconced in my bunk, I read until the lights dimmed at 9 o'clock. Enough illumination filtered in from the dayroom to read the pages if I sat on the floor near the cell opening.

I doubted the night shift cared for this ritual of mine, but they never said anything.

Regular catnaps let me read through much of the night until I passed out and collapsed on my bed to await the institutional matins when the sun rose, stirring the building from sleep.

No one, including the staff, spoke to me in those early days. There were five of us psych patients when I arrived. We existed as phantoms, separate, with no need to acknowledge each other, each of us abiding in our personal slice of time and space. I shunned conversation and avoided anyone who tried to disrupt my self-imposed social isolation and vow of silence.

I learned from the *Upanishads* that silence helped the novice resist the allures of *samara,* or the "world." Something compelled me to ward off the surreal world of the criminal justice system and not internalize the Buñuelian spectacle around me. Images from Buñuel's *The Exterminating Angel* haunted me, where the guests sought to leave the room but could not bring themselves to cross the threshold to freedom.

A staff member administered the Minnesota Multiphasic Personality Inventory, the first of three tests I received while incarcerated. The exam was a standardized psychometric evaluation of adult personality and psychopathology, a therapeutic tool to assess our anxiety, self-esteem, depression, and other social issues deemed *irregular.* The material asked the same questions several times to gauge the validity of the answers.

The test givers wanted to determine whether I was truthful, lying, faking well, feigning illness, being defensive, or evasive. I answered truthfully and completed the exercise in a couple of hours. Yet, nothing came of the activity: no follow-ups, no questions, no subsequent tests, and no interviews related to my responses. Like most things in jail, I found the MMPI a pointless activity and perhaps a charade.

I attended, however, two one-on-one meetings with a psychologist during my six-week stay. The first conference went over feelings and coping, I suppose, to evaluate my mental health and adjustment to my new environment. The last session proved more insightful.

The psychologist, a thin, balding man not much older than me, wearing the requisite white coat and wire-rimmed glasses, sat across the table in one of the conference rooms. He blinked excessively and wore a lingering odor of cigarette smoke on his clothes. Brownish-yellow stains dyed the fingertips on his right hand.

"How are you doing today?" he asked affably, his baritone voice belying his appearance.

"All right, I guess, the same as always."

"What do you consider the 'same as always?'"

"Bored, depressed, tired."

"Suicidal?"

"I don't know, maybe. I guess not."

"You're uncertain?" he asked.

"If I were certain, I might be dead already."

The psychologist flipped through his notes. "How do you feel about your crime?"

"*Alleged* crime," I said. "Not something I should talk about, except for conversations with my lawyer."

"Understood." More note scanning. "Tell me about your parents."

"My mother and stepfather live in California in the house where I lived since I was eight."

"Do you get along with them?"

"Yes. I visit my folks whenever I'm in town and on most holidays."

"What was your home life like?"

"Okay, I guess. I had few friends, so I read a lot in my room. My parents worked, and when together, they always argued. These days they don't bicker. Sometimes they act more like roommates than husband and wife."

"But you had some friends?"

"Until I was twelve. My friends formed a rock band and excluded me because I couldn't play an instrument or sing, so I kept to myself much of the time. I read, hiked in the hills behind my house, or hung out in a cemetery." He raised his eyebrows at this last revelation.

"Why a cemetery?"

"The serenity and peace attracted me. One resident, a young girl, became my favorite."

"Who was this girl?"

"Her name was Charlotte Bell. She died during the Spanish Flu pandemic. I would sit on her gravestone and write in my journal or read poetry and novels to her out loud."

"Charlotte must have been a marvelous listener."

"Yes. Exceptionally attentive."

"Why her?"

"Charlotte lay in a shady but well-lit spot. She died around my age. Although buried fifty-odd years ago, we shared a kinship."

"What do you mean?" he asked, nodding slowly.

"I imagined her alone, scared, dying inside as the illness destroyed her health and carried her off so young. Knowing I wouldn't celebrate my next birthday, what would I do in her place?"

"You exhibit imagination and empathy."

I stretched out my fingers, considering his statement. "Sometimes I imagine too much."

The psychologist fingered the pack of Chesterfields in front of him.

"Go ahead and smoke. I don't mind." He smiled, grateful for the lifeline.

"Smoking is not allowed inside the building." The psychologist placed the cigarettes in his coat pocket. "Give me five. I'll be right back," as he jumped up and ran outdoors for his nicotine fix—unprofessional behavior.

On his return, the shrink acted a little embarrassed.

"You were talking about Charlotte. Do you know whether she suffered alone without friends or family?"

"No. I'm projecting, of course. How could I know? She died in 1919. No one had been buried in that cemetery since 1943."

"How do you know?"

"By looking at the dates on the headstones."

"Oh, right. Tell me about your adolescence, in general."

"Nobody in my circle shared my interests, and I didn't care about theirs, so I became an outsider, unable to fit in. Charlotte cared in my imagination." Silence settled over the room as my confessor jotted some notes.

"You mentioned growing up with your mother and stepfather. What about your biological father?"

"We never lived together. Dad collected me twice a month on weekends."

"Were you close?

I examined my folded hands and thought for a moment. "Not really. We talked a lot about things, but he was guarded, hard to reach, and authoritarian. My alienation extended to him, too, I suppose."

"Would you say your father was strict with you?"

"I'd say so. Seeing eye-to-eye with the man never came easy. He grew up in a different culture, the Dominican Republic."

"In the Caribbean. I spent a week in Puerto Plata on vacation. Gorgeous resort."

"Having traveled since, I matured, understanding Latin American values better. I appreciate Dad more now than when he was alive."

"Tell me about his passing."

"You mean his death?"

"Yes, his death."

"In my senior year of high school, Dad told me he was leaving Los Angeles to return to the DR. We agreed to meet at his Santa Monica apartment on Friday to spend one last weekend before he left. When I arrived, without saying hello, he laid into me about my blue jeans, which he considered working class, and the length of my hair. My hair was a little unkempt, but not too long. He wouldn't let it go, ragging me about how he didn't want a hippie son and how I disappointed him.

"The fact that UC Berkeley, one of the best schools in the country, accepted me didn't matter to him. Disgusted, I said, 'Bon voyage,' and walked out. We didn't speak for four years."

"No phone calls or letters?" The compassion in his voice touched me.

"Some letters, which I ignored. Lots of times, I thought about contacting him but didn't. Looking back, I wish I hadn't been so stubborn. Death puts an end to any sort of resolution." My voice betrayed my regret. I sighed as my hands fell to my side.

"The summer after graduation, I took a long trip to México. Before I left, I got a letter from his new wife, who hoped to encourage reconciliation. She invited me to come to Santo Domingo. Adita left me an open ticket to hop over whenever I wanted."

"What did you do?"

"At the end of my trip, I sat in a little café in Mérida, beer in hand, nursing a hangover, a bit sorry for myself, so I flew to Santo Domingo."

"Go on," the shrink urged as I drifted for a moment, remembering.

"My father met me at the airport, and we tried to rebuild our relationship. I spent a month with him before we flew to New York to stay with some cousins in the Bronx. After the visit, we drove to JFK. Dad hugged me goodbye, and I boarded the 9:30 redeye to Los Angeles."

"You retain clear memories of those events." The dispiriting impact of those days welled up inside.

"Yes," my voice wavered. "The departure gate was the last time I saw Dad alive. Six months later, he died. My stepmother called me the day after to give me the news. The funeral would be on Thursday. Adita wanted me to fly down."

"How'd that go?"

"It didn't. I skipped the service, giving work commitments as a lame excuse. The truth is I couldn't bear to attend another funeral. I hate them."

"Did you achieve any reconciliation or closure over your father's unexpected death?"

"No. I ignored the pain and anger over losing the people I loved for years. How I handle death could use some improvement."

"Dealing with the passing of loved ones is a skill none of us want to hone."

Months of remembering, of reliving, the things I never said, that I will never say, crashed over me in the county jail psych ward like a tidal wave of unresolved emotions, leaving me gasping.

The psychologist pushed over a box of tissues. I missed my dad yet refused to forgive him for his ambivalence, his focus on my appearance, and for not being around or making himself available when I needed him.

Anger, guilt, and regret, commingled with diminished self-esteem, depression, and self-loathing, became my fellow travelers. Exhausted, I collapsed in my chair, overwhelmed by emotional stress and the looming certainty of prison.

"Together, we made some progress today," the shrink said as he closed my file and collected his smokes. I nodded slightly.

On the last Friday of August, a transport crew dropped in to move me back to the central jail. No explanation, no bon voyage party, no exit interview, only a "you're shipping out now," and into the cuffs and belly chains I went. Too bad I hadn't finished Dostoevsky's *Crime and Punishment*, a perfect read for jail time.

CHAPTER 3

The criminal justice system's labyrinthine cavern employed the county jail as its gatekeeper. Stretched across the portcullis warned the flashing red sign: "Abandon Hope All Who Enter Here." Virgil would not guide me after his experience with Dante, nor would Beatrice lower herself to greet me in Purgatory. Navigation of these circles fell to me alone.

On a remote, clear day, the sun rose in the west two days before Christmas. Months of wrangling between my attorney and the prosecutor finally produced a plea agreement I would accept. My lawyer explained that the prosecutor's boss pressured him to clear as many cases as possible since the county DA was up for reelection next year. The agreement shaved two years off my sentence.

A day after my plea bargain hearing, the county remanded me into the Department of Corrections' custody to serve my term. The trial of my character began, my past adjudicated, the present unknown, and the future beyond the horizon.

"Here's your Department of Corrections ID number. Memorize it," said the pudgy corrections officer as he slid the plastic badge toward me. "Keep it with you. Next."

I picked up the photo ID and examined the laminated card: a grainy black-and-white photo, my hair disheveled, my eyes half-closed, a face without emotion, my number stamped in bold type, and my last name misspelled.

The error bothered me, but I decided I was there to be corrected, not for me to correct them.

The next officer down the Intake line glared at me.

"Roll your sleeves up, arms out, palms up. Turn them over."

"What are you looking for?" I asked.

"Scars, tattoos, any distinguishing marks. You're clean enough. Take a seat."

I became a cipher, tagged and cataloged, identified by number, not by name. The buzzing overhead lights gave me a headache. Endless waiting didn't help.

Seventeen newly minted felons sat around me on bare metal benches worn smooth, the finish long rubbed away by men like us who shuffled through this shabby room on their way to prison assignments across the state. Sleepy, hungry, and oblivious, we waited without speaking for the next phase of our indoctrination.

From the onset, my incarceration gave rise to a series of subtractions, a paring away of my old life layer by layer to expose what lay beneath. First, my clothes, dignity, and identity disappeared, replaced by shame. The ability to think slipped away as I languished in a cell, overwhelmed by boredom and angst. The will to resist my fate evaporated until only numbness and ambivalence remained. Exhausted, I settled in among my fellow inmates in a windowless cage to await more humiliation as my IQ dropped another point.

The COs herded us into a desk-filled classroom, the sort of place troublemakers congregated after school for detention. Fluorescent lights emitted an irritating buzz, illuminating walls that were painted Institutional Flesh and had been untouched since the Goldwater era. Not only the room, but the facility itself embraced the Good-Enough-For-Government-Work attitude.

A tired officer perched behind a scratched, unvarnished wooden desk. It reminded me of a bureau one might find at a second-hand store. The proctor drummed his fingers as we took our seats. His long face, oversized glasses, and graying hair endowed him with an academic demeanor. Two stacks of exam booklets and a box of No. 2 pencils waited for us.

"How many of you read and understand English?" About half the hands went up, and the CO handed out booklets and pencils to us: the Stanford-Binet Intelligence Test. He repeated the same question in gringo-accented Spanish. Five hands waved around.

Half the inmates around me appeared Hispanic, some native-born, but most from México or Central America. The officer droned on, first in English and then in Spanish, about how this timed test was mandatory, how to mark our answers, and how we must turn in our pencils at the end. The class fidgeted. At last, he said. "Any questions? ¿Preguntas? Begin. Comiencen."

I opened the test and read the first question—*déjà vu*. I considered that answering every item wrong would be as difficult as answering the questions correctly. DOC would think I had the IQ of a plant or, worse, a smart-ass. Why not play along and perform the exercise as though the results mattered?

Why did anyone care about our intelligence? Were violent misconduct and an individual's intelligence negatively correlated? Jail taught me that those most frustrated were the brightest. The least intelligent found no need to bemoan their fate and accepted what came. Perhaps Thomas Gray was right: *ignorance is bliss*. Orwell would agree.

After completing the exam, I brought my materials to the proctor and laid them out. He regarded me with surprise.

"Done already? Did you answer all the questions?"

"Sure I did. Test-taking is my forte."

"We'll see."

From my seat, I continued examining the faded paint and the cobwebs hanging from the corners where the walls met the ceiling. The CO applied a template to my answer sheet and corrected my responses. I suppressed a self-satisfied smirk and pretended indifference.

From the moment of my arrest, an inescapable impulse compelled me forward like an impending car crash when the crunch of metal and glass became unavoidable. Sentenced to seven years, I would complete thirty-nine months before parole. I endured nine months in the county jail, the rest in a sprawling, pentagon-shaped facility painted battleship gray thirty miles west from downtown, encircled by rattlesnake-infested desert.

The criminal justice system surrounded me as a vast cavern with one entrance and exit. Loyal, underpaid, and poorly educated apparatchiks guarded the realm, subsuming their blind obedience to rules and protocol to make them amenable servants of the bureaucracy.

The cavern operated its roads, buildings, walkways, supplies, and fields, adorned by high chain-link fences topped by well-honed razor wire. The morning dew glistened on its shimmering machined blades and belied its menacing beauty. I hated the cavern but admired its unyielding efficiency for restraining so many by so few.

My droogs and I lived as shadows, our backs to the light, our eyes on the gray cavern walls. We strove to blink away from all that came before and not dwell on the future. Meaningless activity burdened our days and nights until we accepted the tediousness. I sought calmness and contrition in the chaos, knowing someday I would turn and follow the light.

Moll Flanders, the Patron Saint of Criminal Justice, said it best 300 years ago: "We resolve to spend the remainder of our years in sincere penitence for the wicked lives we have led."

Amen, sister.

Chapter 4

Governments built prisons miles from nowhere for "public safety" and to bring jobs to areas where few live. Five days after my IQ test, the department transferred me to a sprawling complex beyond the city. The bus turned off the freeway and followed a road lined with old-growth trees on the facility's leeward side.

We rolled up on a group of battleship-gray buildings clustered around the corners of a pentagon. Perhaps the department obtained a discount on Navy surplus paint. DOC covered every prison throughout the state in the same lackluster color. Such uniformity made perfect sense to the bureaucratic mind.

The architect who designed the prison placed the administrative offices and the law library at the pinnacle. The northeast corner held minimum security, the southwest corner the women's prison, and the northwest hosted the print shop and other prison industries. My Unit, a medium-security facility, occupied the southeast.

Handcuffed and trussed with belly chains, we hobbled off the bus and into a large room. The corrections officers conducted a thorough cavity search before swapping our faded jail garb for standard-issue prison clothes: blue jeans, blue chambray shirts, white t-shirts, and boxers, and brown boots with notched heels to identify us should we escape and not remember to change our footwear. We each received a toothbrush, toothpaste, soap, a comb, a disposable razor, and a spork—all my worldly possessions in a plastic bag.

The officers lined us up outside like military recruits while we waited. A senior citizen idled next to me. Short, gray, stooped but solidly built, he shifted from one leg to the next, trying to shake off some nervous energy.

"Damn it," he said, "I'm back in the army, standing around with a gaggle of whimpering cadets."

"The whining's just allergies from all this dust."

"If you say so," the man said.

The head corrections officer, or captain, gave us a rehearsed speech about how we had been sentenced, and if we wanted to *flourish*, we should be on our best behavior, follow the rules, and all would be well. Blah. Blah. Blah. In a voice a little too loud, the old guy called him a "hotel bell captain," which triggered snickers.

The captain, an enormous black man and former drill sergeant in a previous life, stopped talking and glared at us, freezing us in place.

"You convicts have anything to say?"

Silence. We stared straight ahead or at our feet. The bell captain sermonized for another ten minutes. For the first time in nine months—not counting the psych ward—I breathed fresh but dusty air, standing in full sunshine, content to ignore the harangue, savor the bright sun, and ponder if the prison commissary sold sunglasses.

After the speech, the comedian who made the crack about the bellman turned to me: "I'm Darryl MacDonald. Call me Mac." We shook hands.

Another corrections officer marched us to Intake Yard A. Our group underwent orientation for a week, including another aptitude test, before being assigned to our permanent cells in yards B, C, or D.

"You got a roommate yet?" Mac asked me as we stood in line for our assignments. "My preference is someone who can complete full sentences. Know what I mean?"

"We can choose our cellies?"

"Hell yeah. Watch and learn, son."

Mac approached the officer and explained how we wanted to bunk together. The assignment CO, a military vet Mac had chatted up during the week, made the change.

"See? You gain an edge if you hobnob with the right folks."

Mac and I became cellies.

"Do you mind if I take the bottom bunk? My leg injury makes it hard for me to bend or put too much pressure on it. I got shot in the calf."

"No problem."

On the far end of the last section, Yard D became our *home*. The housing units resembled a two-story Motel 6 arranged like a series of W's, i.e., WW. Each two-man cell held two metal stacked bunks, a sink, and a lidless stainless-steel toilet, and was "air-conditioned" year-round by swamp coolers on the roof. A metal door with a vertical slit of reinforced glass opened on 80 square feet of concrete floor. Two sizable metal drawers on wheels to store clothes and personal items fit in a slot underneath the lower bunk.

We learned to adapt to the shrunken world squeezed into several acres draped with blue skies from east to west and mountains in the north with snow-covered peaks.

Mac said, "If you've ever wondered what it's like to be trapped in a schoolyard surrounded by sniveling brats, you're about to find out."

"That knowledge hasn't been high on my must-know list."

A line of mature trees planted together formed a windbreak to the south, a live channel to protect once-irrigated farms that were long abandoned. Old-growth trees now served to shield the complex from passersby on the Interstate. I stood facing southeast and listened for birds or insects or the wind, my vision interrupted by chain-link fences, always a reminder of where I was.

Gusts out of the southeast carried the muffled rumble of speeding cars moving up and down the highway. Drivers were unaware of the prison except for the ominous sign: *Correction Facility Area: Do Not Pick Up Hitchhikers.*

Armed guards piloted small, white pickups about the facility's perimeter in opposite directions every twenty minutes, perpetual guardians armed with shotguns and radios, ever vigilant for the rare escape.

Only three reliable ways existed for a convict to exit the prison: through the front gate, in a body bag, or by helicopter. Some tried to scale the fifteen-foot-high fences, but never successfully.

"Never try to escape," Mac said one morning as we chatted in line, waiting for breakfast.

"Jailbreaks add five years to your sentence, and you must do every day."

"The thought never crossed my mind." A lie. Every day since I arrived, I fantasized about making a Great Escape like in that movie with Steve McQueen.

Little grew on the prison grounds besides sparse grass kept alive by an unknown water source. Limited moisture, blasts of wind, and constant uprooting of anything green that might conceal an inmate kept the landscape barren. Plenty of choking dust swirled into clouds blanketing everything with grit without water and vegetation to hold the soil.

All sides of the razor-tipped chain-link fences separated bare, raked areas that resembled well-maintained Japanese gardens with uniform combed patterns to capture the footprints of anyone who trespassed in the forbidden zones. Those who approached the boundary triggered a strident warning over the loudspeaker from the panoptic Yahweh on high.

Prisoners without a medical deferment had to take a job, but this was one of the few regulations not strictly enforced. To stay occupied, I spent my mornings raking rocks near the perimeter as any Buddhist monk in perfect mindfulness.

My fellow grunts complained about our tedious task under the hot sun, yet I refused to acknowledge the work as punishment. I smoothed out my assigned terrain in precise rows to resemble ripples in water, removing the larger stones until a mouse could not thread across the sand without disturbing my Zen-like surfaces. The other prisoners thought I was *completemente loco*. We disagreed on the philosophy: *a job not worth doing is not worth doing well*. Still, I put in my twenty hours a week at ten cents an hour without complaint. Who knew Zen gardening was my métier?

I struggled to overcome the relentless ennui, the tendency to disengage, but my mood lightened when I discovered each yard contained a library. With books, I could survive anything. The library, nothing more than a concrete room with a single window, graced the second tier at the top of straight stairs and offered a precarious escape from the monotony of prison. A swamp cooler maintained a tolerable temperature on the hottest days, but the book room was still a furnace.

Two half-filled floor-to-ceiling bookshelves covered the back wall. A metal desk, riveted to the floor, and folding chairs completed the simple décor.

The inmate librarian managed the collection with a plastic box of 3x5 index cards, printing one's name, cell, and ID number on the card for as long as the borrower wanted. No practical way existed to enforce checkout time limits. Prison rules, however, restricted borrowers to two books in their cell.

After gardening, I hung out with a paperback in the hot afternoons or engaged in small talk with the librarian. I dragged a chair near the door to catch a breeze and zipped through several books a week. Acclimating to the heat took a while, but I barely noticed after the first year.

Most inmates, men of different upbringings, life experiences, cultures, languages, and interests, showed no interest in books. The library boasted a dozen regulars out of 120 assigned to Yard D. Few people read because many were either functionally illiterate or unable to read English.

Some disturbed individuals behaved like ordinary guys, and I treated them as such until I learned of their crimes, ideas, or warped outlooks.

Not long after I settled into my digs with Mac, the neighbor next door dropped by one day to borrow a smoke.

"Sorry, I don't have any. My cellie doesn't smoke either."

"Too bad. I'm Fyfe."

"Call me Jim."

Fyfe rolled his sleeves halfway up, exposing scars on both arms. In my naivete, I asked him about them.

"I'm a cutter," he said as though it explained everything.

"All right."

"Yeah. Since I got back from 'Nam, I cut away my sins for the people I killed. Got a few more to go before I'm even."

We didn't understand PTSD in those days, but he embodied it if anyone did.

"Looks painful," I said.

"That's the point, man." Fyfe launched into gruesome stories, about hand-to-hand combat in the jungles, that turned my stomach. Mac rescued me.

"Hey, Fyfe. What's up?"

"He's looking for a cigarette," I said.

"Try Bill in 6A."

"Yeah, thanks, Mac." Fyfe took off.

"Fyfe the Knife's a real burnout. Stay clear of him. Too many jungle drugs."

"So I gathered. I'm never getting high again."

Drug dealing, burglaries, and assaults made up most of the offenses. Most convicts were harmless, but some skirted close to an edge I didn't want to approach. Mac advised me to stick to the less dangerous and more intelligent white-collar types. Excellent advice.

I embodied Heinlein's *stranger in a strange land* who struggled to understand the alien world around him. Over time, however, I located a cadre of kindred spirits with whom an intelligent conversation about something other than the guards, the weather, or the latest episode of *Cheers* was possible.

Brian Sullivan, the librarian, and I became friendly. Brian grew into an autodidact during his incarceration.

"Before, I never had much time for reading. Card games and TV kept me busy, but tedium in this hellhole persuaded me to pick up a book one day and start reading," Brian said as he reshelved some books.

"By now, you've probably figured out not much goes on here. Reading's a worthy pastime. Now it's all I do."

"All I did for four years in college was read and write."

Brian resembled a stereotypical librarian: a slight, soft-spoken nerd with unkempt hair, poorly cut—an inmate barber I avoided—and black-rimmed glasses.

"One year of college was all I could take before I dropped out."

In a chatty mood one afternoon, Brian ran down what brought him to the Joint.

"I used to be the jealous type. Still am, I guess." Brian peered out the window, vacillating whether to continue. "One day, my girlfriend and I stopped at a convenience store to buy beer. The clerk flirted with my chick as though I weren't standing there."

"What did your girlfriend do?"

"She batted her eyes like she enjoyed all the attention. It really pissed me off. I slapped her around when I got home, returning to the store with a baseball bat."

Brian stopped pretending to rearrange the checkout catalog and crossed his arms.

"I put the guy in the hospital for six weeks; broke his arm, collarbone, and wrist and seriously messed up his knee. Thinking back, I shouldn't have done it."

"Stuff like that will get you in trouble."

"No shit."

"And it's bad karma."

"Don't I know it."

For this assault, Brian got five years, eligible for parole after serving half the sentence. To his surprise, the girlfriend dumped him after his arrest. Nevertheless, DOC had recently reclassified him to minimum security and scheduled his transfer to another facility.

Brian wouldn't be the last guy to snap and commit crimes worthy of prison. Convicts often exhibited bizarre behavior and warranted daily medication. Felonious attacks carried a lesser sentence than financial malfeasance. That insight told me a lot about the priorities of the Criminal Justice System. Was it paranoid and cynical to conjecture that financial institutions influenced lawmakers to make property crimes a higher priority and more severe than other misdeeds not affecting these institutions? I had plenty of time to think about this question.

CO Lopez, Brian's boss, dropped by on her tour of the Unit as I thumbed a copy of Ovid's *Metamorphoses*. She reminded me of Minerva, our goddess of wisdom. Since my arrival, I had missed few of her visits. The department regulations mandated inmates' access to books, and Lopez, as head of the Complex libraries, ensured each Unit had them. She made the rounds to all the facility libraries, bringing her by once a week.

Lopez, an attractive Rubenesque woman in her early forties, kept her dark hair pulled back, held in place by reading glasses mounted on her head. On this visit, she greeted me a little friendlier than usual.

Lopez leaned against the edge of the table. "I'm glad you're here. Sullivan is moving to Minimum next week."

"Yes, he told me."

"Yeah, so I need a replacement. Have you ever worked in a library or a bookstore?"

Finding myself in a job interview, I put down my book, straightened up from my slouch, and answered, "Yes, as a paid employee of a university library for three years."

"Excellent. You replace Sullivan when he leaves, if you want the job."

"I'm interested in working here, yes," I said in my most unctuous corporate tone. Lopez pushed down the glasses from atop her head and flipped through the pages on her clipboard. I handed her my badge, and she took down my DOC number and made some notes to herself.

"Let me assemble the paperwork, and you can start next Monday. The position pays 25 cents an hour. Sullivan will fill you in on the duties. All right?"

"Yes, thank you, Officer Lopez. Much appreciated."

Footsteps echoed on the steps as she descended resolutely as though she had someplace important to be. I looked at Brian, and he smiled.

"That was easy. I can move to Minimum, knowing the collection is safe." Sarcasm rang in his voice. Being in the right place at the right time, I received a 150% per hour raise and no more rock gardening under an unrelenting sun.

Several months elapsed before I settled into the routine of the prison camp. When not in the library or the rack, I spent much of my free time walking the quarter-mile oval dirt track located in the Unit's center. The grass-covered interior curved downward, concavely sloping towards the middle. Instead of sprinklers, several black plastic pipes jutted out from the sides, spaced irregularly around the edges.

This construction and other random thoughts kept me preoccupied while I completed my self-imposed penance of ten miles daily, or forty laps, regardless of the weather.

Thoreau once said, "The moment my legs move, my thoughts begin to flow." With Buddha, Jesus, Wordsworth, Emerson, and Nietzsche, I joined a long line of wandering thinkers sans the spiritual or literary pedigree. I coveted those precious instances when a day, a week, or a month had passed, and each step brought me closer to freedom.

One morning, I set out before the heat grew unbearable. Water inundated the track's interior to a half-foot depth to create a small pond. Since the track interior measured less than an acre, I calculated a half acre-foot of water, or about 100,000 gallons, dumped overnight through those mysterious PVC pipes. A drowned field suggested a profligate use of resources, probably sourced from a local well. The facility had no other use for the bounty except to hydrate its crop of felons.

I christened the pond "Walden" because, like Thoreau, I passed many hours by its banks eager to plumb its mysteries, though without the dimpled surfaces or trolling of lines.

After twenty laps, my legs rebelled against the relentless push forward. Unfocused eyes and a wandering mind helped me ignore the fatigue.

Walden reflected three aspects of color: brown, blue, or green, congruent with the angle of the sun and my perspective. To pass the time, I imagined a metaphor to tie the pond to various points of view.

The pool appeared brown and muddied from the corner of my eye. If I slowed to a stroll and glanced upward, my mind calmer, the water turned blue. A sideward glance, my gaze somewhere between the sky and the grass, revealed a shimmer of light green that intensified my daydreaming.

The blazing heat vaporized the pond over several days, its waters escaping this prison. If only continuous evaporation carried me aloft beyond the fences.

Walden reincarnated unpredictably following cycles of filling and vanishing, which continued through the hottest months of April to October. I, too, experienced a kind of restoration after I surrendered to my fate and relinquished the anger and desperation incarceration fostered in me.

One day, I threw off my shoes, rolled up my pants, and waded into Walden, letting the last few inches of water wash over my feet. The warm mud squished through my toes. Anyone who saw me surely figured I went mental as I wallowed in the muck, fully grounded for a few blissful moments.

I passed through not only the desert's seasons but also the stages of grief Kübler-Ross described: denial of what happened, anger at being so stupid, and bargaining I'll never do it again if I can return. Then, confronting depression, accepting the missteps that cannot be undone. Someday I will release the fear, resentment, and self-loathing, the last step in my recovery.

I lived in a prison of my own making, an ambivalent participant and prisoner of the past, unable to break through to true freedom.

The poet said it best in the last stanza of his poem:

> *Stone walls do not a prison make,*
> *Nor iron bars a cage:*
> *Minds innocent and quiet take*
> *That for an hermitage.*
> *If I have freedom in my love,*
> *And in my soul am free,*
> *Angels alone, that soar above,*
> *Enjoy such liberty.*

Did it matter whether my body was restrained if my mind was immobile and forced to stare at my shadow? These reflections and more preoccupied me as I orbited Walden daily for almost three years, walking in circles, my destination always one more step forward. No footstep ever returned to the same place as the timeless desert wind swept away my trackless tracks.

CHAPTER 5

Prison imposed structure and regimentation on the involuntary. Reveille sounded every morning at 6:00 when the cell door locks clicked open. One morning before dawn, I awoke to Mac humming to himself. From the top bunk, I peered over the side, watching him as he sat calmly on his bed, waiting.

"Hey, Mac, how come you get up so early?"

He shifted around so he could talk to me. "Alcoholism and thirty-five years of boozing forced me to awaken at dawn, so I could drink. I used to keep a bottle of vodka on my bed stand. Around four or five, the craving for alcohol woke me up. Now, I wake up out of habit."

"You've been drinking that long?"

"After boot camp, I started swigging every chance I got. During the war, we drank a lot."

"The Vietnam War?"

"No, the Korean. After my discharge, I drank every day and only stopped when locked up."

"My dad was a master sergeant in the Korean War. He never talked about his tour much. Bad memories, I guess."

"Many vets resist reliving their wartime experiences. Some of it was horrible. I joined at seventeen and became an Army Ranger."

"Rangers are an elite outfit, right?"

"Yessir, the Eighth Ranger Company, 24th Infantry." Mac yawned, changing the subject. "This is my third tour of prison duty, and I've had enough. Every bad decision I ever made, I made while drinking."

He remained sober without access to vodka and by regular AA meetings. "Stopping is easy in here, but in the free world?"

"I'm working on it."

"AA works?"

"When I go to meetings, yes." Mac fidgeted, anxious to go eat.

We chatted about his life on the outside. Both he and my father operated their own painting contractor businesses after the conflict ended in 1953. Mac moved through the day, intoxicated from dawn until he collapsed at night. He lived as a functioning alcoholic until the alcohol-induced blunders sent him to prison.

"You and my dad would be about the same age. He died several years ago."

"Sorry to hear it. Both my parents died in a car crash three weeks after I enlisted. The army wouldn't furlough me out of boot to attend their funeral."

"Dad had a heart attack in a Third World country and might have survived if he were in the States."

"Losing people we love hurts," Mac said with a far-off gaze.

"That's right."

Mac "adopted" me and taught me the vagaries of prison life. According to him, always follow the three unwritten rules of the slammer.

"Listen up because these rules can save your life."

"Shoot."

"Never ask a con about his crime, and never wake him when he's sleeping. Convicts become suspicious when one pries into their past, and sleep provides a momentary escape from all this," he said as he indicated our cell.

"The last rule is the most important: no matter what, never snitch."

"Snitches get stitches?"

"That's right. Snitches get pummeled, or worse."

"Thanks. I'll keep those in mind." The door lock released with a loud *clack*.

"Interested in some food?" Mac asked.

"No thanks. I got some stuff to do upstairs."

"All right. Good talk."

Once Mac left for breakfast, I slid to the floor, threw on some clothes, and found a turnkey to unlock the library. Quiet mornings reading or writing before the ruckus of the prison obliterated the serenity kept me sane.

This prison unit conducted head counts four times daily before shift change. Each shift overlapped 30 minutes to complete the count and relay any issues to the new staff. The daily routine seldom varied: count at 5 a.m., cells opened at six, another count at 11:30 a.m., lunch at noon, back on lockdown at 2:30 p.m. until 3:30, and supper between four and five.

Although we were free to roam the yards until 9:30, we remained locked down throughout the night. The only exceptions to this regimen occurred when an event or emergency triggered a Code Red lockdown, where our master's voice screamed over the loudspeakers, "Code Red lockdown! Code Red lockdown! Lockdown! Lockdown! Now!"

We dropped whatever we were doing and immediately returned to our cells. To ignore the call meant a write-up at best, or a day in the Hole at worst.

Six-inch glass slits down the center of the cell doors allowed the COs to spy into every corner. We slipped our plastic badges with our photos and DOC number into the worn weather stripping facing out: the right two men in a cell, a checkmark next to our name on the roster pinned to a clipboard, move to the next one. A cadre of officers counted the Unit in twenty minutes.

The COs initiated Code Reds whenever a fight erupted, a prisoner didn't report for work duty and couldn't be located, or weapons, drugs, or hooch turned up in a shakedown. Perhaps the Administration disrupted our routine as an exercise to remind us of who was in charge.

One evening after chow, a wind surged from the west, seemingly from nowhere. The loudspeaker blared, "Code Red. Code Red Lockdown!"

The call caught me walking on the far side of the track, where I had a partial view of the open desert. Clouds of swirling dust a thousand feet high obliterated the horizon. Akin to a tsunami, this dust storm, called a *haboob*, would overtake the prison and crash over us in minutes.

Haboobs, like living entities, ravaged the countryside, able to bury or suffocate anyone caught outdoors. I cut across the field and ran towards my cell. A CO at the guard shack waved me in, screaming, "C'mon, move it!"

The perimeter of the fence line disappeared as the storm entered my Unit—no time for sightseeing. The building shielded me as Mac held the cell door open, motioning me to hurry.

Visibility dropped to zero as the enveloping darkness descended to blot the yard lights, sun, moon, and stars. One terrified CO trapped outside later told me she understood what it's like to be buried alive. Had the handkerchief not covered her nose and mouth, she might not have reached the shack in time. *I will show you fear in a handful of dust.*

"Quick," Mac said, "Make sure those windows are shut tight and help me stuff some of our clothes in the cracks."

Layers of fine dust collected on the windowsill of our crib. Soon the powdery attritus blanketed the cell, finding its way into every space, on every surface, a gritty reminder Nature governed our lives.

Some cons duct-taped their window edges. Where did they find the tape? Mac laid dirty jeans across the door's base to slow the powder from penetrating the small gap.

Regardless of how well we blocked the openings, the dust insidiously penetrated the cell like a monster from a horror movie that gradually tore away the barriers to reach its prey. Our world became a forbidden planet, menaced by creatures from the Id.

The storm passed slowly.

Dreams of dirt filling my mouth, ears, and nose accompanied the howling winds beating the sides of the building. Inescapable suffocation seized my chest. To be interred alive terrified me. The ordeal was more than a dream, more a nightmare come true. I awoke gasping for air in a dust cloud.

Before I asphyxiated, I shoved off the lid of my coffin as the heavy soil piled on top of me. I dropped to the floor and huddled over the sink to wash the fine particles from my face and hair.

"You all right over there?" Mac asked.

I coughed, unable to speak.

"Grab a pop out of the ice chest," he said. "Or drink some water." Oddly, Mac appeared unfazed by the upheaval.

"This must be your first dust storm. You'll adjust to them. They are standard this time of year."

"How do people live in all this filth?" I said as I wiped my face with a damp washcloth.

"All part of the punishment. Can't take the grime, don't do the crime." Mac smiled at his joke.

"Ha! I see a career in stand-up coming your way. The parole board will love your new direction."

"Me? Bullshitting in a boozy nightclub? Don't think so."

I couldn't go back to sleep until I shook my sheets in the corner of our cell. Exhausted, I returned to a fitful sleep. The panic and anger of my life, restrained by the will to survive, enabled me to endure one more night and day until release.

The lockdown ended the following day. The grit tainted everything: the buildings, the trees, the wildlife, the people, anything not dust. We walked in it, breathed it, overwhelmed by the coarse and desiccated sensation that coated our bodies as we prayed for the rain or wind to blow our tormentor to its next destination, far from us.

We were like dust, trapped in a glass bowl, contained, controlled. Mac and I cleaned our crib. After requisitioning a broom and mop, he dumped some ice chests full of water over the concrete floor and pushed as much dirty water as possible into the yard. Then we wiped down the surfaces and spread out our bedding and clothes. The powder aggravated my allergies. A long shower brought relief.

We emerged into another typical day: hot, dry, expansive blue skies stretched in all directions. A slight, warm breeze kicked up, and most dust moved on by noon.

I usually skipped breakfast, but not today. Sometimes a tiny break in the routine satisfied a repressed urge for rebellion. Skipping the morning meal was not incredibly daring.

For my penance, I often kept myself hungry and suppressed the discomfort with water to alleviate the gnawing. The poor quality of the food made skipping meals easier. DOC still hadn't deciphered that food was essential to maintaining the prisoner morale. Bad food created unrest.

The food restriction regimen exacted a cost, however. My concentration dropped off in the desert heat. Fatigue overcame me, forcing me to nap, often in my chair in the library.

Still, I pushed myself to keep up with my daily ten-mile hikes. Some days I couldn't reach the fortieth lap and cut out a few laps short, which I made up on another day.

Mac said, "You got to increase your calories if you're going to walk so much. Eat more meat. And drink a lot of water."

"I try to. Heat stroke's a problem. I don't crave the food in Chez D." Chez D is the name we gave to the mess hall in our section.

Famished after the storm, I heeded Mac's advice. I visited Chez D, inclined to enjoy a full breakfast until I spotted the fare: buttered white toast; tepid, zestless scrambled eggs that even condiments couldn't revive; slices of orange; and a muffin-like clump. The muffin tasted all right, but I traded my eggs with the guy beside me for his fruit. After two cups of over-brewed coffee, I vowed not to return to breakfast. I lost twenty pounds while incarcerated.

I headed to the library to assess the fallout. Luckily, the seal around the door had kept most of the grime outside and off the books. However, enough leaked through to make cleanup a less-than-trivial job. After tidying the room and wiping down the volumes, some brown stains remained along the book spines where the pages attached to the covers—dust storms marking their territory.

If three or four inmates strolled in during my shift, I considered the day a success. CO Evans dropped by if she was on the day shift to ensure I wasn't doing anything nefarious, such as reading a book with my feet on the desk or jotting away in my prison journal. With only two women in our Unit, she and Lopez, I took advantage of their company. Women gave me a much-needed break from all the raging testosterone.

Distinctive footsteps plodded up the stairs as though the hiker had climbed to the summit of the Empire State Building. The shuffling sound of labored steps indicated she had survived a busy morning. Evans found me before the wiped shelves as I brushed off my next book, a faded paperback of *The Grapes of Wrath*.

"You survived another storm, I see. The place doesn't look too bad," Evans said, anchoring her attention on me.

I put down my book and leaned forward. "You should have seen the mess an hour ago. Is it wrong to say I'm starting to hate this place?"

"To live under a layer of dust can't be pleasant. The dust storms end in the fall. Don't you have a parole hearing coming up?"

"Fifteen months, twelve days."

"Not too long."

"Time is relativistic, according to Einstein. In exile, time crawls."

"Stay busy. That's what I do." She laughed.

"Thanks, I'll do my best."

Under her government-issued cap, she tied her blonde hair with shades of red in a bun. She sported prescription sunglasses and an attractive athletic figure, which suggested she regularly exercised. Her smile, a beacon in the grimness of prison, sometimes evoked sadness to remind me of better days.

Evans browsed the selections like a customer in a secondhand bookshop.

"My dad has a huge library, and my brother and I spent hours reading mostly fiction."

"Me too. I got maximum use out of my library card. I read a book a week. Sometimes two. An advantage of not having a social life."

"I had lots of friends, but I still found time. Sometimes I stayed up late reading in bed. I pretended to sleep and switched on the light once my parents conked out or read under the blanket with a flashlight."

"Yeah. My parents never said anything about my late-night reading habits. They often left me on my own."

I liked Evans, who maintained a sense of humor and, in unguarded moments, blurred the officer-inmate divide. DOC training dictated that officers should never become too personal with the inmates. Sometimes our conversations became so engaging that we forgot our mandated roles for several minutes.

"Got any recommendations? I like historical fiction."

"I don't have it here. Yard B has it, but I enjoyed T.H. White's *The Once and Future King*. About Merlin and King Arthur's Court."

"Really? My dad has that one on his shelf, but I never read it."

"Do you know *A Canticle for Leibowitz* by Walter Miller?"

"Sounds religious."

"The novel's a marvelous work of speculative fiction about how civilizations rise and fall over the millennia and how the Catholic Church maintains the thread of humanity throughout the upheavals. Quite a deep book, but not light reading. A lot of Latin phrases."

"That sounds like something I might go for, being Catholic." Evans laughed.

"Yeah, me too. My baptism at six weeks of age was the beginning and end of my Catholic upbringing. My mom was an obedient Catholic in her early years but not after I was born. She lost faith in the church but not in God."

Whenever Evans asked for recommendations, I steered her towards literature or other worthwhile books that said something meaningful about life. When we spoke, I imagined myself a free man, a cherished, fleeting sensation, and a memory of lost times.

Evans and I chatted almost daily except for her time off or working the swing shift.

One night after the 9:30 lockdown, an officer stepped up to our door to take the count and tapped at the cell door window.

"Look, your sweetie's at the door," Mac said.

Evans peeked in with a smile and a wink. I tortured myself with fantasies about her all night, which is not a wise move in prison. We chatted about whether another dust storm was imminent as I jotted down the suggested reading selections. After Evans left to continue her rounds, I opened my copy of *The Grapes of Wrath*, blew off some grit, and began reading.

Chapter 6

I often drifted into philosophical musing to distract myself, usually while doing something banal. The surrounding universe, the world I lived in, touched, felt, breathed, saw, and heard, was merely the surface. One morning, as I stared into a mirror before shaving, I realized my authentic image represented one of many facets of perception. Flat, without depth, my reflection did not express my true self. I pressed my fingers against my face and touched the glass. One authentic, the other an impression, but which? Perhaps both were representations created by the mind, and neither existed outside my consciousness.

With no shaving cream in prison, I lathered hand soap over my face and dragged the disposable razor across my cheeks. The rasping sensation, true or not, anchored me to this place and time. My doppelgänger in the mirror shaved with me. He stared back, advising caution with the dull blade. Everyone would acknowledge my clean-shaven face if my consciousness desired it.

These ideas stayed with me as I walked across the courtyard to the guard shack to cajole a CO into unlocking the library. Another hot, cloudless, gentian blue, routine afternoon awaited me—one more beautiful contemplative day in the penitentiary.

Walden Pond had retreated to the underworld several days before. After finishing my shift, I circled the grassy interior of the track, and my mood lightened. That afternoon, I realized I had remained drug-free for almost three years. Desire to use weed, coke, or psychedelics had faded like some random memory from an unimportant day.

Unable to hide behind drugs, sobriety encouraged me to confront the number one trait that held me back: fear. Fear of loss, embarrassment, exposing my vulnerabilities, and perhaps the fear of freedom.

Once the clarity of thought and feeling took hold, all my hiding places dissolved, exposing me to the light. Instead of covering up, I put my hands at my side and let the sunshine reach me.

I acknowledged my terror by recognizing it in others. Next to Yard A, the Department of Corrections had installed free weights and benches on the course's western end. I often stopped by "The Weight Pile" to lift, not to buff up but to maintain muscle tone.

One of the regulars, Miguel, camped at the pile to recover from his compulsive jogging. He had arrived at the Yard emaciated and sickly, but exercise and regular meals restored him. After several months, he appeared tan and fit, except for the needle scars that marred his arms and legs. I envied his vigor, but the numerous cicatrices spoiling his skin repulsed me.

Miguel set up an ambitious bench press, and I offered to spot him. He agreed, and I stood over him, ready to grab the weights if he lost control. Miguel struggled but hoisted the bar off the holders and pushed the metal above his head. After exhausting himself with several reps, he let the load slam down.

"Miguel," I asked, "why do you work out so hard every day? I see you lifting like a maniac and then circling the track like your life depended on it. What's after you?"

He chuckled, then his face went slack: "From these scars on me, you can tell I'm a heroin addict. You ever shoot H?"

"No. Needles are the one thing I avoid."

"Ah. Shooting up was scary at first, but you ignore the creepiness of sticking a needle into your vein and someday love it. Anyway, I got pinched for B&E stealing stuff to buy my next fix. Us addicts always need money. I can't change that."

I wanted to interrupt and challenge his assertion, but I listened instead.

"When I get out, I will try to go straight, find a job, and stay away from drugs, but I have nowhere to go except to my old neighborhood, where my people are and where I belong. Falling back into the old crowd means using again. I want to be healthy, so I can get high as long as possible before I return."

"Why not move someplace new, away from all the temptations?"

"Where would I go? The barrio is what I know. I feel safe there, at least for a while, until the horse licks my hand, then kicks me in the head."

Miguel completed several curls before he continued. "This number is my fourth. Coming to this Unit is like coming home." He gestured at the scene around him. "This is my true home, and I only visit the outside. Beyond the fences, I will die. I'm afraid of death. Here I might survive. Where else will I enjoy regular meals, plenty of sleep and exercise, and no smack to take me out?"

We went back to lifting.

After a few minutes, I said, "Being free to strike out alone, to live with the decisions we make, to make mistakes, is scary, isn't it?"

"*Sí*. Life is better here, where there are no decisions. Bad choices are all I ever made. Being locked up may not be the greatest, but I'm alive, *tu sabes?*"

I said *adios* and continued my laps. What Miguel said bothered me. For him, the only reality he recognized made heroin the focus of every conscious thought. Addiction drove and controlled him. Miguel found peace and a respite from fear through the oblivion of an opioid sleep.

The world in the mirror became the world, just as the map became the territory. Guys like Miguel were the rule, not the exception. Too many inmates accepted the misconception that their only destiny was the Joint. Prison became their mother and father, where food appeared on schedule, where one slept anytime, inane conversations abounded, and card games were never far away. Never a joiner, I found that the camaraderie of prison life eluded me.

Incarceration embodied the realm of no bills to pay and no real consequences for much of anything, a village where precise rules outlined the boundaries of behavior. For many, the Yard remained a sanctuary where the stresses of the outer world didn't intrude. Inmates missed their families but learned to live with only weekend visits. Being unable to see their kids grow up weighed on the prisoners but not enough to effect change. Parole arrived, but many returned because they believed rotation in and out of prison was foreordained.

One guy, whose name I forgot, bragged about his lifetime of detention. He walked the track sometimes after supper. Older, perhaps in his late forties or fifties, he trudged along as every arthritic step restrained him.

"This is my seventh go-around, the first one in this state. I did time in Florida, Louisiana, and Texas. Don't go to Texas."

"No chance of that. This is my first and last DOC tour."

"I said that too. I'm unlucky. Twice some guys ratted me out. During a burglary, I tripped over my goddamn shoelace and sprained my ankle. The cops got me easy that time."

"Did you ever think of another line of work?" I already guessed his answer.

"Sure. Many times, but once you got a rap sheet, nobody wants to hire an ex-con. Drugs did me in a few years back."

"That does sound like bad luck."

"I never much had a hankering to do anything that required me to be anyplace on time."

"Aren't you afraid of dying in prison?"

"Not really. Being locked up ain't so bad. Better to drop dead here than in a flop house or an alley."

"What about your family?"

"Lost track of them after I dropped out of high school at sixteen. I had to make my own way. My mom raised me to be on my own, but I do miss her."

The mix of pride and resignation in his voice told me everything. Proud to have racked up so many convictions and years, he accepted his fate. I listened politely but thought: *Loser, he's a seven-time loser and not cut out for crime.* The man sought incarceration, embracing life without ambition, responsibility, or concern about people other than himself.

One of the cruelest aspects of prison life was living with a group of self-centered assholes who only cared about their immediate needs and what they might game out of others. I never wanted to be like them, and as my incarceration continued, I became more resolved to get out and stay out.

I hated late-night TV. This facility allowed televisions in the cells. Some preferred to watch all night and sleep all day.

Some cons bullied gratuities off the weaker guys, like cigarettes or food from the commissary. Everyone got tested eventually.

A guy in his late twenties came into the library once to bum a smoke. His gait and expression suggested he had something to prove.

"Sorry. I don't smoke."

"Yeah, but you got them. I saw you paying off the laundry guy the other day."

"The laundry guy is a high priority. I want my clothes and sheets back clean and folded. You know how it is."

"I'll be back tomorrow. Marlboro's my favorite."

"With or without filters?"

"Tomorrow, chump. I ain't playing."

The guy made me nervous. All talk or not, I asked Mac's advice.

"Is that the balding carrottop with the red mustache and the scar on his left arm?"

"Yes, short with bad breath."

"Forget him. That loser will back down if you tell him to pound sand. But to be safe, I have some *research* I need to do tomorrow, so I'll be upstairs when he shows."

"Thanks, Mac."

Ginger entered the library half an hour before the afternoon count, browsing the bookshelf behind me. Mac sat at my desk reading some poems by Coleridge.

"Can I help you find something?" I said.

"Got my smokes?"

"What smokes? I told you yesterday, I don't smoke."

Mac glanced up from his book. "You heard him. Buzz off."

"Fuck off, old man. What are you gonna do?"

Mac stood and squared off with him, balling his fists. The menacing glint in his eyes zeroed in on Ginger, who glowered back. Mac, in combat mode, locked his eyes on him: "Come over here, and I'll show you what an old man can do."

"Better listen to him. Mac's had training." I stepped back to give them room, thinking I would have to grab Ginger from the back if Mac overplayed his prowess.

Ginger, to his credit, assessed his chances and relaxed, swearing under his breath before he left the library, almost bumping into CO Evans.

"Everything all right up here? Hey Mac." she said.

"No problem, Evans. Ginger couldn't find a book he liked, so I sent him to another yard."

"Ginger?"

"That's our name for him because of his red hair."

"Oh. That guy's a troublemaker. Whenever I see him hanging around, I investigate." Mac smiled and retook his chair.

The incident taught me another thing about prison. Alliances with the right people are essential. Loners are vulnerable. Nothing good happens when a sheep and two wolves meet to decide what's for lunch.

Some days I hated prison enough to spit blood. Disgusted for putting myself in this situation, in this shithole, I stepped up the pace of my daily walks.

My bouts of self-loathing drove me to push harder, as though walking faster and sweating more would accelerate my contrition, my version of mortification of the flesh.

The first and the last couple of miles hurt the most. Mom sent me sunglasses, which helped me cope with living where the sun shone 300 days a year. From March to October, the dry heat haunted every step. I walked at night too, but the sun didn't set in the summer until after nine o'clock.

Sweat rolled off me as I pressed each lap. Copious amounts of water kept me from collapsing on the track as my kidneys diverted every drop to my sweat glands. Kidney stones from all the hard well water I drank, and hemorrhoids from the low-fiber diet, loomed in my future if I wasn't careful.

If pain erupted from my sides or vertigo arose, I dropped off the course to find water and rest.

Tramping sparked constant ruminations about my past and future. I relived the best times of my adolescence and college days. More on that later. Darkness crept in after the lost years following graduation until I hit bottom in an isolated desert enclave surrounded by razor wire and men with shotguns. My only genuine moments of solitude came during forty dusty laps. Forty days of abnegation in the wilderness.

CHAPTER 7

Each day followed the rhythms of the day before. Most of us adapted to the regimentation, and some thrived under the constant supervision and patterns laid out for them. Everyone complained about the food, the guards, and the lack of variety on television, but few protested the loss of freedom. However, discontent resulted whenever the prisoner attempted to synchronize his life with those outside the fences.

A bank of telephones lined the front gate entrances, lifelines to the outside world apportioned in twenty-minute intervals.

If I wanted to make a call, I joined the haphazard phone line with no tangible form in which everyone guarded their position in the queue. Regardless of heat or cold, we waited near the guard shack door for our turn to hand the CO our badge and a slip of paper with the phone number scrawled in illegible handwriting.

The automated feminine voice announced a collect call from a correctional facility, giving the recipient one chance to reject the call or the caller. The first time I called Mom, the exchange went like this:

"This is a collect call from a correctional facility. To accept the charges, please press 1. Otherwise, hang up, and you will not be charged."

"Hello? Who's there? Collect from who?"

"Mom, press 1!" She couldn't hear me.

I hung up and got back in line. Thirty minutes later, my stepfather answered and accepted the call.

"Hi, Jim. Everything okay?"

"Sure, Dad. The same old thing here. I miss you guys."

"We miss you too. Here's Mom." My stepfather didn't much care for talking on the phone, or indeed, speaking at all. He had to be the most taciturn person I knew. Perhaps I got my "man-of-few-words" demeanor from him.

Mom came on the line. "Hello, Jimbo. I'm glad you called. Dad and I went to Vegas last weekend. I won $300 playing Keno and $75 in Texas-Hold'em. Dad lost $500 playing craps and from those damn slot machines. Then yesterday I had to see the doctor again for my foot. It's better now. The doc wants me to have surgery, but I will not do it. I don't mind limping a little or using a cane. I ran into Mrs. Compagno at the Pomona Sears yesterday. She says hello and hopes you're well. After all these years, she's still sad, but let's not talk about that now. How are you?"

"I'm fine, Mom. Still working at the library, staying out of trouble . . . "

"Oh, I wanted to tell you. Your Aunt Lucia called and asked for your address at the place you're at, so I gave it to her. I didn't think you'd mind. She sounded like she wanted to tell you something."

I called my mom more for her sake than mine. My life, always the same, gave me little to talk about, so I enjoyed listening to a familiar voice, ready to reassure her not to worry.

Nineteen minutes into the conversation, a surreptitious tone beeped to encourage a quick but orderly goodbye.

"The call's going to end any second now, Mom. You take care. I love you . . . " Dial tone.

Calls home cost lots of money. One of my semiregular library patrons told me his family spent over $150 monthly for his calls—a fortune for some families. Still, children needed their dads, wives and sweethearts yearned for their guys, and prisoners craved a connection to a life they gave up for their own reasons. Ironically, if these guys had stopped their felonies, they would have been home instead of loitering around a guard shack waiting for an open line.

For the first two years of my incarceration, ambivalence colored my mood for days after calling my parents. Part of me didn't want to be reminded of everyday life beyond my reach, a life I voluntarily gave up by committing felonies. The world continued whether I was free or not. Life went on, and people went on, with or without me.

After a few drinks, my friend Paul once said, "While you were away, it felt like you had died. When Laura and I packed up your condo after the arrest, the whole thing reminded me of, well, you know . . . like before, going through your stuff, trying to decide what to keep and give away. Of course, we knew you were alive, but gone like we'd never see you again."

My world shrank to a few acres of desert connected by some cherished disembodied voices apportioned in measured interludes and three or four flesh-and-blood people who kept me grounded. Loneliness dogged every connection I made to the world beyond the razor-wired fences.

Mail arrived every day except Sunday after inspection by the mailroom staff. The officers slit open each envelope, examined its contents, and resealed it with tape. Before the library job, I passed by the guard shack every day to check for news from the outside. Since I seldom received more than one item a month, this pointless exercise became a depressing ritual, and I stopped.

Officer Evans alerted me if I'd received anything whenever she dropped by the library. Sometimes she brought my mail to me on those rare, rainy days.

"Don't assume anything. I only brought your mail because I'm coming this way," she said, the inflection in her voice suggesting she didn't mind.

"Still, I appreciate you thinking of me."

My mom never wrote except for a Hallmark card at Christmas and on my birthday. Because she left school after the eighth grade to work in her grandfather's bar in Weehawken, her writing skills never developed.

I always looked forward to the infrequent postcard from my college friends Paul and Laura, who had formed a successful jazz quartet, often touring in Europe and Asia. I recognized Laura's distinctive handwriting, but Paul always scrawled an oversized PS on the bottom.

Cologne is an exciting town. Who knew the Germans loved jazz so much? L&P — P.S. Miss you. The herb here is killer.

We love Paris. The city's even better than your descriptions, like a second home. Jazz is fantastic here. We're almost superstars! L&P — P.S. We could really use your language skills. Laura's French is okay.

Doing 5 shows in Tokyo this week. Might have to add two more. The demand is huge. The Japanese people are super friendly. L&P — P.S. We met Chick Corea at our hotel doing an MTV video here.

Tidbits about their travels or impressions of the cities they visited made my day. Sharing their adventures via the terse yet lively dispatches kept me involved in their lives. We'd enjoyed close bonds once, and I missed them more than my parents.

I never received visitors. Inmates were allowed one visit per day on Saturday and Sunday. Wives, girlfriends, and grandparents appeared each weekend to bring the family news and remind the prisoners they had not been forgotten. Many had young children whose brief childhood passed in the Visitation room. Though necessary, the interaction with loved ones highlighted the agony of separation, which swung from tolerable to intolerable, unmitigated by time.

Weeks, months, and years elapsed, rapidly for some and slowly for others. Incarcerated men promised they would never commit another crime, delusions they and their loved ones needed to believe. Families wanted to trust them because the pledge brought optimism and gave their children hope their father would return home someday. Women didn't forget their men in prison. Did the men understand how much their women loved them and sacrificed to keep the family together while the convict lounged around playing cards and watching TV?

Struggles with underwhelming and mind-numbing routines, boredom, lethargy, and loneliness punctuated each day, highlighted by periodic flashes of hope reinforced by letters, visits, or phone calls. I made no long-term plans and resisted the urge to fantasize about how things might be. The past was history, and the future is yet to come. As Baba Ram Dass taught in *Be Here Now*: be mindful of the present, the Now, for that's all that is.

Jason, my regular barber and another recovering alcoholic, earned parole and took his final stroll in June on one of the hottest days ever recorded. Mac and I accompanied him to Administration to give a proper send-off. In a firm and fatherly voice, Mac urged Jason to secure a new sponsor and gave him a list of several local AA chapters.

A month before his release, I suggested, "Hey Jason, why don't you earn a license to work in a barbershop when you get out?" Jason had cut his son's hair but had never considered doing hairstyling for a living. Since he was a welder by trade, he thought welding would pay better, but he admitted he loved barbering.

Some found a niche during their incarceration applicable on release, while others overlooked every opportunity. Too many learned more ways to commit crimes and lengthen future sentences.

For some, incarceration opened new avenues, but not for me. I underplayed my talent for numbers and critical thinking and resisted acquiring the specific felonious skills available to prisoners.

My predicament offered me casual insights into human nature, which I recorded in my journal for use in a book I might write someday. Time was my nemesis, so I stayed busy with books and pens. Confinement would change me, but I hoped for the better.

During the last haircut with Jason, he told me that Vargas, over on Yard B, was the (second) best barber.

"Doesn't he wield some juice around here?" I asked.

"Juice? Man, he runs this place. No one is as well-connected on the Yard or outside as he is. He's kinda like the Godfather, know what I mean? The only difference is he's a Chicano Godfather instead of an Italian one. *Capiche*?"

"*Capsico*."

"Yeah, so he's an older guy, quiet, thoughtful, proper, and he gives decent haircuts. He cuts mine."

Jason always sported an above-average cut, but I'd never thought to ask where he got it. Rumors about Vargas circulated, perpetuated by guys who hung out in the library, shooting the bull about their vast knowledge and insight into prison gossip and politics. Gabby women carried this undeserved reputation of endless blather, but they got nothing on a bunch of cons with nothing better to do. I figured Vargas for another OG, or Original Gangster, as older recidivists were called, and didn't give much credence to the stories about his reputation.

The consensus touted Vargas as a guy who got results or could procure things for a price, although the people I talked to didn't know him personally. Convicts excelled at running their mouths about subjects they knew nothing about.

Luis Vargas had cut hair for three years since his transfer from maximum security. With four years left on his current number, he intended to remain until sentence expiration. The man despised parole for its pervasive monitoring and the severe limitations on his "freedom." He required a clean break and didn't mind serving time since he considered incarceration an occupational hazard. I admired his forthrightness, beliefs, and code, but not his career choices.

Vargas earned respect on the Yard and expected the same from others. He used his barbershop as a neutral venue to mediate disputes, whose parties abided by his "suggestions." Vargas looked about 50 years old, was medium height, and had compact, muscular arms like a boxer. He kept his gray hair short and sported a thin mustache on this otherwise clean-shaven but rough face. Vargas wore the years as a man who endured hardships but gained wisdom, and I supposed he had learned a lot along the way.

A badass in his younger days, Vargas admitted to spending half of his adult life locked up. Competitors had tried to take him down. Were it not for snitches, Vargas would have escaped most of the cases he caught. He grew from his mistakes and vetted those around him more carefully.

Vargas believed this would be his last number. Given his priors and age, any further prison terms would be a life sentence, and he didn't want to die in prison. Time away from his wife and four children wore him down. In a candid moment, he conceded his fatigue over prison life, *"Estoy harto de esta mierda."*

Vargas's code of honor extended to everyone in his circle. To cross him, lie to him, or mislead him in any way, one found behind his dark eyes and intelligent expression lurked a quiet fury that lashed out and exacted retribution. He never became enraged, and the calmer he appeared, the more menacing his bearing. No one wanted Vargas as an enemy.

He attended Mass every Sunday before visitation. Whether he went out of faith in his Catholicism or to manage the impression he had mellowed in his middle age did not matter. I suspected the former. Vargas occupied the front row on the left, surrounded by his crew, a collection of *vatos* he mentored. They watched his back in return. He preferred to receive Holy Communion first, and everyone waited for him to start. Even the priest understood the deference congregants paid him and offered the sacrament to Vargas before the others, which boosted his status among the other inmates. For him, prison rank and respect meant everything.

Of course, I understood none of this on my first visit. Many months passed before we reached a rapport. We did favors for each other only if my participation didn't involve more jail time for me. Vargas acknowledged my reluctance because he did not consider me a player.

Sometimes he sought advice or different opinions and didn't always rely on the people closest to him to give honest answers or insight. I suppose godfathers suffered their share of yes-men ready to kiss the boss's ass. Like any seasoned leader, he acquired facts from all sides before deciding. Vargas appreciated my neutral stances, and, at times, I flattered myself as a *consigliere speciale pro-tempore*, though only in the broadest terms.

Jason mentioned that Vargas preferred Salem Menthols over Marlboros, so I ordered several packs the day before from the commissary. I strolled to Yard B and entered Vargas's realm while he finished with a *vato*. He nodded as I took a seat next to the window. These yard barbershops contained nothing more than folding metal chairs, the kind we used to wear our asses thin in high school.

Like Jason, Vargas had developed his talent for cutting hair behind bars, preferring a smooth Cadillac job with the freedom to hold court and talk to people in neutral circumstances. Working a square gig kept the COs off his back.

Done with his client, Vargas shook out the old bed sheet he used as a salon cape, accepted a pack of smokes in payment, and grabbed a broom behind him to sweep the cut hair into a corner. He moved deliberately, unrushed, as though every gesture carried meaning.

When I introduced myself, Vargas offered his hand with a firm grip.

"You did an excellent cut on the last . . . client."

Vargas nodded and mumbled something I didn't quite catch, motioning for me to sit in the chair in front of him. He covered me with the sheet and judged me how a chef might size up a cut of beef.

"Let's see, you like it tight around the sides, a little longer on the top, medium sideburns, no?"

"Yes."

"From the shape of your head, I can tell what would best suit you," he said, patient for my answer.

"You're right. Jason, over on C, used to cut it that way."

"Many of Jason's people come to me now."

"Jason said you are the best, after him, of course."

He grinned. "*Sí*. I have been busier than usual. Someone will take Jason's place, but I enjoy the extra work."

The room was silent at first as Vargas snipped away.

"You new on the Yard?" he asked.

"No, but it seems like I've been here forever."

"*Cómo no*. I like to stay busy so that time passes. How do you like our little desert paradise?"

"This is my first time, so I have nothing to compare it to, but it sure beats the hell out of the county. That jail's a pit."

"*Eso sí*. You live on Yard D?"

"Yes. On the first tier below the library where I work."

"There's a *typo* from there. Mac is his name."

"Mac? He's my cellie. How do you know him?"

"Mac gets around. We met, waiting in line for the commissary. Interesting fellow."

"He's the best. Mac is reliable, if you know what I mean."

"That's my impression too. Send him around for a haircut."

"I will."

Vargas and I engaged in some neutral small talk.

My recent encounter with Ginger sparked an idea. Emboldened by our congenial rapport, I waited for Vargas to finish before I made a presumptuous move.

"Done," Vargas said as he removed the cape from my shoulders. "The cut looks fine. Check it out when you return to your crib, and if you're unhappy, come back, and I'll make changes."

"Your work speaks for itself," I replied as I stood, reached into my pocket, pulled out two packs of Menthols, and handed them over.

"Only one pack is necessary."

"I wanted to give you two because I might ask a favor sometime."

Vargas eyed me for a moment, face emotionless, calculating, considering. Perhaps my presumptuousness had offended him. He shrugged and smiled, amused.

"*Oye. Tienes unos cajones*, and I like that. Sure, you know where to find me. If anybody gives you trouble, you tell me. Do you speak any Spanish?"

"*Sí, cómo no*." We switched to Spanish using the *tu* form.

"There are *pendejos* on this yard who will test you. Never back down, even if you get your ass kicked."

"Already happened. Mac and I reached an understanding with him."

"Good. How come you speak Spanish?"

"My dad was Dominican—long years of study in school. I've traveled through México, the Dominican Republic, and Spain. I speak French too."

"Not much use for French around here." He laughed. "Though you never know."

Another client wandered through the door.

Vargas held out his hand, and we shook. In English, he said, "By the way, Montez, come back in four weeks instead of six."

"Will do, for sure." Relieved my gambit had worked, I hoped I never needed a favor, but Vargas would consider it if I asked him to back my play.

A little insurance never hurt, though needing nothing would leave me in a stronger position. I wondered how Vargas gleaned I cut my hair every six weeks.

One of the tedious annoyances of the Joint was the surprise shakedowns. I loathed these *polizeiliche Aktionen* because they forced us to confront our incarceration stripped of the veneer that we controlled any aspects of our lives. Inspections came at any time, with or without justification. Snitches, results from a random cell toss, pruno, drugs, or shanks—they all precipitated lockdowns, and the broader search ensued.

Routine shakedowns conducted as training exercises in the early morning occurred soon after breakfast before the desert sun scorched the camp. Whenever a Code Red lockdown blasted through the unit, we drifted back to our cells, uncertain whether we'd be locked in for an hour or a day.

Yards A through D suffered the same treatment. After the count, the officers worked each yard from front to back. My cell was on the lower rear section, so we received the "treatment" last. Once the search teams reached the last few cells, their energy and enthusiasm waned substantially because of the unrelenting desert heat and antipathy from the inmates.

Schmoozing in with the staff paid off since I seldom suffered the disruptive handling others underwent. I prayed Evans would shake down our cell because I trusted her over the others not to nitpick or plant something incriminating.

COs forced selected inmates to strip to their underwear and stand outside as the officers tossed the cell. Officers shook out the bedding and threw the blankets, sheets, and pillows to the floor as though they were infested with lice or bedbugs. They dumped the metal drawers' contents into a pile while latex-gloved hands pawed each piece of clothing. Some inmates, stupid enough to hide contraband, earned a strip search too. I understood the gloves, however. Many convicts were strangers to personal hygiene.

When our turn arrived, Mac and I lingered outside our cell, disheartened by the shattered illusion we retained any privacy. Mac made his bed military-style, which impressed the COs, some of whom were ex-military and often traded service stories with him. Mac's reputation as a no-nonsense vet went a long way to boost our cred with the guards, though he privately held many of them in contempt.

Mac preached, "The guards adhere to what I call the Five I's protocols…"

"What are those?" I asked.

"Incompetence, Indecision, Inadequacy, Indolence, and Idiocy. Most of the COs follow these tenets without fail."

"Brutal, Mac. Not all are like that."

"Most of them are."

Mac's clothes always appeared sharply folded and methodically arranged in his drawer. He taught me to do the same since the COs were less likely to savage a well-ordered cell. Officers picked things up, moved them around, and fingered them with gloved hands but seldom dumped them out for us to pick up and refold.

The desert grime continued its relentless invasion of our cells. Since Mac was a neat freak, he cleaned the crib every two days with buckets of water dumped on the floor and swabbed out. The firm bunks with their blankets and sheets stretched tightly across the flat mattresses left no room to hide anything. The search team lifted the edges to check underneath and moved on.

Our cell never contained contraband, though I always exceeded the two-book limit. If confronted, I reminded the officer I worked in the library and often brought "new" books to examine. This weak explanation satisfied them, and I promised to return the books soon.

In case of a prolonged lockdown, I always stashed several unread selections. Once, a cache of weapons turned up on Yard B in a routine shakedown. To punish us, the administration closed down the facility for three days. Lockdowns were no time to run out of reading material.

These *search-and-destroy* exercises pissed me off. I resented the violation by people who assumed the worst of me. I fumed but said nothing, complied with orders, and feigned indifference.

Tired, thirsty, and angry, I surrendered. I broiled in the hot sun, bored by the officers' work. I experienced an epiphany: nothing belonged to me—not the clothes, the bedding, the toothbrush, the shaver, the soap, the books.

None of these items were mine when I arrived, and I would take nothing with me on release.

The cell I occupied did not belong to me either. Some other schmuck would move in when I departed, and I would not care. With this new insight, I worried less and shrugged off shakedowns over time. Surrendering to events out of my control or losing possessions easily replaceable lowered my blood pressure markedly.

Later that afternoon, CO Evans stopped by the library, looking drawn out and tired, and I said so. Her hair, often nimbly tied back, dangled unkempt despite attempts to push the loose strands under her cap. Sweat stained her underarms, unusual for her. The disheveled presence surprised me.

"I hate these shakedowns," she began. "The work's exhausting and ends up pissing off the staff and the inmates." Evans almost always stood in the library when we spoke, but she settled on one of the empty chairs this time. I listened as she vented a little. These moments were rare when we were alone, away from the rest of the population. Sheltered from the heat and gossipy ears, we commiserated and chatted as friends.

Not accustomed to this level of frankness, I nodded in sympathy and decided to take Evans's side.

"I hear you, but they are necessary. You understand how many fruitcakes roam this yard, and no one is safe with homemade weapons floating around."

Evans's eyes widened with a dazed stare, unaccustomed to an inmate taking a CO's side of things.

"That is true. Most of the time, we find insignificant contraband, but sometimes we uncover weapons, drugs, alcohol, or other things capable of jeopardizing the safety of staff or inmates."

"Well, the exercise is unpleasant, so why bemoan the inevitable? You must do it, and we must let you. Anyway, these massive shakedowns only occur once a month or so. Think of it as part of the rigors of the profession."

"Yes, but I question whether this job is for me on days like this. I'm losing patience in my old age."

I laughed because Evans was only in her late twenties, hardly old. "No job is wonderful every day. A move into management might be worth considering."

"I'd have to go back to school for that. An associate's degree is not enough. But you're right, I've thought about returning for a while. There's no real advancement in DOC without credentials."

"Isn't it funny that pieces of paper carry more weight than actual knowledge and performance?"

"At least a degree says you started and finished something."

Evans had never revealed much of her private life nor seldom asked me for any personal details, but she could have read my jacket and gotten all the sordid facts. Perhaps she already did.

"I graduated from a four-year university in California, and look where it got me."

"You're not the first person I've seen go off the rails despite their education. You are a puzzle, though. You're probably among the smartest people I've met, yet here you are, marking time."

"Yeah, I messed up bad, that's for sure, so now I'm paying."

Evans went quiet, looking out the open door, listening to the desert wind that often kicked up in the afternoons.

"We all make mistakes. Hopefully, we learn from them."

"Agreed," I said, leaning forward.

"I'm optimistic you will not recidivate. Few here show true remorse, but I think you do, James."

Her confidence touched me. "Thank you. That's the kindest thing I've heard all year."

Evans smiled. "Well, thanks for the chat. I'm off to the next milestone in my fantastic day."

That exchange I recalled as the first time Evans spoke my first name. I don't think she realized she had said it, but my heart fluttered.

Moments later, unrecognized footsteps echoed off the stairs. I looked up to find Vargas in the doorway. Since we'd known each other, he had never visited me at the library.

"The CO hassling you?"

"Hi, Luis, No. Evans dropped by to get out of the sun for a minute. Come on in. It's fabulous to see you survived the morning festivities."

Through his sunglasses, he stared at me as though I had spit in his soup.

"No fun for me, standing outside in my *chones* and then a strip search. Do I look like a guy who shoves stuff up his ass?"

"I wouldn't sweat it. The guards want the other convicts to see they can take you down a notch or humiliate you. Don't let them bait you." I explained my revelation about not caring about other people's stuff and how we were all renters here.

Vargas listened and considered what I said.

"*Tu sabes*, Jaime, you look at the world differently than me."

"Glad to help. Now, what's on your mind, since books are not a high priority for you?"

"I have a small problem, and maybe you can help." I gestured for him to sit in the same chair Evans kept warm.

Vargas continued in Spanish to lend an air of privacy. "I need to add another lawyer to my business, and the one I want won't accept cash, and since I prefer to deal in cash only, I need a way to pay him that won't bring the heat down on him or me."

I considered his problem as I took in the mountains, admiring another bright blue summer day. Patient as Job, Vargas scanned the bookshelves behind me as I ruminated.

"There are two ways you might approach this. Is there someone in your circle, a woman in her sixties or older, who you trust?"

"Yes, I think so, my *abuelita*."

"Good. Ask her to open a checking account at one of the smaller banks or a savings and loan. Avoid the majors like Bank of America, Crocker, or Wells. Buy a money order from a supermarket for $100 to open a new account. Make sure she gets an ATM card.

"Put together a crew—use well-dressed women, the older, the better—to visit all the small banks and buy money orders or cashier's checks for odd amounts below $2,000. Don't go to the same bank on any one day."

"Got it."

"Every other day, ask *Abuelita* to deposit checks through the ATM but never more than $10,000 in any monthly statement cycle. Banks must report cash deposits over ten grand, so stay well under the limit. I realize they are checks, but the banks might consider money orders as cash."

"I understand."

"Over time, *Abuelita* will accumulate plenty of cash in her account, and she can use the balance to write checks to your lawyer."

"And the second way?" My scenario really grabbed his interest.

"Yeah, another way is to find a gold dealer who sells one-ounce gold coins, such as Maple Leafs, Krugerrands, or American Eagles. These are best since they are the most liquid. Use companies in another city like LA or Las Vegas, who will accept cash for payment with no questions. This search may take a while, but coin dealers often prefer cash. Buy as many gold coins as you can and keep them in a safe place. Hopefully, the price of gold will increase in the meantime."

Vargas nodded for me to continue.

"When you need the funds, go to a local gold dealer or one in a nearby city and sell them back, but insist on a check, not cash, written to *Abuelita*. You could send her to cash in the coins, but it doesn't matter. Deposit the checks into *Abuelita's* account so you may write personal checks."

"I never thought of doing this. You're sure this works?"

"*Sí, Señor.*"

Back to English. "Thanks for your help. I will consider what you say." He reached out to shake my hand. "By the way," he said, "you don't get visits, right?"

"No. The outside world is only a dream for me. *La Vida es Sueño.*"

Vargas grinned and left, ignorant of the literary reference or too apathetic to ask. Thirty minutes to the afternoon count. I picked up my book and continued, unaware I had steered my journey in an unexpected direction.

CHAPTER 8

Several weeks had elapsed since my impromptu business meeting with Vargas. While cutting my hair, he said, "*Oye*, I did as you suggested. I think it will work out rather well."

"Which idea did you follow?"

"Both of them. Why not? I liked the idea of gold rather than boxes of paper."

Vargas never told me his source of income. I believed it prudent not to *understand* too much. The less I knew, the better. More unwritten prison rules: keep your mouth shut, don't gossip about another man's livelihood or count his money.

I handed him a pack of smokes after he finished the haircut.

"Listen, amigo. *Mi primita* finished a two-year program at the community college, the first in our family to graduate. I think you two might be *simpático*."

"*¿En realidad?*"

"Of all my cousins, she's strong-willed, opinionated, and ambitious, not your traditional Chicana. I don't think she'll ever be one of those stay-at-home types or the kind of *chicas* I grew up around."

Vargas piqued my interest.

"If you don't want to meet her, I understand. Since you never come to Visitation, I thought you might like company."

He handed me a folded piece of paper. "Here's Consuelo's info. If you add her to your list, I'll tell her she may visit you."

"Did you tell her about me?"

"Yes. Consuelo's curious about how I got friendly with a college *güero* here on the Yard." I had never explained the story about how a middle-class, college-educated kid with a Spanish surname got here, nor did Vargas ask.

"Give me a day to think about it."

Vargas seldom did things without strings, and he probably wanted to pay me back for the advice I'd given him. Meeting his family might bind us in ways I wasn't sure I wanted. What if Consuelo and I didn't like each other or we argued? How would this affect my relationship with Luis? Still, the idea of visits from a young woman who didn't wear a uniform appealed to me.

I slept on it. The following day, I trudged up to the administration to add Consuelo to my visitors' list. There was no harm in talking. If she had time to visit an inmate in prison, perhaps Consuelo's boredom matched mine.

Ten days later, CO Evans popped into the library to tell me a visitor had passed the background check. Evans knew I received little mail and no visits. She lingered, perhaps, to find out who this visitor might be. Her furtive interest surprised me. With other inmates unable to overhear us, we became a little friendlier. However, to be seen too cozy with a guard might get me accused of dry snitching or worse.

"If you're wondering, Evans, my visitor is a friend's cousin who I've never met. Perhaps she's got this thing for convicts." I spoke flippantly, but Evans didn't follow.

"When a woman visits a man, she comes because she wants to, or because she hopes for something."

"Sure. The happy couple can fantasize about a wonderful life together once he gets out. Any chance I can sign up for conjugal visits?"

"Absolutely no chance. Only minimum security can earn those and only between married couples." The edge to her voice surprised me.

"Chill. Just kidding, Evans. I am not expecting much. Someone new to talk to would be healthy for me and relieve boredom."

"That makes sense."

"As much as I enjoy our conversations, your rules and protocols keep us as far apart as possible while still in the same town." She gave me a downcast glance, her eyes narrowing as she considered what I said. Evans liked me. I watched how she interacted with the others, keeping them at a distance, and I believed myself lucky to spend time with her. She was intelligent, sympathetic, and curious.

"Well, can't chat today. See you."

Evans breezed out the door. The uniform didn't flatter her much, but the sight of a young woman walking away gave me solace, and I savored every moment for the unexpected and fleeting pleasure her bearing offered me.

The days ticked down. Another haircut, the moon cycled through its phases as the summer's unrelenting heat faded, and we slow-walked into autumn. The nights cooled, and I switched to long-sleeve shirts. My allergies abated somewhat, along with the dust storms. The seasonal winds shifted, and the dew point dropped.

I welcomed the more temperate days as I circled the track, alert to subtle changes, such as the shifting stars, at least the ones that penetrated the prison light canopy. Orion, Canis Major, and the Big Dipper were the most visible constellations that ranged in and out of view during the seasons. How would these stars glisten when viewed from beyond the fences?

Time passed like the desert wind, variable and unpredictable, always relentless.

I remembered Maria and blinked away the tears.

Spiritual books never ranged high on my reading list, but I finished an intriguing volume by Philip Kapleau Roshi, a Buddhist monk. From *The Three Pillars of Zen*, I learned that Zen was not a religion but a philosophy. My counterpart from Yard C found the paperback in the mess hall mislaid by someone who made parole but never returned it to the library. This book appeared when I was most receptive to its message.

I carried *The Three Pillars* back to my cell and read it over several days. After my release, I read many books on Zen Buddhism, but this account remained one of the best written in English. Its comprehensive overview helped me put into perspective some insights I'd gleaned but could not articulate.

The text presented the teachings understandably and gave practical methods to implement them. I meditated according to the instructions. The technique focused on the breath: count each one up to ten, then start over. At first, I couldn't concentrate. At five or six, I lost count and started again. My thoughts bounced around like a troop of monkeys flying from branch to branch. I tried to incorporate this "monkey brain" to let them whirl about, acknowledge their presence, and follow the tally. Twice a day for twenty minutes, while the prison whirled around me, I sat with my eyes closed, relaxed, followed my breath, and waited for calm. With practice, I kept the count as my monkeys rested.

Breathing connects the mind and body. A still mind relaxed the body. Once I retained the count, I added the mantra Mu. When a student asked a Zen master whether a dog had a Buddha nature, he answered, "*Mu*!"

This Zen koan became the first in a collection called the "Gateless Gate." Zen teachers created koans to overcome the barriers between the logical and intuitive mind or the surrounding conceptional fog. No rational answer to the koan existed because the question had no meaning.

Many aspects of my prison life persisted out of my control. Agitation over shakedowns or my predicament was meaningless. Rather than deny my experiences, I attempted to integrate them. When I had used psychedelics, I glimpsed the world's interconnectedness, which I now grasped more clearly—how shapes become discernible when seen from a distance. Once I surrendered the uncontrollable, the unobtainable became possible.

Evans's footsteps echoed into the library as I meditated. She stood in the doorway, casting a shadow, and the flicker of light lifted me to the surface.

"Am I disturbing you?"

I opened my eyes, "Not at all, resting my eyes for a moment."

"Napping?"

"I am learning to meditate. I find it helpful to sit and let this place recede into the background."

Evans listened thoughtfully while I explained the essentials of *The Three Pillars of Zen* and my efforts to apply what I learned.

"Too few of us give attention to the unseen," I said.

"Once I moved from my dad's house, I stopped attending Catholic Mass."

"Your dad's house?"

"I left after high school. I lost my faith after my mom died in my junior year."

"I'm sorry."

"I tend towards the agnostic these days. Working in a correctional facility doesn't reinforce one's belief in a deity."

"Really? Aren't we all God's children, even those of us who have lost our way? Perhaps the penitentiary is broader than the narrow prison we left on the outside."

"You're awfully metaphysical today. Tell me more about this Buddhism."

"Buddhism appeals to me because its practice does not require belief in a god or a higher power, so I can cling to my agnosticism until I decide."

She nodded. "Or hang on to forever."

"May I make another book recommendation?"

"Please."

"Check out Hermann Hesse's novel *Siddhartha*. Siddhartha's spiritual journey of self-discovery is both enlightening and entertaining. Hesse introduces some of Buddhism's tenets without being technical or heavy-handed." I wrote the title on a slip of paper and handed it to her.

"If nothing else, the novel is well-written and engaging whether you buy into Buddhism or not."

"Do you think it's possible to be decent and moral without God?" she asked suddenly, a quiet seriousness etched on her brow.

"Yes. It's possible. Despite my agnosticism, I believe in the Judeo-Christian moral principles."

"How's that?"

"If everyone followed the Ten Commandments, prisons would be unnecessary."

"Hm. Something to think about. Thanks, Professor. Always a wellspring of wisdom. I'll think about what you said."

In the kingdom of Yard D, I was the one-eyed fool in the realm of the blind.

A northerly breeze descended on the camp on an uncharacteristically cloudy morning in late October. I scribbled in my journal at one of the picnic tables in my building's grassy foreyard, available for conversation with whoever passed by. Then the loudspeaker announced my name: a visitor.

I ran to my cell to brush my teeth, comb my hair, and put on my last clean shirt until laundry day.

Today I met the mysterious Consuelo. Like a kid on his way to Disneyland, I raced to Visitation but slowed down halfway to not overheat.

Visitation filled as congregants arrived and claimed their spots among the metal tables and benches bolted to the checkered linoleum floor.

Each inmate underwent a pat-down for contraband on entry and exit. Some were selected for strip searches after the visits if the COs suspected them or if they had a sketchy disciplinary history. The authorities banned anyone caught smuggling drugs or weapons into the Unit from further visits and brought them up on charges. Officers often arrested visitors involved and perp-walked them as a warning. Very few inmates or arrivals jeopardized their visitation privileges.

After the pat-down and metal detector sweep, the officer in charge let me into the hall. Not knowing what Consuelo looked like, I scanned the room for a young woman sitting alone. All the visitors dressed for the occasion, including the children. Some women wore sleeveless, thinly strapped dresses hemmed above the knee in various festive colors. Others sported tight jeans or slacks. Many blouses displayed cleavage, which men in prison appreciated.

One Chicana flagged my attention as she fidgeted in her chair. I approached her, clearing my throat.

"Consuelo?"

"Yes." She smiled warmly, extending her small, dry hand as I sat down on the other side of the table and engaged her brown eyes.

"Thanks for coming."

"Not at all. *Tío* Luis said many positive things about you, so I thought, why not?" She called Vargas *Tío* because it was often customary to refer to an older cousin as Uncle.

"Did it take long to pass through the security gauntlet?"

"Not really. Security is efficient, as I imagine at the airport, though I have never flown. Have you?"

"I have spent more time in airports than you did in college, waiting for flights to Europe, Asia, and South America."

"Why so many places?"

"My import-export business obligated me to travel. I enjoyed running around at the onset, but after days in airport lounges, the enthusiasm for flying wanes sooner than you think. I don't want to discourage you. Everyone should venture beyond the United States. The world is huge, a lot to experience. New people and cultures are always fascinating."

"I went to México twice by car but didn't care for the border towns. They were too dirty and rundown."

"The best parts of the country are where people are less itinerant, families are more stable, and the populace maintains pride in their cities and towns. Of all the places, México and Spain are my favorites, though Paris is most like home."

"I would love to visit Paris."

"Places are what we bring to them and what they reveal to us. May I tell you a little story?"

"Oh yes. Please do."

"In high school, I was a member of a local Rotary Club chapter, sponsored by our school. We conducted a food, clothing, and toy drive for weeks until we accumulated enough to fill a small truck."

"Was this for charity?"

"Yes. One day, in a caravan of several cars, we followed the truck to a neglected orphanage in Tijuana, one of those dirty border towns you mentioned."

"Oh. Sorry."

"No. It's all right. Parts of Tijuana are definitely rundown and abandoned. Our little troupe pulled into the orphanage on the outskirts of town on an unpaved side street where sewage ran in the gutters. We unloaded the truck into a great room while thirty little kids stood by in wonder as we brought more things than they had ever seen."

"I imagine seeing so much food and clothes would be amazing for them."

"It was. I always took my life for granted until I saw how those kids, used to nothing at all, suddenly found themselves rich. Canned food and second-hand clothes and toys, while not much to us, meant something to them. Their joy has stayed with me ever since. Tijuana became a much more meaningful place from that day on." My memory brought a tear to my eye, which I quickly brushed away.

"This visit, it changed you, I think." Consuelo started to reach out and take my hand but stopped.

"Yes. Until then, I never considered the people beyond the neighborhoods I grew up in nor spent a day without everything I needed."

Consuelo scanned the room filled with mixed voices in Spanish and English.

"Do you speak any foreign languages?" she asked.

"*Sí, cómo no.*" We spoke in Spanish. Although Consuelo was fluent, she used the dialect common among those born on this side of the border.

"I want to travel to Europe."

"I've traveled throughout the UK, France, Spain, Germany, Italy, and Yugoslavia. I love Paris, Madrid, and Barcelona, I guess, because I speak Spanish and French. While in Barcelona, I picked up a little Catalan, a beautiful language that melds Spanish, French, and Latin."

Consuelo peppered me with questions about my travels. I had been denied casual female company for so long that I couldn't help but take in her wavy brunette hair, clear complexion, and mocha skin. She was twenty-two or twenty-three while I was pushing the backside of thirty. I wondered if a fifteen-year gap in our ages mattered to her. Lean but not tall, she had a natural grace I found attractive. Her bright eyes, accented with minimum makeup, sparkled with intelligence.

"Your uncle tells me you just graduated college?"

"Yes. Last June, I earned an associate degree in business. Now I'm a bookkeeper for a downtown furniture store."

"I worked in an accounting department for an aerospace company in a previous life."

"Well, it's not my dream job, but the experience helps me gain some skills and build a résumé."

"The important thing is to start. The beginning is not as important as where you land. Surely, not in a place like this," I added.

"Yeah, way too many of my family ended up *away*. I'm not proud of it, but all my brothers and male cousins spent some time in jail. Who can say no to making so-called 'easy money' with everyone around them in the game?"

Consuelo shook her head and shrugged.

"My aunts, sisters, and female cousins cried over their locked-up men." Bitterness crept into her voice. I almost touched her hand. What would it be like to fall in love with her?

Consuelo anticipated my next question.

"I intended to visit sooner. I broke up with my childhood sweetheart last summer, and finding my bearings took me some time. When *Tío* Luis told me you added me to your list, I planned to come immediately but needed more time. It would be unfair to use you to help me rebound from a breakup."

Consuelo placed her hands in her lap.

"Tell me more if you like."

"Miguel and I met in grammar school and agreed to marry someday. Our families expected us to follow the ways of our mothers and grandmothers. He didn't want me to attend college, but I dreamed of going since my *quinceañera*. Education helped me find a different path, leading me away from him and the family business. An early marriage, having kids too soon, would mean giving up my career. I want a life apart from a husband. I will marry later, but why rush?"

"In uncertainty, it's wise to think things through."

"Miguel got into some major trouble. He joined *Tío* Luis's thing and killed somebody by accident. He got fifteen years with no eligibility for parole. I couldn't imagine waiting until 37 to begin my life while spending my youth sitting across from him at a table."

Realizing what she'd said, Consuelo flushed with embarrassment.

"Sorry. *Tío* Luis told me you were due for parole soon; otherwise, I would not have come."

"Thanks for being honest. Listen, please don't feel any obligation whatsoever. Not surprisingly, this place lacks witty conversationalists. I'm happy to talk, that's all."

Consuelo smiled. "What college did you go to?"

"I attended UC Berkeley and graduated with a bachelor's in comparative literature. My languages were Spanish, French, and Latin."

"You had to read books in those languages?"

"Yes. A complete dictionary is handy."

"I only read one book in Spanish in high school, by Julio Cortázar."

"*Rayuela?*"

"Yes, a strange book, but I loved it."

"Quite an ambitious book for a high schooler, with the convoluted timelines and stream-of-consciousness."

"I wanted to read something different and challenging. Most of the stuff we got in high school was lame."

We talked about the Spanish novel for several minutes. Consuelo impressed me with her intuitive knowledge of the book's themes and how much she remembered in the four years since she read it.

"After talking to you, I'm inspired to explore other literature," she said. I gave her a quick list of Spanish novels I thought she might enjoy. She had heard of some of them and promised to look for them.

Our first visit ended when the CO called, "Five minutes!" I hoped she would come next weekend but didn't want to pressure her.

Consuelo circled to my side of the table as people departed and gave me a sisterly *beso* on the cheek. "I'm so happy to meet you, Jaime. May I visit again?"

"*Absolutemente. Espero verte de nuevo.*"

I inhaled the strawberry scent in her hair and complimented her.

We said goodbye. I wanted to see more of her as she walked away in those tight jeans, medium-sized heels, and her torero-red blouse.

CHAPTER 9

After supper one evening, I dropped off my tray and, lost in some idle thought, crashed into a squat Chicano named Hernandez as we both tried to exit simultaneously.

"Excuse me," I said. Hernandez scowled and grunted as though I bumped him on purpose.

He pushed through the doorway ahead of me and wheeled around, confronting me. I stopped, about to maneuver around him, when his fist connected with my temple as he sucker-punched me. My legs crumpled, and I collapsed to the concrete walkway, instinctively breaking my fall with my arm.

Like a Sam Peckinpah movie, all the action unfolded in slow motion. I lost consciousness and revived to find a shadow standing over me, several loud voices, and two brown shirts tackling Hernandez to the ground and slapping on the handcuffs as he resisted.

Nice takedown.

Another CO joined us and dragged my assailant to the Hole. The second officer helped me to my feet.

"You hurt?"

"Yeah. No. I don't know," I said, still disoriented. A wicked headache spread over my skull, and a road rash on my hand hurt like hell.

"You don't look fine. Come on, let's visit the infirmary."

The prison nurse cleaned out the scrape on my hand and wrapped a bandage.

"There's nothing critical. No concussion."

"I'm still a little dizzy."

"Lie back and rest. We got time until the 9:30 count."

She busied herself with other inmates while I strained to remember what had happened and why Hernandez had turned so hostile.

Finally, the nurse gave me some Tylenol and released me to my unit.

The next afternoon, I showed up for a haircut.

"What's this bandage and bruise on the side of your head, *ese*?" Vargas asked.

"Oh, some guy sucker-punched me last night at the mess hall." I explained as much as I remembered.

When I finished my story, Vargas said, "Excuse me," and stepped outside on the tier. A *vato* came over, and the two spoke in soft tones I couldn't overhear. The guys always hanging around the barbershop camped out in case Vargas needed them. How convenient to have staff available to run errands, act as lookouts, and provide personal protection.

Vargas returned and continued the haircut without a word more about my incident.

About a week later, as I walked the track, Hernandez approached me from the other direction. I balled my hands into tightened fists as my heart rate skyrocketed. No way would he catch me unprepared this time.

Hernandez stopped ten feet away, held out his open palms, and approached me.

"*Oye, mano*. About the other day: I had a fight with my wife. Sorry, *ese*. Here, take this, okay?" Hernandez handed me two packs of cigarettes, both Menthols, Vargas's brand.

I accepted the packs and held out my hand. Surprised, Hernandez reached over, and we shook.

"*No hay de que.*"

"*Lo siento*," he nodded and walked away.

We never spoke again, but on occasion, he nodded in greeting whenever we passed near each other. Perhaps Hernandez didn't like me, but he always showed respect. For me, polite deference was enough.

My facility's sixteen hundred or so books, spread across four small library collections, had no organizing principle other than fiction versus nonfiction. As each group of books rotated through my library, I imposed order. First, I divided the nonfiction books into science, history, psychology, and so on, alphabetically by author. General fiction broke down into romance, crime, science fiction, and literary fiction. Resources, and honestly, the inclination to implement anything more elaborate, did not exist.

I implored Officer Lopez to find me a manual or electric typewriter to inventory the titles. A computer with a spreadsheet program would have been better, but for inmates, computers were forbidden for fear we might MacGyver or jury-rig a modem from spare parts and ravage the free world.

One morning when I opened the library, I found a freshly ribboned 1955 Underwood upright typewriter sitting on my desk, like the one I owned as a kid. Too bad I had no paper. The commissary sold bond paper, but why should I spend my money on supplies? I wasn't a public school teacher.

Struck with an idea, I shuffled to the admin building to talk to the head inmate secretary, Larsen. He sat characteristically idle behind his hefty wooden desk like the gatekeeper before heaven. He held the most trusted clerkship in the Unit. The warden's clerk saw documents and overheard conversations inmates shouldn't.

Larsen modeled a shriveled bureaucrat in his eighties with thin white hair, a small nose, and a scratchy voice. Most disliked his quick wit and sardonic humor, both of which appealed to me. He struck me as pouty, forthright, and no-nonsense.

Forty, fifty, or sixty years older, he shared few mutual interests with his fellow inmates. The Yard consensus pegged him with a ten-year sentence for a white-collar beef; others believed he molested a child, but I doubted this latter scenario because he would've been dead already if it had been confirmed. Molesters inhabited the ninth circle of hell, and they deserved it.

Larsen lived on Yard D and visited the library periodically, so he recognized me when I showed up.

"CO Lopez left me a typewriter, but I need some paper. Can you help me out there?"

"Sure. I can rustle up some for you. Why do you need it?"

"I thought I'd create a quick-and-dirty inventory of all the library books."

"All four libraries?"

"Why not? I'll catalog them as they rotate from yard to yard."

"Why bother with a list of books? Few read around here, and management doesn't give a flying fuck," he said in a hushed voice in case the warden overheard us.

"True enough, but the exercise gives me something to do. Also, I want to type up some of my poems and short stories."

"You would be in esteemed company. Thoreau, O. Henry, Wilde, King—all wrote from prison." Larsen's literary history and bookish knowledge surprised me.

"My ego's not that ambitious. I'm just a scribbler at heart." We laughed. "Best of luck."

After his shift, he dropped by with half a ream of typing paper.

I compiled my list for several days, leaving three empty lines between each entry to add books as they came in without retyping the whole page.

Evans swung by as usual and expressed curiosity about the new acquisition.

"Officer Lopez provided everything I needed to organize the unit libraries, except for the paper. That I had to scrounge for on my own."

She asked me the same question as Larsen: why bother?

"I don't have much autonomy around here. This list is one small aspect of my life I control. A small thing, yes, and no one cares, and once I'm gone, the list will go stale, but the exercise is useful and appeals to my sense of order. Besides, I have time. Plenty."

While waiting for the scheduled recycling of books from one yard to the next, I made a field trip to the Law Library, where I located an outdated Yellow Pages on a top shelf, three years old but recent enough for my purposes. From its pages, I assembled a list of local entities such as libraries, thrift stores, and used booksellers that might donate books for a charitable deduction.

With the list in hand, I typed up individual letters to request donations to a worthy cause, emphasizing the rehabilitative powers of reading. I used Lopez's name because DOC wouldn't allow an inmate to solicit merchandise. If she didn't go for my plan, the books on hand would have to suffice.

CO Lopez made her weekly visit to discover me hunched over my catalog.

"Just in time. I've been working on a project to expand the inventory." She took the draft letters and glanced through them.

"You have taken the initiative here. Good."

"Long overdue, Officer Lopez. This meager collection needs some refreshing. Look behind me, a half-empty shelf, the same on the other yards. I don't expect much, but maybe we'll acquire ten or twenty new volumes. Worth a shot, right?"

"Yes, but these can't go out like this."

"Correct. Retyping the letters on department letterhead and mailing them officially would be helpful."

"Fine, I'll tell Larsen to type these up and send them. We'll see if your salesmanship works out."

Lopez took the stack of twenty letters and started for the door.

"You're all right. Thanks for doing this. Too bad there aren't more like you," she said.

"Kind of you to say so. Just trying to model proper behavior."

"Keep doing it."

Only the cynical would point out that building up the library, unasked, might support my bid for parole on the first try. Sometimes looking for an angle isn't always a bad thing.

Weeks later, after breakfast, the loudspeaker blasted my name and ordered me to the Yard D guard shack.

"Some boxes are up in the administration building out of security inspection. Books, I think."

"Excellent." I raced up to Admin, expecting to find perhaps one or two book boxes, but instead, I discovered eight stacked in a corner in front of the warden's office.

Over at the mailroom across from the warden's, I spotted CO Riley chit-chatting with the two officers assigned to our little prison post office.

"Officers. There are several boxes I need to move to the library on Yard D. Can anyone run me down there in the company pick-up?"

"I ain't too busy," Riley said. "Let me bring the truck around so you can load them."

Riley drove my treasure to the foot of the stairs below the library, where I unloaded the cartons. I lugged them upstairs by myself. Everyone scattered when there was work to be done.

The new collection came from three different sources, all on various subjects. Like a kid on Christmas Day, I unpacked them and divided books into two piles, fiction and nonfiction. Before distributing them among the other libraries, I wanted to inventory them and select which remained with me—final count: 102 volumes.

Most of the books were mundane, but some fired my imagination. The first was *The Theory and Practice of Oligarchical Collectivism* by Emmanuel Goldstein, a political tract to bludgeon me with slogans about bureaucratic collectivism, a perfect read while on a prolonged lockdown.

The cache included all four volumes of Lawrence Durrell's *Alexandria Quartet*, which had received a favorable appraisal in the *Paris Review*. The story presented three perspectives on numerous events in the Egyptian city before, during, and after World War II. The author evoked the desert seaside metropolis so richly that it evolved into a significant Levantine character. If only my little desert had a sea nearby. I missed the scent of brine on the breeze.

Spread between two separate boxes, I found Marcel Proust's *Remembrance of Things Past*'s complete paperbacks, translated by Moncrieff and Kilmartin. Why would anyone give up this fantastic work of French literature—one of those novels everyone praised but nobody read.

Each of the three physical volumes contained over 1,000 pages, and I was eager to start.

One morning I awoke from a dream: *Trial by fire cleanses the darkened soul.* Did I hear this phrase somewhere, perhaps a song lyric, a line from a poem I once read, or a sentence from a long-forgotten novel? Dread lurked in the shadows.

My legs ached. Paralyzed. "Mac, you there? I can't move." Silence.

Panic mounted as sharp pains punctuated each breath.

Fear. Cold sweat beaded on my forehead and slid down my face.

Where was I? Now, I remember.

Concentrate by counting each breath.

A dream. I'm still dreaming.

The door locks clicked. Mac left for breakfast.

I willed myself to sit up and slide to the cold concrete floor.

At the sink, I rinsed my face. The fear subsided.

I deserved pain and punishment. No redemption.

Maria, my love, what have I done?
I wish I could relieve your suffering.

Knowing you're near helps, chérie.
I'll be with you forever, mon cher.

Five days before Thanksgiving on Saturday morning, another day to endure. A month had passed since Consuelo's last visit. I dragged myself to the shower to cleanse the night terrors. After dressing and shaving, still drained from fever dreams, I took my book to the picnic table to read before it got too hot.

The loudspeaker barked my name. A flash of relief pulsed through me as though I had held my breath; now, I could breathe.

In my crib, I checked myself in the polished metal mirror, ignored the distortions, and headed to Visitation. Security labored in slow motion but got me inside.

Consuelo waited in a corner with a broad smile, dressed in a short dress, her shoulders bare, her skin flawless. She wore a touch of makeup that accented her eyes, hair around her shoulders, and small studded emerald earrings.

"Consuelo, you look so beautiful."

"Thank you. Why not dress up a little for you? I feel bad that so much time has passed since our last visit. I had to take the weekend shift when one of my coworkers took maternity leave, but my weekends are free again."

"I wondered what happened to you. In a dark moment, I thought perhaps you lost interest."

"I like you a lot, but work is work."

"True." The grin on my face belied the ordeal of the early morning. "You are fashionable. I'll be the envy of the Yard when the news filters back about my chic visitor."

Consuelo blushed. "Thank you."

"Just so you know, I'm inspired by beauty and brains."

"Do you think I'm smart?"

"Definitely. Intelligence is one of your best features."

"I'm glad you're in a sunny mood. I was a little down this morning; I had this weird dream where I had an appointment for a job interview, but I couldn't find the floor. Up and down the elevator I went, getting off on random, empty floors without anyone to ask for directions. Finally, I left and went home. Strange, no?"

"Yes. Losing-your-way dreams are related to insecurity about a decision, choice, new situation, or refusal to acknowledge you're in a rut."

"Makes sense. I am a little bored with my job, and I want to make a change."

"Unfortunately, the dream doesn't always tell you whether to act. You must figure out the next steps on your own."

Consuelo twirled a lock of her hair with her left hand as I spoke.

"Something for me to think about. How do you know about dreams?"

"I used to have a lot of weird dreams and read several books on them. I experienced an odd dream too." I told her about last night, or most of it. After I finished, a long but comfortable pause passed between us. We smiled at each other, waiting for the other to continue.

"May I ask you something? Please don't answer if you don't want to."

"Sure," I said, "you can ask me anything."

"How did a guy like you end up here?"

Was I ready to tell her? Her look of anticipation and sympathy encouraged me to talk aloud about my crime. I hid much of who I was and what had happened to me from my fellow inmates, but I wanted to be friends with Consuelo, so I broke the rule about discussing my case.

"The affair seems so anticlimactic now. I was no master criminal, merely an idiot who trapped himself with no way out. Remember, I told you about my import-export company?" She nodded. "Well, my partners and I made quite a bit of money and earned almost two million dollars before we expanded our San Francisco offices. We slaved to build a good-sized company that would set us up for life."

"What did you import and export?"

"Mostly computer parts, equipment, software, networks, anything needed in a computer data center or a modern office. I was the CFO and handled sales for our more valuable customers. After Reagan's reelection, the Feds clamped down on exporters of American high-tech products to Eastern Europe. We partnered with a distributor in Austria who would buy a lot of stuff from us and supply his customers in Poland, Czechoslovakia, Yugoslavia, and other parts of Europe. High-tech export licenses through the Department of Commerce allowed us to ship. The approvals were *pro forma*."

"Sounds like an exciting business."

"It was. But the process changed, and specific license applications now required secondary approval by the Defense Department. Commerce would approve our licenses and send them to DOD, an abyss where requests vanish forever. No response, no permits, nothing came back. Soon, our business deteriorated without approved licenses, and we exhausted our cash and couldn't pay the bills."

"So, what did you do?"

"We got creative. We found freight forwarders who would ship our goods overseas without asking questions. No matter what we sent, we labeled them 'Electronic Parts' or 'Machine Parts,' which is vague enough to pass through customs. We shipped anything on the proscribed item list, and whatever our customers needed, they got. Before you ask, our clients were insurance companies, banks, agricultural firms, and places like that, only they hailed from behind the Iron Curtain. The American government insisted every piece of technology would help the Soviet Union."

I stopped for a second to catch my breath. Consuelo glanced around the room and waved. Luis sat with his wife several tables over, and they waved back. With a nod, I acknowledged him and his guest.

"Although we sold without export licenses, our business dwindled to a third of what it once was. We all had mortgages, rent, cars, and lives to maintain, and the money kept drying up. Every month it got harder to pay the essential bills like utilities for the office and groceries. I awoke each night drenched in sweat for a year, agonizing over how to cover the rent due on the first of the month. My partners and I tried to do everything possible to rebuild our trade, but the strength of the dollar and the European recession made a recovery a lost cause."

"*Dios mio*, that sounds terrible."

"Yes. I hated my life, the company, and the government. We blew through our credit and couldn't convince our suppliers to advance merchandise, so we used cash. After the first few checks bounced, creditors demanded cashier's checks, which we couldn't buy because we had no money. We put the company into bankruptcy proceedings, but I got *creative* in a last heroic effort to save our dream."

Consuelo gave me a pained look to brace herself for the worst.

"Since we maintained multiple accounts in several banks, I wrote checks from one to another, hoping to cover the bad drafts with accounts receivables."

"Check kiting?"

"Exactly. The bank clearing procedure gave me two or three days to make good on the last bogus deposit with the accounts in different states. The scheme worked for a while, but in the end, the business collapsed. Vendors and the banks called the police, and here I am. I wrote the checks and took the fall so my partners wouldn't go to jail. Everyone knew, but I wouldn't snitch on them. I signed enough bogus paper for about $100,000."

"How much time did you receive"?

"I took a plea: eight months from the Feds for bank fraud and seven years from the state on the forgery charge, eligible for parole after 35 months. The plea deal I signed stated I would do the federal time first and then transfer to state custody. Something went wrong, and the US Marshals never came to collect me. With this federal detainer, DOC classified me as medium instead of minimum security, so I'm here. After I'm done at his facility, I go to Club Fed for five or six months of golf and tennis before my final release."

"Quite a lot of time for so little money. You were a first-time offender?"

"Yes. I caught a prosecutor out to make a name for himself by racking up as many convictions as possible. If I had remained in California, I would have received probation as a first-timer."

"*Tío* Luis knows about this legal stuff like detainers. Did you talk to him?"

"No, not yet. Excellent idea, though. Thanks."

"Sorry about what happened to you. When is your parole hearing?"

"In May coming up. I can't wait. Most guys tell me how hard it is to make parole the first time, but I'll prove them wrong."

"I'll pray for you."

"Thank you, Consuelo. I'm sure you have other things to do on your day off, but I'm glad you came today. "

"I like talking to you. You're worth the time." Consuelo reached over and took my hand. For a moment, I let myself hope all would work out.

"What about your family?" she asked.

"My mom and I talk occasionally. My father died ten years ago in the Dominican Republic. My parents and my father's sisters live in Los Angeles. I have some close friends. They're musicians and travel extensively."

"You're Dominicano?"

"Half. My mother is Italian."

"You never married?"

"I was engaged once."

"I'm the youngest of three sisters. *Tío* Luis is the first son of my uncle. *Tío* Luis went away soon after my *quinceañera*, so I don't know him that well anymore, but he used to babysit my sisters and me."

Looking up at the ceiling, I said, "I'm trying to imagine Luis babysitting a bunch of little girls."

"Luis is not the most open of men, but he is kind to us, and his heart is good, except . . . "

"Except?"

"His business, I hate it. Did he tell you?"

"No, and I never asked. I can't say what I don't know."

"True enough. None of our concern, anyway."

Later that night, I dropped by Luis's cell and found him dozing in front of the TV. He offered me a Diet Coke.

"Consuelo suggested I talk to you. Do you know anything about detainers?" I explained my situation with the Feds.

"A writ of habeas corpus is what you need. There's a guy who's excellent with court papers and such named Carlson. I'll hook you up."

"Sounds great."

CHAPTER 10

Icouldn't be sure then, but I hoped this holiday season would be my last behind bars. Thanksgiving was one of my favorite times, and I longed to spend it with my family.

My third Thanksgiving passed uneventfully. The Camp presented another impoverished dinner in the penitential lights of a monochrome mess hall. DOC served a pitifully lackluster meal of warm turkey, mashed potatoes, biscuits, and a cranberry-like sauce, more like a heated jam. I picked at my plate, ate some, gave the rest away, and headed to the track to put in my ten miles.

Since reading *The Three Pillars of Zen*, I had worked on my walking meditation to maintain equanimity and presence of mind. I stopped fighting incarceration, knowing that someday imprisonment would end and become another faded memory to set aside, not to forget, but to let go.

Near the holidays, the Yard changed as it did every year. The days grew shorter, the skies darkened by 5:30, and the temperature dropped into the 50s and 60s. Reduced sunlight, elevated stress, and diminished immune responses triggered Seasonal Affective Disorder.

Many of us fell ill as cold and flu swept through the yards. Neither inmate nor staff resisted the viral onslaught. CO Evans stayed home for a week with flu and a nasty cough. She didn't sound healthy when she returned, but cabin fever and dwindling sick time compelled her to return to work.

Only those who followed exercise routines escaped the worst of the illnesses. I never succumbed, but my allergies flared up and became chronic nasal congestion. After a three-day wait, I saw the nurse, who gave me some allergy pills, the little yellow ones, which were ineffective.

The Christmas season used to be a time of celebration, yet pernicious negativity rolled over us like eternal death. One would think year-end holidays for inmates would be a breeze: no money worries, shopping lists, store crowds, or traffic, and other things people found trying.

The opposite occurred: no gifts for the kids, no excursions to pick out a tree, and no holiday meals with family or joyful satisfaction on Christmas morning as the children tore into their presents. Prisoners missed the milestones in their kids' young lives. Wives and girlfriends shouldered the burden of single parenthood. Inmates' loneliness reinforced a cycle of stress, fatigue, and suicidal ideation.

We always celebrated the holidays when I was young. Every year, my stepfather and I searched for the grandest Christmas tree our living room would hold. A lot near our house offered hundreds of fresh Douglas and Noble firs. We walked up and down the rows to scout for the perfect tree: the right size, a uniform shape, crisp needles still attached, and the intoxicating scent of pine.

"How about this one, Dad?"

"See how the needles fall off too quickly. Too dry."

We kept searching. At eight years old, I never tired of any Christmas-related activity.

"Here we go," Dad said. "See, the needles are fresh like the tree had been cut yesterday. Mama will like this one."

Dad tied the fir to the roof of his car for the ride home. Mom came out to greet us as we pulled up. Pleased, she put a Christmas blanket over a tarp while we retrieved the tree stand from the garage and fitted our treasure into the holder.

Mom loved the festive holidays and decorated the house with every Yuletide knickknack she'd collected through the years. Even the carnival glass escaped their boxes to adorn our shelves. What I wouldn't give to relive the holidays through those innocent eyes again.

On December 13th, around 1:15 p.m., the powers-that-be called a Code Red lockdown. We remained confined to our cells until supper, which didn't start until 6 o'clock, later than usual. No one said anything or knew why the lockdown occurred, but rumors flew. The next day, the grim story unfolded.

Larsen dropped by the library to return his book and select another.

"Did you know Conrad? A young dude who worked in our cafeteria here."

"I saw him behind the serving line, but we never met," I said, unsure if Conrad was his first or last name.

"Anyway, the guy received a Dear John letter from his high school sweetheart. She dumped him and announced her engagement to a buddy of his. Already in the grips of the holiday doldrums, her rejection only squeezed tighter and pushed him too far."

"Holidays can be rough on some."

"A department-operated garbage truck backed into the rear of the dining hall to empty the kitchen Dumpster. By protocol, a CO would inspect each bin before unloading it. Yard D was the last pickup. The officer who supervised the galley overlooked the final inspection."

"He's in trouble."

"Yeah. DOC won't fire him, but he can kiss off any promotions for a while."

"Conrad's kitchen job put him in the right spot at the right time. He waved to the driver to lift the load before he leaped into the waste bin."

"Sounds like a risky plan to me."

"Whether a premeditated or impromptu scheme, we'll never know. Conrad became part of the prison waste atop the rest of the garbage. Unaware of anything amiss, the operator drove to the dumping ground outside the perimeter."

"COs don't inspect before the truck leaves the facility?"

"Guess not. The clueless trucker hit the compactor switch at the dump site, crushed the contents, and pulled forward to drop the compacted refuse on the ground. According to the report, the roar of the hydraulics and the thick steel walls masked Conrad's screams."

"How do you know all this, Larsen?"

"Who do you think collated and typed the final report?

"So, when the Mess CO realized Conrad had deserted his post without permission, he ordered an inmate to go to his cell to search for him. Conrad's cellie had not seen him. That initiated the Code Red."

"How'd they know where to look for him?"

"Tracing any vehicle on or off the Yard is standard procedure. Somebody checked the truck and its load, where they found him crushed to death among the debris. Both officers who discovered him vomited when they witnessed what a trash compactor could do to a fragile human body."

"Uh. Awful." Larsen's description turned my stomach.

The story spread throughout the unit, inducing more anxiety, stress, and misery. We talked among ourselves for several days about the incident. The faint-hearted and stalwart pontificators on the Yard concluded the guy was just another young, weak white kid who couldn't handle the Joint's deprivations. Disgusted with this ignorant consensus, I stopped talking about the whys and wherefores.

What more was there to say? Some of us barely hung on from one day to the next. The struggle to fend off despair continued. Many searched for a reason to climb out of bed each morning.

No stranger to depression, I preferred sleeping in or wallowing in self-pity some days. Maintaining a positive attitude required constant vigilance. Meditation helped. When Officer Evans noticed me out-of-sorts, I indulged my negativity too much and reoriented my thinking. *He thinks in secret, and it comes to pass: Environment is but his looking glass.*

Loneliness and regret permeated our desert enclosure. Existing issues persisted, as did family members' unrealistic expectations about anticipated holiday visits. More than 80% would likely re-offend and miss more holidays away from their families—a depressing fact I uncovered in a recent issue of *The Journal of Criminal Law and Criminology*.

The Conrad incident only reinforced what many intuitively understood: mental distress and mental illness ran much higher within the prison population than the authorities let on. Either they did not know, didn't care, or acknowledged the problems but declined to act.

Despite the battery of intake tests forced on each inmate, none of the diagnostics mattered. Since nothing could be done to heal mental illness, treat the symptoms. To throw too many unstable people together in tight quarters meant terrible things might happen. The number of fights, injuries, and arguments broken up by staff intervention skyrocketed.

Prison either toughened or broke people. Such stress underscored the day-to-day survival of a subliminal dog-eat-dog mentality.

Some days I questioned whether I would survive until the end. If neurasthenia overwhelmed me, would my response be justified? Would my reaction be human?

Following Conrad's death, CO Evans popped by the library.

"Hey Evans, you're back. Feeling better?"

"I'll live."

Darkened eyes suggested she hadn't slept much. She couldn't mask the fatigue in her voice, or her listlessness.

"A lot of action around here the last week. You heard about what happened?"

"Of course. There's talk of nothing else. The incident over Conrad really upset me. I understand it's tough sometimes for the guys here, but to take it that far?"

"You're assuming he committed suicide?"

"What else?"

"A lousy judgment call under stress. Apparently, Conrad's fiancée broke up with him via a letter." A pain settled in the back of my throat. "Perhaps he wanted to escape and took the chance without considering the risks."

Evans thought for a moment. "Maybe you're right. Five years added on to your sentence for escaping should have been a deterrent, but if his distress was so acute . . . " She stopped and followed a cumulus cloud drifting near the mountains.

"Sometimes, this job wears me out." She began pacing, her fingers restless, as she opened and closed her fists.

Evans was a sensitive woman in a heartless environment. The daily stresses that would push a young man to kill himself, intentionally or unintentionally, impacted us more than we expected. The despair we shared would not likely dissipate soon.

"Neither of us will be here forever. I'm up for parole, and you could transfer to another facility or a desk job."

"I enrolled for next semester to finish my bachelor's degree in criminal justice."

"Excellent news. Once you graduate, you can move to a better situation."

"That's the plan." Evans sounded flat and devoid of enthusiasm.

My intuition sparked a question.

"Is everything all right otherwise, at home and all?"

Evans turned her attention back from the window and refocused on me. My inquiry only increased the tension in the room. "Nothing I care to go into just now." Her terse and distracted answer suggested she had other worries, but I didn't press further. Only at a chance Starbucks rendezvous two years later would I understand her marital problems had begun long before her separation.

She turned the tables on me and asked, "Everybody here is depressed except you. How so?"

"I choose not to complain. If I gave into despair, I would never survive. Prison is not a place for someone of my temperament, so I work on cultivating no expectations of good or bad or anticipating much from the outside. Whether I receive letters or visitors is out of my control. Besides, I'm too exhausted to put any more energy into resistance. I want to go with the flow, as they say." I didn't quite live what I told her, but I wanted my sentiments to be true.

"Makes sense. I see your point: accept the things you cannot change."

"Right. Do you recall the Serenity Prayer?"

"No. Isn't that an AA thing?"

"An American theologian named Reinhold Niebuhr popularized the saying by its use in his sermons. In the 1940s, Alcoholics Anonymous and other Twelve Step groups adopted the prayer. It goes something like this:

God, grant me the serenity to accept the things I cannot change,
The courage to change the things I can,
And the wisdom to know the difference.

"Would you write it down for me?"

"Sure." I fed a piece of paper into my typewriter and banged out a copy for her as she whispered the words.

"May I suggest something? Tape this to your bathroom mirror and read the prayer every morning."

"Will do. Thanks, James. My husband will think I'm crazy, but so what? You've cheered me up a bit, despite recent events."

"We're both prisoners here in our own way. Strange, isn't it?"

"Like you implied, it's temporary." Evans sighed, and the tension in her shoulders relaxed.

"At the Yard D library, we tend to the mind and the spirit. One-stop administration of enlightenment and healing."

She laughed, "You're too much sometimes. I'll catch you later."

Too bad my upbeat attitude did not extend to my compatriots. Despite my efforts not to let this place pull me down, I endured low moments throughout the holidays that snuck up on me and whacked me in the head. And Evans shared my predicament.

Consuelo missed the next weekend, and I girded myself for disappointment throughout December without her lovely face and cheerful disposition to encourage and console me.

Saturday came and went. Sunday a.m. I walked the track to exploit the cooler mornings, skipped lunch, and climbed into my bunk to read. Mac barged in and startled me awake.

"Rise, Sir, from this fully recumbent posture! You have a visitor." Mac loved paraphrasing this line from Oscar Wilde's play *The Importance of Being Earnest*.

"Really?" I straightened myself out and headed to Visitation.

Consuelo waited for me at our usual table in the back, dressed in black. She appeared lovelier than ever. Some guys sitting with their girlfriends or wives endured cold stares when their female visitors caught them eyeing the young woman waiting for me. A part of me enjoyed their envy as I sat across from her. We waved to Vargas and his wife, huddled on the other side of the room, immersed in their customary heads-down *tête-à-tête*.

We engaged in small talk. Consuelo told me about her job at the furniture store, the holiday rush, and the Christmas shopping she still hadn't completed.

"How are you holding up?" she asked. I gave her the same answer I'd given Evans—a question formed on her lips.

"I remember you said you were engaged once, but no girlfriend now, on the outside?"

"I had some girlfriends throughout the years. Most didn't last. Either she or I split amicably. Once I reached my late twenties and early thirties, I formed a better idea of what I wanted and felt it dishonest to pretend when I realized we weren't right for each other. Some self-knowledge comes with age."

"Yes, I agree."

"I dated a woman before my arrest. I don't blame her for breaking up and laying low after blindsiding her with all my legal and personal problems."

"I knew several people who disappeared for years until the stress wore them down."

"Yes, exactly," I said. "I carried my disappointment like an anchor for a long time, but I want to let it go. I seldom think about those times anymore."

Consuelo's questions conjured memories of Maria. I fought back a wave of anguish. Tears welled, and I wiped them away.

"I'm sorry if I upset you. I didn't mean to."

"Just some memories from the distant past. This is not the place to talk about them. Why do the good times fade at once but not the painful ones?"

"We internalize the pain because suffering is personal to us."

I held her gaze as I considered her astute observation.

"Yes, well said. Once I'm released, I hope we can remain friends and talk more candidly. I want no secrets. I have developed this need for truth-telling." Consuelo and I searched each other's eyes.

"I want to be open with you too. You're a sweetheart, and I'm sad you're here. You should be doing other important and useful things."

"I put myself here and must accept the consequences and perhaps turn this time into something positive, a growth experience, if you will. Misery, crushed dreams, and disappointments teach us a lot." I caught myself when I said *crushed*, but let it go.

Consuelo and I moved on to more minor heart-wrenching subjects for the remainder of our visit. With Christmas next week and other family obligations, she apologized for not visiting until January.

"Thank you for the time you've given me. It's a Christmas gift I'd never expected."

Consuelo smiled as her eyes glistened. "You ask so little of me. I wish I could do more for you. I'm touched that a couple of hours a week would mean so much."

"I feel blessed to have known you, Consuelo."

When they called the end of Visitation hours, we hugged each other, and for the first time, Consuelo kissed me on both cheeks in the Latin style. I savored every second and committed to memory her soft lips and sweet breath. Buoyed by her visit, I strolled back to Yard D, more optimistic than ever, humming *Jingle Bells*, grateful for an authentically joyful moment.

Vargas turned me on to an excellent jailhouse lawyer with a reputation for competence. After my shift at the library, I wandered over to Yard B to find him. Carlson hung out in the library most days, so he was easy to locate.

Tall and dark-haired, Carlson wore black-rimmed glasses that gave him a professorial demeanor. He reminded me of my friend Paul.

I explained the plea deal I'd signed to do the federal time first and return to the state with credit for time served and how my situation went awry.

Carlson took notes as I spoke.

"I assume you have some court documents? Could you bring them by later tonight?" His soft-spoken but authoritative voice gave me confidence.

He said my case seemed straightforward.

"We'll file a writ of habeas corpus to compel the Feds to detain and transfer you to a federal facility and then remand you to finish the state sentence."

"What is habeas corpus, exactly?"

"It's a recourse that allows you to report an unlawful detention or imprisonment and petition a court to determine if the detention is valid."

"And when I'm back in state custody, I'm eligible for parole and release?"

"Correct. You should be back by fall with time served on the federal charge."

Two days and two packs of smokes later, I signed the pleadings Carlson prepared and mailed them to the Court. *Nothing to do now but wait.*

During my holiday haircut, I informed Vargas I'd filed the writ. He looked pensive momentarily and suggested, "Since you did almost three years, why don't you ask the Court to give you time served on the federal beef? Stay here and go up for parole in May."

"Carlson mentioned that but said he couldn't do it. He said I needed an outside lawyer to present my petition in person to the federal court. Without $2,500 for a retainer, I am stuck."

Vargas agreed the cost of a lawyer in my position would be a problem.

"My parents don't have that kind of money either, so I'm forced to do an extra few months if I make parole at the initial hearing."

Vargas accepted my Christmas offering of three Menthol packs instead of two to thank him for steering me to Carlson and Consuelo.

"*Feliz Navidad,* and *gracias* for all your help, Luis. I'm grateful to have you as an ally."

Luis seldom showed much emotion, but he appeared genuinely touched by my words. He accepted the cigarettes.

"*No hay de que, Jaime.* You have been a great help to me as well. I pray everything turns out well for you. *¡Si Dios quiera!*"

He reached out and shook my hand.

"*Oye*, let me think about your legal problem. Maybe I can come up with something."

"Sure, Luis, I always welcome your help. *Hasta luego, Carnal.*"

CHAPTER 11

Cloudless blue skies and a slight breeze out of the northwest foreshadowed the last remaining months of my incarceration. A short rain the night before had dampened the dust and pollen and left the air fresh and breathable. Save for the memory of rain patter against the window, no evidence of precipitation remained as the reduced humidity dried the ground by mid-morning.

Tuesday, January 3rd, the day after the New Year's holiday, proved uneventful. I opened the library around ten and stayed open until the 2:30 count. After the count, the door lock popped, and Mac and I went to supper. While we picked at our desserts, an officer found me and ordered me to report to the shack to retrieve a message.

Curious, I dumped my tray, wiped my spork, and tucked it in my shirt pocket. After identifying myself to the CO in charge, I waited as he shuffled some papers, looking for something.

"Here is the order. Yeah, you're shipping out tomorrow morning, be ready by 6:00 a.m. You're returning to county to await transport by the Marshals to a federal facility."

The court had acted on my filing. The writ of habeas corpus greased the wheels to slide me out of here and into federal custody. I strolled to the next yard to say adios to Vargas.

"Give my thanks to Consuelo next time you talk, in case I don't return to this Unit."

"Here, take her phone number." Vargas wrote it down for me.

"How long do you think before the Feds show up?"

"The Marshals are quick. I'd say within ten days."

"Ten days in the county jail is ten days too long," I said.

"*Así es*. I did two years at a federal minimum camp in Duluth. You'll be all right once you get where you're going."

Vargas ran his fingers through his hair.

"Let's walk up to the phone banks. I need to make a call tonight."

Stepping lightly, I returned to my cell to brush my teeth before completing my final laps of the day. The irrigation sluices opened last night, and Walden Pond, in all its murky greenness, shimmered under the overhead lights that immersed us in eternal Hollywood night.

I'll miss you, old friend. You've been a steady companion.

At six in the morning, whatever personal items I owned went into a plastic bag for storage until I returned to state custody. The administration processed me, slapped on the chains and handcuffs, stuffed me in a van, and headed east to the downtown lockup.

County sheriffs booked me in as though I had come off the streets. They photographed and fingerprinted me, then removed my prison clothes and replaced them with standard blue pajamas and plastic flip-flops. For a meal, they handed me a paper bag with an unappetizing bologna sandwich on white bread, a seedless orange, and a small carton of milk with a straw attached.

Finally, they dumped me into a holding cell jammed with thirty other prisoners for fifteen hours. During the interim, I witnessed a guy kick heroin. The wretch shivered uncontrollably in the warm cell and could not sate his thirst. Miguel, the perennial track star and weight lifter, came to mind as I considered he went through something similar to pay his way back to Mother Prison.

Guards most likely monitored the addict over closed-circuit cameras for any life-threatening medical complications. Still, he spent hours with his head near the toilet in convulsive dry heaves after he had nothing left to vomit. I hoped his nightmare would end soon for him and us.

I slept as much as possible until the night shift marched me up to my pod on the fourth floor, which, not surprisingly, resembled the fifth where I had stayed during my first visit almost three years ago.

Placed in an empty cell on the upper tier, I rinsed my face in the tiny sink and fell asleep among the snores and clangor one grew accustomed to in jail. Everything was uncomfortably familiar. Did I dream the last few years, or had I been here forever anesthetized?

There was no way to gauge how long before the Marshals would collect me. I hoped the delay would not be too lengthy because, after the Yard, county struck me as more oppressive and claustrophobic than ever.

On the morning of the third day, the loudspeaker called me to report for an escort to Visitation. Surprised, I wondered who knew I was at county. The sheriff ushered me two floors down and stuffed me in a locked room for law-yers' consultations. Momentarily, the door swung open, and a middle-aged woman in a gray business suit entered. She sat in the chair across from me and opened an expensive leather briefcase. Her hair, streaked with gray, was braided. The darkness under her eyes suggested she didn't sleep much.

"Hi. I'm Johanna Friedman. I've been retained to assist you with your detainer issue."

She reached out to shake my hand, and I obliged, introducing myself.

Puzzled, I said, "I appreciate the help, but I didn't hire you."

"Understood. I received a retainer of $3,000 from a . . ." the attorney flipped through some pages, "from a Ms. Consuelo Vargas." I spotted a ca-shier's check clipped to the document she held.

Luis came through for me. I owed him big-time now.

Ms. Friedman continued, "As I understand the facts, we will petition the Feds to waive your transfer to the federal penitentiary, with credit for time served on your eight-month sentence, which you fulfilled via the state over the last three years. Are these facts correct?"

"Yes, ma'am. And I'll receive credit for county jail time as well?"

"Indeed. You are eligible for parole in May, so we can arrange a transfer back to the same unit. Once back in state custody, with the detainer removed, DOC will reclassify you from medium to minimum security. I suspect you'll be relocated to a minimum unit if you don't make parole. Any questions?"

We spoke until I made sure I understood the details.

"Would you let Ms. Vargas know she may visit me if she likes?"

"Certainly. Oh, by the way, no need for you to appear in court. I'll file the petition this afternoon and appear on your behalf if necessary. These pro-ceedings are routine, so I don't expect any issues."

I thanked Ms. Friedman. A massive burden of uncertainty lifted, allow-ing me to recognize the end of my ordeal.

Back in the pod, I found a nineteenth-century detective novel by Wilkie Collins called *The Moonstone* about the theft of a gemstone. I climbed into my bunk to read for the rest of the day, my mood lighter, illuminated by a glimmer of optimism.

Although my attorney believed the legalities would take less than a month, her confidence appeared misplaced. Five weeks after our first meet-ing, she returned to apologize for the courts' slowness and to assure me she sought to spur them along.

Meantime, I spent my days reading. The cellblock continued its unique temporal frame of reference without outside windows. For the inmates, the world beyond the concrete walls did not exist. Only the strict routines of the lockup persisted mercilessly around us.

The jail provided Catholic Mass every Wednesday and Sunday. To break up the monotony, I attended. The sheriffs escorted the parishioners to a cramped chapel on the second floor. We passed through an exterior corridor that wound around the building and whose windows afforded us a glimpse of natural sunlight.

Although I questioned the belief in a personal god, I found the Mass uplifting. The rituals intertwined with Judeo-Christian mythology instilled a curious yearning for something outside myself. I hoped that God existed and felt the need for God in man. Baptized as an infant, I was eligible for communion, which I accepted as a dutiful Catholic.

Consuelo did not visit. After the sixth week, I assumed she would not turn up. Although I had memorized her phone number before leaving the prison, I debated whether to call her. Did I want to join the bevy of collect callers from a correctional facility? Her thinking of me as another hanger-on who cost her money bothered me, so I did nothing.

Waylaid in purgatory, I embraced the passage of time. I read, meditated twice a day, and watched some TV whenever the news or a movie came on, but I slept as much as possible. Without money deposited on my books, I couldn't buy anything from the commissary but borrowed a pencil and pad from my cellie, who had inherited them from his previous cellmate. Writing in French gave me a little privacy.

I taught my cellie, Karl, how to meditate in return for the writing materials. We got some strange stares when other inmates or the sheriffs passed by our cell and saw us cross-legged on our bunks, our palms turned out with eyes closed, quiet, just sitting, still.

Karl was a resourceful illegal immigrant who had bought a fake passport, clothes, and a plane ticket to escape East Germany. From West Berlin, Karl landed in México. A bus from México City brought him to the border. Dressed in clothes he purchased used, he crossed unnoticed with the regular migrant flow.

He spoke little Spanish and English, but he taught me some German, and we managed to communicate. My acquaintance with Karl helped kill some time. Although he had a working-class background, he was self-educated, ambitious, and strived to build a better life. He caught a shoplifting charge from a supermarket, but the Sheriff reported him to Immigration, so he expected to be deported if he couldn't acquire political asylum.

We parted in March, eight months before Mr. Gorbachev tore down the Berlin Wall. Perhaps Karl returned to a better country.

At last, Consuelo arrived. The sheriff escorted me to the visiting room, where I found her waiting quietly at one of the small tables. I expected to speak to her across plate glass connected through a disease-laden phone, but that was for high-risk, high-security prisoners. We sat across from each other, forbidden to touch, so close, unable to narrow the insurmountable gulf between us. Nevertheless, being near her again heightened my mood considerably.

My visitor wore business attire, with shorter hair than our last visit four months ago.

"You look well. You grew a bit of a beard."

"The razors here are awful, but I'm getting plenty of rest, as you can imagine. Thank you so much for your help with the lawyer."

"Thank *Tío* Luis. I was a go-between and happy to help. Any news on your case?"

"Things are in the works. My lawyer says the court nullified the transfer order to federal custody. Once the time-served paperwork clears, I'll return to the Santa Cruz Yard. How have you been?"

"I changed jobs. I work in the accounting department for American Express. I am happier and have more money, responsibility, and longer hours. The work is challenging. The company will pay me to earn a bachelor's degree after one year of employment." Consuelo sounded prosaic, without her usual optimism, with the barest hint of a smile.

"That's fantastic. I had no doubts you would advance. I'm happy for you. We are all getting what we want these days." Consuelo's smile faded as she toyed with the ring on her right hand.

"I have to confess something to you," she said as her voice tightened. "I met someone. We've been dating for the last two months."

Consuelo explained how she'd met this guy in college and ran into him at American Express, where he worked in a different department. They met for lunch, then romantic dinners until their friendship became something else.

"I'm not surprised, Consuelo. A lovely woman like you was bound to find someone. My situation, being what it is, was long odds regardless." Although sincere, I held back my real disappointment. Life on the outside moved on without me, and I'd allowed myself to hope I might participate from the inside, which was never the case. Still, those who have never been locked up do not realize the importance of *normal* relationships with people beyond the criminal justice system.

She lived up to the meaning of her first name and provided me with consolation, comfort, solace, and relief from the self-absorbed negativity I struggled with every day.

"Once you are back in Santa Cruz, I'll try to visit. I told my boyfriend about you, and he's okay with it. Not that I need anyone's permission."

"Only if you want to, Consuelo. I will be out in June, regardless. We can meet for lunch. Anyway, I hope you will concentrate on your new relationship and build a life away from prison and prisoners."

"I'm doing that. Thanks for understanding." She spoke in a subdued voice with her eyes cast down.

No one spoke for a few moments.

"My ordeal is almost over, and you helped make the journey easier. I am blessed to have met you, and I'll pray that only the best comes to you. You are a kind, loving person, and I am richer for knowing you."

"I've never known anyone like you. If things . . . "

"It's time." The sheriff intoned in a stern voice. "Wrap it up."

We stood, and Consuelo hugged me and kissed me before the guard admonished us about the no-touching rule.

Her slim figure passed through the heavy double metal doors as I slumped back in my chair, wondering if I would see her again.

The pain in my chest only increased as the sheriff escorted me back. I pulled the pillow around my head to block the chaos of talk and TV reverberating throughout the pod. Soon, I surrendered to a fitful sleep, emotionally, physically, and spiritually exhausted. Would this disappointment and loneliness ever end?

I attended my last Mass on Sunday, March 26th. Given my chat with Consuelo, this communion offered more solace than previous ones. The following morning at o'dark thirty, DOC arrived to transport me back to my prison oasis. The sheriffs processed me out of their system. I dressed in my prison-issue jeans, boots, and blue chambray shirt before they slapped on the belly chains and cinched the cuffs around my wrists.

My ten-week ordeal in the central jail had ended. Strange how prison felt like a satisfying relief and a welcome change from the county's suffocating weariness. Even trussed, I savored the ride back to the penitentiary, the sun rising behind us.

My old spot on Yard D had just become vacant. Mac had had a new cellie for several weeks who had already transferred to another facility. The department reclassified Mac to a minimum unit, and he would likely relocate soon. He still had another year before his parole hearing and was sure he'd earn release from minimum security.

Back in the fresh air, I headed to the track to catch up on my forty laps, ready to exercise after weeks of enforced inactivity. When I reached the weight pile, I paused to lift. Miguel, my spotting partner, had left the Yard last November, buffed, healthy, and resigned to continue his slow suicide by heroin.

That evening, I dropped by Vargas's crib, where I found him absorbed in some crime drama on TV. He turned down the volume.

"I'm not keeping you from your show?"

"Nah. It's a rerun. Welcome back. When you'd get in?"

"This afternoon. Thank you, Luis, for hiring the attorney. The ordeal took long enough, but here I am. I intend to reimburse you once I'm out."

"*No es nada*. I was happy to help. The night before you left, I called Consuelo, and she insisted on helping you. I got her the money, and she took care of everything. We used the cash from our business account to pay the lawyer." Vargas smiled.

"She is something, isn't she? I owe Consuelo big time too."

"Consuelo won't accept anything from you. Hey, listen, I have a little bad news about her."

"Yeah, she visited me in county. She has an *amante* now." I glanced down at my hands and back at Luis. "I tried not to get my hopes up. I'm happy for Consuelo. Anyway, *civilians* shouldn't be around people like us. Too many complications," I said.

"True enough. I liked the idea of having you in the family if things had worked out between you two."

"We'll always be friends, Luis, perhaps not cousins-in-law, but friends, yes."

"*Eso, sí, mano.*"

"Did I miss anything while I was downtown?" I asked.

"Not really. The usual crap. Some dudes got busted on Yard C for hooch. It was a pretty decent batch for a change. The warden locked us down for three days. One of my homeboys pushed a brother down the stairs. He'll get another nickel added to his time. And CO Evans is mooning over you."

"Oh, bullshit."

"Yeah, since you left, she looks lost and grumpy. You didn't think nobody noticed how much time she spends at the library when you're there?"

"We talk, that's all. I'm sick of yakking to guys all the time. No offense."

"I hear ya. *No te preocupes.* I vouched for you, so nobody will hassle you about it."

Luis and I chatted for another half-hour before I returned to Yard D, showered, and crashed a little before the 9:30 lockdown. The image of Consuelo had already faded despite my desire to hold on to her.

Officer Lopez had replaced me in the library, so I had time to run around and assemble my application for parole. Although we were supposed to have a job, nobody said anything, and I didn't seek or volunteer for any work. I retained a hundred bucks on my books to tide me over. All my free time went to the track, reading, or writing in my journal.

CO Evans lit up when we crossed paths on Yard D.

"Welcome back. Good to see you." Her cap and dark sunglasses shielded her face.

"Although I hate to admit it, I'm glad to be back here. The county jail is really a pit. I missed you, too."

Many of my fellow inmates had no use for the staff and would ostracize, or worse, anyone who did.

In a hushed voice, she said, "I haven't had an intelligent conversation with anyone since you left."

This was the first time I recalled her surreptitiously disparaging her co-workers, although ever so gently.

"Everything going all right for you? Getting enough rest?"

"About the same."

She still wouldn't tell me what bothered her, though she was clearly distracted, and I did not insist.

Every day I visited my old library. The new librarian, named Buchner, kept the place clean and well organized. I offered to cover for him whenever he needed the head, and we became friendly. Ruggedly handsome, he was another white-collar type, immensely proud of his moneymaking schemes, even though he got caught.

This new librarian liked to talk too much but managed to weave a fascinating tale.

"The trick, you see, is to keep moving and stay flexible, so I bought a used mobile home and installed a scanner and high-end color laser printer."

"Those are very expensive," I noted.

"Worth every penny. Every day I'd go to a different bank and buy a $30 cashier's check, scan it, and change it to $3,000 with some cool software I found."

Gesticulating, he continued. "Then I printed several copies on check stock paper with magnetic ink and a MICR font. The only flaw in the scheme was the required watermark, but I had a workaround."

"Why did you need an RV for this?"

"I drove up and down the state to different cities, cashing my new checks. The best time to go into the bank was when the tellers were the busiest. I scoped out the prettiest one and flirted with her as she processed my transaction. Distracted, the tellers seldom looked for the watermark."

He claimed he separated over $400,000 from the banks in six months, most of which he moved offshore into interest-bearing accounts.

"The best part? The prosecution only tagged me for about $50,000, so I'm only doing time on that."

"The incompetence. What a waste of tax dollars," I said.

This minor three-year vacation here on the Yard became an acceptable business expense. I don't know if he told the truth or exaggerated his fable of financial intrigue, but I enjoyed the story and the amusing way he spun it. With $350,000 waiting for him upon release, maybe it was worth it. Were I inclined toward criminal activity, the Joint provided a tremendous learning center for new ideas and techniques.

By letter, I informed my parents of my scheduled parole hearing on Wednesday, May 10th, at 10 o'clock. I completed all the paperwork, composed a short essay to bolster my petition, and submitted the application two weeks after returning from the county jail.

With the federal detainer off, DOC reclassified me to minimum status but held me over until after the hearing. I reveled in my short-timer standing and indulged in moments of optimism as the real prospect of release sank in.

Even Evans mentioned that I smiled a lot more.

"You must be excited to be near the end of your time here."

"One day at a time, Evans."

"What are your plans? Going back to California?"

"Not right away. I can transfer my parole, but I'll stick around here for a while, find a job, and start afresh. I love the desert."

"What? I thought you hated it."

"Yeah. Just kidding. I don't mind it anymore now that I'm used to the dryness and the heat. The sun does wonders for my complexion."

"You always look tan. Well, I'm happy for you just the same."

Over the following weeks, we still chatted in the Yard D library or out by the picnic tables in the quad after the sun dipped below the rooftop. On my way to the track, I waved to the guard shack whenever I knew she was there, although I couldn't see inside because of the glare on the windows. It was enough to imagine she spotted my furtive wave. I would miss her more than she knew.

The day arrived. A little nervous, I presented myself to the administration building. The Inquisition clustered at the front of the room: seven parole board commissioners, six men and one woman, all middle-aged. However, what shocked me were the visitors who had arrived to support my bid for release and sat in the folding chairs 25 feet behind me. Although the rules prevented us from speaking, I turned and acknowledged them with a grin and a nod of thanks.

Behind me sat Mom and Dad, my fiancée Maria's parents, my two aunts, Paul and Laura Stern, with their son, Paul Jr., and Consuelo Vargas. I took a deep breath, overjoyed everyone had taken the time and expense to fly here to the middle of nowhere to support me.

My mother had written to as many people as possible and asked them to endorse me, an effort I never expected. Later, I discovered many of them had written affidavits supporting my release, which cinched my making parole on the first attempt. Officer Evans also provided a statement about my behavior and readiness for discharge.

The chairman acknowledged my visitors by saying, "Sir, I see you garnered considerable support from your family and friends. Indeed, the Board appreciates this, and we believe such backing helps in the rehabilitation process."

I relaxed and answered their questions as best I could. The Board asked how I'd spent my time during my incarceration, what I learned about myself, and my plans if granted release. Most importantly, they wanted to hear how contrite I was about my offenses.

After the *petite interrogation*, the Magnificent Seven conferred among themselves. Subsequently, the chairman stopped talking, wrote something down, coughed, and began his standardized recitation.

"Sir, before we announce our decision, would you like to say anything?" I stood, certain this would be my only chance to drive home what we discussed.

"Yes, Sir, if it pleases the Board, may I make a personal statement?"

"Please proceed."

"First, I appreciate the opportunity to present my petition." My voice quivered. "I'd like to thank friends and family for their support today. I freely acknowledge I violated the law and accept the punishment meted out to me. I broke the rules of civil society and community norms and deserved the sentence I received. Reflecting on those terrible days three and a half years ago, I cannot believe I was so reckless and stupid. My imprudence and lack of judgment are now behind me, and I must assess the present and chart my future. After nine months in the county, I vowed to atone and re-engage to ensure I never found myself in this situation again. Prison life was hard on me, its lessons were learned, and I am certain I will not re-offend." I sat down. Several Board members nodded.

"Thank you for your statement." The members whispered among themselves until the chairman pushed his glasses off his head to his nose. "By unanimous decision, the Board grants you preliminary release to a halfway house until you have gained lawful employment. You must acquire a place to live and comply with all the conditions stipulated by the Department of Corrections, as overseen by your duly assigned parole officer. If you comply with all requirements, you will satisfy your parole and earn early release from supervision eighteen months from now, on December 16th. You may not leave the state without your parole officer's express permission until discharged from DOC oversight. Do you accept these terms as outlined?"

"Yes, Sir. Thank you. I assure you, none of us will meet here again."

"We'll hold you to that, sir. Dismissed."

My visitors arose and filed out, herded by a CO who was ready to prepare for the next petitioner. I waved to them, beaming.

When I returned to the Yard, I spread out materials on the picnic table near my cell and wrote thank-you letters to everyone, tailoring each one to its recipient, elated to reach out to the friends and family I had lost touch with. All the letters went to my mother so she could forward them. Evans passed by as I finished my correspondence.

"Your smile tells me the proceeding went well."

"Yes, ma'am. The Board released me to a halfway house. How long before I'm out of here, do you think?"

"Admin takes about a month to process the release paperwork. I'd say mid-June. Congratulations. I had no doubts. I'm happy for you and believe it's time for you to move on. You've profited from the ordeal." Evans laughed, and I shook my head.

"That's an understatement."

I didn't have Consuelo's address, so I asked Vargas to thank her for me.

"Consuelo came to my parole to support me."

"She attended the hearing? I hadn't heard."

"I figured she came on her own." Luis detected a tinge of sorrow in my voice.

"You miss my *primita*, no? *Lo siento.*"

"*Ese novio suyo es afortunado.*"

To celebrate my success, Vargas unveiled two Snickers bars. That I made parole on the first attempt astonished him since most did not in his experience.

The weeks dragged on. May and June were hotter than usual, and every blistering day scorched and desiccated my bare skin. With no tasks to occupy me, I walked the track and read. Walden Pond appeared before my departure—the beginning and the end. I told almost no one about my pending release into the free world. Some convicts noted my unusually upbeat demeanor, while others continued in their blind cluelessness.

I received my release date: June 9th. Three days before, Evans dropped by my cell to let me know after we came off the 2:30 lockdown.

"Not too long from now," she said, "you'll be at the halfway house on North 23rd Avenue, not quite free, but a lot more than you are now."

"Thirty-nine months is a long haul, but I don't expect to be at the halfway house long. I'll be on my own by autumn."

"I believe if it's possible, you'll succeed. I won't bet against you."

"I'm grateful for your confidence, and I mean that."

Friday morning, I walked out of my cell for the last time, across the Yard, and stopped at the shack. Evans pushed the door open and peeked out.

"This is our goodbye, then?" She sounded wistful.

"Yes."

Officer Evans offered to shake hands. I realized this was the first and only time I would touch her, as I did not expect to see her again. Not much would I miss about prison, but some positive relationships arose from bad situations.

With no one in earshot, I said, "Thank you, Evans, you made this experience tolerable. I appreciate your treating me like a human being, not another felon. I'll miss our chats together."

She appeared embarrassed by my gratitude but smiled and accepted the gesture. We parted, and I continued to Administration, sad to leave Mac, Luis, and Evans behind but eager to exit the prison. I trod contemplatively for several hundred feet on the track I knew so well, past Walden, Yards A, B, and C, the weight pile, and up the path to freedom, leaving behind an awkward familiarity.

Mac came out of the commissary with his purchases.

"I'm glad I caught you before you left," he said, shaking my hand.

"Thanks for everything, Mac. Take care."

"You too. Maybe once we're both off parole, we can go to dinner or something."

"Sounds good."

I stopped in to say farewell to Larsen. Few Yard events escaped him, and aware of my release, he came out from behind his desk to take my hand.

"Glad to see you muddled through. Admin has your paperwork ready to sign, and you're out of here. Great job on making parole."

"Thanks, Larsen. I'm obliged for your help. Hold down the fort, as the cliché goes."

"Will do."

A tedious twenty minutes passed, signing various papers I did not bother to read. After the last signature, I passed through the first door of the sally port and waited for the second door to open. The CO behind the glass in the control room gave me a wry smile as he pushed the button to allow me to leave.

I sat on a bench, waiting for the bus, enriched by a check for $125.42 comprised of $50 gate money and the $75.42 from the cash left unspent on my books. A government check defined my net worth two weeks past my last birthday. Despite the dash of impending freedom, the bittersweetness of a squandered life and virtuous poverty left me empty.

The coach arrived after half an hour or so. Other civilians boarded, and I climbed in behind them. I was the only inmate released today from my unit. How unfamiliar it was to ride in a vehicle unshackled. We exited the deep desert and breached the city limits, welcomed by civilization's sounds, odors, and movements. The air became fresher, cleaner, and freer.

PART II

CHAPTER 12

Some remnants of life must be forgotten before they can be remembered, such as the buried, suppressed, or perhaps merely abandoned memories of a time lost forever. Whatever past I had was only what I remembered.

In one of my earliest memories, I lay on a couch in a sunroom three steps down from the kitchen in front of a black-and-white TV when stations broadcast test patterns rather than late-night movies or talk shows. My tireless and uncomplaining electronic babysitter entertained me for hours by presenting nonstop cartoons and clown programs to distract me from the painful itching of measles.

My older brother and two sisters had already suffered from childhood diseases and had no qualms about joining me in the sunroom to watch television. Ronnie, who was twelve, liked *Gunsmoke, Have Gun—Will Travel,* and *Wagon Train.* Joyce and Beth, already teenagers, preferred *The Danny Thomas Show, I've Got a Secret,* and *The Loretta Lynn Show.* I only watched what I wanted when they weren't around.

My siblings argued every night.

"*Have Gun—Will Travel* is my favorite show," whined Ronnie.

"But *I've Got a Secret* is more educational," Beth said.

"Don't you want to improve your mind?" Joyce added.

"It's too easy to guess the secret. Westerns are educational too. It's history."

"All right. We'll let Jimmy decide. Which is it, kiddo, the dumb western or the show that teaches us something?" Beth asked.

"I like *Lassie.* Someday I want a dog like her."

"That's not one of the choices."

Somehow we worked it out.

During suppertime, no disagreements occurred. Our family ate at the big oval table in the dining room—no televisions in there.

Bill Harris, our dad, selected the dinner music. "What shall we listen to this evening?"

"How about rock 'n' roll for a change?" Joyce suggested.

"Too discordant. How about some sweet jazz?" Bill said.

We listened to Big Band jazz—Duke Ellington, Benny Goodman, or Peggy Lee—every night, except on holidays when Gladys Harris, Bill's wife, chose classical music.

During the day, when it was just Gladys and me in the house, we listened to country. She was from Galveston, Texas. While others watched TV on Saturday nights, Gladys and I often huddled around the big radio in the living room as she swooned over the Grand Ole Opry straight from Nashville.

There was no happier child in the San Fernando Valley than me. Except none of it was real.

Four times a week, a young woman, not much older than Joyce—the person I thought of as my eldest sister—dropped by in the mornings or evenings.

"Jimmy, time to change out of your jammies and get dressed. Your mom is coming to see you."

"How come I have two moms, you and Teresa?" I asked.

"You're lucky. Your mom has to work a lot and can't take care of you all the time, so you live here with us. You're part of our family too. You are our youngest son. Don't ever forget that." Gladys hugged me as she explained.

Everything made sense to me. Only when I was a little older did I understand. The Harris family were caretakers employed by my mother for $15 a week to look after me. That's $150 in today's dollars.

Before my mother found the Harris family, she bounced me around from one caretaker to another for the first year and a half of my life. A coworker mentioned a family in the Valley who would shelter a child for a reasonable fee. Desperate to provide stability while she waitressed to support us, my real mom agreed to place me with Bill and Gladys.

When I reached six or seven, Teresa, my biological mom, explained what had happened.

"I worked long hours at several Hollywood restaurants famous in those days. Do you remember the Brown Derby and Schwab's Drugstore? We drove in the car."

"Let's go to Schwab's Drugstore. The hamburgers and chocolate malts are my favorite. The restaurant that looks like a funny hat is too dark."

"Yes, that's called *atmosphere*. I lived in a shabby apartment two blocks off South Hill Street near the Angels Flight. Do you remember the little cable cars we rode from one street to the next?"

"Yeah, but the ride was too short. It was steep, though."

"I had to live close to work then because I didn't own a car. Since you were out in the Valley, I took the bus or borrowed my girlfriend's car to visit you."

Mom understated her sacrifices to keep me with a family while she put in long hours on her feet. Mom braved the metro bus for ten miles, a 90-minute ordeal through the Cahuenga Pass, past the Hollywood Hills, and into North Hollywood to reach me.

"Dorothy loaned me her old Ford on rainy days. Shame on me, but I never told her I had never applied for a driver's license. I couldn't read the signs because of my near-sightedness. Without help from gas station attendants giving me directions, I never would have made it."

The Harris's backyard butted against a storm drain that fed into the LA River. Off the sunroom grew an expansive oak tree whose broad leaves sheltered the yard where I played. The kidney-shaped swimming pool, built years ago when the Harris kids were young, drew me like a magnet. Everyone thought the chain-link fence with its locked gate would impede me from entering the shimmering blue water that proved irresistible on those hot LA summer days. But I was a climber, and six feet was no obstacle.

So often in the county jail, I dreamed of that pool and swimming. I loved swimming in pools, lakes, rivers, and oceans. My father used to say, *la playa es el lujo mas barato*. Indeed, the beach was the cheapest luxury; I missed the openness of the sea and the salt spray most of all.

The Helms Bakery truck passed through our neighborhood in the mornings, filled with millions of pastries. My favorites were the glazed doughnuts, the old fashioneds, and the elongated ones twisted like a rope, infused with jams, and covered with sprinkles. Lucky for me, my primary teeth fell out on their own. Otherwise, the sugar would have rotted them away.

The Helms deliveries ceased in the late 1960s, but a few trucks remained in museums, a testament to an era that forever vanished. The old bakery neighborhood is now called the Helms Bakery District, home to retail shops and design firms. Hollywood of the fifties might be gone, but I remembered those days the way only a child would.

Two months before my fifth birthday, as I waited for the Helms truck, a stranger pulled up in a blue car and parked in front of our house. He rubbernecked the street, looking for something. After a minute, he climbed out, pushed through our wooden gate, and stepped on the porch. I ran over and opened the front door before he knocked.

"Hi, my name's John. You must be Teresa's little boy."

"Who are you?"

"I'm John."

"Okay, but *who* are you?"

Gladys and my mom came behind me and invited the man inside. My mother greeted him with a kiss. He blushed a little. The man, quiet and shy, looked me over and smiled. Our house rarely received visitors except for my sisters' teenage girlfriends.

"Gladys Harris, this is my friend John Hartmann. He's an aerospace engineer."

"Pleased to meet you, Mrs. Harris."

"Oh, y'all can call me Gladys."

"And, of course, my son, Jimmy."

"Yes, the irrepressible son. Your mom's told me a lot about you." John said.

"What's unredressable mean?"

John sat on the sofa. We could now see eye-to-eye.

"Irrepressible means impossible to hold back. It's a good thing."

"You don't spend much time around kids, do you, John?" Gladys said.

"Not for a long while. I'm the second oldest of four brothers, and I have a slew of nieces and nephews, but they're all back home in Pennsylvania."

"I know where Pennsylvania is. It's a state in the east," I said.

"That's right! How did you know?"

"It's on a map in Ronnie's room. You wanna see it?"

"Sure." I grabbed John and dragged him into the bedroom I shared with Ronnie, who helped me sound out the names of the states.

John examined the map. "So, this is Pennsylvania," he said, pointing. "Which state are we in?"

"California." I reached up and touched it on the map. "This is Nevada, here."

"Correct. And what's this book?" John picked my book on fish that Gladys helped me select from the library.

He flipped through the pages. "Isn't this a little difficult for a four-year-old?"

"Why?"

John opened to a random page and pointed. "What's this word, Jim?"

"Oxygen."

Over the next several weeks, John and I warmed up to each other during trips for hamburgers, French fries, and milkshakes at this funny place with yellow arches.

"This is my favorite hamburger place, Jim. What do you think of it?" he asked me as we sat on one of the outdoor benches to eat.

"Pretty good," I said between bites. "I like the shakes, but the hamburgers and malts at Schwab's Drugstore are still the best."

"You've been to Schwab's Drugstore?"

"Sure. My mom used to work there. She works at Oldy's now."

"You mean Aldo's. That's where we met."

John and I played at the park near our house in the afternoons, where we tossed back and forth a new toy called a Frisbee.

In August, my mother and John went to Lost Vegas and were married. When I first saw *The Wizard of Oz*, I asked John, "Is Lost Vegas like Oz?"

"It's *Las* Vegas, and yes, the town is much like Oz, except more expensive."

The morning Mom and John arrived to take me away from the only home I knew and from the people I loved had to be the worst day of my young life.

Bill, Gladys, my mom, and John sat me on the couch before the bay window that framed my world.

"Jimmy, do you understand what marriage is?" Bill asked.

"Two people are together, like Mom and John?"

"Yes. And your parents want to make a home for the three of you. They have a new apartment in West Hollywood all ready to go."

"I like it here."

Mom put her arm around me. "Honey, you'll love it there too. You get your own room to play with your new train set."

"Can I have a picture of the United States like Ronnie's?"

"Of course. And guess what?" John said. "In a few weeks, school starts. Do you know what kindergarten is?"

"No."

"A fun place where you can play with many kids your age and learn to read books," Gladys added, trying to sound cheerful.

They described the adventure of living in a new neighborhood, attending school, and making new friends.

"I want to stay home. Can't I go to Kinner Garden here?"

Everyone who tried to convince me looked sad.

"We'll see you soon, little brother," Joyce said as she and Beth sobbed, each giving me long hugs. I didn't want to cry, but I couldn't help it.

Ronnie stood in the hallway with a sullen stare before disappearing into his room. I would not see him again until he returned from active duty in Vietnam, an army chaplain with a Purple Heart.

I wanted to stay, fighting back, vice-gripping the arm of the sofa, determined to remain. Bill and Gladys betrayed me as they helped usher me to the street. I refused to climb into the car.

"Jimmy, please give your mom and John a chance to care for you." Gladys's voice shook a bit as she held the door. "We will always love you, and I'll be your second mom forever."

Bill and my sisters stood by with expressions of desolation as I was lifted into the car.

Resigned, I let them pack me into the rear seat of John's 1954 Chevy sedan. I would miss the mature trees, the pool, the milkman who left bottles of chocolate milk on our porch, the bakery trucks, the ice cream trucks, and the television in the warm and cozy sunroom off the kitchen.

Devoid of all hope, I sulked as my parents spirited me through the pass from North to West Hollywood to my new home on Detroit Street.

Chapter 13

Memories of Bill and Gladys faded as I adjusted to my new surroundings in West Hollywood. I attended elementary school, learned to roller skate, and rode my first bicycle, a shiny black English three-speed my aunt bought me on my seventh birthday.

Once I was old enough for him to take an interest, I met my biological father for the first time. The divorce decree gave him visitation rights, but he never bothered to visit until I was almost six.

One Saturday morning, I awoke to my parents' angry voices. I climbed out of bed and slid open my door to listen.

"Where was he all these years? Why is he showing up now?"

"The court says I have to allow reasonable visitations. What can I do?"

"It's simple, Teresa. Tell him no."

"But he's paying child support now. He promised to catch up on the months he missed."

"So now he's buying his way in? We don't need his goddamn money. I make enough to support this family. Anyway, Jimmy is my son now. I'm going to adopt him."

"He'll never go for that."

"We'll see. Will you call him and tell him the visit's off?"

"I . . ."

"Where's the number? Is that it by the phone?"

"Yes."

John dialed the number and slammed the phone down after a minute with no response.

"He must be on his way," Mom said in a barely audible voice.

"Dammit." John slammed the front door, jumped into our car, and drove away.

I entered the living room as my mother sat on the couch, crying, sitting beside her and resting my head on her shoulder. She hugged me and wiped her tears with a handkerchief. We sat, comforting each other, until she said, "Come, I need to dress you. Your father is coming to see you."

Confused, I replied, "But he just left in the car."

"No, not John; I mean your real father."

"Oh, you mean my other dad," by whom I meant Bill.

"No, your actual father. The one who I married before your birth."

"Okay," I said, still perplexed but accepting the answer.

After my sponge bath, clean clothes, and a breakfast of toast and juice, my mother and I sat on the couch, entertained by cartoons. The doorbell rang.

"I'll get it."

I pulled the door open. A man with thick, wavy dark hair and a clean-shaven face towered above me with a brief smile capped by two small dimples with a minor cleft on his chin, like Kirk Douglas. His clothes reeked of tobacco. I stared up at him but did not recognize him.

"Come in, please," my mother said behind me.

The man entered and took a chair by the bay window. He and Mom chatted for several minutes while I stood by. His voice ranged deep, like those men on the radio. He kept glancing at me, smiling.

"Here's this week's child-support check of $15, plus $600 more toward what I owe you. Sorry it took so long."

"Thanks. Is this going to be a regular thing?"

"The checks? Yes, of course."

"No, I mean the visits?"

"I want to get to know my son, and I believe it's important he knows his family, so yes. Let's say once a month to start and see how it goes from there." The man spoke in a confident voice.

Mom walked us out to the stranger's car, telling me I would go someplace fun. I nodded dutifully and climbed into the seat next to him. Cars didn't have seat belts in those days. Whenever we came to a sudden stop, the man would hold out his right arm to keep me from flying off the bench. We drove through parts of the city new to me before arriving at the Santa Monica pier for my first visit to Pacific Ocean Park, a nautical-themed amusement center.

John hated the return of his wife's ex-husband to our lives. He and the man never spoke. John never said his name, calling him *Hickey-Doodle*. My mother escorted me to his car to meet him whenever my dad arrived since John would not let him enter the house. He detested the man and resented his interference. John tried to adopt me several times, but my birth father would not give up his parental rights.

Arguments about the visits and my father's interference stopped almost immediately. John remained mute. My mom said he refused to speak for hours and remained sullen and unresponsive. He disappeared into the garage to work on one of his projects.

"Shouldn't we talk about this?" my mom demanded one night during dinner.

"What's there to talk about?"

"You could be civil, if not to him, then to us."

"I'm civil. You know I won't talk to Hickey-Doodle. There's no point. I'll talk to you when I have something to say."

"I don't like the silent treatment you're so fond of."

"Sorry. I wasn't a big talker when you married me."

Some variation of this conversation continued until the visits stopped. The pressure abated once I turned sixteen and drove my car to see Dad instead of him coming to the house. John's passive-aggressive behavior plunged our household into prolonged bitter silences that pushed me into my room to seek escape through the numerous books I collected.

The charm of West Hollywood wore off quickly for my parents. Tired of urban life in rambunctious Hollywood, they decided, under the GI bill, to buy a modest three-bedroom house 45 minutes due east in a new LA suburb called Diamond Bar. My stepfather had not lived in a house since he'd left his family home in Pennsylvania for military service. He looked forward to some space between him and his neighbors among rolling hills and grassland, away from noisy and crowded city apartments.

Throughout the 1962 holidays, I helped my mom pack our things into boxes. On December 26th, three men arrived to load our furniture and boxed items into a truck. We climbed into our over-packed car and headed off. I asked to ride in the moving van, but they said no. We raced east through Los Angeles to beat the movers to the new house and even stopped for lunch at McDonald's.

I remembered endless weekends all over LA, exploring hundreds of developments, but I did not recall the one we bought. To an eight-year-old, they all swirled together in a mélange of perfect model homes.

I loved our new house, mostly because I got a much better room than my old one, and the backyard stretched three times larger than our yard on Detroit Street. Hills loomed behind us, grassy slopes to the east and snow-capped mountains to the north. I had not seen such peaks since those long weekends in the Harris's Big Bear cabin near Baldwin Lake. Unlike Hollywood, the clean sidewalks contained no cracks or uneven surfaces to impede roller skaters. Everything was fresh: our house, the streets, the hills, and the air.

Flat, sedimentary shale rocks blanketed the yard. John demonstrated how to throw them for maximum glider effect. No one threw stones in Hollywood, at least none of that sort, and I spent hours at the edge of my yard while my parents directed the crew where to put the furniture.

Rock-throwing ended once I split one open and discovered a fish skeleton's imprint pressed into the rock. Our house sat on a hill far from any ocean or lake, and I pondered how fish got there. I brought the fossils to my stepfather, who examined the samples for a minute and said, "This is interesting. Perhaps this part of LA existed underwater several million years ago."

"You mean when there were dinosaurs?"

"Maybe not that far back."

I imagined our hill on the seafloor and realized the world around me was not as I had assumed. Creatures older than anything I might conceive had left their imprint in shale. Did other things exist below my feet, waiting for my vision to clear?

The first five years in Diamond Bar passed unexceptionally. I was always a good student who spent more time inside than out. I never took to sports. Still, when my parents bought a new color television, I spent several evenings captivated by Grenoble's 1968 Winter Olympics in the French Alps. That year marked the first Olympics to be broadcast in color.

The city's picturesque views inspired me to learn French, a harmonious and precise language. In my third year of Spanish, I added French and discovered many similarities between French and Spanish grammar. I enthusiastically studied both languages throughout middle and high school.

While I loved figure skating, speed skating intrigued me more. I wanted to zoom across the ice on two thin blades and lean into the turns like the Olympic competitors.

My mom dropped me off Saturday night at the Ontario Ice Skating Center. The rental skates were ill-fitting. After stumbling around the rink for an hour or two, I picked up the basics. Many years of roller skating helped me adapt to the ice.

My ankles, weak at first, gained strength by the third visit. I glided around the oval so fast that the skate monitors yelled at me to slow down. Every stumble on the ice moved me closer to mastery, and I didn't mind the embarrassment of tumbling as much as the cold from my wet pants and sweater. Management kept the building at 50 degrees, so I stayed damp and chilled the rest of the evening once I got wet. Proper clothing helped.

My mother bought me leather gloves and a black beret on a trip to Sears. She said I looked European in the *berretto*, although drawing attention to how I dressed made me uncomfortable. Once I realized no one cared, I embraced the new style.

Blisters from ill-fitting rental skates plagued my feet. Skates, either too tight or too loose, forced me to rent a half-size larger and double my socks. Nevertheless, the poor fit impaired my skating technique and diminished my enjoyment of the ice. I needed custom skates, which cost almost a month's mortgage payment.

My hard-earned skill and improved wardrobe encouraged me to confront my social awkwardness and dare socialize with the cute girls who showed up at the rink. I did my best to smile as we passed each other but never summoned enough courage to speak to them. The prettier the girl, the more intimidated I felt. These girls always had guys hit on them, so what chance did I have? I didn't know what to say, having never learned the art of small talk.

The rink followed the same schedule every Saturday night: an hour of mixed skating, resurfacing by the Zamboni, girls-only, boys-only, couples-only, and back to all-skating. Many girls sat on the bleachers, hoping the boys would ask them as couples-only rolled around. Since few guys invited them, the boy-girl ratio favored me, if only I could overcome my awkwardness.

By the fourth week, I asked someone to couples skate with me. Terrified, I hobbled over to a bevy of girls clustered together in a protective ring, careful not to stumble, and asked the closest one. In subsequent efforts, seldom would anyone turn me down; if they did, one of the others would jump in and say, "I'll skate with you."

The small talk proved to be a significant obstacle. After we introduced ourselves, my partner often went quiet, with pressure on me to say anything to lessen the awkwardness. Sometimes we held hands, but only if she grabbed mine first. I regretted the gloves when holding hands as I imagined how the warmth of her soft hands would feel against mine.

To overcome my nervousness, I rattled off the descriptions of the books I loved. Most feigned interest and nodded graciously, smiled, or asked a question, but few cared much for literature. It didn't matter. Five minutes, the length of the couples-only session, was all I needed to describe the plot of the latest novel on my nightstand.

One Saturday in August, I arrived early and made several warm-up spins around the rink as the newcomers filtered in, changed into their skates, and spread out on the ice. A new trio of friends entered the rink. They gesticulated wildly as they talked among themselves, oblivious to the rest of us, absorbed in conversations about school, boys, and their restrictive parents.

An unexpected sensation rippled through my body as I zeroed in on the middle girl: petite and slender, with long dark hair, olive skin like mine, and translucid green eyes. She wore tight jeans and a sweater that revealed her well-formed contours, unexpected for someone her age, or so I believed in my limited experience. I savored her tenor-like voice that reminded me of classical music. When she saw my beret, similar to the one she wore, she stared at me for more than a moment and smiled.

The girl broke away from her pack to skate beside me on the next pass.

"Hi. I love your beret. Are you French?"

She must be teasing me, so I followed her lead and answered in French.

"Mais oui, je suis français dans mon cœur."

"J'ai pensé que oui. Moi aussi."

For fun, I switched to Spanish. *"Yo también seré español, depende."*

"Oh? ¿De qué depende? ¿Tu humor?"

"Exactemente."

"¡Hasta luego! À bientôt."

The girl smiled and rejoined her entourage, leaving me nonplused.

Shaken, I dropped off the ice and stood sidelong while she glided past as a serene champion born to float on the ice. How could such a girl be here without a boyfriend? *Is it possible she doesn't have one?* I struggled to calm myself and channeled patience until the couples-only session.

Time slowed. Every minute stretched to an hour. I admired her graceful movements during the girls-only skating as she practiced her turns and skated backward, balanced and confident.

The couples-only session arrived, yet I hesitated as fear belayed my earlier eagerness. The girl flashed me a flirtatious smile as she stepped toward me. Taking the cue, I shuffled over.

"May I have this skate?" My overture sounded corny as I mumbled the words, but I couldn't think of anything better.

"Of course. I'd love to." She took my hand and led me to the rink. Self-assured, she stepped on the rink, turned around backward, and held out her hands for me to take them. I reached for her, and we skated a lap before she spun facing forward to allow us to glide side-by-side.

"So, you are American, not French or Spanish?" My companion said in a playful tone.

"I love to practice my Spanish and French."

"You speak both languages beautifully, though your French has a Spanish accent."

"It does?"

"It's not a bad thing. I do too."

Hand-in-hand, we relaxed and enjoyed the thrill of the moment.

"I'm Maria."

"My name is James, but you can call me Jaime if you wish."

"Pleased to meet you, Jaime."

"Is this your first time here?" I asked.

"No. I skate on Friday nights."

"That explains why I've never seen you. You skate well."

"Thank you. I took some lessons. After the Winter Olympics, I wanted to learn how to figure skate."

"The Grenoble Olympics? Those games brought me here too. I want to be a speed skater."

"I wondered about those long blades. Most use figure or hockey skates."

Maria shared my passion for literature. We raced through the list of books we'd read and our opinions of them. Somewhere in the final session, we slid off the ice and sat to talk without distractions. She neglected the two companions she had come with, who happily skated without her.

Maria sat close to me, almost touching. My nervousness dissipated the more we spoke. I loved the soothing musicality of her voice. How strange to feel so at ease.

"You're easy to be around, Jaime. You listen. I like that. Lots of guys talk too much. And don't say very much."

"Except for school, I don't spend much time with people."

"You have friends, though, right?"

"Yes, but most aren't readers or share my interests."

"Well, I do. So maybe we can be friends."

"I'd like that, Maria."

"I love the idea of having someone to skate with who's also *simpático*. There's my friend Laura, but she's not always around."

"We can practice our languages too. Speaking French or Spanish with you is fun."

"Let's. We speak some Spanish at home, but I seldom practice French except in class."

Enthralled by her enthusiasm, I planned to rush to the library soon and check out Maria's recommended books. Throughout our conversation, we maintained eye contact. I dared not glance away as we embraced each other without touching, enwrapped in mutual interests and the thrill of our first meeting.

The evening ended as our respective parents arrived to take us home. We promised to rendezvous next week. Unfortunately, we attended different middle schools.

The week dragged on as I kept busy, anxious for Saturday night to arrive. Maria stayed with me every minute of every day. Was I on her mind too? I wished I had a picture of her. Her green eyes, so full of light, radiated intelligence that filled me with a sensation I had only read about in books.

Maria arrived alone. She mentioned that the girls she had come with last week were mere acquaintances and that her best friend, Laura, was sick.

"I would like you to meet her. She wanted to come, but her parents said no. I'll bring her next time. Laura also likes books almost as much as we do."

"How's her Spanish and French?" I asked in jest.

"Oh, quite good. We study together."

Maria and I skated for an hour before exiting the ice to talk more privately.

We chatted about our upbringing, how alike our families were, the foods we enjoyed, our favorite music and holidays, and whether we were too old for Disneyland. I said yes, and Maria said possibly.

"What do you want to study in college, Jaime?"

"I'm leaning toward linguistics or Romance philology. The origin of languages and how they change over time fascinates me."

"Do you want to teach?"

"Well, with a PhD in those areas, there are only two professions."

"Which are?"

"College professor or analyst for the C.I.A."

Maria slanted her head to one side as she decided whether I was joking.

"I think you will be a fantastic professor. Let the government hire the backbenchers" Ignorant of my academic prowess, Maria based her opinion on her initial impressions. "You seem like a deep thinker to me. Quiet guys often are, I think."

"And your plans?"

"Comp lit."

"What's that?"

"Comparative literature studies literature, culture, and art across many languages. Of course, I want to study French and Spanish, but I'll add English, maybe Italian, and at least one ancient language."

"Latin?"

"Latin, Greek, or Sanskrit. The three big ones."

"Do you want to teach, too?"

"I want to be a novelist."

"Wow. Do you? That's really cool. Will you come to my class and give a guest lecture after you're famous?"

"I would love to."

"Do you think we'll know each other in twenty years?" I asked.

Maria glanced around the rink, her eyes widening as she considered her answer.

"Twenty years is a long time. My dad has a master's degree and doesn't associate with anyone from his high school or college, so I'd say the friendship would have to be really strong."

"Just wondering. Let's skate."

The last call sounded. We stared wide-eyed at each other, surprised. The previous three hours had raced past with no sense of the outside world.

While our parents waited outside, we drifted around the rink, anxious to hold on to one more minute until they kicked us off. Before we exited the building, Maria gave me a friendly *bise* on the cheek. My heart fluttered.

Maria never showed up the following week, the week after, or for the rest of the summer and fall. Worried, I arrived at the rink each Saturday only to suffer disappointment.

Why didn't we exchange phone numbers or last names? Stupid. I clenched my teeth as my pulse raced, and the anxiety destroyed my concentration. I could hear the blood rushing through my head. Although I was usually excited about the new school year, I mustered little enthusiasm for this one. My listlessness provoked my mother to ask what bothered me. I did not know how to explain the abiding grief and confusion.

Dreams of Maria's face, tresses, voice, perfume scent, and our brief time together kept me preoccupied. Daydreams of us, hand in hand, circling the ice rink, filled my days and nights. Heartbroken, I relived every conversation, conjuring what I could not remember, even reenacting our encounters in Spanish and French. On frequent trips to the library, I checked out the authors and works Maria liked best and read them to bring us closer.

Thoughts that something terrible had happened to her forced me awake at night, soaked in a cold sweat. Was she injured, or worse? In feverish bouts of insecurity, I imagined she wanted nothing more to do with me. Anguish made me sick. I missed several days of school, too miserable to leave my room.

Withdrawn, silent, and morose, I woke each morning hoping it had all been a nightmare. Each week faded into the next. By Halloween, I had lost my eagerness for ice skating. I never returned to the ice.

The holidays came and went, and Maria's countenance faded from memory after my sadness and self-loathing lifted, but I knew she had awakened something in me. If I found her again, it would be the beginning of everything.

CHAPTER 14

My first week of college launched in late September. I washed dishes at the Diamond Bar Country Golf Course during the summer, where my mother worked as a coffee shop waitress. I hated the job. Being on my feet in a hot, steamy kitchen for twenty-five hours a week left me exhausted and greasy after my shifts. The experience reinforced my resolve to study hard and leave manual labor behind forever. I vowed never to work in a restaurant kitchen again.

When my friend Paul Stern invited me to his parents' beach house in Del Mar for two weeks, I decided I had saved enough money and quit.

Labor Day weekend, I drove to north San Diego County in the used VW Bug my parents had bought me as a graduation present. The kid across the street bought the motorcycle my stepfather and I had restored to pristine condition, but he wrecked it within weeks.

The beach towns up and down the Pacific Coast Highway celebrated the end of the season before the weather turned. Early in the afternoon, I arrived at Paul's to enjoy 75 degrees, a warm and salty August breeze, some high clouds, and an ocean mirroring the sky's blue.

Paul Stern and I met in high school but never hung out. We shared some classes, said hello in the hallways, chatted sometimes, and remained friendly throughout our junior and senior years, but we never uncovered any shared interests. He was a tall, lanky Jewish kid with long, black hair, often pulled back into a ponytail, who kept to himself and didn't socialize much beyond a terse greeting. Paul lived one overriding passion: the piano.

A month before graduation, I attended a party where Paul played with his hair unrestrained and draped across his face and shoulders. The pianist glided back and forth between rock and jazz, blending them into a melodic and propulsive fusion, invoking Keith Emerson or his hero, Keith Jarrett, to display a mesmerizing virtuosity. The partygoers pushed into the room, desperate to see him play, spellbound by his long hands as they danced over the keyboard. The kid was a genius.

However, around campus, he remained anonymous as though two Pauls existed: the rock star and the laconic, nondescript teenager who few people recognized, a Clark Kent waiting for the call. Shy away from his instrument, he only seemed himself when immersed in his music. During a brief encounter between classes, we stopped to chat.

"Any plans after graduation, Paul?"

"Sure. I got accepted at UC Berkeley for the fall term."

"No way. So did I. I have to send in my dorm application this week."

"Need a roommate?"

Del Mar was paradise. Those long hours on the sand allowed Paul and me to reminisce about our junior high and high school days, preferences, and passions.

"When did you start playing the piano?"

"I was four. My parents used to listen to classical music on the radio and hi-fi. My mom played but stopped in high school. She took me to a piano lesson, and I was hooked."

"You play really well."

"Until the eighth grade, I played classical music, but I listened to rock and roll like all of us. One day, flipping around the radio, I discovered KKJZ."

"Don't know that one. KRLA is my go-to rock station."

"So rock has its roots in jazz, classical, country, and rhythm and blues, which made it easy for me to adapt my style. My parents hated it when I started jazzifying Chopin." Paul laughed, then coughed as he passed me the joint.

"I wish I had some musical aptitude."

"You never tried any instruments?"

"No. I can't sing either."

"How do you know you can't play if you never tried?"

"Well, I spent all my time reading, so I just assumed . . ."

"Later, I'll show you some simple stuff. Everyone can play 'Chopsticks.'"

"Sure, why not?" I said, unable to hide my skepticism.

Paul surveyed the waves crashing on the beach. "So what do you read?"

"Everything, classical literature, history, crime fiction, science fiction . . ."

"Scifi is excellent. My mom buys the *New York Times* best-sellers, so I read those too."

A breeze rolled off the ocean.

"You must have done other stuff besides reading," Paul asked.

"I used to ice skate."

"Never tried it, myself."

Chuckling, I said, "You probably get quite a workout using your hands and feet when you play. You move around a lot."

"That's right. Sometimes after a jam, I feel like I ran the track a few laps. I sweat too."

"It's easy to keep cool ice-skating. I went every week for nine months, where I met a girl and fell in love. Now and then, I dream about her."

"What happened?"

"She stopped coming to the rink, and I didn't know how to find her."

"That blows. Speaking of . . . " Paul took the joint back from me.

We shifted on our towels, watching the breakers. The sun hovered over the horizon. Only an hour of beach time remained.

To offset the melancholy, I changed the subject back to music.

"How much do you practice each day, Paul?

"At least five hours a day, and more before a gig."

"Your dedication has paid off. It's amazing how you intertwine rock classics we all know and change them up with jazz riffs."

"I change the tempo, transpose chords and notes. You hear the changes in Eric Clayton, Jimi Hendrix, Keith Emerson, and guys like that. Many rock musicians started with classical or blues, so jazz is a natural progression. Jazz means freedom," Paul explained, his eyes slightly glazed and squinting from the sun.

"Just when I think I know where the song is going, you take it in a new and surprising direction. You must have a blast playing it."

"I love playing, especially for an audience that's into it."

The holiday weekend ended far too soon. Paul invited a small group of people over Monday night, older and mellower. Paul performed, and we listened as we passed around the bong.

The next afternoon, he and his mom drove into La Jolla on some errands. Following Paul's instructions, I went to Torrey Pines south of Del Mar and found the access road to Black's Beach. At the end of a long hike down the path, I wandered north to an empty stretch of sand.

Offshore, surfers in black wetsuits bobbed like seals on the waves until another rideable set rolled in. Few sunbathers found their way to the shore mid-week, except for the occasional ultra-tan nudist.

I spread out on the white sand and absorbed its heat, with an occasional dip to cool off. I catnapped, lulled by the cadence of the breakers. The sun descended through the billowy clouds to hover above the horizon as the midafternoon waned. The ocean offset the high bluffs behind me, delineating a much narrower beach than Santa Monica's, where the surf line to the sand extended 800 feet. Black's spanned less than 400 feet between the escarpment and the backwash.

The breakers induced a tranquil rhythm as my breath synchronized with the undulating motion. My thoughts drifted over the sea as I followed some gulls whose carefree flight speckled the sky.

I was eighteen. Alice Cooper's song *I'm Eighteen* kept rolling around in my head. Somewhere between a boy and a man, I was in the middle, yearning to break away and discover my life.

Paul and I would head north to Berkeley soon to start a new adventure. Although doubts plagued me, optimism tempered my insecurities. The newfound freedom I anticipated loomed ever closer, along with the endless possibilities, many too fleeting to capture.

The surfers loitered about until a distant swell surged forward, and they paddled methodically to gather momentum and catch the wave cresting toward the shore, their patient efforts rewarded. I, too, floated on the sea of possibilities waiting for my wave to propel me into a miraculous future, buoyed by the optimism of youth.

The first term at university approached. Paul and I made the pilgrimage from LA to Berkeley up Interstate 5 through autumn hills and farmland, our belongings stuffed into my car with whatever we thought we would need to furnish our dorm room. The music turned up, the windows down, and a soda and gas stop punctuated the six-hour drive.

After we turned off from I-580 North to the Warren Freeway, we entered the last stretch of highway before our destination. We turned left on Dwight Way from Telegraph Avenue and arrived at the dormitory that resembled one of those utilitarian apartment buildings built after World War II.

The RA checked us into our room, an unassuming box on the second floor above the Dwight and Dana Street intersection. The single window permitted afternoon sunlight, but the massive trees shaded the interior and granted us an autumn afterlight. Street noise wafted up, but the neighborhood generally quieted in the evening.

The room came furnished with two beds, small dressers, desks, and chairs mirrored on either side and the door in the center directly opposite the window. We plopped on the floor whatever luggage we thought we needed for the night; the rest we would retrieve from the car tomorrow. I took the right side and Paul the left.

We unpacked our bags and stuffed the drawers with our clothes before we headed downstairs to join the kegger party already in progress. Our first day, late Friday afternoon, was free of parents and family, with nothing to do but a freshman orientation the next day and classes on Monday. Whatever fatigue lingered after our drive dissipated when we finished the first beer. The excitement of our new surroundings rejuvenated us.

I awoke a little hungover and dehydrated the following day around 8:30 a.m. Paul got up earlier and dressed, prepared to head out. He detected the question on my face when he slipped on his yarmulke.

"This is a kippah or yarmulke; I wear one during prayers, part of the tradition. I'm not religious, but I find prayers relaxing and uplifting. The experience helps my music."

He examined himself in the mirror and continued.

"I promised to attend Chabad of the East Bay over on the north side to keep my parents happy. Let's meet here at 11:30, and we can walk over to the noon soirée."

"Cool. I'll see you later."

The university proffered an enormous lunch during our afternoon freshmen orientation. Most agenda items recapped the materials in the orientation handbook we received weeks before. We slipped out and returned to our dorm during one of the breaks.

We retrieved the rest of our luggage from the car and assembled Paul's stereo and speakers. Paul had brought numerous cassette tapes of Monk, Oscar Peterson, Coltrane, Miles Davis, Chick Corea, Weather Report, Mahavishnu Orchestra, and other lesser-known jazz groups.

To start, Paul put on something called *Return to Forever*. This album had only been released in Europe, though Paul managed to procure an import copy before its debut in the US market. A friend of Paul's attended Cambridge and mailed him advance copies of music unavailable in the States.

Halfway through *Return to Forever*, someone knocked at the door, and I rose to answer it. Paul jumped up ahead of me and cracked the door open. One of the guys on our floor, who I didn't know, handed Paul a cellophane package. Paul reached into his pocket and gave him a twenty-dollar bill.

"Is that what I think it is?" I asked.

"Yeah, I'm told it's the best Windowpane around."

I had heard about Windowpane acid but had never sampled it.

"This is a full dose, which we should cut in half if you're game."

I pulled out a hand mirror and a new razor blade from my overnight bag, and Paul gently took the blade from my hand, laid out the gelatin square on the glass, and carefully bisected it.

"There. Pick which half you prefer."

I acted impulsively because I might not have done it if I had had time to consider what I was about to do. Wetting my index finger, I picked up my half and placed it on my tongue. The tab was tasteless and dissolved instantly.

Paul swallowed his hit, and we kicked back while the music played.

"We're committed now."

"Yep, no turning back," I said, my voice trembling.

Once the full effect of the acid surged like a tide rolling in on the shore, time and space assumed a new dimension. Boundaries, always sharp and well-defined, became indistinct and fuzzy.

I opened my eyes to walls that cascaded as glistening colors like a polychromic waterfall. Paul looked at me and smiled. He mouthed something like "God assists you," or perhaps "Good acid."

The music stopped, but something echoed so loud I covered my ears. My aura bounced off the walls and swirled around the room before my body reabsorbed it. Blood coursed through my veins like river rapids. This sound ricocheted and stung me like needles, an uncomfortable but tolerable pain. My energy, bottled up in this room, wanted to disperse into the world. Only through conscious will could I move my body.

"Paul. Paul!" His eyes blinked open. "Let's go outside."

We moved down the stairs to the ground level and exited the front door. Some guys were hanging out in the dayroom and waved to us. All I saw was the walls liquefied behind them, and their hand waves fluttering through liquid color.

Paul and I merged into a festive Saturday evening on Telegraph Avenue. Many people paraded the street between Blake and Bancroft, shopping, going out for dinner, meeting friends, and everything people do in a city.

We walked to campus in awe of all the intense colors and lights, street musicians, reverberating sounds, and food's sweet and pungent odors. Irrationally, we laughed about nothing.

Swept up by an invisible current of space-time, we flowed into Sproul Plaza, the campus's central square.

Late-summer foliage from Sproul trees shed droplets of green and amber fire. Bright, multicolor fireflies winked in and out while the landscape trembled in an eerie preternatural glow. Sacred plants blossomed, worthy of respect and veneration.

Fascinated, I stood by as people rushed around me like I was wading in a stream. Minutes or hours may have passed before I remembered Paul. I turned around, but he had disappeared. I walked towards Sather Gate and beyond, entering another world through the portal, a threshold into something unknown covered with a bluish mist.

I wandered for a decade before I laid down on a grassy knoll somewhere on campus, staring into the twilight. Up in the sky, I became a viewpoint in space. Wispy clouds moved across the stars, dissolved in and out of focus, on the edge of awareness. In a moment of clarity, I realized I had no head, only a vast emptiness before me, coexistent with unity. A warm breeze scented with citrus touched me briefly.

I dreamt a dreamless sleep.

When I awoke, chilled and damp, I glanced around, looking for Paul. I was lost. I arose near a copse of trees where squirrels leaped from branch to branch. The familiar scent of grass and leaves conjured the transition from summer to fall, energized by Greek mythology's ethereal fluid that is the blood of the gods.

Off-balance, I rose and set out in a random direction, but it turned out to be the correct one. Later, I stood on the steps of our building where a loud and crowded party splashed out the first-floor windows: the time was 12:10 a.m., Sunday morning. *Tempus Fugit.*

A girl handed me a cold beer, which I guzzled, surprised by my thirst. The dayroom had an old upright piano, and there he was in all his glory, playing one of the jazz tunes we'd listened to earlier—Paul. I stood by until he finished and sat on the bench next to him. He hit the final chord, and we embraced like the long-lost brothers Antipholus and Dromio.

"There you are. Did we separate?"

"Only for a while," I said, "but everything comes together again."

"Fantastic. Listen to this song I made up."

Paul turned to the keys, and I moved away as he launched into a jazz-rock fusion piece that catapulted the partygoers to their feet dancing. I found a spot on the overstuffed couch and settled in. The acid had worn off mostly, but my legs still tingled. Colors radiated brighter and sharper, my hearing acute, while my heart rate slowed to normal as fatigue crept in.

An attractive brunette sat beside me.

"I'm Kara."

"James."

Most of the insights of the last few hours faded beyond reach, the way a memory of a vivid dream upon waking dissipates too quickly to grasp. Paul played as intensely as ever; he poured himself into his music, ignored the extraneous, and exhibited only the essential. I envied his creative focus.

"I haven't seen you all night. Is this your dorm?" Kara asked.

"Yes. The guy on the piano and I are roommates. We had another gig earlier."

"He's really fantastic. I'm so excited about being here and starting on Monday, aren't you?" Her face was bright and soothing.

"I've been looking forward to it all my life." She laughed.

The girl smiled with childlike innocence. I knew I was going to like college.

Chapter 15

The end of our first term at UC Berkeley arrived sooner than we imagined. Paul and I completed our final exams the same day and returned to our dorm, exhausted by the late nights, impossible workloads, and relentless deadlines. Most of the building cleared out for the winter break. Some remained for a day to rest after the term. Paul ordered a "kitchen sink" pizza with every topping offered (except pineapple) and borrowed two beers from our neighbors. We jettisoned our shoes, put on some music, and ate, anticipating the three weeks of leisure.

"Any plans for the winter break?" Paul asked.

"I thought I might go by the country club to see if I can get my old job back during the holidays, but I don't need the money that bad, and standing in a hot kitchen for hours would suck."

"I hear you. I've never had a real job because of my music, but it doesn't sound great."

"Well, you get into it, and the time passes. The paychecks are nice when they finally arrive, except for all the deductions."

"Didn't someone say we young people are all socialists until our first paycheck?"

"Someone from the Nixon administration, I think."

"Anyway, I'm going to unwind, play music, eat, and sleep. My parents want to spend the holidays in Del Mar."

"Do you celebrate Christmas?"

"We observe the holiday. My mom puts up a small tree. Chanukah ended last week, but she likes to keep the festive mood going for as long as possible."

Paul and I loaded our backpacks full of clothes and books into my car and drove to Diamond Bar the following morning. The drive down I-5 through rolling grasslands and corporate farms always made me sleepy, so we blasted the stereo and cranked down the windows despite the cold air. Paul managed to nap a little, making the six-hour drive uneventful *for him*. I dropped him off at his parents' house, and we didn't speak again until the 29th of December.

We spent much of our winter break idle. Overcome with boredom, Paul convinced me to return to Berkeley early for the New Year's Eve parties put on by friends who had moved out of the dorms.

A chilly and damp 50 degrees heralded the second day of the new quarter. Six months passed before I acclimated to the colder and wetter climate after moving from the Los Angeles coastal desert to the Bay Area. Over the Christmas break, my mom had taken me shopping for warmer clothes to replace my summery shirts and LA jackets. I bought my first dark-brown leather waist-length coat with a detachable lining. I wore it almost every day through April.

In the main library, I rummaged through the stacks hunting for books to provide historical context for my survey class in European literature. Each floor or tier contained efficiently aligned seven-foot-high shelves. Numerous stepstools were sprinkled throughout to help reach the top books. Also, individual cubicles and tables provided places for students to examine books or study.

With my items in hand, I sat down at one of the study carrels to thumb through the finds to decide if I wanted to check them out. Dust covered some bindings, which suggested no one had handled these volumes in some time.

Later in the year, as a library employee, I would work on the Blue Dot Project. A team of us examined every book, shelf, and tier in search of volumes unborrowed in over twenty years. Older publications received a sticker on their spine. Every blue-dotted book went to an offsite storage facility to accommodate newer acquisitions.

On a top shelf, I discovered a dusty book of poetry written by Ethel Carnie Holdsworth, unread since 1921: 52 years without a single checkout—five decades on a gray shelf overlooked by three generations of students and faculty.

The slim volume, *Voices of Womanhood,* spoke of working-class women's plight in the UK, a subject I knew nothing about. This publication may have been one of the harbingers of the Women's Movement. Writers who foresaw changes in our politics or culture before they became mainstream must have been rare.

I considered checking it out but decided I had enough to occupy me and affixed the blue dot—another text consigned to Erewhon, where forgotten works languished.

That afternoon I camped in one of the carrels focused on a book on French history and blocked out all extraneous noises and commotions. I did not detect someone motionless behind me.

A woman spoke. "Are you still ice skating?"

Turning, I stared at a petite, slender brunette with olive skin and soft green eyes. The voice, the way she stood, could it be? I recognized her as I rose to my feet.

"Maria?" I held out my hand. She hugged me tight enough to knock the breath out of me, her body so close I caressed her bones. Astonished, I held her and took her in, those eyes I now remembered, the Maria I believed lost forever, here, now, holding me.

We stood motionless, spellbound, searching each other expectantly, unable to speak for a moment. Every forgotten emotion erupted as I flashed to the two of us standing outside the skating rink, saying goodbye for the last time. Pain, elation, and relief swirled within as I savored an event I'd believed would never come.

"Oh, James. I never thought we would meet again. So awful the way we left things, but I didn't know how to contact you."

"I tried to find you too . . . " We gazed at each other. I studied Maria's face to rediscover everything about her, every faded detail in the labyrinth of memory. Too many since our last meeting. I drew in the scent of her skin, hair loosely tied back, and signature beret atop her head.

"How wonderful we both attended Cal. If only we had run into each other sooner."

"What better place than a library to reconnect?" I said.

"I missed you and have so much to tell you."

"I thought you might have forgotten me."

"No way. You've been on my mind forever. What? Four years, no?

"Yes. A long time. Almost a lifetime."

Maria let go of me, still standing close, intimate. I wanted to kiss her, hold her, touch her cheek, and push the locks of hair behind her ears adorned with emerald earrings.

"Hey, listen," she said, "I have some things to finish here, then I'm free. Let's meet somewhere for a coffee and catch up?" She consulted her wristwatch, "Say at 4 o'clock? I hang out at the Renaissance on Durant. Meet me at four?"

"Café Renaissance? Sure, I know it. I'll meet you there." Maria squeezed my hand and headed toward the opening elevator. She hesitated as though she had changed her mind about leaving and waved, smiling.

I gathered my books and headed down several flights of stairs toward the checkout desk to work off my nervous energy. I could not think clearly. Too many emotions: surprise, elation, relief, dread. But why fear? I needed time to reflect.

3:30 p.m.: thirty minutes to walk, clear my head, calm down, and grapple with the chance encounter that had caught me unprepared. I took the long way to our rendezvous by walking up South Drive to Piedmont Avenue and south. I meandered, unaware of passing cars or people.

At the café, I ordered a cappuccino and found my customary table in the corner, with the walls behind me and a clear view of the entrance, to monitor the patrons as they filtered in.

She said she hung out in the Renaissance, yet I had never seen her there. Her schedule must be the opposite of mine. Otherwise, I would have spotted her.

I preferred the Café Renaissance's coziness, its pleasant mix of natural and overhead light, optimal for reading, and the better-than-average coffee. Paul and I had sampled every cappuccino made on the campus's South and North sides, and this coffeehouse stood out as the best for espresso drinks. The carefully roasted beans, fresh milk, and expensive espresso machines operated by skilled baristas made the café my favorite.

Halfheartedly, I flipped through one of my books with a nervous eye on the door. By 4:05, Maria had not arrived. I returned to the counter to order another cappuccino. Considering how much espresso I drank, I wondered how I fell asleep at night.

Several minutes passed. Maria rushed in, her hair windblown with her powder-blue backpack swung over her shoulder.

Maria ordered and scanned the café while the barista pulled her espresso into a cup. We waved at each other. She smiled back, her mouth barely parted, her eyes full and focused in a way that made you believe you were the only person who mattered.

A jolt of adrenaline surged through me, a flash of sexual desire as she casually leaned on the bar. I recalled the contours of her body and the warmth I had absorbed earlier when we embraced.

Coffee in hand, Maria walked towards my table, her gaze fixed on me, ignoring the heads of other patrons who turned as she strolled between the narrow rows as though a movie star had unexpectedly appeared among them. Incongruous in Berkeley, her cowboy boots clacked against the concrete floor.

"Sorry to be late. Today's only the second day, and I'm swamped." She sat down, placed her bag under her chair, and stirred a packet of brown sugar into her macchiato. We waited for the other to start.

"At first, I didn't recognize you in the library. I stood behind, checking you out. The beard threw me. Your hair used to be short."

"I stopped the haircuts last summer. No reason to cut it, I guess."

Maria reached over, stroked the side of my cheek, and twirled a lock of my hair. "I kinda like it. Let your hair grow a bit more." Her caress made me shiver.

"Is my hand cold?"

"No . . . your touch is warm, actually."

She pulled back her hand and scanned the café. "I'm usually here in the early morning or early evening."

"Late morning or late at night for me."

I smiled to shield an awkwardness I didn't expect.

"I'm sorry about how we ended," she said. "Remember the last Saturday night when we said goodbye? Well, my grandfather on my mother's side died the next day. The services happened the following weekend, so I missed skating. Without your phone number, I had no way to reach you. I remembered you went to Fremont, but I didn't know anyone at that school."

"I skated every Saturday up to Halloween, waiting for you." She gave me a pained look.

"I didn't start skating again until after the new year." Maria glanced out the window, searching for the right words, "The truth is I met this older guy who went to Claremont High. Brett lived two doors from my grandparents and used to help Grandpa Vidal around the house. My grandmother invited him and his mother to the house after the funeral. He came on to me, and we started going out, but he didn't like to skate, so I stopped.

"My friend Laura urged me to return to the rink and explain what happened, but Brett insisted on tagging along, which would have been too awkward. A private conversation would be impossible with Brett nearby, so I bagged the idea, but I felt awful I didn't tell you myself. I'm sure I hurt you, and I'm sorry. Not an excuse, I know, but 14-year-olds aren't known for mature decisions." The regret in her voice sounded sincere.

"And Brett?"

"Brett turned out to be a real jerk." Maria hesitated and scratched her neck, about to say something further. She arched her eyebrows. "Let's leave it at that."

In the momentary silence between us, Maria spun her coffee cup clockwise.

"I went back to skating in January, but you never came. You should read my journals, full of laments about not finding you, losing the one guy I liked and had so much in common with. I hope you will forgive me for disappointing you."

"I was upset for a while, but I got over it. What's the point of living in the past? Of course I forgive you."

"Good. I messed things up, and I want to make amends. Please don't be bitter."

"It happened a long time ago. I'm happy we found each other again."

"Me too. I'd like to be friends."

Maria leaned over and settled her hand on my arm, and I brushed my fingers over hers. I finally relaxed, not realizing how tense I was meeting her again.

"I tried to look up your phone number but never knew your last name. To answer your original question back at the library: I no longer skate."

Maria pulled a notepad from her bag and ripped out a page to write. "Here. My name, number, and address. I don't want to lose you again."

She handed me the page. I read aloud, "Maria Isabella Compagno."

"Yes, a pleasure to meet you."

"James Alexander Montez, *a su orden*."

We shook hands across the table to formalize our reunion and create an official reset point, which in a way, it did. I dashed my information on the bottom half of the paper she gave me and tore it in half.

"So you live on the Northside?" I asked.

"I live near the Berkeley Rose Garden. It's a pricy yellow cottage that looks like a ski chalet."

"I'm in the dorms on Durant.

"It was too late for the dorms because I didn't accept the admission until late spring. My roommate Laura and I were planning to attend Stanford. I got in, but she didn't, so we both came to Cal."

"You gave up Stanford for your friend?"

"Laura's my *best* friend, my sister; *mi comadre*. Berkeley's cheaper, and I don't care about prestige and all that."

"I applied to UCLA and here. Both accepted me, but I wanted to get out of LA."

"UCLA accepted us both, but we preferred Berkeley for the same reason. I've always loved northern California, especially the cooler and less humid climate."

"My roommate Paul is an acquaintance from high school. We're good friends now. In fact, he's my only friend."

"Friends don't come easily to you."

"Not really."

"I remember how shy you were when we first met."

"Still am. I have several acquaintances, but no one I would call a friend."

"Other than Paul and me?" Maria smiled.

"Yes, exactly."

The noise level in the café rose a few decibels. Maria and I leaned in to hear each other better.

"I have a younger brother. My older sister goes to UCLA."

"I had an older sister, but she died."

"I'm so sorry."

"She died before I was born from Rh hemolytic disease. No cure existed in the 1950s. My mom never talks about it. I didn't find out until two years ago."

Maria placed her hand on my arm to comfort me.

"I never talked about her before. Not sure why I am now."

"I'm touched you would share something so personal with me. That's why I liked you from the start. You're a deep person, and deep people feel deeply."

Maria searched my face as she spoke. I would have told her anything at that moment.

"What of your parents, Maria?"

"My dad's VP of Finance for Enterprise Resource Planning at the Global Dynamics plant in Pomona. And my mom's an RN supervisor at the Pomona Valley Hospital."

"My stepfather's a Quality Control engineer for an aerospace company in Seal Beach. My mom's a waitress."

"Where's your real dad?"

"He lives in the Dominican Republic. We're not speaking to each other right now." I explained our falling out over my clothes and haircut.

"I hope you two patch things up. Life is too brief to be at odds with a parent. In my opinion."

"We're both stubborn, but you're right."

"My grandparents run a small ranch in the San Gorgonio Mountain foothills outside Beaumont, about an hour east of Pomona. That's where I board my mare, Smokie. She's named after her gray coloring."

"I've always wanted to learn to ride."

"Laura and I have spent the last seven summers out there. We ride a lot."

"Your grandparents raise horses?"

"Some. We own a few and board several others. The ranch lives off the income from the three hundred hens. That's a lot of eggs."

"Oh, you have a chicken ranch."

An hour passed in an instant.

"Listen," she said apologetically. "I need to go. I'm meeting my roommate and boyfriend for dinner at seven."

When she said "boyfriend," my heart dropped to the floor. Throughout the afternoon, she'd never mentioned a boyfriend. I hid my disappointment, but she detected the flash of sadness I could not disguise.

"I loved our afternoon together. It's so fantastic we reconnected," Maria said as she grabbed my hand and squeezed it to reassure herself my feelings had not changed.

"Oh, all right. I'm on my way back to the library anyway."

Maria and I stepped out into the street, partially lit by streetlamps. We shared one Spanish class that met every Monday, Wednesday, and Friday from 3 to 4. The administration had canceled the Monday class, so we had missed each other yesterday.

We strolled through Sproul Plaza and across campus. I hesitated to reach out and take Maria's hand, distracted by her perfume and the reddish highlights in her hair, accentuated by the ambient light.

Before dropping me off at Moffitt Library, she hugged me briefly.

"Thank you so much for the afternoon. Seeing you again makes me happy."

"If you're free, let's have coffee after class on Wednesday. We can practice our Spanish together."

Maria pulled out a pocket calendar. "Perfect. I'm free after class Mondays, Wednesdays, and Fridays."

We parted. Maria continued to Northside, and I ambled toward the library, full of conflicting emotions and overwhelmed by the afternoon's surprises.

After our encounter, her presence gripped me as firmly as the first time. A nagging voice urged me to restrain my enthusiasm. Since I could do nothing about the boyfriend, I decided to let the situation go and not worry about the other people in her life. She was only dating, and couples seldom stayed together for long at our age. Besides, we had a connection and a bond—perhaps a tenuous one now, but I remained optimistic. That should be worth something.

Over the next several weeks, we strolled to the Café Renaissance after class, often chatting in Spanish to reinforce our lessons. Although she stumbled over the less-used verb tenses, such as the subjunctive, Maria spoke fluently and often corrected my diction. Under her tutelage, I lost much of my American accent.

Over coffee, we talked about a wide range of subjects in English or Spanish, or sometimes French.

"I love all animals," she said one afternoon, "particularly horses. Horses, because of their gentle, sensitive nature, can heal. They are like dreams you can touch. And dreams are portals to healing."

"Do you mean from dreams we can heal ourselves?"

"Yes. Let's say you hurt your leg and can't walk. If your leg is healed in your dream, and you're running again, there's hope for healing."

"How do horses heal?"

"Whenever I'm sad or not feeling well, I take Smokie for a ride. In no time, whatever's bothering me disappears. Horses exist in the moment and love unconditionally. Smokie transfers that energy to me because we are in intimate contact with each other emotionally and physically. I ride bareback to feel her as part of me."

"This works with dogs and cats, too, doesn't it? My dog used to sit next to me when I was down. My mood improved quickly."

"Exactly. We cannot live outside or away from nature. Can you imagine living in a high-rise apartment without trees, plants, or pets? Such a life would kill me." She waved her hand around to emphasize her points.

"Do you or Laura have any pets in Berkeley?"

"No, though we talked about getting a cat."

"Well, I live in a dormitory, but Paul and I plan to move to an apartment or house this summer."

"I love living in the Bay Area. The weather is better than in LA, and it's more convenient. We can jump on BART and reach downtown San Francisco in thirty minutes. In LA traffic, it takes thirty minutes to drive five miles."

"In Diamond Bar, where I grew up, it's still rural. I like the city but miss the grassy hills behind my house and the long walks with my dog."

"I know, right? I enjoy Berkeley only because I know I'm returning to the woods around my grandparents' ranch after each term."

"I like the freedom of being away from parents, to do whatever we wish."

"That's true. Don't you feel like you can really be yourself?"

"Yes. In a way, I'm finding out who I am." Maria nodded, knowing exactly what I meant.

"I miss my family, though," she began after a moment. "But most of all, I miss Smokie. I don't like being away from her so much. Can I tell you a secret?" She leaned closer, lowering her voice in a faux conspiracy. "I call my grandparents most evenings to check on her."

One subject we avoided, however, was Maria's boyfriend. My curiosity about him prodded me to ask an occasional, oblique question.

"Did you guys do anything fun last weekend?"

"Friday nights, Robert works in the computer lab. The three of us ate dinner on Saturday and went to a movie. We saw *The Groove Tube*. The show had its moments, but it was dumb."

"I saw that movie. My favorite scene is the opening where the guy is chasing that girl while both are stripping off their clothes."

"Yeah, that was a good one, especially the accompanying music. I love being naked in nature."

At first, I thought I had misheard her. I recalled the scene from the movie, replacing the girl with Maria.

"Where'd you go, James?"

"Oh, just imaging you running through the woods."

Maria smiled, her expression demure. "Maybe I shouldn't have been so forthcoming."

"You are honest and forthright about who you are. I love that."

I tried not to think of Maria and her boyfriend having fun together, sitting arm-in-arm in a movie theater, going home, tearing off their clothes, going to . . . Why did I torture myself?

Still, she detected the change in my mood whenever he came up.

"He's fun to be around. I told him about you, so I'm sure you'll meet him someday."

"Looking forward to it." From her expression, I gleaned her disapproval of my softened snide remark.

"Let's not spoil our time together." She leaned back in her chair, staring out the window at the passing traffic.

"I'm getting another coffee. Another for you, James?"

"Sure. Thanks."

Maria returned to the bar and ordered two cappuccinos, deliberately keeping her back to me as she chatted with the barista.

In her less-than-subtle way, Maria intimated that I should accept her relationship with her boyfriend if I wanted to be around her. Acceding to this condition proved difficult. I ached to know what sort of life she shared with him and whether theirs was as good as I imagined ours might be, but I dared not ask. The truth might not have set me free.

Somehow, I adopted the role of the impassive admirer, kept my ardor under control, and subdued the urge to declare myself to her, an effort of self-restraint I suspected she appreciated but which disrupted my tranquility.

Still, Maria running through the woods as a leafless nymph . . . I couldn't unimagine that, nor did I want to.

On another occasion, I risked everything for reasons I still can't fathom and asked her directly about what was on my mind.

"Robert's a computer science major, two years ahead of you, and you're in literature, so what's the attraction between you?"

She tensed slightly, rotating her coffee cup. Her head tilted as she pondered whether I could endure her answer.

"We only see each other on weekends since he's buried in the bowels of Evans Hall, working on his computer programs. That gives me the time I need during the week, but I like to relax too."

"Sure, makes sense."

"He makes me laugh. He can be charming. We like the same music and share the same taste in movies. He's not deep like you, but I don't expect him to satisfy all my needs. And in case you're wondering, the way all guys do, Robert's not bad in bed. Anything else you want to know? Because I want to get all this out in the open."

Her words left me nonplussed. I gathered my hands beneath the table, ashamed of irritating her and receiving her rebuke. Once I memorized every ring in my coffee cup, I raised my eyes to hers, a gaze that bore a hole through me.

"I'm sorry to annoy you, Maria. I hope I'm not jeopardizing our friendship. It's just . . . "

Maria softened. We both exhaled, unaware we were holding our breath.

In Spanish: "I know you like me; I adore you, too. We talk about all kinds of things together, and I love that. If we had met before Robert, things might be different. I'm sorry, but I couldn't bear not having you as a friend. I need you to accept things as they are for now."

I reached across the table, taking her hand with both of mine as I marshaled my thoughts in Spanish. Tears were about to well in my eyes.

"Our friendship means everything. Please forgive me. I'm an idiot sometimes, but relationships between two people who care about each other are sometimes *demanding*. Is that the word?"

She laughed. "Close enough." Maria raised my hand to her lips and kissed it. The tension dissipated just as the sun emerged from behind a cloud. A promising sign, perhaps.

My nemesis, Robert, became an abstraction, so I did not recognize this broad-shouldered, dishwater-blond guy with squinting blue eyes and a copper mustache as he hustled to our table like a bull to a red cape. He struck me as more the lumberjack type who looked out of place without a plaid flannel shirt and leather boots. The man before us did not register as the computer wunderkind I imagined.

"Hi, Maria. May I join you?" Before she could respond, he grabbed an empty chair from an adjoining table and muscled beside us. Dressed in faded blue jeans, white sneakers, and a green pullover, the intruder glanced back and forth, a glint of menace in eyes spaced too narrowly on his face as he tried to piece together what we had been doing before he arrived. I suspected this visit to be a deliberate ambush, not a chance encounter.

Throughout several seconds of uncomfortable silence, Maria crossed her legs and folded her arms across her chest, her jaw tightening as she met Robert's gaze and supercilious grin.

"Robert, this is James, the friend from LA I told you about."

I extended my hand. Robert merely nodded and spoke to Maria as though I were invisible.

"I wondered why this joint was your favorite, so I figured I'd find out. Is this your so-called Spanish partner?" he asked her with his pinched mouth and stiff posture. My blood pressure shot up, my jaw tightened, and my fingers curled. Though I'd never been one for violence, Robert was an interloper, a *terzo incomdo*, who disrupted our *tête-à-tête*, and I wanted to smack him.

"Yes, he is. Don't be rude. You know I don't like that." Her clipped voice and narrowing eyes bored into Robert, who softened his smirk. "I'm surprised you found the time to leave the computer lab. Lovely to see you." Maria's eyes constricted into pinpoints. Despite his brutishness, Robert caught on that his name had moved to the top of her shit list as he reclined to create more room between them.

Her brow darkened with a cautious glance at me as she twirled her cup.

"Yeah, I miss my girl." He leaned in clumsily and kissed Maria on the cheek. She did not respond, her face slack. These junior-high antics embarrassed us.

"Don't be an asshole, Robert."

"Kind of hostile today, aren't we?" he said with feigned surprise. "I thought you'd be glad to see me."

"I don't like you hanging all over me like you're marking your territory. What's come over you? And you're treating my friend like he's not here. Do I do that to you?"

Robert leaned back and smiled. "Sorry, hon."

"Don't call me *hon*; I'm not your hon. And if you don't lay off, I won't be your anything, *capiche*?"

"I said I'm sorry. Jeez." He shrugged. "Sorry, Jim."

His faux contrition failed to register. I checked the time. "It's late. Friday night, and I have a date. Nice meeting you, *Bob*. See you in class next week, Maria," I said as I stood to go. I stared at him, almost a direct challenge, annoyed by his leer. Maria sighed and sagged back into her seat. Her expression broke my heart.

"All right. *Oye, Lo siento mucho por esto. Te llamaré más tarde, ¿de acuerdo?*"

"*Sí, está bien.* Goodnight, all," I said.

As I walked away, I overheard Robert ask what we had said to each other but missed her curt answer.

The sun dipped below the horizon as I raced back to my dorm, angry and crestfallen, my chest restricted. I stopped into Moe's Bookstore, browsed the fiction section, could not concentrate, and left. Maria had held her own, but I prayed she laid into him after I left the café. He deserved a solid verbal beat-down, *Latina* style.

My heart rate returned to normal when I reached my room, and my mouth felt less dry. Paul had not come in yet. I dropped my bookbag on the floor, kicked off my shoes, and laid down, my arms over my eyes to block the light from the street. Someone on my floor played Elton John.

Six weeks had passed since our first meeting at the start of the term. I mulled over our time together, second-guessing what I'd said, what I should have said, and the lost opportunities to convince Maria of my sincerity. Still, she held fast. She was with Robert, preferred him, and I had to accept her (misguided) choices or not hang out with her.

I fell asleep. Someone knocked loudly on my door.

"Hey, you got a phone call."

Shoeless, I crossed the hall to the waiting phone.

"This is Maria. I apologize. Robert's behavior really upset me. He's usually not rude, but I suppose he's jealous of you," she blurted out, breathless.

"All right. Robert probably misconstrued the situation. He understands we are just pals, right?"

"I made it clear to him after you left." A long pause. "Am I keeping you from going on your date?" She waited for me to respond. "You never mentioned seeing anyone—"

"I'm not. I didn't want to give him the wrong impression." She sounded disappointed, though I couldn't tell if it was because I was dateless or because of the possibility I might have been seeing someone and didn't tell her.

"What are you doing tonight?"

"I'll find some supper and head to the library, the usual Friday night routine."

"Why don't you come over? My roommate and I were about to put on some pasta and make a salad. We even scored a bottle of chianti."

"Will he be there?"

"No, we fought. Robert's history until the weekend, or longer. Will you come?" I almost said no thanks, but wanted to see her and agreed.

"Sure, thirty minutes?"

"Perfect. *Ciao*."

A weight fell away and allowed free breathing to return. I showered, shaved, and headed to Maria's house, about a twenty-minute trek across campus. I walked fast, not surprised at my eagerness to reach her. My appetite also returned along the way.

Chapter 16

Maria lost some of her *joie de vivre* after our first dinner.

"Are you guys getting along better?" I asked one afternoon following Spanish class, bracing myself for her answer.

"Yes and no. We've had several heart-to-hearts. Robert knows how I stand now, though talking to him sometimes is like wrangling a wild goat."

"Something you have experience with?"

"I trained our goats on the ranch. They're like two-year-old children, but eventually, they get it."

"You look tired."

"I haven't slept as well as I usually do. I hate conflict. I prefer to get along with people, not confront them on their issues."

"I'm sorry."

"I have my issues as well, I guess," she said, sighing.

"You're one of the happiest people I know. It bothers me when you're unhappy."

Maria reached over and took my hand.

"You're the best, James."

I squeezed her hand and let myself hope I might have an opening.

Every part of me ached to hasten my rival's departure. I cherished each moment with Maria and loved that she was a one-guy-at-a-time type of girl, only I wanted to be that guy. She often hesitated to depart after our *tête-à-têtes* at the Renaissance, reinforcing my belief she shared my sentiments. Whether she was ready to admit her ambivalence remained to be seen. Perhaps Robert also discerned an aloofness widening between them.

Like the weather, life changed. One chilly Friday afternoon, we strolled over to the café. Maria behaved sullenly and downcast in Spanish class. Something bothered her, perhaps an illness taking hold. We picked up our coffees, and I followed her lead to a quiet table in the back.

"Maria, something's on your mind."

She looked up at me as she collected her thoughts, slowly turning her cup, a tell that she was upset. I was alarmed by an errant idea that she might be about to curtail our time together. She noted my concern.

"Don't worry. It's nothing about us. We're fine. Last night my boyfriend and I had another huge fight." She looked around the café, at her coffee cup, and back at me. I nodded for her to continue, suppressing *schadenfreude* about Robert.

"He told me he questioned whether we should continue as a couple. He admitted that, besides sex, we didn't have much in common, and he thought we should take a break. Well, he blabbed for a half-hour before conceding he wanted to date someone else in one of his classes and confessing he was hanging out with some girl in and out of the lab. Then, he admitted that they had been sleeping together already. I thought he was working all this time, but the *petit enculé* was cheating on me, *pardonne-moi*."

"*Certainement, ma chérie.*"

Maria began to sob. "I hate when people lie to me, especially someone I'm close to. For me, that's unforgivable. To sleep around on me is the ultimate betrayal I can't forgive." She slipped a handkerchief from her pocket and wiped her eyes. "When I'm with someone, I'm with them all the way. I don't hold back. This isn't the first time I went for the wrong guy. Haven't I learned my lesson?"

"Maybe it's because the cynical or unscrupulous will accept the challenge of coming on to you."

After rubbing her eyebrows, she said, "What do you mean?"

"Because of your looks, most guys are too timid to approach you. A narcissist would, though."

"My looks?"

"You're beautiful, Maria. That intimidates a lot of guys, including me."

"I don't think I'm that attractive."

How could Maria be so confident, mature beyond her years, and demure?

"As a biased observer, you are the most attractive woman I know."

She mulled over my words for a few moments.

"Please tell me I don't intimidate you now."

"No. Not now. When we first met at the rink, I summoned a lifetime of courage to approach you."

"Funny. In some ways, I think of you as the bravest of all my friends. You speak your mind, and you're honest. Lies are easier to tell than the truth."

"Lies are harder to keep straight, so I prefer honesty if possible."

Maria recovered from her initial outpouring of emotion and put away her handkerchief.

"I guess I saw this thing with Robert coming. The sex over the last few weeks has been so-so, like he's not into me. And to be honest, I'm not thrilled with him, either." She stopped when my face telegraphed my uneasiness. "Is my frankness making you uncomfortable?" She gently grasped my hand.

"Not at all." I hedged as she gauged my sincerity. Her penetrating stare exposed my vulnerability. Maria glanced behind her and bared her neck as she tugged her coat off her shoulders to the back of the chair. I removed my jacket too.

"Robert's history. I lost my temper and threw him out of the house and my life. Just the thought of him pisses me off." Maria shook as she spoke. "What kind of guy can lie to your face week after week? His new *copine* and he were together during that little stunt he pulled last week. We left ten minutes after you did, and where did he go? To *her*."

Maria's anger poured out of her, and I considered it best to stay clear until she had purged all of it.

"How could I have misjudged him for so long? Last night, after Robert left, it took Laura an hour to calm me down. I knew he wasn't for me, but I hung on out of misplaced loyalty. I don't need this aggravation. School is more important, and I should concentrate on my studies. I realize this sounds melodramatic," she attempted to laugh, but the bittersweetness stifled her, "but he wants to move on, so let him." I nodded.

"What are you feeling?" she asked, her eyes wide, pleading.

My breathing had stopped. I let myself breathe again. Fear, relief, and a guarded joy swirled inside me.

"Please forgive me if I upset you." She reached out again and placed her hand on mine. Her tenderness sent a warm surge through my body, and I relaxed. My heart rate slowed to normal.

"Maria, I have almost no experience with these things. I don't know what to say, and perhaps I shouldn't say anything." I took her hand. She tightened her fingers around mine and relaxed, locking her eyes on me expectantly to confirm our bond. "I want you to be happy. You know I'll do anything for you."

"You do care about me."

I hesitated. *Should I be entirely honest?*

"Maria, what I feel is much more than caring. I have tried to hold back my feelings because I didn't want to make you uncomfortable or scare you away. I enjoy every moment with you. Weekends, when we're apart, are pure agony. You are always with me. Now, I sound melodramatic." My voice trailed off.

Maria let go of my hands and pulled her chair next to me as she rested her head on my shoulder and wrapped her arms around me. Lulled by our heartbeats, we held each other in perfect synchronicity.

Time passed: minutes, hours, days, weeks . . . Perhaps Maria had fallen asleep. The sun had set, and the streetlights flared in the twilight to bathe the streets in their yellowish, unearthly glow.

The warmth of our bodies penetrated and infused us with a familiar yet undefinable sensation. No need to speak, we remained in flawless silence. Everything disclosable passed between us as though a direct link bridged our nervous systems.

The café had emptied some time ago as calm settled over the tables in anticipation of the early evening crowd's arrival. Maria whispered in my ear in the half-light, "Thank you for being here for me."

"Always."

"I'm starving. Come to my house, and I'll make some of my grandma's spaghetti and meatballs. It's Friday night, and I want to be happy."

Maria and I held hands as we strolled across campus toward her house, the warmth from our revelatory confessional stronger than ever. She wore one of her berets, of which she owned several in varying colors. The temperature dropped at sunset. The weather forecast called for possible snow after midnight, but it seldom snowed in the Bay Area, and I discounted the report, though the air whiffed sharp and crisp the way mountain air did.

We crossed Hearst Avenue to Euclid and ran into Paul, returning from a prayer session at Chabad of the East Bay. I made the introductions.

"Pleased to meet you, at last, Maria. I've heard almost nothing about you." She tilted her head as she pondered whether Paul was kidding, unaware of his ironic sense of humor.

"James and I are headed to my house for dinner. Join us, won't you? I'm making a home-cooked meal."

"If I'm not intruding."

"Not at all. My housemate's waiting for us. Let's go."

The three of us entered Maria's cottage as her roommate, Laura, emerged from the kitchen wearing a red apron. I had mentioned Laura to Paul, but they had never met. She gave me a peck on the cheek. "Welcome back." Turning to Paul, she extended her hand, "Hi, I'm Laura Shapiro."

"This is Paul Stern, my dorm roommate," I said.

"I invited them to dinner. We have enough, don't we?" Maria added as she helped us slip off our coats.

Paul stood for a moment, pleasantly surprised, staring at Laura, who clasped his hand, saying, "Paul? Have we met before? I know you from somewhere."

He thought for a moment as he took her in. Laura was tall like Paul, with dark blonde hair, hazel eyes, and an oval face. Clearly, he found her attractive, judging from his growing smile. Paul told me he liked girls with slender builds and full breasts, and Laura had both attributes.

He recovered his voice. "Ah, no, we haven't met. But didn't I hear you guys went to Claremont High?"

"Yes."

"So maybe our paths crossed at some school event."

"Maybe that's it."

The four of us stood in a cozy living room with a small couch, coffee table, and an armchair. Maria dropped our coats on the sofa and said, "Let's go into the kitchen."

Paul and I sat at the round, wooden table. Maria poured us glasses of red wine. "I hope you guys like wine because we don't have any beer."

"Wine's great," Paul said, and I nodded.

We chatted as Maria and Laura prepared supper. Laura finished cutting up vegetables for a salad while Maria opened a cupboard filled with various kinds of pasta, deciding which one to use.

"Tonight, we're serving one of the oldest dishes in my family, and the first one I learned to make. It's spaghetti and meatballs but with a few Compagno innovations."

She poured a batch of marinara sauce into a pan from a two-quart Mason jar and set it on low heat.

"The sauce is the secret to this dish. The recipe is committed to memory, so you'll never find it in any cookbook."

The aroma from the heating sauce stimulated my appetite. I took another sip of wine.

"My grandmother mixes ground beef and chicken to give the meatballs a lighter flavor. Instead of regular spaghetti, I substitute bucatini."

"What's that?" I asked.

"Bucatini's like traditional spaghetti, but more round, and a hole through the middle giving each noodle a hollow center. This makes it a little thicker than spaghetti noodles."

Maria dumped the bucatini into simmering water, added some spices, then brought the water to a boil.

Laura said, "Maria is a tremendous cook. You guys are in for a treat."

"I wondered about those secret recipes. My mom keeps several of her own," I said.

Maria joined us at the table and sipped her wine. "Wait until you try it. My grandmother taught me to prepare this sauce when I was ten and made me promise to pass the instructions down to my daughters."

"How do you know you'll have daughters? Or if you will marry?" I asked, teasing her.

"Girls run in our family. You know me a little by now." She returned to the stove. "Do you think I'll have trouble finding a husband?" She smiled as she stirred the sauce. The subtle Hispanic lilt in her voice, which emerged at her most relaxed, aroused me as I imagined us together, married with children.

"No. I believe all your daughters will be brilliant chefs." I almost said *all our daughters.*

As she poured her vegetables onto the bowl of lettuce, Laura said, "Maria says you both attended Ganesha High, our crosstown rival?" Laura looked at Paul as she spoke.

"Yes. I thought Ganesha was a decent high school until I got here and discovered the curriculum didn't prepare me for college work," Paul said.

"That's true for most public schools. Claremont High wasn't much better."

"James said you play the piano?"

"Yeah, I play a little."

"Didn't you play at a party in Diamond Bar last May, at a big house in a cul-de-sac?"

"I did. Were you there?"

Maria took a sip of wine. "I remember you now. You're the pianist we heard!"

Laura nodded. "There were people everywhere, inside, outside. We tried to push our way into the living room where you performed but couldn't break through."

Astonished, I said, "You two stood in the driveway while I camped next to Paul? Damn! If only I had peeked out the window."

That singular recognition event initiated a bond of friendship that tied us to each other. How close Maria and I came to rediscovering each other *last year*, and how Laura found the man she would spend the rest of her professional and private life with, a certainty yet to materialize.

Laura said, "Although I'm not a music major, I play the violin, piano, and guitar. My parents are musicians, too."

"I also play a little guitar. My folks don't play, but they made sure I practiced. I used to spend five or six hours daily, but now I'm down to three, with school and all." The excitement in Paul's voice was palpable. "Tell me about the music you play."

"My parents got me started playing the piano at six. Then, I switched to the violin so my mom and I could play duets. She plays the cello and piano. I love the sound of the violin, plus it's easier to carry around." We laughed.

Paul turned serious. "Hmm. Do you know the music of Stéphane Grappelli or Jean-Luc Ponty?"

"I've heard their music, yes."

"Well, I'm writing this piece and thinking about adding a violin part. Would you be interested in helping me?"

"You write your own music?"

"Sure. Half of everything I play, I composed myself."

"Why not? Sounds fun."

"Fantastic. I'll book us a practice room some evening next week."

Maria tossed the empty wine bottle. "Hey Paul, would you pick up some more wine for dinner?" I had mentioned that Paul and I carried fake IDs.

"Sure can. What can I buy?"

Maria pulled $30 out of her jean pocket, enough for a week's groceries. She believed a little wine with dinner was not a luxury but *de rigor*. My parents didn't drink, so complementing dinner with wine was new to me. Maria once told me, "Drinking for drinking's sake is immature, and I always prefer to have food with my wine."

"Laura, could you drive Paul to the Monterrey Market on Hopkins? Here's the money. Please buy a bottle of chianti and a pinot noir, like the ones we got last time. We will finish up here. Hurry back. Dinner will be ready in ten minutes."

Laura led Paul out of the kitchen to the garage. Maria continued with supper while I "helped."

From behind, I embraced her, kissing the back of her neck.

"Thanks," I said.

"For what?"

"For confiding in me, trusting me, and being my friend. And for cooking."

She turned and hugged me, her head on my chest for a moment before letting go and returning to the counter: only the necessary words or gestures, no more, no less.

"Paul and Laura sure hit it off," I said.

"Smitten with each other, I'd say. I'm glad."

"Paul's a great musician. Laura sounds like she's no slouch, either. And now they're composing together."

"When we were young, I hung out at her house and listened as Laura and her mother practiced. Laura is a fantastic musician."

"They have music, and we have literature and languages in common. A nice symmetry."

Maria paused, thinking about something. "Like it was meant to be."

Laura and Paul returned with two bottles. Laura opened a cabinet and pulled down four pinot glasses. With a waiter's corkscrew, she skillfully uncorked the pinot and poured an inch of wine into each glass. Paul and I followed her motions, impressed by her oenological expertise.

"Swirl the glass first," Laura explained, showing us how to aerate the wine. She took a sip and inhaled air to allow the fruit to pass over her tongue. We did the same and grinned as the flavor unfolded in our mouths.

"Where did you learn to taste wine, Laura"? Paul asked.

Laura smiled and turned to her side, pointing at Maria. *Elle là-bas.* Maria took a slight bow.

We sat at the table which I set earlier. Maria apportioned the pasta and meatballs into bowls and ladled generous amounts of sauce over each serving. She took a Parmesan block and grated the pungent cheese carefully before adding a sprig of fresh parsley. Then she served an elaborate green salad with homemade balsamic and olive oil dressing on separate plates.

I said, "A toast to our beautiful hosts, Maria and Laura. *Bon appetit.*" We clinked glasses and enjoyed our meal.

Maria unveiled a homemade tiramisu, another secret Compagno family recipe.

"I use only fresh Italian mascarpone and ladyfingers. That's most of the secret."

"My mom still visits the same Italian delicatessen to buy everything Italian," I added.

"Absolutely," Maria said. "Food is a religion for us, right up there with Catholicism."

After supper, we cleared the dishes and moved to the sitting room with our glasses. We polished off the wine. The scent of the savory marinara sauce, the delicately flavored meatballs, and the light-bodied pinot noir lingered in the air and our memories.

A comfortable, understated intimacy emerged among us as we huddled on the couch like friends who had known each other for years. Whatever barriers separating Maria and me dissipated, leaving space for us to grow. Laura and Paul clicked so spontaneously that I dared to believe love might exist at first sight. *Le coup de foudre,* as the French say.

The evening passed swiftly.

"Spring break arrives in three weeks," Maria said, "and I'm going to my grandparents' ranch. Would you guys like to go with me?"

"I told my parents I would visit. They want to go to Del Mar, but thanks for the invitation," Paul said.

Maria glanced over at Laura. "My parents expect me home too. Sorry. But put me down for a couple of weeks this summer."

"Of course. It's our annual ritual."

Maria turned to me as I smiled, pushing the hair off my forehead. "I'm free. Visiting a real ranch and meeting your grandparents sounds great. One condition, though."

"Oh, what's that?" Maria asked in a playful tone.

"That I get some more of grandma's cooking."

Maria laughed. "Be prepared to pack on some pounds. You will eat more food in one day than here in a week."

Laura and Paul excused themselves as Laura took Paul to her room to show him her guitar and violin. Moments later, music wafted in from the bedroom as Laura bowed a melody and Paul strummed along on the guitar. Maria smiled and shook her head: "A match made in Heaven, as they say. It doesn't hurt that they're both Jewish."

"How did you know Paul's Jewish?"

"By his yarmulke." Maria smiled. "I saw him remove it and put it in his coat pocket when we ran into him."

Paul and Laura serenaded us. Maria took my hand into her lap and laid her head against my shoulder. I remained still, wanting to savor every moment, absorb the warmth of her body, and remember every detail, just in case.

"Do you mind if we don't sleep together tonight? I want to jump your bones, but I need more time."

"I understand," I said, careful to keep the disappointment out of my voice. I shouldn't have expected Maria to transition almost overnight from one guy to another. After waiting four years, I could wait a little longer.

"I'm so happy and calm right now with you," she said. "I didn't realize how amped I could get being with Robert. What a disaster. Can you forgive me?"

"Nothing to forgive. It was inevitable that you would circle back to us."

"You have the patience of Job."

"When we met four years ago, something told me that our destinies were intertwined, and we would be together forever. Just an intuition."

"I'm starting to believe in your clairvoyance. "

"I had faith in you, in us. When we met at the library last January, it only reinforced my belief."

"But how did you know?" Maria leaned further against me, whispering.

"It was a certainty that's hard to explain. I just knew."

Maria kissed my neck, my cheek, and then my lips. That moment stayed with me for the rest of my life.

The night grew cold and overcast. The girls bundled Paul and me into our coats and sent us out into the evening. We hurried across campus as I labored to keep up with Paul's rangy gait and reached the dorm, oblivious to the twenty-minute walk.

Paul was smitten. Laura was smart, funny, and alluring. He said, "Beauty, brains, and musical talent, how can I ask for anything more? And my parents will be happy she's Jewish."

"When I met Laura last week, I had no doubt destiny would bring the two of you together." Maria later confirmed Laura had found her "soulmate," and Paul walked around, convinced he had won the lottery. In a way, he had.

CHAPTER 17

The following evening, in an impromptu decision, the four of us went to a coming-of-age movie, *American Graffiti*, about teenagers in a 1962 central Californian town at the dawn of the Vietnam War.

On Sunday, we drove in Laura's Mustang to visit Petaluma Boulevard, the star avenue depicted in the movie. We cruised up and down the famous street as though we were high-schoolers from the film.

Tired of cruising, we lunched at the rustic Metro Hotel and Café and ordered grilled-cheese sandwiches.

"At least the kids in the movie didn't have the war hanging over them like Paul and I did."

"You guys aren't in danger of the draft, are you?" Laura asked.

"The lottery system took the place of the draft. My number was 243. What was yours, Paul?"

He thought for a moment. "About 125, around there."

"Only numbers below 100 had to report for the physicals and induction."

I took another bite of my sandwich. "When I registered, I put myself down as a conscientious objector. If I went in, they'd have to put me in a noncombat role."

Paul shrugged. "I hear the weather in Canada isn't always shitty."

"It's unfair that only men have to serve. In Israel, both sexes must do a tour of duty," Maria said.

"You would go in?" Laura asked.

"Probably. I'm not squeamish around blood. I've seen enough of it at the ranch. I'd make a good nurse like my mother, no?"

"I'd want you by my bedside, that's for sure," I said.

"The war's winding down. Peace negotiations will end the conflict." Laura lifted her glass of iced tea in a toast: "To the end of the war."

The winter term closed with only one week off before the spring quarter began. Maria's grandparents' ranch rested in a little town north of Beaumont, California, called Cherry Valley. Nestled in the foothills at the foot of snow-topped mountains, the rural hamlet guarded the San Gorgonio Pass, 3,000 feet above sea level, where its orchards and farmhouses escaped the hottest summer days.

On the 120-acre spread, Maria's family bred and boarded horses and raised goats and chickens. My mother expressed disappointment when I told her I would not be coming to Diamond Bar but sounded hopeful to learn about my new girlfriend—a nice Italian girl—who had invited me to meet her family.

Laura offered to drive Paul down to LA while Maria and I took my car to the ranch. Paul and Laura planned to play music together throughout spring break. Before Paul left, we stopped by the Renaissance for coffee, where he related the story of Laura's call to her mom. He couldn't wait to try out the grand piano Mrs. Shapiro bought when they moved to Claremont. According to Laura, her mother began to sift through the family music library, searching for piano, violin, and cello pieces they might play together.

"Laura's mom thought trios might be too difficult. When Laura mentioned I had taken first place in the Los Angeles International Piano Solo Recitals in 1968, she seemed impressed. I played *Chopin's Étude in G# minor, Op.25; No.6.*"

"I take it that piece is hard to play," I said.

"Yes. It took me four months to get it perfect."

Early Saturday morning, I bought two cappuccinos *para llevar* from the Café Med, picked up Maria, and set out on the seven-hour ride southeast. Highway 99 wound through homogenous farms, rambling grasslands, and numerous small towns with picturesque names such as Turlock, Merced, and Tulare.

We practiced our Spanish and French while we drove.

"There's an advanced French course offered this term. Let's take it together," Maria said.

"Do you think I know enough?"

"Sure. It's only second level, intermediate. I'll help you through it." Maria's near fluency in Spanish made French easy for her. "Also, there's a four-week intensive Italian class for beginners in the summer. That would be fun, too, no?"

"I'm not sure my finances will stretch that far. Did I tell you I applied for a job at the Main Library?"

"No. Doing what?"

"Research, I guess. The department's called Intra-Library Loan. Professors submit requests for books or articles; we locate and deliver them to their offices. Fifteen hours a week."

"Does it pay well?"

"A dollar above minimum wage. It's a work-study program."

"That would be wonderful, James."

"I'll find out next week."

"I've never had a straight job. Every summer, I worked on the ranch. I'm glad my parents can afford to put me through college without me having to work. I can't imagine working and studying at the same time."

"If I get up an hour earlier and stay up a little later, I can make up the time. We'll see."

"I hope your working doesn't mean we'll spend less time together."

"No. Time with you is sacrosanct."

Maria leaned over and caressed my cheek. "I don't deserve you."

"Yes, you do. All of me."

The passage through the Tehachapi Pass, over the summit, and through snowy alpine valleys was breathtaking as we advanced out of the Central Valley and into the Mojave Desert.

"Are you sure everybody's okay with me dropping by for a week?"

"Of course. You'll meet the whole Compagno clan. My parents, my brother, my sister, and my grandparents."

"All right."

"If I bring you, everyone assumes you're significant because I never invite my boyfriends to the ranch."

"So, am I your boyfriend?"

"Let's not fly off the saddle, cowboy," she said playfully.

"This will be my first real ranch."

"I hope you'll love it as much as I do."

The afternoon temperatures spiked to 85 degrees in the desert, and the ubiquitous winds pushed my little car back and forth on the two-lane highway.

The ranch house capped the end of a quarter-mile private lane fresh with new gravel that branched off the principal highway. The San Gorgonio

Mountains towered above the valleys, its highest peaks layered with winter remnants.

A sizable barn or stable bordered the left of the house. On the other side were two corrals and a fenced pasture with massive hay bales stacked to one side. Foraging goats ranged in another fenced-in field nearby. Horses grazed lazily in the late afternoon shade. Based on the noise, the chicken coop stood behind the stables. At the turn off the main road, a hand-painted sign read "Fresh Eggs, $2/dozen" in bold, white lettering. The scene came right out of a 1940s movie.

Maria's parents and grandparents greeted us as we pulled our bags from my car's trunk. Maria's older sister and younger brother were with them.

"Everybody, this is my friend James Montez." Maria hugged everyone in turn.

"I'm Nico, and this is my wife, Ana." Maria's grandfather stepped up to shake my hand, easily a man in his seventies who carried a slender build, yet massive shoulders and arms built up from a lifetime of strenuous labor. Blue eyes, like cerulean stones, offset his tanned, craggy face.

"Welcome, son." A petite woman younger than her husband showed signs of reddish hair in her youth. Both of Maria's grandparents exhibited the rugged demeanor of people unafraid of hard work.

"It's so nice to meet one of Maria's friends at last," said her mother.

"I'm Angelina Compagno." She shook my hand and kissed my cheek. She had arrived in the US as a teenager and still spoke with a slight Columbian accent. Small gray streaks ran through her dark hair. "And this is Maria's father, Marc."

Mr. Compagno gave me a firm handshake. "Welcome, James. Glad to meet you finally." Marc favored his father with the same strong face and blue eyes but without the sun-darkened complexion. Clean-shaven and well-coiffured, he struck me as the quintessential corporate executive, including the nascent bags under his eyes from overwork.

Around thirteen, the younger brother Jon stepped up and shook my hand without speaking. I couldn't tell if he was too shy or not thrilled to meet me.

Maria's older sister, Alicia, introduced herself.

"So great you could visit us. What Maria told us about you is true," she said, smiling.

Alicia resembled her younger sister, though her hair was shorter and black instead of brunette. She was taller and favored her father, while Maria took after her mother. Both sisters had the same contralto voice and similar inflections.

After the introductions, Maria's grandmother showed us to our rooms. Maria claimed her childhood room at the back of the house, and I took the one across from hers. Alicia and Jon stayed down the hall; Maria's folks slept in a small cottage in the back, while the grandparents enjoyed an extensive suite at the other end of the house with expansive views of the mountains.

"Leave your stuff on the bed and come with me to the stable. I want to check on Smokie."

We exited the house through the kitchen door and headed to the stable, where the Compagnos boarded six horses.

Maria opened the first stall where her black-gray mare stood. "This is Smokie. I got her for my tenth birthday as a yearling. Grandpa and I trained her."

"She's beautiful." Smokie recognized her instantly and shuffled her legs in excitement. The horse lowered her head down and nuzzled Maria's hair. Maria wrapped her arms around her neck, and the two hung there like long-lost lovers reunited after a terrible absence. I had never considered the deep affinity between an owner and her horse until now. The love between them was palpable.

"I've missed you so much, Smokie. How's my girl? Did you miss me?" In response, Smokie gave a soft neigh. Maria grabbed a brush and explained the proper way to groom her.

"Grooming creates a bond between you and the horse. Usually, I like to do it every day before or after riding. It also gives me a chance to check for injuries. This is a mane comb. See how I comb out any tangles." Maria gently ran the brush over Smokie's mane while she held her head with her other hand. "Tomorrow, I'll give you a full lesson and let you practice on the other horses. If you want to, that is."

"I'd love to. Thank you for sharing all this with me."

"No problem. I'm glad you're finally seeing me in my world."

She finished brushing Smokie and kissed her snout. "I'll give you a proper brushing tomorrow, my darling." Smokie, a sensitive creature, responded to Maria's mood, tone of voice, and touch. Seeing the two together made me choke up a little.

"It's beautiful to watch you two."

"I connect with my animals the way I do with people. I give them everything I have from the heart. That's just the way I am."

I took Maria in my arms, and we kissed, letting some *bonding* flow between us.

Once the sun slipped below the horizon, the eight of us sat down to a sizable Italian-style feast of salad, pasta, grilled chicken, goat cheese, and plenty of red wine. Maria's family drank wine with every evening meal, and she had been sipping since she was thirteen. Even little brother Jon had a quarter-glass, which he barely touched.

Grandpa Compagno stood before we dug in and said grace in Italian:

"Benedici Signore noi e il cibo che stiamo per prendere, fà che non manchi mai a nessuno in nessuna parte del mondo, specialmente ai bambini. Amen."

Later that evening, Maria said, "More or less, it means: '"Bless us, Lord, and the food we're going to have, let no one lack it anywhere in the world, especially children.'"

During the meal, I said, "Alicia, your sister tells me you're graduating from UCLA this spring, in finance?"

"Yes. I only have to finish my senior thesis. It's on a new derivative asset-pricing strategy theory that some are calling the Black-Scholes model."

Maria and I gave each other a bemused look.

"Can you explain it for us Lit majors?" Maria asked.

"Sure. It's a mathematical model that gives a theoretical estimate of the price of stock options, showing the option has a unique price given the expected return and the risk of the security."

She briefly explained stock options. Only Alicia's dad followed her curtailed but technical explanation, nodding knowingly as she spoke before the dinner chatter soon reverted to the daily challenges of ranch management.

Grandma served homemade cannoli to top off one of the best meals ever.

"What do you think of the wine, James?" Marc Compagno asked as he topped off my glass.

"Delicious. A good chianti, no?"

He looked both surprised and pleased. "Yes. That's right."

"Maria has been teaching me about wines. This is one I remember."

"Oh? You're telling me it's easy for university students under twenty-one to buy the best vintages?" Marc's joke calmed me down after I feared I had given away some secrets. I didn't want to admit I carried a fake ID.

Maria jumped in to save me. "Dad, most of the school is over twenty-one. Laura and I have connections. Anyway, did you really think I would give up a family tradition that easily?"

"Good point. Please drink at home and not out and about."

"Don't worry. We're responsible."

Maria placed her hand on my thigh; her foot rubbed mine beneath the table. I doubt anyone caught on except Jon, who spoke little but glanced at me throughout the evening as he pushed his food around his plate. Perhaps he merely safeguarded his older sister.

After supper, we moved into the rustic living room adorned with high arched ceilings, long oak beams, wooden wainscoting, and original oil paintings. One of the pictures depicted the mountains above the house in exquisite detail.

"My Uncle Jon painted that scene as part of a series," Maria explained.

"Such detail. It's like a photograph."

"He pioneered the technique called photorealism. Unfortunately, he died in a car crash soon after he finished it."

The room went quiet, her family eyeing the intricate patterns of the parquet floor. I inquired no further.

Maria and Alicia chatted about school.

"Westwood is a gorgeous place to live, a little noisy perhaps. After all, it's in the middle of LA, but UCLA has been a good school for me," Alicia said. "I'm ready to finish and get on with my life."

"What are the job prospects?"

"Two so far. One for an investment banker here in LA and the other for a firm in New York City. I'll probably take the New York one. Remember that trip we took as kids? I really loved it."

"New York would be fantastic. We'll have to visit you."

"Excuse me," I said. "What's investment banking?"

"Investment banking organizes mergers and acquisitions, initial public offerings, and complex financial transactions."

"Sounds like long hours to me."

"The hours are brutal, but the salaries are obscene by our standards."

"You would live in Manhattan?" Maria asked.

"Yes. As close to the office as I could get." While Alicia spoke, the almost photograph-like painting kept drawing my attention. The artist must have had tremendous patience to render it so perfectly.

Alicia continued, "How do you like the Bay Area and Cal?"

"Cal is awesome. The caliber of the students is lightyears beyond Claremont High. I feel like I'm a part of something there. The classes are challenging, and the workload is relentless. Each quarter is ten weeks, so we must cover the coursework quickly. What do you think, James?"

"Well, my high school, Ganesha, was bush league. Maria's right. We're competing with the top tier of all the other schools. I spend a lot of money on coffee to keep up."

"That won't change, even into grad school," Alicia added. "The Bay Area's nice too?"

"Definitely. I don't miss the LA heat and traffic. James and I are thinking of staying over. We'll enroll in a summer course."

Alicia listened intently as Maria spoke, her eyes moving back and forth between Maria and me, sizing us up. I don't know; perhaps she was trying to decide if we were a suitable couple. Alicia struck me as someone with strong opinions.

Jon sat quietly, half-listening but somewhere else, not too interested in our "adult" conversation. I suspected he sought a lull to excuse himself and return to his room. A strange kid, taciturn, sullen, he reminded me of myself at his age.

Mr. Compagno never spoke. Suddenly, he stood and said goodnight. On his way out, he grabbed a book from the shelf before retiring to the cottage behind the house.

"Excuse us, we're going to clean up the kitchen," Grandma Compagno said. Maria's mom followed her.

"I'll help out. You guys will be okay for a minute?"

"Let me go, Maria," Alicia offered.

"No. Stay and keep James company. We won't be long."

Jon also mumbled goodnight and left Alicia and me to stare at each other with only a coffee table between us.

"You and Maria almost sound alike. With my eyes closed, I wouldn't tell you apart."

Alicia laughed. "Maria's three years younger. When she was fourteen, she would answer the phone when my boyfriends called and pretend to be me. She was quite a prankster."

"That sounds awkward."

"I got her back when I took her calls and said I was her." Alicia chuckled. "Our house was wild then."

A black Siamese cat jumped on the sofa. She edged toward me and cautiously sniffed before climbing into my lap.

"Looks like you might join the family if Olivia adopts you," Alicia hinted.

Olivia purred as I pet her, content as though nothing existed except my hand on her fur.

"She's Maria's cat and never cozies up to strangers, indifferent to us most of the time."

"Olivia, a regal name for a ranch cat."

"There's a story behind it if you're interested."

"Sure," I said.

"Some years ago, on a trip into town for groceries, we saw a lady sitting at the entrance with kittens to give away. Maria looked them over and picked this one," pointing to Olivia.

"'What's the breed?' Maria asked. The litter's a black tom and Siamese mix."

"Olivia's a gorgeous cat," I said, stroking her back.

"Yes. Maria decided she would be an excellent mouser. As it turns out, soon dead mice appeared by the kitchen backdoor, deposited by Olivia, to remind us she intended to earn her way. Olivia only rests on Maria's lap. Until now."

"I didn't realize I was a cat person. How did Maria know about the kitten?" I asked as Olivia settled in, her soft purr calming.

"She has this thing about animals. You'll see. Even the chickens do her bidding."

"How's that?"

"Whenever Maria appears in the hen house, egg production increases by five percent. Grandma tracks these things and can prove it. After she leaves, production goes back to normal. Odd, yes, but my sister is a strange girl. If this were Salem, she'd be in peril."

"Animals want to please her?"

"Yes, particularly primates." We laughed.

"That I'm sure of."

When Maria returned, she stopped, surprised at a contented Olivia curled on my lap. She sat down beside me.

"Olivia, what are you doing over there?"

Maria smiled as the aroused cat slipped off my lap to hers.

"Olivia likes you. She's an uncanny judge of people. "

"Cats enjoy a quiet, wide lap." I reached over and scratched Olivia behind the ears.

The senior Mr. Compagno came in from the outside, removed his coat, went to the wet bar, poured three small glasses of what might be whiskey, and headed into the kitchen. He did not offer us any.

"I think I'll turn in," Alicia said as she rose to her feet, yawning. "See you all tomorrow."

Maria, Olivia, and I leaned against each other, three happy mammals snuggled together.

I stifled a yawn. Maria lifted Olivia to one side and took my hand.

"Let's go to your room for a little while. I'd like to lie down."

She led me down the hall. We stretched out on the bed, our legs and shoulders touching, with the door open to the hallway.

"Shall we read a little from *Cien Años de Soledad*?"

Maria yawned. "I'm suddenly tired. What a long day."

I closed the book and put my arm around Maria's warm and alluring shoulders. We nibbled each other with little kisses, mindful of the sounds of running water and the jangle of dishes echoing from the other end of the hallway. Olivia surveilled us from the doorway before disappearing into Maria's room.

Around 9:30 p.m., we entered a Dickens novel where three spirits would visit us before the night ended. Thanks to the creaky wooden floor, we heard anyone approaching my room.

The first spirit appeared as Maria's mom. While Maria favored her mother, she had inherited her grandmother's nose and cheeks.

"You kids need anything before we close up the kitchen?"

"No, we're fine, Mom. Thanks."

"I'm going out to the back house. Enjoy your evening. Don't stay up too late."

"We won't. Goodnight."

Several minutes later, the second spirit arrived, heralded by heavy, sliding footsteps as though he couldn't lift his feet entirely. I half-expected chains to clatter. His parents had come from Cosenza, Italy, and bought a farm where Mr. Compagno was born in Texas.

"Oh, hi, Grandpa. You going to bed?"

"Yes, ma'am, I wanted to say goodnight and ask your young fella here if he'd be up to helping us with some chores this week," he asked in his Texas drawl.

"Sure. I'll help any way I can."

"Glad to hear it. Y'all have a g'night."

"Goodnight, Grandpa. Love you."

"Love you, too, darlin'."

"Goodnight, Sir. Thanks again for having me."

Once Grandpa moved down the hall, I told Maria, "I like your family. Everyone's made me feel welcome."

"The family likes you and sees how we are together and how smitten I am with you."

"You are?"

"Not really. I always lie beside guys on a bed making out when I don't like them."

She leaned over to give me a long, passionate kiss. Maria exhaled a sigh of frustration when the boards creaked for the third time as the last nightly visitor loomed in the doorway.

"You two all right for now? Need anything to eat or drink?"

"Sure, how about a triple bourbon and a beer chaser, Grandma?"

Grandma chuckled. "We'll see, maybe tomorrow," she said with a wink and a smile.

"We're still stuffed from the fabulous dinner you made, Grandma," Maria said.

"Mrs. Compagno, thanks for all your hospitality. I'm so happy to meet you all."

"Glad to have you, son. All right. Maria, don't you think it's time to return to your room and get some sleep? Busy day tomorrow."

"Oh yeah, right. For tomorrow, I planned something fun for us."

"What?"

"A surprise. Be patient."

Maria slid off the bed and gave me a peck on the cheek.

"Goodnight, *mi amor, mi corazón*, sweet dreams."

She followed her grandmother out into the hall and winked at me as she eased the door closed.

Too restless to sleep, I went into the small bathroom attached to my room, took a quick shower, and brushed my teeth for five minutes. My mother had taught me to brush three times a day, and I had skipped the noontime brushing.

While brushing, I pondered how close Maria's family was. Her uncanny rapport with animals also intrigued me. I didn't quite know what to think of it all, but my curiosity was aroused. We had only parted moments ago, and I already missed her.

I donned clean boxers and slid between the cotton sheets. The songs of crickets and frogs echoed outside. Though it had been windy when we arrived, the air had settled into a breeze. Stars sparkled through the window as wispy clouds drifted by. My pulse slowed; my limbs relaxed as sleep overcame me.

I awoke several hours later and checked the time: 2:37 a.m. Awake, I listened to the house fluttering to its well-worn rhythms as the wood expanded and contracted. A hinge creaked in the hallway. The moonless night lessened my vision as the door to my room swung open and closed, and Maria's silhouette flittered past as she climbed into bed beside me.

Maria said, "I took a nap to recharge my batteries, but I couldn't sleep with the thought of you all alone here in this cozy bed," her hot breath on my cheek.

Her body against mine, she ran her hand down from my shoulder to my thigh and back. "I'll keep you warm, so you don't need to wear anything." She reached down and pulled off my boxers before removing her t-shirt and panties and kicking them to the floor.

Aroused, I wrapped my arms around Maria and pressed against the entire length of her athletic body. I had never been in bed with a naked woman. She placed my hand on her breast to show me how to touch her. Her nipples stiffened as I massaged them. Her breathing became shallower as she relaxed.

Her hands ran up and down my back, hip, and legs. Each stroke evoked a shiver and concealed the world as our excitement mounted. Soon, we mapped out each other's erogenous zones. Desperate to feel her skin, I pulled her tighter toward me.

Maria brought her nipple toward my mouth. I gently sucked as her breathing grew more prolonged and more profound. She pulled herself up and kissed me, long and slow, as our tongues explored each other, tentative at first and then more insistent.

I ached for release. Maria rolled on her back, pulled me atop her, and pushed my head between her legs. Despite my inexperience, I had read enough erotic fiction to know what to do. Lightly, I caressed and sucked her clitoris as she writhed beneath me, her wetness slippery like nectar. Her hands grabbed my head to direct me. Soft, slow, harder, faster, I varied my cadence and pressure until her soft moan signaled perfection. I reached up, cupped her breasts, and slowly kneaded them, intensifying her pleasure until she spasmed and arched her back.

I surfaced for air and reveled in the myriad sensations, the scent of her skin, the wetness against my legs, her breasts against my chest, and her arms wrapped around me, pulling me closer.

I hesitated, reluctant to break the mood, "Don't we need protection?"

She whispered, breathless, "I'm on the pill," as she reached down and guided me inside. She felt wet and hot inside; I'd never expected so much heat.

"Go slow, real slow . . . like that."

We found our rhythm. Maria sensed my excitement and slowed to a stop until I recovered. We threw off the covers and lay exposed on the bed, ignoring the cold temperature of the room.

The wind picked up, and a synchronous rustling of leaves vibrated with us.

Our skin glistened, drenched in sweat. The scent of Maria's hair, and her sex, intoxicated me as I floated softly, lost on a quiet sea, outside my body, so close to Maria, yet wanting to fuse with her until we became one being, transcendent.

I exploded, and seconds later, she with me, our bodies seized as though electricity arced through us. We collapsed on top of each other, silently enwrapped in the softness of receding breathlessness, only the sound of murmurous leaves somewhere beyond.

We lay there, listening. I pulled the sheet over us to reduce our vulnerability. I thought Maria might have fallen asleep. She kissed me and slid out of bed into the bathroom. When she returned, she covered us with a blanket.

"Wow. I never imagined it could be like that," I whispered.

"That was incredible. You didn't disappoint."

"I was a little unsure, this being my first time."

"Sex is always a little awkward the first few times, but no, you were so sensitive and giving. Also, you're willing to follow my hints about what I like. If this is what you're like now, I can't wait to warm you up."

"I think I'm rather warm now."

We hugged before she pushed me back on the bed.

"I hope you're rested because I can't seem to get enough of you."

Maria massaged me until I was hard again and lowered herself on top of me. I entered her so deeply that I imagined it must hurt her. She assured me she was fine and shut me up with her kisses. Her body enveloped me until I reached places no one had ventured before, and in the darkness, I wandered astray, lost in the moist and soothing heat.

I lost count of how many times we made love. I didn't know we had so much stamina. Spent, we fell into a dreamless sleep.

At cockcrow, I drifted in and out of a fading awareness. Marie nudged me, climbing out of bed. "I'd better get back to my room before the household wakes up. Sleep now, rest. You'll need it later. Thanks for the organic sleeping pill."

I rolled over and fell asleep again. No one needed an alarm clock on this ranch. How loud those birds were. Not much of an early riser in those days, I pulled the pillow around my head and slept more, worn out from my romps with Maria, but it was not to be. Once the smell of bacon, eggs, and brewed coffee lured me awake, I did not resist breakfast.

Was last night a dream? No. I lay naked in my bed, imbued with Maria's intoxicating scent. Several spots, now dried, decorated the sheets. I wondered what Maria's grandma would say. I let it go; Grandma was young once too. I rolled out of bed to take another shower.

And so began the second day of our vacation.

Everyone appeared for breakfast after last night's meal long digested, the new day a stimulant to appetite. Fresh eggs, smoked bacon, buttermilk biscuits, orange juice, and endless cups of coffee were set out. Famished and dehydrated from our nighttime marathon, Maria and I each downed two glasses of juice, two cups of coffee, and double helpings.

I said, "Maybe it's the clean country air, but I'm famished this morning despite last night's meal." Maria smiled at me over the rim of her coffee cup from across the table. Her little brother caught our exchange because he made a transient face like something "icky" had happened. I guessed he had not quite reached the age where girls would be a focus in his social life.

After breakfast, Maria's family loaded the car for the return home. Alicia had classes on Monday since her spring vacation fell on a different week than ours. The family hugged everyone goodbye.

"I wish we could spend more time together," Maria said.

"School's out in two months. Let's meet back here for another visit," Alicia suggested. Everyone agreed.

"You're welcome too, James."

"Thank you, Mrs. Compagno. I would love to come back."

Maria's dad waited patiently in the car after he said his goodbyes. The rest piled in and drove off, leaving us waving.

"No rest on the Sabbath. We've got work to do," Grandpa Compagno said as he headed toward the chicken coops.

Maria and I changed into blue jeans and boots. Her grandfather had a pair of old cowboy boots he thought might fit me. I tried them on, and they worked well once I switched to thicker socks.

Dressed for "ranching," we headed to the stable.

Maria spoke to the horses as she groomed them from head to toe.

"I speak to them softly because it calms them and reinforces our bond. Animals may not talk, but they communicate if you attend to their reactions." As Maria brushed, the horse's muscles rippled. "Notice how I move slowly, no sudden or jerky moves. I'm always reassuring them and demonstrating that I love them."

"They seem to love you back."

"Yes. Remember, horses are prey animals. It's the herd that keeps them safe. Here, I convince them I am part of their herd, so they don't feel alone and vulnerable."

Maria's interactions with her animals, love, and desire to care for them revealed an aspect of her personality that surprised me and deepened my love and admiration for her.

"I don't know if I could live without my menagerie. Being with animals centers me. Berkeley's great and all, but I need to spend time here to help me connect with life. I can only take so much of the city, the noise, and the concrete before I crave to return here."

"Is that why you get a little down after a while?"

"Spending time with my family and animals is a part of who I am."

"Compared to you, I feel estranged from my family, like there's always an unbridgeable distance."

"I'll share my family with you if you'll have us." Maria stopped brushing, noticing the tears in my eyes. She put down the brush and hugged me.

"You'll have a family as long as we're together. I promise." Caught off-balance, I held her, hesitant to let go.

"Come, we have one more horse to get to, *your* horse."

"I have a horse?"

In the last stall stood a sturdy yellowish male. "This is Old Yeller. He's about twenty, mellow, perfect for a beginner."

"You're going to teach me to ride?"

"Of course. After you give him a quick brush, we'll saddle up. Besides, I can't leave you idle while I gallop over the countryside on Smokie. Grandpa will put you to work if he sees you standing around."

After I gave Old Yeller the once-over with the brush, Maria showed me how to put the bridle on, properly saddle him, and cinch the straps.

"I'll bridle Smokie, and we're off."

"You ride without a saddle. Wow, how Amazonian."

"There's nothing like the sensation of the horse rubbing against me," she replied, unabashed.

Maria and I led Smokie and Old Yeller to one of the corrals and returned to the stable to fetch the other horses and release them into the adjacent pasture. The water trough sat on one end of the field, and the feed on the other. This forced the horses to wander back and forth, giving them a modicum of exercise. Later in the week, we rode them to ensure a real workout.

In the corral, Maria conducted my lesson.

"Take hold of the horn and the reins, place your foot in the stirrup, and lift yourself, swinging your leg over. To dismount, reverse the process."

I practiced climbing on and off a few times.

"To direct the horse, pull the reins in the direction you want to go while pressing against him with the opposite knee, making a sound to make him go. Pull back on the reins like this to stop or slow him down." Maria slowly demonstrated all the steps.

I needed several attempts before I followed her directions successfully, but soon I had Old Yeller walking around the corral under my control, more or less.

"You're a natural, James. No, I mean it. You got a knack."

"If you say so. Dare we venture outside the corral?"

"Absolutely. You're ready for a trial run in the wild. Hang on just a sec." Maria dismounted and ran into the house. While I waited, I trotted Old Yeller around to reinforce the rhythm of our movements together. I directed him, though it didn't take long to learn horses have a mind of their own. Sometimes he didn't obey. Or maybe I didn't signal right.

Maria returned carrying a small leather saddlebag, worn smooth by years of use, and attached it behind me.

"You're in charge of lunch. Be careful with it."

"Will do."

Maria deftly mounted Smokie, levitating over her back in defiance of gravity. This woman, who before I had only known in the context of urban Berkeley, moved through the world in harmony with nature. Her horse infused her with beauty and spirit. Maria's rightful domain was not the ice-skating rink, the classroom, or the café. She reigned queen of the undulating hills, green with spring and snowy mountains that bounded the landscape.

Atop a 1,000-pound creature who loved her, like Ovid's Hylonone, the centauress, Maria and horse were fused mentally, physically, and spiritually. Both woman and mare, now thoroughly coalesced, full of fire and grace.

Maria and Smokie trotted away, interrupting my poetic musings as I followed them along a trail approaching the mountains. Like Rocinante, my new friend carried me surefooted, content to shadow the mare before him.

A country mile from the ranch house, we arrived at a creek nourished by the melted snow. We dismounted and left Smokie and Old Yeller near a patch of sweet grass growing in abundance in the margin between the water and the trees, the perfect spot for horses to graze.

"We train them not to wander off," Maria said. "Smokey and Yeller will stay put as long as they can see me."

The creek's embankment sloped towards the water's edge. Maria pulled a blanket out of the saddlebag and spread it across the grass. About 40 feet from the horses, the spot she picked had partial shade and provided cover from the direct sun. Not all the spring buds had fully sprouted this early, but they gave enough shelter to make our lunch spot ideal.

"I come to this spot whenever I can. Like you and your cemetery, I spend hours reading, writing, napping, sitting, thinking, or daydreaming. It's where I feel the most centered."

"Such a beautiful and serene place. Thank you for sharing it with me."

The soothing water flowed over the polished rocks. The warm breeze shook the leaves while the birds sang and flittered about, their mating songs on display, submerged in the aroma of spring grass flowering around us. Black and yellow butterflies swirled like dervishes.

"So peaceful. If I lived here, I would visit every day," I whispered to avoid disrupting the scene around us. "I feel like we're sharing in something humans have done for thousands of years."

"I'm happy in my woods. My thoughts are clearer. When we're in the city, we become enmeshed in all the activity, much of it pointless, but in this place, I slow down, I'm more relaxed, clearer, in the moment, able to gain some perspective on things."

"What sort of things?"

"Oh, you know, life, liberty, and the pursuit of happiness, the usual goals." We laughed.

"Seriously, I've wanted to study literature, for instance, since I learned to read. Once I discovered literature, music, and art, I was hooked for good. People say we're too young to know what we want. Perhaps being alone in my room with books and music instead of outdoors with my friends helped." She gesticulated while she spoke.

"And I thought I was the one who spent much of his time in his room. I find it hard to imagine you hidden away in your bedroom, away from the world. You're so outgoing most of the time."

"Laura and I matured early. We were the only girls in the seventh grade with big boobs. Being modestly good-looking, I got lots of attention, which I liked. Soon, I realized boys only wanted to feel me up and get into my pants."

"Those teenage boys, always rutting."

"Throughout middle and high school, I preferred my time alone. Laura and I joined the tennis team, but I didn't do much else. I dated on weekends and liked making out as much as the next girl, but we had nothing to talk about afterward. The characters in my books, the novels, and the poems I loved spoke to me and put what I experienced into words."

I reached over and ran my fingers through her hair. "I know exactly what you mean."

"I was so taken with you when we met at the ice-skating rink. We read many of the same stories, and your shyness attracted me. You summoned a lot of courage to ask me to skate."

"We seemed like kindred spirits. Plus, I had a huge crush on you."

"Likewise. I prefer being around people who know what they want, where they're going, and who have some ambition to do something worthwhile. Brett and Robert were like that at first, or so I believed. Taking up with them was a big faux pas." Maria shook her head. "Let's forget about them. Regrets don't get us anywhere. I want to write novels like the one I started last year. I'm up to 200 pages. The draft's not very readable now, but it will be."

"What's it about?"

"The novel's a coming-of-age story about a girl who grows up in Huntington Beach in the late fifties and early sixties during the transition from the Beat Generation to the Surfing-Hippie era. The story contains some autobiographical material, with characters disguised as Laura and me. I let her read a draft, and she gave me plenty of ideas, some of which I incorporated into the next version. Someday, I'll share it with you."

She stopped and gazed at something floating on the creek before she continued. "I also wrote a slew of short stories, vignettes, and hundreds of dreadful poems over the years—the usual teenage angst, but in iambic pentameter. I like to write in my journal every day."

"I write almost every day too."

"Two things I do before sleeping: write a little and read, if only for five minutes. This has been my routine forever. My ex couldn't understand my need for a few moments to myself. As soon as we climbed into bed, Robert insisted on having sex. I went along at first, but it grew old fast. I prefer my routines. Some might call me selfish, but I didn't want to give them up."

"I don't think you're selfish. In fact, the opposite, you give a lot of yourself."

"Thank you," Maria pressed my hand. "After we were done and Robert crashed, I wrote or read a bit before sleep. My way of smoking a cigarette after sex, since I don't smoke. I don't know why I stayed with him for so long. I guess that loneliness, the excitement of someone new, being away from home for the first time drew me to him. He had his moments."

"I have a different take on those moments," I said.

"When you and I reconnected in January, I doubted my judgment. Maybe I'm a little naïve. Everything I wanted in Robert, I discovered in you. I fell for you too, long before his awful surprise visit to the Renaissance."

"I get you, Maria."

"You do." Maria grabbed my arm and laid her head against my shoulder, one gesture that defined our intimacy. She liked to listen to my heart.

"Your heartbeat calms me, " she said.

We lapsed into silence again. The birds filled the serenity with their songs. Maria lay down and put her head on my lap as I stroked her head. My fingers combed away all the loneliness of the past. I never wanted to move from that spot. If only time would slow and allow us a few more moments to absorb the richness of each other's company. A ladybug crawled around the edge of the blanket. I closed my eyes and let the breeze waft over us, still between the seconds.

At last, she sat up, and the trance dissolved. "Let's have lunch."

Her grandmother had packed us some peanut butter and jelly sandwiches on sliced Italian bread.

"Do you like PB&J? It's one of my favorites."

"Mine too."

"Yeah, my grandma makes the bread, the jam, and the nut butter from scratch. She taught me how to bake bread. I should make some loaves when we get back."

We found two red apples in the picnic lunch, a small canteen filled with orange juice, and a gigantic homemade chocolate chip cookie.

"With all the food around here, we'll gain ten pounds if we're not careful."

"True. These ranch meals are for people who work outdoors. Grandpa will help us burn it off, don't worry."

"Looking forward to it. Though I like some exercises more than others." We laughed.

Maria closed the saddlebag after finishing everything in the lunch except for the juice. The sun moved, and we lay on the blanket in the warm shade. Smokie and Old Yeller still grazed blithely on their patch of grass, with an occasional meander to the creek to drink.

Maria kissed my neck, my ear, and finally, my mouth, the excitement accelerating between us. She pulled off her blouse and turned her back to me.

"Help me unhook my bra."

"Here, outside? Won't the horses see us?" I teased.

"The horses won't mind. My grandparents' is the nearest house, and they rarely come out here. We are on private Compagno land. There's nobody around, so relax."

The bra fell away, and I admired Maria's full breasts. She grabbed my hands to cup them. "Did I ever mention how much I love to have sex outside?"

"Not that I recall," I said. "Though when I imagine wood nymphs, I only see you."

"There's something so primordial about making love in the open, like in the Garden of Eden. I love the feeling of the air and sun directly on my skin, as though they caress me."

We helped each other undress and made love on our tiny blanket island, the experience more intense and satisfying than the night before.

Afterward, back in Berkeley, we drove around searching for secluded spots. The Berkeley Rose Garden, Live Oak Park, Indian Rock Park, Remillard Park, Grizzly Peak Park, and Tilden Park became our refuges for lovemaking. Sometimes people would come upon us, which would make for some awkward moments, usually with us more excited than ever, or leaving us collapsed on the ground laughing hysterically.

Spent from our postprandial lovemaking, we reclined in each other's arms and dozed. Near sleep, my love for her surged like light emerging from the shadows. Maria turned to her side and put her hand on my chest. I placed mine over hers and felt them as one while my eyes closed as she fell asleep.

Chapter 18

Throughout the rest of our first spring break, Maria and I helped around the ranch, tended to the horses, collected fresh eggs, milked goats (a task not well suited to my talents), and did other chores Grandpa Compagno found for us.

We rode out to our bountiful Eden beside the creek each day, relished our lunch, made love, and napped a little as the sun darkened our olive skin. Grandma treated us to another evening meal, much to everyone's satisfaction.

The evenings gave me a chance to get to know Maria's grandparents. After washing the dinner dishes, we relaxed in the living room.

"The missus and I were childhood sweethearts and married forty-six years ago in our hometown church in west Texas."

"That's right. We attended one of those one-room schoolhouses where all the grades were mixed. Nico was one of the older students, but I fell for him the first day. Of course, he didn't look twice at a girl six years his junior."

"You were way too young, Ana. But once you hit sixteen, something came over me, and I was smitten. You were the prettiest girl in town."

"Oh, Nico, stop."

"Did the Great Depression prompt you to move away from your home?" I asked.

"Nope. We got hitched, picked up, and moved west in . . . "

"1927. In the spring of 1927," Mrs. Compagno filled in.

"The papers said California had a mess of suitable land available. So why not? Farming in west Texas was never that easy."

"Nico and I cleared all the pastures you see outside while I was carrying Marc. That was some work. We used the trees to build this house."

Mr. Compagno pulled out a bottle of Kentucky bourbon and poured everyone a dram. At first, I didn't care for the sharpness, but I soon appreciated the spicy, sweet fruit aroma, with caramel, vanilla, and oak flavors.

Mr. Compagno continued his story. "Our sons Marc and Jon grew up on this ranch. Jon's the younger one who died in an auto accident three years ago. Marc went to college and stayed in the city."

"There was nothing for him here, Nico. Marc never took to ranching."

"True enough."

"In college, he met a sweet Columbian gal; the rest is history, as they say."

"I'm certainly glad that worked out," Maria said.

"As are we. At least Angelina's Catholic," Mr. Compagno said, chuckling. "Italian and Spanish culture ain't all that different. We all love to cook and eat. We all believe in family."

The Compagnos went to bed early. Olivia, Maria, and I lounged on the sofa for a while.

"Were you close to your Uncle Jon?"

Maria thought for a moment. "We saw him on holidays, but he didn't socialize with the family much. He was a loner. The accident devastated everyone, but more so my little brother. The two of them were probably the closest. Dad named my brother after him."

"Is the accident the reason your brother's a little stand-offish?"

"Jon was only ten when his uncle died. He never got over it."

Olivia jumped up and headed for her water bowl.

"Your uncle's art is amazing."

"Yes. My grandparents have numerous paintings stashed away somewhere. The mountain scene picture is the only one they show. You know, your room used to be his."

"I thought I saw a shadow in the corner while we were making love."

Maria slapped my shoulder. "Don't joke about that. Ghosts give me the creeps."

"Sorry, just kidding."

"I miss Jon. A lot. You remind me of him, the quiet, resilient type, creative and intelligent."

Half-serious, I said, "I'm perfect for you."

Leaning against me, Maria whispered, "Yes, you are. I'm a lucky girl."

Exhausted, we turned in and slept for several hours before Maria slipped into my bed for our nightly tryst.

The sunrise, regardless of clouds, never slipped past the roosters, who faithfully signaled Maria's return to her room before her grandmother woke us for breakfast. I longed for this routine to continue, wishing it was summer vacation.

Sunday, we arranged to return north since classes started the next day. I asked Maria if we might stop at my parents' house to say hello and go out to brunch. She agreed, and after early-morning coffee, we loaded up the car, said our goodbyes, and drove west on a chilly morning, the blithe sun rising behind us.

"Anything I need to know before I meet your folks?"

"Let me see. My mom's the typical Italian mother, so eat everything on your plate when she cooks."

"Check. That part, I guessed."

"You can offer to help in the kitchen, but don't be offended when she says no. She seldom lets anyone cook or clean. She's territorial that way."

"Got it. And your stepdad?"

"He doesn't talk much. It doesn't mean he doesn't like you if he ignores you. He's about as guarded with feelings as one can get."

"Good to know. I have ways of getting through. Your dad's probably shy. I bet you get your introversion tendencies from him."

"You may be right. John was my role model for many years."

We pulled up on a medium-sized ranch-style tract home. John had moved his pickup to the edge to give us room in the driveway.

I tapped the horn to let them know we had arrived.

Mom stood at the front door as we emerged from the car.

"Hey, Mom, this is Maria Compagno, that sweet Italian girl I told you about."

Mom held out her hand, but Maria hugged her instead.

"I'm so happy to meet you finally, Mrs. Hartmann."

"Come in, come in." So far, so good. I didn't remember when I had last seen such a broad smile on Mom's face.

Dad stood in the dining area waiting for us to enter.

"This is my husband, John. This is Maria." John wasn't a hugger, so I held my breath waiting for Maria's greeting.

She held out her hand and gave him a firm handshake. "Thank you for inviting us, Mr. Hartmann."

He nodded.

Mom had already returned to the kitchen to whip up some waffle batter. "We decided to cook at home instead of going out. Anything I make is better than a restaurant. I bought some fresh Italian sausages at the delicatessen yesterday and want to use them."

"Sounds delicious. Can I help with anything?"

"No, Maria. Relax. I got everything under control. On second thought, would you and Jimmy mind setting the table?"

"*Jimmy* and I would love to," Maria said, teasing me over my nickname.

I pulled out the silverware and napkins from their respective drawers.

We set the table and sat down. Dad in his usual head-of-the-table spot, me in my childhood seat, and Maria in the guest chair. Mom brought us full mugs of hot coffee, fresh from her new Mr. Coffee. The electric cord on the old percolator had frayed beyond repair.

Knowing my mom was sensitive about her coffee, I parroted a TV commercial we had heard a million times: "Mom, this Folger's Coffee is great. Can I have another cup? Happiness is another cup of your coffee."

She gaped at me. "You're funny. It's Hills Brothers, not Folgers."

"He said it just like the commercial," John added. Another milestone—Dad amused.

Playing along, Maria said, "Well, I don't get it, but this is a delicious cup of coffee, Mrs. Hartman. Can you show me how you brew it so I can make it at home for *Jimmy*?"

I finally witnessed a living example of *chortling* because we all did it.

Mom served breakfast.

"Delicious sausages, Mrs. Hartmann. Are these from Luigi's Delicatessen on West Orange Grove?"

"Yes. How did you know?"

"My mom buys stuff from them all the time. The shop is near the hospital where she works. She's a nurse."

"Your mom's Italian too?"

"No. She was born in Columbia, South America, but came here as a young girl."

Maria turned to my stepfather. "Mr. Hartmann, James tells me you're an aerospace engineer?"

"Quality Control Engineer."

"My dad works at Global Dynamics on West Mission. He's in finance."

"I've thought about applying there. I work in Seal Beach, only forty miles away, but the traffic gets heavier each year."

"My dad could get your résumé to the correct department manager if that would help."

"Thanks. I'll consider it," John said, nodding. I think the offer may have touched him.

After breakfast, Maria jumped up and started clearing the table. Mom let her do it.

While Mom washed the dishes, Maria dried and stacked them.

"Do you like to cook, Maria?"

"Very much so. My mom taught me a lot, but my grandmother taught me the most about Italian cooking. I enjoy cooking for my friends and family."

"The dorm food isn't the greatest. Maria's an amazing cook, Mom," I said.

"I love cooking for him." Maria smiled broadly. "Our family has lots of recipes, not written, of course. I hope to pass them down to my daughters."

Mom nodded. "Since I don't have any daughters, maybe you would be interested in some of my recipes."

"You'd share them with me? That's wonderful. Of course, I'd love that."

Observing this exchange, the hope that my parents would treat Maria as their future daughter-in-law grew more likely.

With a long drive ahead, we departed soon after brunch and headed north through Tejon Pass and up the Central Valley.

"What a vacation. This has been one of the best weeks of my life. Thanks for inviting me, Maria."

"We had fun, didn't we? Best of all, I think our families like us together. That's important to me."

"And if they didn't like us as a couple?"

"Then, we'd have more work to do. I don't give up easily."

I reached over and took her hand. "Maybe it's too soon to say this, but I'm falling in love with you."

"I'm in love with you already." Maria leaned over and kissed me. "I've fantasized about being in love with you since we met ice skating. Only during our time at the Café Renaissance did those feelings become real."

Tears welled in my eyes as she spoke. Maria confirmed everything I hoped to be true. On our way to Berkeley, we sped by endless miles of farmland, and another moment remained etched in my heart forever.

We arrived at Maria's cottage in the early evening. I helped her carry her bags inside.

"I'll see you tomorrow, James." Maria gave me a long, tender hug followed by a kiss that lasted a century.

A few minutes later, I strolled dreamily up to my room.

Paul listened to music on his headphones while propped up on his bed. He pulled them off to talk.

"Laura and I rolled in about two hours ago. Guess what? I think I'm in love."

"I'm not surprised. Laura's perfect for you."

"We spent the entire week together. I dropped Laura off at her parents' last Saturday around 4 o'clock. Several hours with the folks satisfied her. She called me all blasé at nine and asked me to take her out. Of course, I said yes, drove her into the Claremont Hills Wilderness Park, and parked under a new moon, where we chatted for hours, among other things.

"We had a wonderful time under the stars." Paul grinned as he savored the memory.

"I went to her house every day, playing her mom's piano while Laura accompanied me on the violin. She's also quite talented at the piano. We played duets, and her mom often joined us on the cello. What a fantastic collaboration."

"I can imagine. You liked her parents?"

"Definitely. Laura's dad plays a fantastic Spanish guitar. I could have sworn it was Segovia playing."

"What a talented family," I said.

"When the time to leave for Del Mar arrived, I convinced Laura to drive down with us. Of course, she brought her violin, and we continued our duets at the beach house. I found an old pickup and an amp, which we attached to her instrument, and she went full Jean-Luc-Ponty on me. I can't wait to play the stuff we wrote for you."

"You guys are writing music together. Man, too serious," I said, teasing him.

"Yeah, Laura's amazing in more ways than one."

"I'll bet she is. Laura impressed me from the first. What about the collaboration you guys started after our first dinner?"

"Oh, we finished it and played it for her parents, who enjoyed the classical aspects but not the jazziness."

"How can anyone not like jazz?"

"Right? Beats me. And the ranch, how was it?"

"Maria taught me to ride a horse. Can you believe it, me, an equestrian?"

"Good deal. I imagine riding is more complicated than it looks."

"Maria's family is incredible. Grandma Compagno cooked us fabulous meals. Her grandfather worked us all week, from sunup to sundown."

"And you and Maria?"

"I love that girl more than anything in the world."

CHAPTER 19

Monday, the term started, and the next ten weeks passed in a blur. Maria and I continued Spanish but added conversational French and a survey course on nineteen-century French literature. Maria, always practical, confirmed a minor in business to have a fallback if the literary career didn't work out. Also, she figured skills to manage all the royalties she planned to earn from her forthcoming novels would help.

Without much resistance, I let her convince me to do the same. We declared our majors in comparative literature with minors in business administration.

The summer before, Maria's sister, Alicia, had convinced Laura to pursue a business degree on one of their many long horseback rides. It was strange how Maria listened to her best friend over her sister, who gave similar advice.

"It's not so unusual," Maria began. "Don't we weigh our peers' opinions greater than our families'?"

"Sounds right. Someday, we'll look at our parents and say, 'they were smarter than we thought,' once we realize how right they were about stuff."

"I already think that. Besides you and Laura, my parents are the smartest and wisest people I know."

"The fifth commandant: *honour thy father and thy mother*."

"Exactly. Good advice."

Laura's infatuation with Paul reinforced her enthusiasm for music. She confirmed a minor in music. Of course, they were thrilled to take music classes together. Paul, fully invested, focused on his two loves: music and Laura.

I spent three or four nights a week at the Northside house during the term. Paul slept over, too, so we often enjoyed supper together and studied the rest of the evening. We brought our laundry, which saved us a lot of time, and Paul and I shared in the groceries, supplying the beer and wine and, on occasion, sprang for a bottle of Maker's Mark, Maria's favorite bourbon.

The only thing missing was a piano for Paul. The music department made many keyboard instruments available in private rooms, but traveling to campus to play them proved inconvenient. In the meantime, he strummed Laura's guitar until he bought himself a used Fender King with rosewood back and sides at a music store on University Avenue.

Without anyone noticing, only three weeks remained until the end of the school year. We loved our time together as a foursome, and after supper one evening, we worked out how to stay together as a *family*.

"If I go back to LA, I'll have to quit my job at the library. I'd rather hang on to it."

Maria said, "James and I want to take an intensive Italian class during July. We'll keep this cottage for another year."

Paul drummed his fingers while he ruminated. "Laura and I talked about enrolling in an advanced music-theory class. The seminar is hard to get into, and live auditions are required. Are you still game, Laura?"

"I'll have to ask my parents to cover my summer expenses, but I want to take that class."

"So, we've all agreed: no southern California for us this summer, except for a fun visit to the beach?" I said.

"And the ranch," added Maria.

"I have an idea," Paul said. "This place is really too small for the four of us. Why don't we rent a larger apartment together? Split four ways, we could afford something charming. I did a little research and found a reasonably priced three-bedroom flat on the southside, available June 15."

A week later, we rendezvoused at a remodeled spacious apartment on the second floor of a 1920s house that had been converted into flats.

Two of the bedrooms were enormous. The second one offered a glass door to a small patio on the roof facing west, filling the room with afternoon sunlight. Laura suggested the third would be perfect for a library/studio or another roommate if we needed one.

The living room would hold two sofas with enough space for entertaining. The north-facing oriel window let in plenty of sun with a bench wrapped around the inside, overlooking a schoolyard. Maria and Laura sat in the cushioned window seat and scanned the tree-lined school through the weathered panes.

"I would welcome the sound of children at play," Maria said.

Laura agreed. A dog barked in the distance.

Maria loved the extended kitchen with ample counter space and a deep two-sided porcelain sink. Off the kitchen, we discovered a modest utility room with a stacked washer-dryer unit and back stairs that descended into a garden tended by the bottom-flat tenants.

The four of us signed the one-year lease the next day.

Maria and I took the bedroom with the door to the patio. Paul and Laura wanted the other bedroom because it was large enough to fit the piano he planned to rent.

After a half-hour of tactical maneuvers, two burly guys muscled the beast upstairs into the bedroom, and Paul sat down to play.

Immediately, he realized the slightly worn Kimball Upright begged for tuning. He called around and located a guy who would come over cheap and tune according to his specifications. Since Paul possessed absolute pitch, he sat with the tuner, and the two went string by string until Paul was satisfied that each vibrated correctly.

"You know, Paul, if we were going to have friends over, wouldn't it be better to have the piano in the living room?" Maria asked in her sweet-as-pie voice.

"As long as you guys don't mind hearing me practice out there."

"No problem at all."

Paul and I moved the instrument one morning. I nursed a sore back for a week, but Maria's skillful massages helped my recovery.

"How did you get such strong fingers?" I asked.

"Massaging horses isn't much different from your back."

"When you're done, why don't you take me for a ride?"

"Well, you know how much I like to go saddleless."

Our first summer in the Russell Street house ended mid-September when a cold breeze swept inland over the ocean. Time passed swiftly because we paid little attention to clocks and let ourselves drift on the emotional content of each day's activities. Before classes started, Paul, Laura, and Maria hatched a surprise which afterward Maria recounted to me at length.

Several weeks earlier, while Maria prepared a meal, Paul camped at the kitchen table to keep her company while she hummed a Columbian folk tune her mother had taught her.

"You have a lovely voice. Have you ever sung in a choir or at church, Maria?"

"Not really. I like to sing, but I've never had any lessons."

"Do you trust me, Maria?"

She stopped and turned towards him. "I trust you, sure."

"I could bring out the best in your voice."

Paul convinced her to learn a song by the Brazilian singer Flora Purim, who toured with Chick Corea, Paul's favorite jazz pianist. While I worked my shifts at the university library, Maria and Paul practiced in the afternoons. Laura joined them, adding the violin part. After dinner one night, the three surprised me with their shortened *Light as a Feather* arrangement.

Paul said, "Come sit down. I want to try out a new piece on you. Grab me a beer, will you?" Maria and I settled on the couch while Laura and Paul warmed up with some B-minor scales.

"I know you like this song, but we decided to adapt the arrangement to add a new vocal part." Paul smiled and nodded toward Maria, who stood between them. Maria's clear and harmonious contralto voice floated across the melody.

After Maria finished the verse, Paul launched into a solo, followed by Laura on the violin, which substituted for the saxophone on the original recording.

Speechless, I listened, enraptured by my girl's perfect voice and moved by the blending of their creative talents; I could not have loved those three more than at that moment. Afterward, we formulated a plan to introduce our artistic sanctuary to the people in our circle.

The four of us often gathered in the kitchen on weekends. "Here's what I'm thinking," Maria said, one Sunday morning over coffee. "Let's invite people to the house interested in the arts, and provide live music and an opportunity to share some creative writings, like story excerpts or poems."

"Kind of like the salons of Paris in the early twentieth century?" Laura said.

"Exactly like that. I've been reading about Gertrude and Leo Stein's accounts of their soirées. Why not do the same? You and Paul can play. We'll invite other musicians. James can read his poems . . . well . . . "

"Some vote of confidence," I said. "And food and drink?"

"Potluck, finger food, nothing fancy. BYOB to start."

"Let's do it," Paul said. "We can try out some of our new arrangements in front of a small audience."

Drafted to play Alice B. Toklas to her Gertrude Stein, I helped Maria invite our classmates, teaching associates, and professors to our monthly Saturday night salons.

Because parties were seldom quiet affairs, out of respect for our neighbors below, we invited Jim and Lila to attend our soirées. Lila Perl was a professional photographer and an amateur filmmaker. Before the guests arrived, she came up the back stairs to our kitchen, her camera equipment in tow, to help Laura and Maria prepare *hors d'oeuvres*.

"Do you mind if I take a few pictures during the party?" Lila asked.

"Not at all. I'd love it if you'd captured the mood on film," Maria said.

"Yes. I'd also like to get some footage of the musicians in action."

"That'll be great," Laura said.

Lila's partner, Jim Hoffer, graduated from Harvard with a bachelor's in English and a minor in philosophy and now attended Boalt Law School as a first-year student. Lila revealed he was a genius with an IQ of 175.

We told everyone the salon kicked off at seven o'clock, knowing most would arrive late. By eight, we had our full complement of guests. Since Maria completed all the kitchen work beforehand, she greeted everyone as they hiked up the two flights to our flat.

I knew everyone either casually or by sight except for one.

Maria opened the front door using a lever at the top of the stairs built into the banister.

"Hi, Professor Gunn. Come on up." Professor Gunn was tall and bearded, with short dark hair.

"I'm so glad you could make it," Maria said. "This is my boyfriend, James. This is Thom Gunn, a poet and returning professor, is that right?"

"Yes. I taught at Cal a few years ago but have returned." Gunn was a Brit, judging by his accent.

"Would you mind reading one of your poems later, Professor?"

"Sure, Maria. I brought a couple with me. Let me know when."

"There's snacks and drinks in the kitchen. Help yourself," I said.

After everyone had settled down an hour into the party, Paul and Laura played some of their latest arrangements. While most enjoyed their jazz-rock pieces, my favorites were their modern classical compositions, now known as New Age.

Paul's virtuosity never failed to astound people, even those who had heard him before. One afternoon, to escape a downpour, we ducked into the Renaissance. I asked him why he didn't strike out and start his music career.

"I love music, but I'm also interested in literature, history, philosophy, and science. I can learn from my professors and my classmates. I'm in no rush to tackle the music world. It will take hold of me soon enough."

"That makes sense."

"Besides, times are changing. In the old days, jazz musicians were often self-taught. They learned whatever they could from jamming with others. Now, all these academic programs and professional training exist. What's wrong with learning jazz systematically and codified by my teachers, who hold credentials in music and are experienced musicians in their own right? This might sound strange, but I see preparation for a jazz career the way a future lawyer or doctor views his studies leading to his profession."

"What do your folks think about your direction?"

"My folks are supportive, though they'd prefer I become a classical musician. I run through my favorite classical pieces to warm up before switching to jazz whenever I go home. They would like to see me as a concert pianist in an orchestra, or a soloist." Paul sipped his coffee and grinned. "I want to perform at the Monterey Jazz Festival. Last year, Thelonious Monk, Herbie Hancock, and the Modern Jazz Quartet played, and I missed the whole thing."

"What does Laura want to do? She's into business, but the girl can jam."

"I kid you not. Laura is one of the best musicians I've ever played with. Not only on the violin, but she's fantastic on the piano and guitar. Remember the song *Spain*, by Chick Corea, with the flamenco part by Paco de Lucia?"

"Sure, on the live recording, not the studio album."

"Laura is learning the flamenco piece. Very difficult. We sent Laura's dad a copy last week, and she begged him to learn it. Every night they call each other, play over the line, and work through fingering and chord progressions together."

"Oh, God. There goes the phone bill."

"Don't worry. Laura's good for it."

"I'm kidding. So why doesn't Laura want to be a professional musician?"

"Her parents hold her back. Both are excellent musicians and skilled enough to go pro, but they're too risk-averse and don't want Laura to gamble on a musical career and fail. They tell her she's competent but not talented enough. Such bullshit. Better to keep music as a hobby and secure a real job. Oh, like playing music for a living isn't work."

"That has always been her plan, right? To work and play on the side."

"So far, but I think she's coming around. She's much better than good. Laura will be a superb jazz musician with the right encouragement and direction. Perhaps she will outshine Jean-Luc Ponty."

"Is that your unbiased opinion?"

"No. I'm biased as hell, but I'm not wrong."

Thom Gunn sat in a corner digging the last jazz piece Laura and Paul performed. Maria slipped next to him and whispered in his ear. He listened, nodding.

The salon jumped to its feet at the final bar line and applauded our musicians. Once the praise simmered down, Maria spoke.

"Listen, everyone. Professor Gunn would like to read one of his unpublished poems. Let's give a listen."

"Thank you, Maria. Another applause for Laura and Paul. Fantastic music."

Gunn waited as the room clapped.

"This one's tentatively called *To the Air*." I watched Maria from across the room, her eyes closed so she could concentrate as he recited the poem in his expressive free-verse style. Gunn's work displayed a concise philosophical elegance we appreciated, even if we didn't understand it initially.

The Salon increased in popularity as Paul and Laura strove to maintain variety and innovation in their compositions. Chopin's *Nocturnes* lent themselves to jazz arrangements with the violin added in creative ways. Jazz-classical fusion, although not unheard of, was still relatively novel. Paul's passion for Chick Corea's music, incorporating Latin and progressive techniques assisted by percussionist Manny Molina, proved immensely popular with our guests.

Paul implored his parents for a Fender Rhodes electric piano, which revitalized many original pieces he and Laura composed or arranged. The music sounded "jazzier" with the electric piano. With the new instrument, they expanded their repertoire to include piano duets.

Maria and I adored the personalities, intelligence, and creativity that imbued our lives.

In one of her bursts of realism, she said, "I love that we can indulge our zeal for learning and take the time to discover new things. But you know it could all end one day, so we should make the most of it."

"Of course, we might leave academia and forego this lifestyle, but we don't have to," I said.

"You want to live and teach in a liberal arts college in some small town, but what about me?"

"Why can't you teach and write too? Lots of professors write novels."

"I'm not sure I want to spend another five years in school."

"Why five years?"

"That's how long it takes to get a PhD in comparative literature. I might finish in three if I switched to English or Spanish."

"There you go. That's a plan worth considering."

Maria reflected for a few moments.

"Wouldn't it be awesome to recreate our literary circle and resurrect the Salon in a new incarnation?"

"Now you're talking," I said as I reached over and pushed a lock of her long hair behind her ear.

"*Querer es Poder.*"

While we craved every opportunity to live untroubled, we never took our blessings for granted. We remembered those who did not possess the advantages we enjoyed.

The specter of war still raged in the world, and while US involvement in the Indochina War ended in 1973, most guys from our high school returned. Some did not.

Paul and I were lucky that we drew high lottery numbers. Those of our classmates who joined or were inducted fought in our place. Violence terrified Paul and, more specifically, any damage to his hands.

"I'm glad this war is winding down," he said one day over morning coffee. "If I'm a coward, so be it, but I don't want to hurt anyone or get hurt."

"Right. Ever notice how the sons of elites never fight in these wars?"

"It has always been that way. The poor and middle class do all the fighting and dying."

"I know. The horror stories I dragged out of my father made me a pacifist." Like many of our generation, we rejected war outright.

We marched past numerous antiwar rallies filling Sproul Plaza on our way to classes, punctuated by inane slogans. We were not interested in the protests though we wanted the war to end. The Vietnam conflict had been front-page news since 1965. Our generation grew up bombarded by images of brutal conflict beaming into our living rooms and psyches.

I also suffered from Paul's fear of bodily violence, avoiding movies and shows that depicted senseless mayhem. I wouldn't say I liked horror movies with their gratuitous and exaggerated gore, maiming, and torture. Films about jails and prisons also churned my stomach. The thought of imprisonment frightened me as much as physical violence. A thrashing could be a one-time thing, but prison and its brutality might extend for years.

I lost count of how many soirées we hosted while living as a unified household on Russell Street. Some were lively, others more relaxed, but most ranged in between. Paul and Laura always prepared a piece or two and took requests. One party towards the end stood out because it was one of the few times Maria and I argued, and for us to squabble or clash about anything was infrequent. We respected each other's idiosyncrasies and sensitivities when we needed space, lessening the potential for conflict. I always found it strange when other couples bickered. We seldom did, and I assumed we were the rule and not the exception.

That night, I drank a little more than usual. Every time my wine glass emptied, more found its way into it while Maria bounced around from guest to guest in her customary way. She settled into a conversation with Monica, one of her female admirers, who never let a chance to flirt with Maria pass by. Stranded across the room, I could only guess Monica's pick-up line while she gesticulated wildly.

Despite the ebullient mood invigorating the Salon, I tuned most of it out, lost in thoughts of the evening ending so I could go to bed. A grad student in French, Heather, whom we called Lady Heather because she was fascinated with B&D, slid beside me and wrapped her arm around me like we were old pals. We had chatted a few times after our twentieth-century French lit seminar, but that's all. Judging from her breath, she drank her share. The way she hung on Maria's every word got me thinking she had a thing for Maria, too.

"Why so forlorn at your party?" Heather asked.

"I'm resting before I return to the social pool. I'm a little tired tonight."

"I have something for you. Let's go someplace private."

Heather pulled me to my feet and led me to the back bedroom we used as a library. I glanced over at Maria, who, I believed, spotted us exit the gathering. Heather pulled the door shut. We sat at the small table as she pulled a compact mirror and some coke out of her tiny purse.

She chopped and shaped four lines. "This is the last of my stash, so why not share the finale with someone blow-worthy, like my host?"

"I appreciate that. I could use a pick-me-up."

"Poor Monica never gives up, does she?"

Heather had taken in the situation in the living room. "If Maria wants a dalliance with Monica, I guess I'm fine with it," I said, more to convince myself than Heather.

"Awfully modern of you. Would Maria accept you having a fling of your own?"

"Excellent question. I've never wanted to engage in one."

We each snorted our lines in turn and threw our heads back to let the numbing sensation spread.

"Maria's a lucky woman. Some gals would like a little time with you alone. That includes me."

"Really? Don't you go for the more submissive types, Lady Heather?"

She laughed. "I like the sobriquet. So, you believe the whispers?"

"Are any of them true?"

"Probably. Why deny my kinky side as long as no one gets hurt? I'm not the only fan of *Justine* and *La Philosophie dans le boudoir*. My current favorite is *Histoire D'O.*"

"Another French erotic novel? I don't know it."

"Yes. Pauline Reage wrote it in the 1950s. Mademoiselle O eagerly agrees to submit to every desire of her male lovers, regardless of how degrading. She reverses everything on them in time, and they become her submissive slaves."

"So they had to dominate to be subdued, their *vrai désir*?"

"*C'est ça.*"

We switched to French. Heather spoke impeccably because she had attended a year of high school in Paris, but I managed to keep up.

"O is like Dolores Haze in *Lolita*?" I asked.

"Yes."

"Sounds interesting. I should read it."

"I'll loan you the French edition and bring it to class next week."

"Thanks, Heather. You put yourself out there, don't you? No pretenses, no guilt, no feigned coyness. I admire that."

"Life is too fleeting to play games. I'm not getting any younger."

"How old are you, if I may ask?"

"I'm 25."

"Still quite young, though you are older than most of us undergrads. I like you, Heather. I'm sorry we didn't become acquainted sooner."

"I wanted to be certain about you and Maria. I have my way of choosing those I get to know."

"How's that?" I asked, now more curious.

"You'll laugh, but whenever I detect an erotic charge between another person and me, I get wet."

"Isn't that normal when one feels an attraction?"

"Not for me. Most people do not elicit much reaction, but I notice when they do. Think of it as *radar vaginal* or vagdar." We laughed.

"Any soundings now?"

"Definite echoes. The love interest is near."

"Are you making an offer, valid until midnight?"

Smiling, Heather arose from her chair, stood behind me, and massaged my neck and shoulders. She uncovered the tension and kneaded more vigorously.

"That *hurts* so good," I moaned.

"That's the spirit. Just relax," she said as she attacked the knots in my muscles "You are tense. It could be the blow, or you're a little nervous about me rubbing on you."

"*Nerveux? Moi*? I'll give you twenty minutes to stop that. In fact, I am quite energized now." Heather leaned over and nibbled on my ear. Her hot breath on my cheek aroused me.

Dropping her hand to my thigh, she whispered, "I would love a threesome with you and Maria sometime. I'll bring some fun toys you guys might like."

Startled by the suggestion, I appreciated Heather's unapologetic and forthright declaration of her intentions, traits I applauded in Maria.

"I'm not sure we'd be up for it. An offer like that would have to—" I stopped as the doorknob turned, and the door swung open. Maria stood in the doorway.

"*C'est un cours de français*?" she said.

We reverted to English.

"Is this a private party, or can anyone join?" Maria said in a timbre divergence from her usual middle-C range in a tone I dreaded.

"Just a friendly chat, Maria. Would you like a neck rub?" Heather asked, her voice calm and friendly.

"No, thanks. I wondered where our host had disappeared amidst our *ongoing* party. Sorry to interrupt." She returned to the party, the door left open.

Lady Heather removed her hands from my shoulders, smiling at me. "Think about my offer. It's open anytime."

"I will. Thanks for the lines." Heather brushed the mirror against her skirt, replaced it in her purse, and headed down the stairs. I called after her, "See you in class, Heather."

After the gathering, Maria and I cleaned up and went to our room. We exchanged less than ten words.

"You and Heather looked rather chummy." She squinted as she spoke.

"So did you and Monica."

Maria stared at me for a moment, working out what had happened.

"You don't have to be jealous of Monica. We're just friends."

"Are you?"

"You don't trust me? Really? I should be suspicious of you. Everyone at the party watched Heather put the moves on you, whisking you out of view to do drugs in the back room."

"It was just a little coke. Not my usual thing, as you know. I'm more of a psychedelic connoisseur." Maria ignored my little joke. "Anyway, haven't Monica and Heather flirted with you?"

Maria hesitated. "Well, yes. They have been rather *attentive*. Don't change the subject. Do you have the hots for Heather or not?"

"She is quite attractive and sexy. I like her full lips and lascivious smile. Her French is flawless. I could learn a lot from her. You're right. She did make an enticing proposal." Maria waited for me to continue, holding her breath. "I would never accept without your consent, though. I'm not interested in anyone but you. You know that, right?"

"If you want to fuck her, go ahead." Maria crossed her arms, her eyes narrowed.

"You're not hearing me. You misunderstand. Heather wants *you*. She wants us to have a *menage-a-trois*. I think she's using me to get to you."

Maria's face relaxed as she held her hand out for me to take it. We sat on the bed, her demeanor softening.

"I'm sorry. I should have realized. Funny. We must be the hot couple tonight because Monica hinted at the same thing. She figures I wouldn't be comfortable without you there too."

"Perhaps the four of us should get together."

"Ha! You'd like that. Let's go to bed. I'm drained. And since you have some energy left, why don't I lay back and let you pleasure me?"

"Maria. You make me blush."

CHAPTER 20

Nineteen seventy-six lived up to expectations as a leap year because it initiated a new phase in my life with Maria. On Sunday, February 29, the sun rose to clear skies after three days of intermittent rain. We lay in bed after making love. Maria rolled over to me and said, "Do you ever think about being a father?"

Surprised by her question, I concentrated momentarily by closing my eyes until I settled on her expectant face. "Are you off the pill? Just kidding. Not really. I suppose someday. But to be honest, having kids never appealed to me."

"Why's that?"

"I'm too focused on graduating, finishing my PhD. You know, all the academic things we've talked about before."

"But after that. We said no marriage until the end of grad school, but I'm rethinking that. We'll be in our late twenties by the time we're done. I'm not sure I want to wait that long since I'm 99.9% sure I want to marry you."

"Do you want to have kids early?" I asked, in a tone more solemn than I intended.

"It's safer to have children earlier rather than in my thirties. Besides, I think you'd make a wonderful dad."

"Would I? I have trouble picturing that, given how my family life went, or what happened between my dad and me."

"You hardly ever talk about your dad. He's still in the Dominican Republic, isn't he?"

"Yes. I think so. Dad wasn't around much for me growing up. I'm afraid I'd be a so-so father like him."

"But your stepdad, John, is cool, right? He and your mom are great with us. You and John get along pretty well, I think."

"That's true. John is my actual father in some crucial ways, although it's my biological father who I miss and regret not getting to know better."

"Isn't it a two-way street? Did he want to spend time with you?"

I considered this question, staring at the uneven plaster on the ceiling above our bed. Some jays made a racket in the tree that dominated the apartment's garden.

"I think he did but didn't know how to bridge the gap that started when I was born. My stepdad hated my dad and would never let him come into the house for a cup of coffee. Perhaps he always felt like an intruder in my life."

"So, maybe you have some things to work out between you and your two dads. Being a father yourself might help. Can't you be the father you've always wanted for our children?"

"Sounds reasonable. I take your point. You truly believe the two of us will be good parents?"

"No doubt in my mind," Maria added in a soft yet firm voice that came with certainty. She lifted my arm around her shoulders as she snuggled up to me. "I want to have a life with you. We've been great together these last three years. I don't see that changing."

"Nor do I. I love being with you, our life together. Let's not allow anything to come between us."

"No chance of that. We have sixty or seventy years ahead of us."

"You're confident in our healthful longevity," I joked.

"Our love for each other will sustain us. We'll take care of each other and our family. I've nurtured and disciplined horses, goats, and cats. You name it. Raising children will be an extension of that."

"You are the original Earth Mother."

Maria thought about that comment, pondering whether I was making fun.

"I'll take that as a compliment. I care deeply about all sentient beings."

"Exactly."

Several moments later, Maria said, "My grandmother once told me, 'One evening, you'll go to bed and wake up fifty years later. Live every day as best you can. Time is precious.'"

"*Carpe diem*. Let's not waste a day."

"In my imagination, I see us sitting on the porch of our ranch house with our grandchildren, maybe great-grandchildren playing with goats, riding horses, or whatever."

"Are we living off the royalties from your novels as a bestselling author of literary fiction?"

"Why not? I'll take it further. You have a gift for writing. Why not use it?"

"I have a secret."

"Tell me." Maria moved closer to me.

"I've had this fantasy about writing international crime novels where the protagonist solves a cold case in each European city. Of course, I'd have to spend time in each one doing research."

"*We'd* have to spend time, the kids and me."

"Yes, that's what I meant."

"Remember what Thoreau said in *Walden*. I'm paraphrasing, *build your castles in the air; that's where they should be. Now put the foundations under them.*"

"A wise man, that Henry David," I said.

A silence settled between us as Maria slipped into one of her contemplative moods, staring unfocused into the room, thinking hard about something. She could center her thoughts, blocking out any distractions, a power that I envied.

I climbed out of bed and cracked the door to our bedroom balcony. The cool air filtered in as I slipped under the covers and pulled the duvet around us. I couldn't come up with any downsides to getting married sooner rather than later. Having kids while working on our doctorates might be challenging, but I figured we would make it work. Our parents would help us with our new family if we stayed in California during grad school.

Maria and I had previously applied to PhD programs. We waited to hear back from the three schools on our list: UC Berkeley, UCLA, and Princeton. Whichever program accepted us both, we would attend.

The next three months would be manic. We had to complete our regular coursework and our senior theses. I estimated mine would reach over a hundred pages with footnotes, and Maria expected the same. Until now, the lengthiest paper I had ever written was thirty pages.

Paul and Laura had formed a jazz ensemble with two other talented musicians who had become regular jam partners, Will Charles and Manny Molina. Will plucked the bass as though it were an extension of his nervous system. Manny played any drum placed in front of him. On some pieces, he kept the beat on the vibraphone.

Maria stirred beside me, giving me that *uncaffeinated* look as I threw on my sweatpants and shuffled to the kitchen. No sounds emanated from Laura and Paul's room. Now that they had played a few gigs around Berkeley and Oakland, they were night owls in various live venues.

We sipped our espressos with a splash of milk, propped up in bed, surrounded by books and notebooks while we procrastinated studying.

"So," Maria began after a long reflection, "let's get married in June after graduation."

A tinge of nervousness sparked through me. I took a deep breath.

"All right, let's." I sat my coffee down, climbed out of bed on my knees, and took her hands. "Maria Isabella Compagno, will you marry me?"

Maria considered her answer.

"I accept your proposal, James Alexander Montez." We kissed.

"Let's be married on the ranch, surrounded by the people and the animals we love. I think an outdoor wedding would be wonderful. The weather is a little toasty in June, but we can set up some tents."

"Sounds like an excellent idea. What about a honeymoon?"

"While I'm planning the wedding, I'll figure out something. You just need to show up; I'll handle the rest."

"Can you plan a full-blown wedding and finish school too?"

"Mom and Grandma will help. It will be a lot, but I'll make it happen."

"I have no doubt. You are Supergirl."

"Right. Superwoman, to you." Maria took my hand. "Do you mind if I keep my maiden name?" If I take your last name, everyone will think I am trying to emulate a 1940s movie star, so I prefer to remain a Compagno if this doesn't bother you."

"Not at all. I take your point. Only old movie buffs remember the actress these days, but it might strike some as odd if you took her stage name. But if you wrote a screenplay and assumed the leading role, you would be set: the reincarnation of the Queen of Technicolor. You are an exotic beauty as she was. You might play her in a biography. You look like her too."

Maria laughed. "Okay then, I'll get started over Spring Break."

Four weeks later, the winter term ended. My boss asked me to work in the library over the break, and I agreed. Saturday morning, after final exams, we arose early. I made coffee while Maria packed a bag for her trip to LA.

"I am so looking forward to this week off at the ranch. I wish you were coming."

"So do I, but I can't say no to the extra money." Despite her disappointment of our parting for a week, Maria walked airily, her happiness effusive.

The reality of our forthcoming marriage finally settled in, and she loved the idea with each passing day. I didn't know what to expect, but my excitement burgeoned with hers, thinking that the girl I loved more than anything wanted to spend the rest of her life with me. I could not conceive of being with anyone else. If Plato's *Symposium* was correct, our two split souls had found each other and longed for reunification. While I was unsure I believed in soulmates, our joining embodied a vital synergy that bound us in this life and the next.

"C'mon, I'll be late for the flight."

I carried Maria's overnight bag down the stairs and held the front door open for her. The house was quiet. Laura had already left for LA, and Paul was out somewhere.

She took one last wistful look.

"I'll miss this flat if we have to leave. We've had some awesome times here."

"I love it here too. I'll never forget the life we lived together in this place."

On the ride to the Oakland Airport, we promised to call each other every night until her return the following Sunday. I escorted her to the departure gate after passing through the metal detectors.

We spoke quietly in the lounge, our heads together, almost touching, a little sad at being apart for a week, and waited until the last moment.

"I'll miss you. Give Old Yeller a big hug for me."

"I brought one of your dirty socks so he can smell it."

"You did?"

"I'm kidding. Maybe next time."

"Who will make me laugh while you're having fun on the farm?"

"You and Paul will come up with something. We'll talk every night."

The last call for Maria's flight came over the loudspeaker.

"Olivia and I will sleep in your room this week to feel closer to you."

"I'm going to sleep on your side of the bed."

The jetway door was about to close. We kissed long and passionately until she broke away. Before running toward the plane, she whispered, "I love you, James."

After our farewell, I drove home with the radio off. A light spring drizzle began as I parked in the rickety carport next to our building. We'd been apart less than thirty minutes, and a void had already formed. I consoled myself with the thought she would be on her ranch, the place she loved, with a wedding to plan—*our* wedding. I could hardly believe it.

A month had passed since we agreed to marry. Both excited and terrified of marriage, I told myself ours would not turn out like my parents. We would be happy, always in love, care for each other, and never live estranged in the same household.

The sound of Paul at the piano filled the living room while he picked out a melancholy tune. I trudged up the stairs, but he didn't hear me because I surprised him when I slipped in and sank into the sofa.

"A new song, Paul?"

"A melody rolling around in my head." Paul usually kept his long hair braided in a ponytail. Today his hair hung around his shoulders.

"It sounds sad."

"Melancholy. 'Melancholy is the happiness of being sad.'"

"A quote from Victor Hugo?"

"I think so. The tune is in C# minor. I'm feeling a little down."

"I know what you mean. I dropped off Maria for her flight to Ontario. With Laura away, we're carefree bachelors this week. Maria suggested you would make me laugh. No pressure."

"Laura left yesterday. She might as well have been gone for weeks," Paul mused.

"Since we met Maria and Laura, I don't think we've been apart for more than a day or two. Perhaps too much togetherness isn't healthy," I said.

"I suppose not. Congratulations, by the way. The wedding plan is in full swing?"

"Yes. Right after graduation."

"Since I'm the best man, I think I'm in charge of the bachelor party."

"Don't worry about a party. We've thrown enough to last a lifetime."

"True enough. What fabulous times we've had here. I'm going to miss this place."

"Maria said the same thing. If she and I attend graduate school at Berkeley, we'll stay on, so you guys will always have a place to crash."

"Yeah. We start the tour in late July. Our first gig is in Hollywood at the Whisky A Go Go. We open for John Mayall."

"How did you manage that?"

"Remember the music symposium at Stanford last month, where I told you I met an incredible acoustic guitarist?"

"Bill Atkinson."

"Right. Bill started his own label called Random Hill Records. After the symposium, he invited Laura and me to his home in Portola Valley. Once we played for him, he pledged to produce our first album when we're ready."

"I recall."

"Bill is also friends with Mayall. He sent John our demos, and he loved them. Bill convinced him to let us open for him. We'll do our signature jazz-rock fusion thing. It'll be a blast."

"This is a huge step. I assume Will and Manny will join you."

"Yes. We call the four of us the *Paul Stein Quartet*. Not my idea of a name. Bill suggested it, and the rest of the band insisted."

"Well, you *are* the creative musician force and child prodigy." I chuckled.

"I help, but I need the others to spark my ideas. Together we are the source of our Swing."

"Swing?" What do you mean?"

"I'm sure you've noticed how a group of musicians displays this rhythmic cohesion that holds them together."

"Sure. The group sounds like they're not in sync when bands don't jive."

"Correct. You can detect a lack of unity. Even listeners who aren't jazz buffs can tell when the instrumentation sounds a bit off. Musicians adapt to each other but also insist on doing their own thing. This dynamic is what makes jazz so cool. The give-and-take among the musicians provides the energy that emerges from the blend of personalities. The music feels alive and potent, and meaningful. That's what I mean by Swing."

"I never thought of it that way."

"The bass provides the rhythm and the beat. I listen for Swing by how the percussion and bass lock together. When Will is in the zone on the big bass, Manny follows him, and Laura and I tune into this rhythm."

"Hold on a sec. Let me get some beers."

I returned with two open bottles and handed one to Paul. He took a sip, swiveled to the piano, and continued pecking out his melody.

"Did I ever mention I suffer from stage fright?"

"No. You do?"

"For the first 30 seconds or so, I'm terrified. I'm convinced I cannot hit the right notes. I relax. Something takes over, and I play, the anxiety disappears, and I'm fine."

"I thought you would move past the fear after years of recitals."

"Nope. It happens every time. I'm petrified that I will freeze in front of the audience. If I go blank at the John Mayall concert, the Quartet is sunk before we start."

"You're an extraordinary musician, Paul. You will not disappoint your audience. You haven't before. Why start now?"

"Laura says the same thing. She keeps telling me stage fright is normal. Even she gets a flutter of panic."

Paul seldom exposed his private anxieties. I assumed he spoke to me because he missed Laura, but perhaps his calm, laid-back demeanor hid something more profound.

"Don't feel like the Lone Ranger. I struggle with anxiety encroaching on my self-esteem all the time. Maria's my best cheerleader, always ready to contradict my harmful indulgences."

"Yeah. Laura does the same for me. God, where would we be without them?"

"Adrift at sea in a *bateau ivre, j'imagine*."

I hated this angst of never measuring up, never being an above-average writer, poet, teacher, husband, or father.

Paul interrupted my musings. "One last thing about Swing." He finished his beer. "When the ensemble works together, we don't need to play so many notes. Whoever's doing the solo can toss off casual phrases, and each one lands home. One of the others can underplay, and the group will still swing. We are tired when the rhythmic cohesion flounders, and we're tempted to overplay. We like to time our sets and rest before fatigue compromises the sound."

"Now I understand why the band carries your name. You understand how to make the art happen."

"I guess. *Une autre bière, mon ami?*"

"Wow. Your French is improving. *Oui, je nous en apporte une autre.*"

The next day I put in a long eight hours at the library. Most of my colleagues wanted Spring Break off, so I volunteered to cover for them. The real reason, though, was I needed the money. Fees, books, and rent became due soon, and my meager 15-to-20-hour-a-week job didn't cover all the expenses. I hated asking my parents for money, but I would survive another month with the extra hours and their contribution.

The starving-student motif grew tiresome, and I considered dumping grad school to land a real job in a moment of anxious self-doubt. Still, Maria and I were already committed to advanced degrees. Who was I kidding? What else would I do? I had dreamed of an academic career since junior high school. Too late to change directions now. We both carried 3.75-plus grade point averages, and all our professors encouraged us to continue. Some wrote some flattering recommendations. Besides, while some of my business courses had their moments, I struggled to maintain enthusiasm for accounting and finance.

I loved reading, analyzing, and writing about literature. So did Maria, but creative writing was her true passion. Over the last three years, she had written almost twenty short stories and two novellas while carrying a full course load. Maria's ability to organize her time and focus was impressive.

After work, I fell asleep and fumbled for the receiver as I shook off the drowsiness. I missed the start of the conversation, but once awake, I asked Maria how things were going.

"Planning a wedding turns out to be a bigger job than I imagined. So many things to consider."

"Any help from the family?"

"Sure, everyone is pitching in, but I want to do the preliminary stuff myself."

"Is it that much work?" I asked, clearly oblivious.

"How's this: determine the budget. Fortunately, we know the venue. Figure out what vendors we need and hire them on short notice. Buy a wedding dress, outfit the bridesmaids, line up a tux for you, book the honeymoon, and do hair and makeup. Grandma's going to make the wedding cake. Write the vows. Figure out the invite list, make the invitations, and mail them. I'm sure there's more."

"Sorry I asked. What can I do to help?"

"Make a list of everyone you want to attend. Do a rough draft of the vows, if you please."

"Got it."

We both took a deep breath over the phone.

"How're the critters?"

"Old Yeller sends his best. Mopsie and Flopsie are the same as always." Mopsie and Flopsie were Maria's pet goats. "Smokie and I went on a long ride to the creek this afternoon."

"I hate missing that."

"By the water, I put down a blanket and stripped off my clothes for about an hour. The sun felt so good on my skin."

"Now I know I'm missing out."

"I indulged myself in a fantasy or two. I'll leave it to your imagination."

"Not fair you teasing me like this. I wish I were with you at the ranch. If only I had been born rich instead of good-looking."

"The money issues will ease once we marry. My family is generous."

"I am not sure I'm up to being a kept man."

"Things won't ease up that much." Maria laughed. "Oh, and one more thing."

"Yes?"

"No masturbating while I'm gone. I'm off the pill now and want you good and potent."

"Yes, ma'am. *À ton service.*"

"I love you so much; see you on Sunday. I land in the morning, so let's go to brunch somewhere. Afterward, we can do whatever you like."

"I have some ideas. *À bientôt ma chérie, je t'aime.*"

The doorbell rang. Paul's favorite pizza, a large vegetarian with extra chicken sausage, had arrived.

The following evening, Paul and I met for stirred fried rice at a Vietnamese bistro near our house.

"How's Laura's visit going?" I asked.

"Well. She and her mom play music daily, and her dad joins them in the evenings after work. Laura tried out some of the flamenco guitar she's learning."

"Are you going to work it into your sets?"

"Eventually. Manny and I are exploring some Latin jazz pieces for our debut in July. How's Maria?"

"She's fine. We'll chat tonight."

We returned from dinner around seven.

Maria didn't call. I figured she must be busy, so I didn't give her silence much thought. At 8:00 p.m., I called her grandparents, then her parents: no answer.

After a long, hot shower, I climbed into bed, read five pages of Victor Hugo, and fell asleep.

Around 9:30, the phone rang. I scrambled for the receiver in the darkness.

"James? Marc Compagno here. Listen. You need to fly down here right away."

Mr. Compagno sounded uneasy, aloof, and stern. "Maria had an accident."

"What happened? Is she all right?" I could barely control my panic.

"Maria fell off Smokie this afternoon. We helicoptered her to Pomona General in serious condition. I bought you an open ticket, pick it up at the counter, and I'll collect you at Ontario."

"But . . ."

"Please hold your questions. We'll fill you in when you arrive. Call me at the house once you book your flight. I gotta go, son. See you soon."

He hung up. I still held the receiver to my ear, the phone thrumming. Unable to think or move, I mentally replayed his taut message. Maria's dad was terse. Paralyzed by anxiety, I sat in the shadows as the cold numbness of shock constricted my body. I fought back the tears, willing myself to get dressed.

After numerous flights to Ontario, I remembered the last flight left at 11:30 p.m. I threw some clothes into a bag and banged on Paul's door.

"Paul!" I pushed the door open. He lay on his bed, dozing with a book in his hands.

"What's up?"

"I just got a call from Maria's dad. She had an accident. I need you to drive me to Oakland airport." Paul slipped on his shoes and grabbed a jacket from the closet without a word. I tossed him the keys to my car.

"You remember how to manage a stick, right?"

"Ah, I can drive Laura's Mustang."

"Close enough. Let's go."

I rattled off what I knew on the way to the airport. Paul tried to reassure me and persuade me not to presume the worst. He was scarcely able to mask his fears for Maria. We double-parked at Departures, and I jumped out.

"Let me know when you find out what's going on, please." I promised to call him tomorrow, grabbed my bag, slammed the door, and ran to the ticket counter, the sweat running down my back despite the cold temperature and ice congealing around my heart.

I drowsed during the short flight, in and out of confusing dreams.

I stood alone in a desert with tall mountains on either side. The unmoving and blood-orange sun rested above the skyline. In the distance, a silhouette beckoned me: Maria. I followed the bare footsteps in the sand and ran towards her. Suddenly unable to move my legs, I struggled to wade through deep sand, sucking at my feet, willing myself to push through.

Desert winds carried her voice, her words unintelligible. She spoke in a familiar yet ungraspable language. Maria moved away as I fell behind. I screamed for her to stop, change course, and return, but she shrank away, absorbed by the light receding below the horizon. I cried out to her one last time before she winked out, and I collapsed to the desiccated ground, exhausted.

I awoke as the pilot announced our descent into Ontario International Airport. My face awash in a cold sweat, I wiped it with the sleeve of my jacket, craving a sip of water to relieve my thirst and rinse the dust from my mouth and nostrils.

Maria's father met me at the gate at 1:00 a.m. His face was drawn-out, unsmiling, eyes reddened. I nodded hello.

"Thanks for coming, James." Never unduly demonstrative, he hugged me as I emerged from the jetway into the lounge.

The overnight bag slipped from my shoulder.

"Here, let me carry it."

I let him, not because the satchel was heavy but because he needed to distract himself and do something within his control.

Often deserted this late, the passenger lounge echoed with the midnight stragglers' footfalls. The odor of cleaning supplies filled the air as a lone janitor mopped sections of the floor and wiped down the faux leather seats. There would be no flights until dawn.

Mr. Compagno set the pace as we plodded along, marching towards a destination we resisted.

He explained, his voice subdued and tense, "Maria was training Smokie in the corral to the side of the house." He stopped to get a better grip on my bag. "My dad saw the whole thing. He sat on the porch watching her put Smokie through her moves. Smokie gave out a loud neigh, reared up on her hind legs, and Maria lost her grip on the reins and fell back on the corral railing. She hit her head."

"God, no!" I cried, terrified.

"Maria never falls off a horse, but riding bareback, there's nothing but the reins to hold on to. Dad ran to the enclosure, stumbling on a giant rattlesnake that Smokie had crushed. Maria still breathed but was unconscious. He tried to revive her but couldn't."

We passed through the glass doors out of the terminal. The night chill resembled the Bay Area.

I forced my legs to move as we looked for her dad's car. My heart raced as he continued.

"Mom flew out of the house. Dad screamed for her to call 9-1-1. The ambulance arrived, stabilized her, and took her to a Beaumont hospital, where they medivacked her to Pomona's trauma center."

We climbed into the car and drove off. "Maria has a severe concussion. The doctors induced a coma while they evaluated the injury. Angelina is at the hospital waiting for us."

Mr. Compagno went silent and concentrated on navigating airport exits to I-10 West towards Pomona General. I sat stunned, unsure of what to say.

"She's alive, thank God. That's the good news."

"That's the best news," I said.

Maria's grandparents, mother, and little brother sat in the waiting room when we got to the medical center.

Angelina hugged me. "*Jaime, Estás aquí, m'hijo. Gracias por venir.*"

"*Yo tenía que venir.*" Maria's mother wiped the tears from her eyes.

Mrs. Compagno kissed me on both cheeks, and Grandpa Compagno shook my hand. The vacancy in his eyes revealed the fear for his granddaughter's life. The bond between Maria and her grandfather went deep.

Jon curled up in a chair, in and out of sleep, under the overhead lights. Maria's sister, Alicia, visited friends in Santa Barbara and would arrive in the morning.

We huddled silently, everyone ensconced in their world of grief and fear.

I said, "Is Smokie okay?"

Grandpa perked up. "She's . . . she fine, I think. No physical damage anyway."

"That's something, anyway."

He continued, "While Maria lay on the ground, Smokie nudged her like crazy, trying to wake her. I'll be damned, but that horse knew something was wrong. When I tried to take her back to the stable, she wouldn't leave Maria. I could get her out of that corral only after the ambulance left."

Grandma Compagno took Angelina's hand. "What do you think?"

"Maria's getting the best care. She has some swelling that they're trying to control. She's a strong girl."

The answer didn't satisfy her. She shook her head and crossed herself while silently mouthing a prayer.

That ubiquitous hospital odor suddenly sent waves of nausea through me. The tightness in my chest, compounded by angst, made breathing difficult. The usual cacophony of hospital noises, such as bells, PA announcements, and gurneys wheeling by, didn't help.

Grandpa Compagno and his son, Marc, sat rigid in the padded hospital chairs, legs crossed, staring at their feet, silent. Father and son held the same posture; it must be genetic.

Jon startled himself out of a dream. "Maria?" Realizing where he was, he frowned and went back to sleep.

Unable to keep still, I paced around the waiting room. Angelina followed me with a worried look.

I said, "Don't mind me. All this nervous energy."

Maria's mother regained control of her emotions, perhaps from years of dealing with trauma on the job. Her mother-in-law fingered her rosary.

All of us were bone-tired, numbed by the waiting, and apprehensive under the constantly flickering fluorescent lights. Around us, even at this early hour, the hospital staff moved back and forth with routine business. I suppressed as best I could the churning panic of not knowing.

Marc Compagno said, "I'm going to the cafeteria. Anyone care to join me?"

Already standing, I said, "I'll go. I could use some coffee."

Angelina followed us down the hallway to the hospital dining hall. The rest remained.

Maria's parents and I sat at a corner table beside a window, drinking strong but bitter coffee. We surveyed the parking lot surrounded by tall trees while the sky grew lighter. None of us had slept.

Mr. Compagno appeared worn out, his eyes bloodshot, hair disheveled.

"What about your job, James?" Mr. Compagno asked.

"I'll call and let them know. No worries."

He stirred his coffee desultorily.

"The whole thing was a fluke. That damn snake should never have crawled into the corral. Maria would have missed the railing if she had been angled a few degrees to the left or right. Damn it." His anger caused some others in the cafeteria to pretend not to listen.

Mrs. Compagno took his arm and leaned against him.

"It's not fair. Maria's a fighter. She'll get through this." That night we all told ourselves whatever we needed to hear.

Angelina glanced at her wristwatch, "I need to run home and change to get ready for my shift. I will be down later, but Marc, if you hear anything, page me."

"Will do."

Angelina stepped away without her usual buoyancy. "How does she stay so calm?" I asked.

"Angelina's been a nurse for over twenty-five years, used to long hours on her feet, with little or no sleep, working under time constraints and pressures we can only imagine. She works with the doctors here and is confident Maria is well cared for. Besides, she has overseen thousands of trauma cases and can focus on excluding all else."

"But it's not just another case; it's Maria."

"I know, son. She knows it too. She remains outwardly calm because she's trained not to telegraph her true feelings. We're all worried."

We fell silent again. I absentmindedly spun my coffee cup counterclockwise as dawn emerged, now a reddish glow. I fought off a numbness that worked its way down my spine. My feet ached like I had hiked for miles over rough terrain.

"I'm going back to the waiting lounge, son. I'll see you there." He placed his hand on my shoulder as though to steady himself. I nodded as Marc Compagno rose from his seat, having aged twenty years in the last hour. He walked toward the exit, shuffling, his head sagging instead of his usual erect posture.

Only the first day and exhaustion wore us out. Half a lifetime passed, and resignation was our only recompense. Maria's fate belonged to a power greater than our will. God, if you exist, why?

The brightening sky from the cafeteria window evoked a memory from weeks ago when the Santa Ana winds had blasted through the Bay Area out of the east, bringing summer weather amidst winter. We enjoyed the seventy-degree days and warm nights. The overnight rain left the air fresh and moist.

The unseasonal winds abated overnight as we returned to temperate weather and slightly cloudy skies. Maria snuggled against me as I pulled the bedspread up to cover her. We left the door to our little patio ajar to allow circulation, and now a brisk draft chilled the room.

Her breathing slowed as she fell back into a light dream. Quietly, I slid out of bed and went into the kitchen to make some espresso. I heated milk in a small saucepan and layered it over the thick Italian roast coffee. The aroma often aroused Maria in the mornings. She sat up against the pillows in anticipation as I brought her the cup.

"My hero. Thank you." She sipped her coffee as the warm liquid pushed sleep away. "All we need now is the Sunday paper."

"That would be lovely, but today's Saturday."

"So, we can do this tomorrow, coffee and paper in bed?"

"Yes. Today is a practice run."

She laughed. "I will enjoy being married to you."

I smiled. "Do you think anything will be different? Our life now is good. Will our legal status change us?"

"Wait until we have several kids bouncing around, begging for breakfast. That will be different. My sister and I used to wake up my parents every weekend."

"Hmm. I'm not sure about that." Mària locked eyes with me. "I think we're going to enjoy a great life together. Only two?"

"As many as we like. The trend is now 2.4 kids. Two kids and a hunting dog would do. I want at least one of each, a boy and a girl."

While we drank our espresso, the sun rose further, and the rooftop visible from our bed reflected the morning light filtered through the lingering rain clouds.

Maria said, "I want to raise our kids to be self-reliant. Of course, we must protect them as much as possible, but we won't always be there."

"I agree. Let them enjoy their childhood with all its bumps and bruises."

"Before Jon was born, my sister and I ran around the ranch, getting into all kinds of trouble. Alicia fell from her horse twice, but Grandpa encouraged her to brush herself off and try again. It made her stronger."

"There are many ways to injure yourself, that's for sure. No one's invulnerable." I held out my left arm to show the small scar I got from scraping against a nail during one visit.

"And we survive them. I believe in allowing kids to be kids."

"Most children don't want their parents hovering over them like helicopters. I know I didn't."

"That's right. I remember convincing Laura's parents to let her come to the ranch and learn to ride. Laura and I begged them for weeks until they finally gave in."

"You're tenacious. Laura's a good rider, so it worked out."

"Yeah." Maria chuckled. "I recall the first time Laura visited. We were twelve or thirteen. Her parents wouldn't let her drive with us. They had to bring her in their car."

"So protective?"

"Exactly. They almost wouldn't let her stay after Grandma gave them the tour. But Grandma sat them down in the kitchen with a big pot of coffee and some fresh muffins and convinced them there was nothing to worry about."

"Did Laura get hurt during that trip?"

"Yes and no. One of our goats knocked her to the ground playing too rough, bruising her knee. We covered it up with long pants."

"I love those goats."

"Yes, like most animals, they love to play."

Maria sipped her coffee, remembering something.

"I taught Laura how to ride. At first, she wouldn't get near a horse. She said horses were big and scary. Like I did with you, I showed her how to groom them. Forming a bond with animals is easy for me, but it took some time for Laura."

"How did Laura go from the terror of horses to riding bareback?"

"Practice over a couple of summers." Maria laughed. "You should have seen the look on her parent's faces when they pulled up one Sunday as Laura and I cantered on the scene bareback, wearing halter tops, our long hair flowing in the wind like Amazon warriors."

"A look of shock and awe?"

"Mostly shock, I'd say, their mouths open invitation to flies. We trotted up to the car. Laura dismounted as though she had been doing it all her life. Her dad said, 'Where's the saddle?' And Laura said, 'I stopped using a saddle and stirrups ages ago. This is my horse, Old Yeller.'"

"She rode Old Yeller?"

"Yeah. On that day, she did."

"I wish I had grown up in a place like that. Diamond Bar was cool but tame compared to the ranch."

"Long summers working with the livestock, running the egg business, and training horses shaped who I am. I want to share that life with you and our family."

I wrapped my arm around her shoulders and kissed her.

Maria changed the subject: "What a gorgeous morning. Let's walk over to College Avenue, the long way." I agreed.

We read while we finished our coffee, made love, and dressed in our winter clothes before discreetly slipping down the stairs and out the front door, careful not to awaken Paul and Laura. The household stored several umbrellas near the door, and I grabbed a small one and shoved it in my jacket pocket, just in case.

We strolled up the south side of Russell Street, past Telegraph, towards the hilly part of Berkeley into the Elmwood district, through tree-lined streets where old single-family houses sat majestically and appeared as mansions to us. The aroma of damp earth infused the air.

"I love the smell of soil and plants after a rain," I said.

"I never feel more alive than on mornings like this."

"Yes. The gentle drip of water off the trees and the fresh breeze makes life worth living somehow."

"How can people live in the desert?" she asked.

"The desert has its charm. Some say the desert in bloom is quite spectacular. I wouldn't mind driving to the Mojave to find out for ourselves."

"Do you still plan to work over Spring Break?"

"Probably, though I would rather spend it with you."

"Well, we have a lifetime to visit the desert in spring," Maria said as she wrapped her hand around mine.

We passed the Elmwood neighborhood's beautiful homes and commented on the ones we liked, particularly those on generous lots with well-manicured gardens.

"Let's find a gigantic house someday with room for all our friends and family," Maria said. "Or perhaps a big farmhouse."

"You mean, like your grandparents' house?"

"Yes. I think the ranch will be ours someday, but where would you teach if we lived there?"

"UC Riverside is about twenty miles away. We should investigate the literature departments. Perhaps I'll become a rancher and bag academia. I can write novels like you in my spare time when I'm not toiling from sunrise to sunset. I may only have time for a poem or two." Maria squeezed my hand, smiling at my little joke.

The lightness in my step, arm-in-arm with the woman I loved, the spontaneity of our banter, and the fearlessness that everything would work out compelled me forward, undiminished by the tenuousness of happiness that hung on by an invisible thread.

We meandered through the neighborhoods until we reached College Avenue, one of many tree-lined streets typical of the area east and up against the hills, and headed south towards Oakland. We strolled past restaurants, cafés, boutique shops, and window shopping up one side until we found a spot neither of us had visited called the Chestnut Tree Café. Inside, we took a seat in one of the front bay windows.

I ordered cappuccinos and two warm croissants. The fruit bowl looked appetizing, so I bought one to share. The café brimmed with patrons. Several couples sat talking while lone customers read newspapers or books.

While we enjoyed our continental breakfast, people ambled up and down the street, pursuing their Saturday morning rituals. A half-hour passed, and the café almost emptied.

Maria leaned in a low, tentative voice and said, "I need to tell you something. Maybe this isn't the best place, but I wanted to tell you when we first reconnected. Now that we're getting married, it has been on my mind, and I need to get it out. Only Laura knows, and I hate carrying it around. Perhaps it's not so important since it happened so long ago, but I thought you should hear the full story."

I reached over and placed my hand on hers to reassure her.

"Remember Brett, my first boyfriend, the one I met after my grandfather's funeral?"

"Yes, the one who interrupted our ice skating."

"Yes, him. The first few times we had sex, he used a condom, which was cool. On the third occasion, we drank some wine and got in the mood. This time he didn't bring any condoms, so I said no. At first, he said okay, but then got aggressive in a way that weirded me out. He held me down, pulled off my pants, and screwed me without protection. I tried to fight him off, but he was too strong."

"He date-raped you?" I gasped.

"Yeah, he did. Right then, I dumped the son-of-a-bitch."

Maria paused, watching a woman with two dogs cross the street.

"I missed two periods and took a test: I was pregnant. I never told Brett, though. I confessed to my parents what had happened, and they made sure he left me alone."

Her story dumbfounded me as I conjured the fourteen-year-old girl I knew then, raped and impregnated by a guy she trusted. Anger, shock, and empathy swirled inside me in an amalgam of confusing emotions. I admired how calmly Maria related her trauma. Perhaps the years had provided enough distance.

"Well, at nine weeks, I lost the baby, a girl." Maria wiped her tears away. "Now you understand why I didn't return to skating until months later and why I spent a lot of time by myself during high school."

I hugged her to comfort us both.

"Are you worried you can't have children?"

"No. I had some tests done, and I'm fine."

"What did Laura say?" I asked.

"She was very supportive."

I squeezed Maria's hand to say I loved her.

"It's not the assault that bothers me anymore, but the loss of my daughter. I wanted to have that baby." Maria sobbed. I pulled a clean handkerchief from my back pocket and gave it to her.

"If I were the father, I'd want the baby too."

"You're not upset with me for not confiding in you?"

"Of course not. Your past doesn't change anything for us. I'm so sorry you carried this pain around for so long. Did you really think I would react badly or think less of you?"

"No. I pushed the incident away and tried to forget it, but, you know, something like that is hard to let go of. I love you so much. Laura said I was silly for keeping my past a secret."

"She was right. Nothing you might tell me would lessen my love for you." Maria placed her warm hand against my cheek, her eyes filled with tenderness. I put mine over hers and pressed it against me, savoring the sensation for as long as possible.

"I love you, Maria. Always. No matter what."

Clouds had rolled in while we lingered in the window of the café. Outside, I unfurled the umbrella in the doorway, and we squeezed under its canopy.

"Don't you love the intimacy of walking beneath an umbrella, arm in arm, huddled together, protected from the world's extremes?" Maria said.

Where was that shelter now?

We arrived home still a little wet from the drizzle, stripped off our damp clothes, and showered together. Afterward, we climbed into bed and piled books around us as we started our daily studying routine. Final exams were three weeks away.

I finished my third cup of coffee and rejoined the waiting room. Alicia arrived at eight. Maria's sister and I were not close but shared a tentative affection we seldom exhibited. After she hugged her family, she came to me, pulled me into her arms, and held me the way Maria did. She smelled like Maria, which surprised me.

"I'm so glad you're here, James." Tears formed as she broke away and sat beside her grandmother.

Soon after, Laura rushed in, her eyes red from crying. She went to me first and squeezed me so tight I couldn't breathe. I embraced her with a desperation that frightened me. The errant thought of losing Maria terrified us as the possibility flashed between us, a prospect none of us dared acknowledge.

Around 10 a.m., Mrs. Compagno took an early lunch. At last, the doctor arrived, a middle-aged man with short dark hair streaked with gray and with dark puffiness below his eyes. We gathered around.

"I'm Doctor Shepherd. Maria's stable. She suffered some brain swelling, which we relieved. We're keeping her under, allowing her skull and brain to heal. If all goes well, we'll attempt to bring her out of the coma. Angelina, please fill them in on the procedural details for me, if you don't mind. There is not much any of you can do now. I suggest you all get some sleep. I'll call if any changes in her condition arise."

"Doctor, so it's only swelling? No permanent brain damage?" Marc Compagno asked.

"No damage that we can see. We don't think there's any."

"How long will she be in a coma?"

"At least three days, but it could be longer. The swelling is subsiding, but we need more time to evaluate."

Doctor Shepherd maintained his neutral, cautiously optimistic stance.

I asked, "Doctor, will Maria suffer any memory loss?"

He paused, thinking. "Hard to say. Maria may experience temporary lapses, but her long- and medium-term memory should be unaffected."

The doctor's briefing helped relieve our palpable anxiety escalating the last several hours.

Maria's mother spoke, "Thank you, Doctor Shepherd."

"If you have further questions, please let me know." He turned and hurried to the elevator.

"I suggest we all get some rest while we can. Please go to our house and rest. I'll be over as soon as my shift ends."

We followed the advice and drove to the Compagnos' house in Claremont.

After an impromptu breakfast, I went to Maria's room, comforted by being around her things. I pulled down a volume from her bookshelves but couldn't focus.

After a short nap, I called my job to inform them I wouldn't be back on campus until next week. My boss sympathized with my family emergency and told me I'd still have my job when I returned. Right then, I didn't care.

I called Paul and described Maria's condition.

"She's stable and on the mend, according to the doctors. We won't know for sure for a few more days."

"I'm flying down tonight. Manny offered to drop me off at the airport." Paul gave me the flight details.

"Laura and I will pick you up."

"See you guys soon." Paul didn't shield the concern in his voice. None of us did.

Draped across Maria's bed, I fell again into a fitful sleep, dreaming of horses grazing next to a lazy creek that echoed in a clearing under the shade of ancient oak trees, far from any deserts.

Chapter 21

A week passed. Maria had not emerged from her coma, so we returned to Berkeley to start classes, the last term of our college careers. After two weeks, the medical center moved her out of intensive care into a single room. She breathed without the respirator, with the IV forever in her arm attached to a feeding tube. Angelina washed her hair, gave her sponge baths, changed her catheter, and popped in often, although such attention fell outside her duties. The hospital sanctioned her activities, and her colleagues covered for her. Maria's doctors said the recovery would take time, how much no one guessed.

Every weekend I flew down to see her, to sit next to her bed, helpless. I held her cool hand and searched her face, alert for any sign of her emerging from unconsciousness. I kissed her on the lips, hoping she would awaken.

Grandma Compagno often dropped by.

"I've prayed nonstop since the accident. Maria will wake up."

"I know she will," I said.

"Do you believe in God, James?"

"Yes." I was agnostic but didn't want to start a discussion.

"Pray for her. Ask God to restore her to us."

"I will, Grandma." For weeks I begged God to bring Maria back. I promised to take her place, to do anything in exchange for her life.

We sat together in a silent vigil while Maria's dad visited. The dark circles under his eyes paid testimony to his suffering.

One day, he interrupted our watch and said, "You're a good man, James. Maria chose wisely. I'll be honored to have you as my son-in-law."

"Maria's lucky to have a father like you. I look forward to calling you Dad."

Angelina dropped by on her breaks. More of her hair turned gray every time I saw her. She checked the equipment, the IV, and the catheter and brushed Maria's hair. Her constant attention to Maria's physical needs helped her cope with our shared anguish.

Where did those days go? Maria slept.

After a month, the Compagnos transferred her to a long-term care facility near Beaumont. Her grandparents called upon her every day. Maria's parents drove out often. Her little brother, Jon, could not bear to visit his sister unconscious in bed with tubes and monitoring equipment. Alicia flew in from New York for several days, sat at Maria's side, and left. She called her mother daily for updates, and I imagine she screamed voicelessly at the injustice meted out to her little sister.

I boarded the 7:00 a.m. flight to Ontario every Saturday morning and returned late Sunday afternoon. Mr. Compagno paid for my tickets and refused my offer to reimburse him.

"Maria needs you by her side," he said." I have money, don't worry about the cost. It's trivial."

I sat beside Maria for hours, inhaling that slight antiseptic odor ubiquitous in medical facilities, and charted her slow breathing. Her serene facial expression suggested tranquility, as though she enjoyed a quiet afternoon nap and would awaken refreshed at any moment.

Having you by my side is such a comfort, my love.
Please come back, Maria.
It's out of my control. I want to live, to do all the things we planned.
I know. What can we do to help you return?
Stay close by. Talk to me. It's dark, but your voice and touch give me hope.

Someone trimmed and shampooed Maria's curled tresses and painted her nails. But no, her slumber continued uninterrupted. I half-expected her to jump out of bed, ready for a night of dancing. How often had I lain beside her and watched her sleep, my heart so full of love? How many times until the last one?

Flowers arrived from her well-wishers, but only her closest friends and family continued by her side as the weeks progressed. From her favorite books, I read out loud as I stood vigil and hoped for a flicker of recognition.

Nothing yet, but I kept reading. I caught up on my studies and related details about our classes and what Paul, Laura, and our friends were doing. Everyone missed the Salon and prayed for her return to host the soirées that many enjoyed and viewed as essential to their Berkeley life.

"I ran into your friend, Monica, the other day. She prays for you to recover. Professor Gunn asked about you. He seemed genuinely distraught. Jim and Lila also wished you a speedy recovery. You see, the whole world is anxious for you to wake up, Maria."

Laura flew with me twice a month to spend the weekend by Maria's side, at her own expense. Paul visited less often. Laura and I needed each other because we shared mutual anguish and misery. I begged her to tell me more about their lives before I met them. Knowing something new about Maria tied me closer to her. I had faith that, if Maria overheard a bit of her life story from her best friend, the recollections might lead her away from whatever dark place she inhabited and revive her.

"Maria and I met on the first day of school, September 6th, 1965."

"How do you remember the date?"

"Konstantin Mostras, the Russian violinist whose music inspired me to switch from piano to violin, died that day."

"I grew up around the San Fernando Valley and never wanted to move to Claremont, leaving all my friends behind."

"First days in a new neighborhood are often disconcerting. How old were you then?"

"Eleven. Mom dragged me to school on the first day. I remember the principal, an older lady with bluish hair who reeked of lavender. After we filled out the forms, she escorted me to my new classroom and handed me over."

"My first day after we moved to Diamond Bar was scary, so I know what you mean. All the new faces in a strange place, nothing familiar, not sure what to expect."

"Exactly, and I couldn't do anything about it. The unfamiliar classroom terrified me. The desks in the sixth-grade class were tandems, where two students sat side-by-side. Mrs. Hammer put Maria and me together in the back row. We were the furthest point from her oak throne, which sat in the front between the window and the chalkboard."

"The Los Angeles County School District must have received an exceptional deal on those desks. My school used the same ones, " I added.

"Right. Some kids turned around to gawk at me: the tall, blondish girl with freckles, which I hated, and a deer-in-the-headlights stare. Maria tapped my arm to reassure me, 'Don't worry about them. They're curious. I'm Maria. Welcome to our class.'"

"She has a knack for making people feel comfortable. That's why everyone had a good time at our Salon."

"Maria knew everyone at school. People didn't move around much, so she and most students went up through the grades together. Small for her age, Maria projected fierceness and intelligence, confronting the other kids, especially the boys, with her fearlessness and courage to talk and argue, always willing to stand her ground. Maria would make a superb lawyer someday. She took me under her wing and acquainted me with the kids in our grade. I trusted her and got through those first awkward weeks."

"It's surprising how she can be almost shy and unassuming one minute and then transform into a bold and persuasive force without warning." I detected a change in Maria's breathing and glanced at her. "Do you hear us, *mi amor?*"

Laura continued. "She and I walked home together after school. Since I lived nearby, my mom gave us a snack before we went to my room and sat on my bed to do homework. I learned fast, but Maria was smarter. She excelled in every subject: math, English, science, history, and Spanish. I'd never studied a language before, except for a little Hebrew, and Maria drilled me on Spanish pronunciation and grammar. Her mother spoke only Spanish with Maria, Alicia, and Jon until they reached six. Maria understood everything but had to work on reading and writing. By year's end, she and I spoke together easily, much to the envy of our classmates, but to the delight of Mrs. Hammer, who spoke Spanish well, according to Maria."

"Yes. Maria honed my diction too." Maria's chest rose up and down slowly as she breathed.

"We took French in high school. French was so easy for her. What an amazing gift. Maria resembles one of those Europeans who learns to speak four or five languages."

"Comparative literature is the perfect venue for her language skills."

"She's fantastic at whatever she does."

"Through the sixth grade, Maria and I were inseparable. We went to each other's houses every day after school. Sometimes she sat and listened to me practice the violin, piano, or duets my mother and I played. She often scribbled in a notebook to capture the thoughts and moods the music aroused. Maria sat quietly with her eyes closed. Live music enchanted her."

"Maria likes classical music, but I didn't realize how significant an influence you had."

"Perhaps Catholicism influenced her love of lofty music. Her family went to Mass on Sundays. She felt everything so intensely and often disappeared into worlds she conjured as she sat absorbed in the music. Sometimes my mom stopped playing to ask her if she was all right. Maria wrote poems to reflect her feelings about our friendship. At the time, I thought them brilliant. Only much later did I understand how deeply she penetrated her emotions. She was courageous and willing to open herself to life in ways I could not. I wanted to follow her into those hidden places, but on some paths, she traveled alone. Like now."

Laura stopped talking and stared at Maria for several seconds. Tears slid down her cheeks after an anguished sigh. I pushed my chair alongside her and held her hand while a nurse slipped in unobtrusively and handed us a box of tissues.

We huddled together for several minutes as Laura released her bottled-up pain.

"Would you mind playing something on the violin, something she loved to hear?"

After she composed herself, Laura rendered a soft Jewish ballad so evocative that even Orpheus would be moved.

After Maria's accident, nothing prepared me for those nights when I awoke before dawn and reached over to her side of the bed to find emptiness, just a blank, vacant depression where she should be sleeping. I supposed she'd slipped away for a moment and would soon return. She hated the cold and loved her cozy bed. Maria adored her flannel sheets and heavy comforter, two feather pillows, and the small throw rug to shield her feet from the frigid hardwood floor.

"Why is it always so cold here?" Maria often complained during the winter. "Is that radiator doing anything?"

I climbed out of bed and touched it. "It's warm."

"Come back to bed and snuggle with me."

I missed her breathing like a metronome, keeping time throughout the night.

Nothing fortified me for the sickening realization that she lay in a hospital bed in those early hours, hooked up to a feeding tube, in a coma, four hundred miles away, alone.

For weeks, I avoided washing the sheets or any clothing imbued with her scent. I clung to anything reminding me of her essence as though life depended on its preservation. How I pressed on is a mystery, perhaps as an automaton shifting from moment to moment, oblivious to my surroundings, barely cognizant of the people near me. Yet the days slipped away whether I acknowledged them or not.

Several thick envelopes arrived by mail from Princeton and UC Berkeley. Both had accepted us into their graduate programs, which we hoped to attend as married doctorate candidates.

What about the wedding? There would be no wedding until she woke up. Would she still want to marry me? Yes, I thought so. Why not? I spent hours by her side, voicing my fears, my hopes, and our plans, whose outcome I harbored no doubt about except on a subconscious level. She listened to every word, understood me, and struggled to answer. Our fate relied on this belief: rest, Maria, no need to talk now. We'll speak after you recover.

In early May, Alicia greeted me at the gate as I came off my flight. Because she favored her sister, for a second, I thought Maria's astral body had stepped forward to hug me.

"Dad asked me to collect you. I am only in town until Monday."

"You went by? No change?"

"No, she's still sleeping." We never referred to Maria's condition as a coma.

We rode in silence as we headed east on Interstate 10. Alicia drove Maria's car. "The family appreciates you giving up your weekends to sit with her, but we understand if the burden's too much. It can't be easy for you."

The thought crossed my mind that she might ask me to stop my visits. I dismissed the notion.

"Stressful, yes, but I want to be by her side. I must be there. To not be with her would be like holding my breath. Please tell me you understand, Alicia."

"Of course. I have never been in love the way you two are, but I understand. We do not expect you to sacrifice your life for her."

"Maria *is* my life. Without her, my life as I know it would be over."

Alicia reached over and put her hand on my knee as she held back her tears. "Maria is fortunate to have you in her life. I envy her in a way," she said in subdued agony.

"I have no doubt you will find your love someday, none whatsoever," I replied as I put my hand on top of hers.

For the first time, I experienced the depth of Alicia's sorrow and fear for her little sister's fate and understood how profound sibling love ran, something I, as an only child, would never experience.

Not one of the faithful, my belief in God never surfaced as an issue. Yet, I continued to bargain with Him to return Maria from whatever forbidding realm entrapped her. Daily, I renewed my promise to do anything in exchange for her return.

Paul took me to visit his rabbi. My mother begged me to attend Mass on Sundays, but I struggled with the concept of God's Will. Laura stared into my eyes and sympathized. She and I maintained a silent covenant, bound to each other through the girl we loved, who had transformed our lives irrevocably with her love—the girl, now the woman who slept alone, beyond our reach.

Without warning, the end of the term, once so distant, loomed. I emerged from my dissociative fugue state near the final week of my university career. *Where had the previous nine weeks gone? Did the world end yesterday? Who am I?* After a long shower, I donned the last of my clean clothes. The laundry was long overdue.

Little time remained to write two twenty-page course papers and prepare for a final essay exam next Wednesday. I had submitted my senior thesis ten days ago. I scarcely remember writing the massive 100-page epic entitled *The Emergence of Magical Realism in 20th-century Latin American Literature.* I phoned LA to let the Compagnos know I would not fly down that weekend but on one of the midday flights next Thursday morning.

The rest of my undergraduate papers languished in unconscious confusion, waiting for me to sort them out. Days slipped past, writing, rewriting, and retyping. Incapable of eating, I lost several pounds. How could I eat when Maria lived off an IV drip? I forced myself to snack, making concentration easier once my nausea subsided.

Laura gave me concerned glances, and I ate some of her cooking to alleviate her fears. Despite my haggard condition, I wrote forty-odd pages on two disparate subjects in a seven-day marathon of adrenaline and caffeine-infused insomnia.

I spent all my time on campus. The flat depressed me because Maria still slept; I hated being alone in our room without her. I left her things where I found them. She wouldn't want me to mess up her system.

My roommates also found the apartment oppressive and did not hide their listlessness. They tiptoed around me, giving me space, checking in on me the way my mother used to when I lay sick in bed.

Paul only played songs in minor keys, not consciously, but because he couldn't shake the depression of Maria's fate, and the music expressed his real feelings, which he couldn't always show to the world.

Laura suffered. When Paul went out, she sometimes came in and sat on my bed.

"I hate this, James. The not knowing. I can hardly think of anything else but Maria lying there with all those tubes." Laura sobbed as she spoke. I wept with her in a forlorn embrace. Two lost souls powerless to resist our torment.

"We have to hang on, for her sake. Maria needs us to be strong."

"I'm trying."

"You have Paul and me. We love you."

Laura laid her head on my shoulder the way Maria used to.

"She's going to wake up soon."

"Please, God, bring Maria back to us," Laura cried in a voice tinged with hope and fear.

To relieve the tension, I suggested the three of us go to supper. We walked to a French bistro on Telegraph called Le Bateau Ivre (*The Drunken Boat*, a poem by Rimbaud). I ordered the Coquilles St Jacques, Maria would have requested the salmon with a panko crust, and Laura and Paul shared a Mesquite-grilled ribeye steak.

Laura ordered a bottle of a 1971 pinot noir. Paul motioned for us to make a toast. He topped off our glasses and steadied himself. Seldom demonstrably emotional, Paul summoned the wherewithal to speak publicly about his struggles.

"Here's to my best friends, now and forever, and Maria, who lives in our hearts. I love you all, especially you, Maria, *ma petite amie chérie*." Paul's French pronunciation was perfect. We touched glasses twice, took long sips of wine, and ignored the darkness. The previous ten weeks receded while we savored our meals and sought comfort in each other's company.

We passed a homeless panhandler outside the restaurant, crouched in a doorway. I carried no change but bore a doggy bag with my leftover supper.

I said to him, "Hey, have you eaten today?"

"Not today. I need some change to buy some food."

"Do you like seafood?"

"Yeah . . . I guess."

"Here, take this—it's still warm." I handed him the bag; Maria would have done the same. I suspected he had never enjoyed such a meal as the man tore into the sack.

On Wednesday afternoon, I took the essay exam final, writing savagely for almost three hours, filling two of the exam booklets we called Blue Books. Exhausted, I returned home and lay down.

I awoke the following day at sunrise, surprisingly rested after a dreamless night. I packed my dirty clothes into a gym bag, made myself a coffee, and called a cab to take me to the Oakland airport. Laura and Paul slept, and I tried not to wake them.

I placed into envelopes the letters I'd typed the day before, to inform the graduate programs that Maria and I would not attend in the Fall 1976 academic year, citing the circumstances of Maria's illness. I asked if we might receive preferential consideration when we reapplied next year. The letters fell into a mail slot at the airport, and I never thought of them again.

That afternoon, I sat beside Maria, who still slept serenely. I relayed how my finals went and how I would help her complete the last term to receive her degree. I told her I wouldn't attend commencement without her. We intended to wear the cap and gown and graduate with the rest of our class, which now struck me as an unnecessary and frivolous gesture. Let the Comp Lit department mail the diploma.

I read parts of my senior thesis, some poems by T.S. Eliot, some of Ezra Pound's *Cantos*, and Allen Ginsberg's *Howl*.

The first line from *Howl* now made sense. Having experienced a bit of madness, the absurdity around me, I became delirious, unable to accept why bad things happened to undeserving people.

Perhaps we were not as noble as we believed. My selfishness and self-absorption were personality traits ameliorated by Maria's loving kindness and understanding. She made me better and inspired me to want to be better. *Maria, please wake up.*

Graduation arrived. Four years of university training ended one foggy afternoon in June punctuated by anxious *Sturm und Drang* and then nothing.

I moved into Maria's old room at the Compagno house, careful not to disrupt her space too much. She had kept a set of clothes in LA to avoid packing a bag whenever she visited. I stuffed my clothes into an empty drawer and cleared a small section of her closet. Every article of clothing expressed her personality, from bright grays to rusty reds to faded pastels. I pictured her standing before the mirror, her finger on her cheek as she pondered her mood and how she wished to express her emotions through fashion.

I love that you're staying in my room.
I didn't think you'd mind.
Pas du tout, cher, reste pour toujours.
Merci, mais seulement jusqu'à ce que tu te réveilles.

From her bed, I gazed mindlessly through the window at the small bay tree, which swayed in the breeze and cast a green shadow across the cream-colored walls. Lilac wafted up from the garden. How often had Maria reclined in the same spot, her back supported by several pillows as mine was then? She used to lounge on this bed, read, write in her journal, do homework, and live the life of a teenage girl. I intuited her presence all around me, crying openly and without shame.

A shelf on one wall held all the books she'd read through the years, principally volumes of fiction, literature, essays, and criticism. Arranged in alphabetical order were several books in Spanish and French. This place, her sanctuary, became mine as well. Everything around me reflected her and instilled hope we would lie beside each other soon.

I visited the extended care facility every day. Since Marc and Angelina Compagno worked weekdays, I borrowed Maria's BMW for the 45-minute drive. Maria kept several cassettes of her favorite rock tunes in the car. She loved Bob Dylan, the Beatles, Cat Stevens, and It's a Beautiful Day. The music gave me the idea to buy a portable tape player for Maria to listen to her music while she slept.

Always watching for any reaction, I rotated among our chats, music, and reading aloud. Sometimes Maria's eyelids fluttered, or she exhaled more forcefully than usual. The attending physician said these autonomic reactions occurred. Maria still exhibited brain activity, which was a hopeful sign. The staff never gave me false hope but assured me she might awaken at any time.

Another week elapsed. I returned to Berkeley to fetch my car and drove to Los Angeles down Highway 101, reluctant to face another long drive through the monotonous farmlands adjacent to Interstate 5. Despite my itinerary change, I remained unaware of the trip or time passing. My thoughts focused on Maria and whether I should search for a job.

My savings dwindled almost to nothing, and I could not impose on the Compagno household forever. I considered moving to Diamond Bar but preferred being closer to the facility. Her grandfather offered me a bed at the ranch, but I couldn't decide. Usually resolute, I grappled with every decision, no matter how trivial. I drifted from one day to the next without my sleeping beauty, confused and indecisive.

Paul and Laura busied themselves with music rehearsals to prepare for their debut summer tour as a working band. Laura visited twice for several hours, powerless to withstand the emotional strain of her friend's condition. She clung to me as she sobbed. I supposed my presence helped her cope, and I was grateful to be there for her. Laura was my lifeline to Maria as her oldest friend.

My parents and I agonized over Maria's plight whenever I visited.

"Any signs of recovery?" my stepfather asked, the concern in his voice palpable.

"No change yet. She's steady."

"I'm sorry this happened, Jim. Maria is my kind of gal."

I didn't know what to make of his comment. He had never expressed strong emotion about Maria before, yet his sorrow was genuine.

Mom loved Maria, the daughter she'd always wanted. Too wrapped up in my grief, I did not understand how profoundly Mom endured her loss, not only of Maria but also of my older sister, who died soon after birth.

"Gabriella lay helpless in that hospital for several weeks, alone. I visited her as much as possible, but I had to work. I cried every time they let me into the N.I.C.U. to see her."

"What about her father?" I asked.

"Oh, he died six months before. A heart attack at 46, can you imagine?"

The scene crystallized: my mother's older husband died suddenly, leaving her alone and pregnant. And then her daughter, born healthy, suddenly turns ill and dies six weeks later.

"I know what Angelina and Marc are going through, the fear, the uncertainty, the heartache. And what you're suffering too, Jim." Mom put her arms around me and held me the way she used to when I was small. I became that little boy again and sobbed into my mother's shoulder. John, perhaps overwhelmed, left the room.

For Mom, it wasn't just Maria's condition but the monstrous possibility of losing another daughter that demoralized her.

"Try to be strong, Jim. I can't lose you too. I couldn't bear it."

Sunday, June 29. The day began as one of those perfect early-summer days in Los Angeles before the substantial heat set in. Marc, Angelina, and I drove to the facility to spend the morning with Maria. Our moods had lightened when the doctors reported that Maria's brain wave patterns showed increased activity during a routine EEG.

"Doctor Yang said the readouts indicated she's still responding to outside stimuli and that our voices, now more than ever, might help," Angelina said.

"So the three of us should sit in the room and chat? Sounds good to me," Marc said as he merged into the fast lane and increased our speed.

"I've been talking to her since the beginning," I said. "Maybe it's finally paying off."

We arrived at the facility and parked in an almost empty parking lot.

"Where is anyone today?" I mused out loud.

The usual weekend receptionist hung up the phone when we entered the lobby.

"Hi, Miranda. How's it going?" Her normally pleasant face appeared ashen. "You're not feeling well?"

"I'm okay, Mr. Montez."

"Good. We'll go on in, thanks."

"Wait. The doctor said not to let you back until she's talked to you."

Doctor Yang pushed through the double doors with a hard cast on her face; a wave of cold terror tore through me. I held my breath as she spoke.

"Hello. Can we sit for a minute?" Doctor Yang motioned us to the leather chairs in the lounge area next to the front desk.

"This morning at 6:39, approximately . . . Maria passed. We believe from a brain aneurysm, but we won't be sure without an autopsy. I'm so sorry."

I slumped into my chair. Angelina Compagno let out a muted howl and fell against her husband. For a moment, I registered nothing around me as though expelled into the vacuum of space.

I'm still asleep; this is not real, were my first thoughts as I struggled for breath. Maria's father held her mother as she sobbed inconsolably. Marc stared at the wall, tearful, his breathing rapid and shallow. My clammy hands shook.

Doctor Yang looked at me with compassion and anguish. How many times had she given awful news like this?

The receptionist glanced over but averted her eyes, concerned she intruded on our grief. The poor girl's face reflected our misery as the reality of Maria's death tore us apart.

Somehow, I moved to the Compagnos and wrapped my arms around them. Angelina grabbed me, and we hung on to each other like we were in the last few seconds of a plane crash. Marc wrapped his arms around us. We grappled for oxygen. I went numb, unable to feel my legs.

Time stood still. We collapsed on the sofa. I glanced outside through the glass doors to the parking lot as a wind arose out of the east, deforming the palm trees. We held each other to prevent the gust from carrying us off.

No one spoke. Doctor Yang stayed with us until we recovered from the initial wave of incredulity.

"Mr. and Mrs. Compagno. You may come back and see her now if you wish."

Marc nodded and helped his wife to her feet. Angelina's years of training must have kicked in as she composed herself. Years of exposure to the fragility of life and grieving families must have given her the strength to walk down that long hall to view her daughter's body.

I struggled to my feet to accompany them but could not stand.

Doctor Yang touched my shoulder, "I'm sorry, Mr. Montez. Immediate family only for now."

Unable to object and unsure I wanted to see her lifeless, I lingered as the lounge compressed around me, immobile, except for my hands shaking. I sank into the chair, inhaling citrus and lilac from the flowers on Miranda's desk.

The doctor took them back for one last view of their daughter before transferring her to the coroner for an autopsy.

Miranda wiped tears from her eyes as she greeted other visitors filtering in. Silent, I stared out the window, questioning why I believed today started out better than any other day.

We returned to Claremont. I have no memory of the journey except for fastening my seat belt and suddenly pulling into the Compagnos' driveway.

Maria's grandparents and Jon arrived soon after, followed by Laura's parents and my mother. My stepfather, unwilling to expose his emotions to others, remained behind.

"Dad wanted to come but couldn't," Mom told me. "He's here in spirit."

Alicia took the next flight out. Paul and Laura raced down Interstate 5 after breaking off a rehearsal.

Everyone congregated in the Compagnos' living room, bewildered, silent, floundering in our disbelief and disillusionment. Grandma Compagno lit several candles. Until then, I loved the large, airy seating area with its comfortable sectionals, stylist pillows, and overstuffed chairs. Now, without Maria, the space struck me as cold and impersonal.

Had no one anything to say? The tapers flickered. One went out, and I relit it.

We huddled together, united by grief accompanied by wordless raw emotions, each of us lost in our somber reflections.

Grandpa Compagno held his daughter-in-law as she sobbed. Grandma Compagno and Laura's mom went to the kitchen to prepare food.

Laura's dad, Joshua Shapiro, put his arm around Marc's shoulder.

Maria's mom recovered after several minutes and spoke, "Josh, did you bring your guitar by chance? Would you mind playing some music my daughter liked?"

"Let me get it from the car," he said, thankful for a reason to leave the oppressive sadness of the room.

In the meantime, Grandma Compagno served some improvised cheese and crackers and poured white wine for whoever wanted some.

Joshua Shapiro removed his Spanish guitar from the case and tuned it.

"Let's see. How about this one?" I recognized *Capricho Catalán* by Isaac Albéniz in C minor from the first few chords.

How often had we sat in our living room on Russell Street as Laura played this soulful melody, with Maria in enraptured silence, her eyes closed as the music transported her?

"Laura, would you play that one more time, please?" Maria begged.

"Sure. Would you like to hear it on the piano instead?"

Maria's dad arranged the funeral and scheduled the burial for next Sunday. They wished to bury her near her maternal grandparents in Oak Park Cemetery, a serene oasis in the middle of the city.

For the first time in many years, I wandered to the abandoned cemetery where my childhood fantasy, Charlotte, remained buried. This graveyard crouched, hidden and neglected at the bottom of Elephant Hill, less than a mile from Pomona along a railroad right-of-way.

Within sight of the old gate, I turned away, ready to retrace my steps, incapable of entering. A faint voice called to me. The hairs on the back of my neck stiffened. I glanced over my shoulder at the burial ground—nerves, the cry of someone I couldn't see, or the gusts through the fence. I tried to walk away, but my feet would not respond.

I relented and pushed open the rusty metal entry. Vines entangled themselves throughout the creaking hinges, and I ripped them away until the gate yielded.

In early July, rampant growth clotted the graves. A musty odor lingered. Compelled to wade deeper into my boyhood sanctuary, I shuffled towards the stone I remembered, to the one place that provided solace throughout my adolescence. Soil and vines covered poor Charlotte's gravestone. I cleared a spot with my hands and sat down.

I remained for a long time in numbed silence, watching the sun dip below the oak trees. "I'm sorry I didn't visit sooner. You know how it is, life and all."

Of course. For me, almost no time has passed.
Is there no time where you are?
Time flows like the wind, always in flux.
I see.
I'm sorry for your loss, my friend.
You know what happened?
You have been unbeguiling ever since your teenage years.
I've never hidden anything from you.
Yes. You make Purgatory bearable.

Paul, Laura, Alicia, and I congregated on the Shabbat for the first day of our modified Shiva. The darkness under Paul's eyes suggested he had not slept much. He recited the Mourner's Kaddish in Hebrew, which affirmed the Jewish Faith and reminded us that no mourner is alone in their grief. These rituals existed to console the living—the dead required no solace.

After the ceremony, Alicia brewed some green tea for us.

Paul asked her, "How do you like living in Manhattan?"

"I have mixed feelings. Such a vast and noisy city. Sometimes I dream of the ranch, though I don't know if it will ever be the same without Maria."

"Nothing will be the same without her," Laura said.

I asked Alicia, "What happens to Smokie?"

"She'll be my horse from now on. But you guys can ride her whenever you want. I won't be on the West Coast that much."

"And the job? Is investment banking the dream job you imagined?" Laura asked.

"It's a great business if you like sixty- and seventy-hour weeks. I'm putting my career on the line, being away for a week, but I don't care. This is my sister." Alicia broke down sobbing. Laura moved to comfort her.

"Maria had so much to live for. I feel so selfish not spending more time with her when I could," Alicia moaned.

"There's never enough time," I said. "Maria and I spent almost every day together for the last three years, and it wasn't enough. What I wouldn't give for one more minute with her."

Everyone nodded. We retreated inside ourselves and finished our tea.

Sunday morning was dry and hot. I arrived at the empty chapel twenty minutes before the scheduled ceremony. The unopened casket had already been laid out surrounded by flowers. Numerous lit white candles lined the walls. From the back row, I found a place to wait. The funeral director entered.

"I'm here to open the casket for viewing. It won't take but a second."

"Please," was all I said.

My mom and stepfather arrived. John hated funerals.

"Thanks for coming, Dad."

He shook his head and mumbled something.

Mom once explained his aversion: "John was a teenager during the Second World War but too young to enlist. Over half the boys he grew up around came home in body bags, including his older brother. For two years, all John did was attend funerals. Now, he can't stand them."

The Compagno clan filed in. Marc shook my hand, and Angelina hugged me every time we met. Alicia herded her brother Jon, who clearly wanted to be somewhere else. Paul and the Stern family entered the chapel and found seats, followed by the Shapiros. Everyone wore black.

Paul excused himself and came back to talk to me.

"How're you holding up, James?"

"I'm numb. Everything feels so surreal. I've given up hope this is all a nightmare. If it is, I'm never waking up."

"Yeah. We're all still in shock. Laura constantly cries and can't eat, sleep, or play music."

"Nothing will be as it was. We must learn to cope, I guess."

"It will take time."

"You got that right," I said, sighing.

Tears flowed, and quiet, unabashed sobbing echoed throughout the chapel.

After a few minutes, Marc Compagno walked to the flower-strewn casket to pay his final respects. He recited a prayer and crossed himself. With a deep breath, Angelina and Alicia followed. Both uttered a blessing and made the sign of the cross.

Furiously counting her rosary beads, Grandma Compagno did not approach. Her husband leaned over and whispered something in her ear, but she shook her head. He ambled upfront, wobbling slightly, and stood before the open coffin, grasping one side to steady himself as he beheld his beautiful granddaughter for the last time. His sobs reached me from the back of the chapel as my stomach, already in knots, tightened further. Finally, he crossed himself and returned to his seat, half the man he was when he entered.

My folks, followed by Laura and Paul's parents, paid their respects. No one lingered for long.

I compelled myself to approach the casket to gaze one last time at my lovely girl lying motionless as though asleep, her head supported by a pale blue satin pillow. The pallor of my dark-skinned beauty, drained of sunlight, left me bereft of sanity. I wanted to scream but could not find a voice. I fought the urge to reach out and touch her cheek, a face I had felt, kissed, and loved for eternity. How could I remember her flesh as cold and lifeless? I needed to hold on to my memory of her: warm in our bed, her soft breathing after making love as we drifted together in some quiet place.

I love you, James.
I love you more, chérie.

Mr. Compagno offered a heartfelt eulogy in a subdued, monotone voice. I listened without understanding until he retook his seat and nodded to signal my turn. I moved to the front to acknowledge the expectant faces, red and tearful.

"Now it's eight years ago, I saw Maria across the ice at our local rink, wearing her favorite beret." The audience nodded as they, too, remembered.

"That first meeting changed everything. One look, one casual glance, captured my heart forever. Maria had a way about her. You all know what I mean. People and animals who came under her influence responded positively. So full of life, so full of love, she brought out the best in everyone. The best in me, for sure. I loved Maria; I will always love her . . . I know she would want us to celebrate her life, to move on with our own. Honestly, I don't know how to do that yet."

I stopped as emotion strangled my voice. The teary-eyed heads nodded in agreement as they waited for me to continue. Before publicly weeping, I concluded, "Maria was the best of us, and we are all the better for . . . " My heart was about to explode. I collapsed on the nearest seat and buried my head in my hands.

No one spoke. Like leaded weights, we endured in silence the immense ache that gripped us in a relentless vice of agony and bitterness over our loss. First, one attendee and another stood, glanced at the casket shrouded with orchids and roses, and filed out into the pitiless blue sky of that hot July morning that any other time would have been glorious.

The priest sprinkled the coffin with holy water and incense at the gravesite. We sang a farewell hymn in subdued voices carried on the wind. After the Rite of Committal, we stood motionless as they lowered Maria's casket into a plot sheltered by mature laurel trees.

After the service, we traveled east to the ranch for the reception. Grandma Compagno already had prepared refreshments. She served hors d'oeuvres and chianti or tea. Most of us drank wine.

Olivia decided the crowd was too rambunctious for her, and she disappeared down the hall to Maria's bedroom. Grandma told me she had slept there every night since the accident. Olivia knew.

Since this was my parents' first visit, Grandpa Compagno offered them a tour of the ranch. Mom declined, but John agreed. He grew up in a rural area, and the farm reminded him of home.

Paul and Laura's parents camped on the couch, discussing Claremont's Jewish community.

Paul, Laura, Alicia, and I headed to the stables.

Smokie immediately came to the front of her stall when Alicia approached. I think she was happy to see her. She grabbed a brush and went to work on her mane.

"How is my darling? Did you miss me?" Smokie stamped her hoof.

"Do horses have good memories?" Paul asked Alicia.

"Yes, for people who treat them well."

"Do you think she knows Maria is gone?"

"That's a good question, James. It's possible." Alicia continued brushing.

Old Yeller stuck his head over the gate and neighed. I stroked his head, and he licked my hand.

In a loud voice, I said, "Let's take the horses out."

Alicia and Laura agreed.

"I'll sit this one out, guys. You have fun. I want some more wine anyway." Paul never showed interest in learning to ride and returned to the house.

We bridled the horses. Laura helped me saddle Old Yeller.

Laura took one of the boarded horses, a chestnut-colored ten-year-old named Miss Daisy, while Alicia rode Smokie.

The stable carried a stash of cowboy hats, so we each grabbed one to keep the afternoon sun from causing heat stroke. We pointed our horses in a familiar direction, where they made a beeline to the creek.

Once the horses reached the trees, Alicia revved Smokie into a fast canter, and Laura followed. Old Yeller, not to let the girls get the best of him, picked up speed with no prodding from me.

After our run, we left our mounts near the creek and found a shady spot on the grass a few yards down from where Maria and I had spent many afternoons picnicking, among other things.

"This was Maria's favorite spot," Laura said. "We always came here during the summers."

Alicia added, "My sister and I started coming here when I was seven and she was four. We rode bikes until we got horses."

"How come you never got your own horse like Smokie?" I said.

Alicia tossed a pebble into the creek. "Smokie was supposed to be mine, but Maria wanted her so bad I gave her up. After that, I lost interest in owning my own, though Grandpa would have bought me one any time I asked."

"But you love horses," Laura said.

"Yes, I do. More than anything, but not as much as my little sister. Smokie and her took to each other. I wanted them to both be happy."

Alicia teared. "I love Maria so much." I wrapped my arm around Alicia and pulled her toward me. She buried her head in my shoulder and wept.

Laura moved closer. The three of us consoled each other in what had to be one of the most stressful and exhausting days of our young lives.

PART III

CHAPTER 22

Paul remained in LA after the funeral to meet with a promoter and planned to join us in Berkeley later in the week. Laura and I headed north in separate cars. I drove for a hundred years, ignoring the six-hour ordeal through the San Emigdio Mountains, the Central Valley, and the Altamont Pass, until I arrived at Russell Street for the last time.

I drifted into the living room and lay on the sofa in the warmth of the afternoon sun. This room often stirred pleasant memories from another lifetime when we believed our naïve idyllic existence would extend forever.

Death and tragedy only happened in books or to other people, but now we confronted realities we never anticipated and were ill-prepared for. Of course, I spoke for myself, yet I was sure Laura and Paul had similar outlooks. At least they had a new life to step into, their music career about to take off. When I informed the grad schools I would not attend in the fall, I had no plan, no goals, just overwhelming grief and fatigue that made reflection and decision-making almost impossible.

I fell asleep. Laura stood over me as I awoke.

"I'm sorry to wake you," she said softly.

"Giving my eyes a rest. How was the drive?"

"About like yours, I suspect—long and tedious."

"Yes."

I slid over to allow room for Laura beside me. We held each other's hand in silence, lost in our separate worlds of sorrow. Twilight fell across the room. Still, we sat. An occasional car passed under our bay window, a dog barked nearby, and water gurgled through the pipes underneath us as our neighbors ran the faucet. I shivered in the warm room. Laura rested her head on my shoulder as Maria used to.

We curled up together on the sofa until Laura dragged herself to the kitchen and boiled some water. I joined her at the wooden table we had scoured Berkeley to find, a table on which we shared countless meals and conversations, a surface wide enough to spread out and study, a communal table for an elegiac community now dissolving.

Laura fed a handful of vermicelli into the simmering water and added salt. I opened a bottle of red wine and poured two glasses as she served the pasta *al dente* sprinkled with Parmesan. Habitual movements we performed in silence. We picked at our meal, lost in our cheerless musings.

After I cleared the plates and rinsed the dishes, we remained at the table to finish our wine.

"I'm so tired, Laura. I want to sleep, but I'm not sure if I can."

"I'm scared. What happens next?" She swallowed the last of her wine. "I don't want to be alone tonight. Stay with me."

Laura took a shower and opened her bedroom window to let in the night air. She changed the sheets and pillowcases while I bathed. I needed a shave, but let it go; perhaps tomorrow.

Laura already lay in bed when I entered her room. Her eyes opened and beckoned me to her. I dropped my robe on the floor and climbed in beside her. We embraced as she sobbed, clinging to me, afraid of what might happen if she let go.

"I miss her, James, so much. Will it always feel this way?"

The enormity of our loss pressed down on us and would have crushed us without the strength we sought in each other.

"Promise me we will be friends for the rest of our lives, no matter what happens after this."

"I promise, Laura, for as long as we live, maybe a little longer."

She hugged me tighter, and we fell asleep, exhausted. Several hours of oblivion granted us some ephemeral peace.

I awoke at dawn and stared at the ceiling, unsure of where I was. Laura slept beside me, her hair spread across my chest, the warmth of her body offering comfort. Birdsong filtered through the window. I sat up and watched her sleep for several minutes, contemplating a plan to leave, to escape somewhere, to a place emotionally untainted. Change my life. Maria talked about a tour of México. Self-imposed exile to a foreign county seemed like the right idea and perhaps the only path left.

I eased out of bed, found my robe, and returned to my room, careful not to wake Laura. To let the chilled morning air refresh the staleness, I cracked the door to the patio. Expanded sunlight reflected off the windows of the surrounding houses. I fell on my bed with my feet dangling and glanced up.

Why did I keep staring at ceilings? Because they stretched flat and empty like me. I projected my misery upon them like overhead canvases. Would this dull ache ever subside? So many questions and never an answer. Prospects menacingly loomed overhead, resembling the uneven, stuccoed canopy, with imperfect cobwebs in the corners, devoid of meaning. *What will I do without her? How can I live? Should I?*

When I sniffed coffee brewing, I ascended through various layers of fitful dreams until my eyes opened. The sun shone brightly as the heat of midmorning poured into the room. I pulled some clean but wrinkled clothes out of my overnight bag, where I'd dropped them the night before. I washed my face, almost afraid to stare at my reflection—what a mess. My eyes were puffy, my face unshaven, and I hated my long hair.

Laura poured hot milk over the espresso and slid my cup towards me as I settled into a chair like I was 80. She had not slept well either.

"We are a sight, aren't we?" she said.

"The last three months have been pure torment."

"Awful, yes."

"I've been thinking." Laura waited for me to continue. "I decided to make the México trip Maria and I discussed."

"Sounds right."

"Also, I'm moving from Berkeley forever. I'm paid up to the end of the month. If you can't find someone for my room soon, I'll pay for another month and leave all the furniture. Renting a furnished room should be no trouble."

"I'll ask around. I think Will needs a place."

I chuckled. "If you moved Manny into the other small bedroom, the whole quartet would live under one roof."

"Paul and I decided to keep Russell Street until October or November. Then we'll move back to LA. Why pay rent when we are traveling much of the time anyway?"

The unspoken realization between us sank in. We were splitting up not only our household but our futures too. Our lives together vanished in a breath. Our college days ended moments after they began.

"I will never forget our time with each other, here in this house, in this town. The last four years have been fantastic. You are a great friend, Laura. I will keep our promise."

"I know you will. You can always reach us through my parents or Paul's. What are your plans today?"

"Maybe it's too soon, but I must pack up my room. I want to be on my way tomorrow or the next day."

"Paul will be up tomorrow. At least wait for him."

"I will. Would you help me with Maria's things?" Laura suppressed a tremor.

"Of course."

We pulled some folded boxes out of a closet and retaped them. Laura helped me pack Maria's clothes. I suggested she keep whatever she liked, and the rest we would donate to a nearby thrift shop. I bundled the clothes I might need and threw what remained into a carton, along with our favorite books. We consolidated Maria's journals and creative writings to return to her parents. I wanted to read them but dared not, afraid I might collapse from emotional fragility.

Laura found a wrapped package in the back of the closet.

"This has your name on it, something for you."

Maria had concealed a birthday present for me. *Maria, if only you were hidden there too.* I carefully removed the diaphanous blue paper: a book of poems by José Gorostiza called *Muerte Sin Fin*.

"Laura, my heart is breaking," I said as I collapsed, sobbing while Laura comforted me, cocooned in the agony of loss. "Why did this happen?"

I had hoped you would like the poems.
How ironic I would give you poetry called Death Without End, *considering.*
Are you really dead, Maria?
My body is gone, but I am not.

Our history together was packed up, crated, and consigned in less than a day. I dusted, swept, cleaned the windows, vacuumed, loaded my car with whatever I planned to take, and waited for Paul. He arrived the following day and found Laura and me sipping coffee in the kitchen. We spoke of mundane subjects until Paul broached the topic we dreaded.

"So, this is the coda to our four-part harmony?"

"We can't play the same tune forever. The rondeau always comes last, " I said.

"Yeah, that's right."

"How long will you be in México?" he asked.

"Six to eight weeks. That should be enough to clear my head. Mr. Compagno said he would find me a job at the plant when I return."

"Send some postcards to the Del Mar house. After the LA gigs, we booked further appearances in San Diego through August and September. We'll be back in the Bay Area after that. In January, we go to Amsterdam."

I nodded. "I have a long drive." The reality of saying goodbye to my best friends finally took hold.

"I'll miss you, James. You've been a great friend. I love you, man." We hugged each other. "Let's stay in touch."

"We will. I love you guys."

"Our debut is July 23rd. I left you a ticket at the Whisky a Go Go's will call, if you're still around."

"Thanks."

"If you need anything, please reach out to Paul or me. Be safe, okay?"

Paul and Laura accompanied me to the car and stood by while I backed out of the carport for the last time. I sighed when I caught their wave in the mirror as I headed down the treelined street I had grown to love.

I surrendered Berkeley, the university, my career, my optimism, and the life I cherished. That part of my life ended there, and a darker, protracted period of desolation commenced.

CHAPTER 23

I arranged an excursion to México and the Dominican Republic to visit my dad for the first time since our falling out years ago. Guilt plagued me whenever I acknowledged that I never gave him much thought, though I'm unsure why. I was an afterthought in his life, so I made him one in mine, perhaps unfairly.

Several letters had arrived, scribbled while he was drinking, no doubt, and I'd ignored them. Now I needed to talk, to show him his assessment was wrong. My long hair and manner of dress did not preclude me from earning a college degree from one of the best universities in the world. The need to prove something to him compelled me. That, and the intense loneliness and urge to connect to some tangible past.

I loaded a backpack and flew to San Diego, where I took a bus to Calexico, crossed the border into Mexicali, and boarded the train to Guadalajara, a 1,200-mile, 30-hour journey. I dozed off and on, waking to glimpse the scenery slip past.

Once past Mexicali, we traveled through the desert until the insufferable heat and humidity of coastal Mazatlán made sleep impossible. Further south, the stops became more frequent as we approached Guadalajara.

The trip did not vanish entirely in a haze, though many details faded almost as quickly as they occurred. I had no plan, itinerary, or goal but to travel through a strange land where I was an untethered transient, free to wander.

The sun had already set when we reached the end of the line. I took a cab to a no-name, rundown hotel near Guadalajara's center, one the *taxista* recommended. Checked into my room, I collapsed on the small, lumpy bed. The narrow, cracked ceiling stared back at me as the street noise echoed around me. *Why am I here?*

I slept for twelve fitful hours.

After a day in Guadalajara, I found nothing memorable or charming about the massive city. I drifted southwest on local buses to other towns on my map and passed through so many places whose names I cannot recall.

So many towns, filled with people I would never know, went about their lives as I passed unnoticed through their cities. The pain of the last few months subsided into a dull ache. Paranoid about drinking the water, I bought beer *bien fría* or spirits wherever I traveled, grateful for the anesthetizing effects of alcohol.

Small hotels near the center of town, a little outside the tourist zone, sheltered me. I seldom spoke English. The people treated me cordially and were often curious about a gringo who spoke Spanish. I mentioned my Dominican father, Spanish grandfather, and Italian mother and adopted the Spanish version of my name, Jaime. Sometimes, I experienced a real kinship whenever I forgot to think of myself as the *el otro,* the other.

One day, I shed my American clothes and bought brands made locally. Adept at accents, I assumed Mexican intonations and vocabulary until people stopped asking me where I was from. Despite the camouflage, youthful alienation influenced my solitary travels through a country at war with itself in ways unfathomable to an outsider. Perhaps I projected my unconscious struggles into my environment to externalize my inner turmoil.

I spent a week in Oaxaca, hanging out at outdoor cafés and bars, alternating between coffee, beer, and spirits. I read some books I bought at a local bookstore and scribbled in a leather notebook I carried. At night, I sat inebriated on a bench in the *zócalo*, listening to local music and chatting with whoever happened by.

One morning, I took a bus headed northeast toward the Gulf of Mexico. Along the way, I jotted more observations in my journal. Distracted or perhaps a little drunk, I left my notebook on one of the buses headed to Mérida. The bus pulled away with my diary still on board. With Maria gone, I realized how many absentminded things she had saved me from. Would I ever manage to live without her?

Ten days passed since my sojourn in Oaxaca—ten blank days lost forever. I awoke from a dream ensconced in a darkened hotel room, unsure who or where I was. An empty bottle of tequila rolled around on the floor, which I kicked as I climbed out of bed. The plaque on the door said Hacienda San Marco, Mérida. What day was it?

I checked out and brooded in a café on one of the *zócalos*. My father's new wife, Adita, had consigned a plane ticket at the Mérida-Rejon Airport counter, and today seemed like the right time to skip town.

After a quick layover in Puerto Rico, a crowd herded me through Dominican Customs, where I paid a $5 entry fee and exited among a throng of people who waited for passengers. Against the railing, with a bemused grin, leaned my father, wearing his signature *guayabera*. As he straightened up and sauntered over, I noted that he had aged in the last five years, heavier and grayer. We hugged briefly. He asked about my flight, and we headed to the parking lot.

"What did you think of México?" he asked in Spanish.

"A fascinating country, impoverished, but the people are warm and big-hearted."

"I think you'll find the Dominicans are the same. It's good to see you, son. I've missed you."

On the way back to Santo Domingo, he pulled out a bottle of Brugal, and we sipped rum as we drove. Some laws were either more liberal or unenforced. No minimum drinking age existed, and few looked skeptically at open containers in the car unless an accident occurred.

We made the 34-kilometer drive without mishap and arrived at Dad and Adita's luxurious townhouse as a rain shower descended. I commented on the neighborhood's tranquility, given the building sat two blocks from the Capitol, a sizable, park-like compound surrounded by a tall wrought-iron fence and guarded by a detachment of soldiers armed with automatic weapons. In a deadpan response, Dad described the instability of Latin American governments like this: "If they ever start a little war in there, this neighborhood will be the hottest place in town."

Adita, thirty-something, tall, and beautiful, shared her home with my father and her three young children. The youngest son gave up his room for me. Adita worked in the travel business and spoke fluent English and French. The Dominican government had stationed her father, a former military officer in the U.K. and France, as a military attaché. He educated his only daughter in foreign schools, where she absorbed the local languages quickly. She married young, had children, and dumped her husband when she caught him cheating. Wrongs against her were seldom forgotten or forgiven.

Adita and I warmed to each other immediately and often chatted away in French, much to my father's annoyance.

"Why can't you two speak Spanish or English? Are you trying to hide something?"

"*No, mi amor*," Adita answered in Spanish. "I don't often get to practice my French, and your son speaks so wonderfully. I feel like I am back in Paris." Although I had not yet visited Paris, my *professeurs* hailed from France and drilled Metropolitan French into us. Countless hours of French films had also honed my accent. However, I could not fool real Parisians, who spotted my foreign inflections immediately.

We relaxed in Santo Domingo, passing the time sightseeing, visiting Dad's friends, eating, and drinking lots of rum and a satisfying beer called *Presidente*. I gained several pounds back from the fifteen I'd lost. Adita said I looked too thin, but the daily rice, beans, plátanos, and yuca soon filled me out.

I'd trimmed my hair before I left California. In his less-than-subtle way, my father now suggested I would be more comfortable in the torrid heat with shorter hair and offered to take me to his barber. The barber draped the salon cape over me and awaited my instructions.

"Give me a *corte de equipo*." The term "crew cut" escaped me, so I guessed. The clippers ran up and down my skull as hair fell in clumps to the floor, liberating me from a long-carried burden. I decided never to grow my hair long again. My life had changed, and my appearance must change with it.

Dad waited for me next door in a café. When I walked in, he looked pleased. "Now, that's the right style for this climate."

"Why not get your money's worth?" I dropped into a chair across from him and ran my hand over my closely cropped skull. "My head feels lighter and cooler."

"You look better." Dad waved to the waiter and ordered two more espressos, "*Trae dos cafecitos, por favor*." The haircut cost me nothing and kept peace in the family. I was too depleted to fret over things that no longer mattered.

After my father had left California for Santo Domingo several years ago, he arrived without much of a plan. Uncle Francisco, his eldest brother by 20 years, retired and sold his business to my dad. Francisco employed Adita, a part-time bookkeeper who wielded a firm grasp of international markets and decided to stay on once she met my father.

Adita split her time between the travel agency she started after her divorce from her first husband and the Montez export business, keeping her busy and providing enough money to live well by Dominican standards. Intermittent financial assistance from her ex-husband also helped. While Dad handled the operational aspects of the company, Adita managed the back-office functions and client relations.

Dad explained the business this way: "I'm in the forestry business, but more like mining than tree cutting. I mine lumber for export."

"How can you mine lumber?"

"The Asian shipping industry uses a wood derived from a tree called Lignum Vitae or *Guyancán*. We also call it Ironwood. Typhoons knock these trees down and bury them in the soil. The Dominican Republic is full of *Guyancán*. My crew digs them up, mills them into manageable sizes, and ships them off to Hong Kong."

"But why would ships need lumber? No one builds wooden ships, do they?"

"Lignum Vitae is a super-dense wood infused with natural oils, which gives it reduced friction and high load capacity. The shipbuilders make wood bearings for use in propeller shafts. Since these bearings wear out, they replace them as needed."

Dad sipped his beer before continuing. "I ship four to six loads annually at 12 to 15 grand profit each. That's in dollars, not pesos. We only work six to eight months yearly because of the rain, which is not a bad life."

"*Guyancán* sounds like a profitable business."

"I'm about to start another harvest cycle next week. Why not come along and see how it's all done?"

"Sure, Dad. My schedule's open."

One morning after a drinking binge, we climbed into Dad's Jeep and headed west to the *campo,* to a place near Jaraqua National Park. Dad had to secure permits from a government agency to dig for Lignum Vitae after paying a modest *mordida*. All exporters paid bribes as a cost of doing business with the authorities and passed the costs on to their foreign customers.

We roamed from town to town, from site to site, searching for harvestable wood. Digging and cutting the ironwood was backbreaking work. Dad paid his crew to follow us in a large flatbed truck and load the cured logs for shipment to a Santo Domingo mill.

On occasion, to show them he was not above doing the work himself, Dad stripped off his shirt, grabbed a shovel, and helped liberate his quarry from the ponderous, wet earth. In poor shape, given his drinking and smoking, he soon tired but made his point. I watched from the sidelines, happy to monitor from under a shade tree. The heat and humidity would have stopped me after five minutes. The more time I spent in the tropical climate, the less I liked the swelter and stickiness. Iceland sounded like paradise.

At day's end, we bivouacked in the nearest town at one of the many pensions or boarding houses Dad frequented. The proprietress offered to cook our dinner for a fee. Sometimes we went to a local restaurant. If we stayed in, he gave the kids hanging around some pesos to go to the *colmado* and bring back some cigarettes, cold beer, or rum.

Dad and I started drinking in the late afternoon and continued through the night. This routine became natural after a week or so—*something in the genes*. I smoked a cigarette or two to give my hands something to do, but I didn't like what the tobacco did to my lungs and soon stopped. Dad smoked two packs a day.

We took time off to swim in the warm surf if we were near the sea. Palm trees bordered the deserted sandy shores. Dad warned me to keep a watch for sharks that lurked beyond the breakers. Because of this forewarning, I enjoyed brief swims close to the beach.

Dad and I got along well. We never discussed the incident that had separated us for so many years. Somewhere between the airport and the city, we tacitly decided to leave the past alone and start anew. If I had foreseen the future, I would have reconciled sooner and not lost so many years of the father-son relationship. Still, we enjoyed each other's company, lived for the moment, and wandered around the incredibly green countryside of his youth, drinking and earning money as miners.

"You know, some miles from here, our family owned a large *finca* of coffee and sugarcane. Before the Great Depression, your grandfather was one of the wealthiest men in the region. Our family had prestige and respect. He was friends with the dictator Rafael Trujillo, the president, who grew up in San Cristóbal with your grandmother. My mother and Trujillo attended school together."

"How come you never mentioned any of this before?"

"Our family became relatively impoverished. It's not something I like to dwell on."

Dad sounded wistful.

"Anyway, Papa used to ride up from our house in Barahona atop his favorite horse in his impeccable suit. We spotted him coming from a mile away in his white Panamanian hat. He surveyed the fields daily and stopped to talk and drink coffee with the foremen as though he were one of them. He could be complicated and cruel but fair, and we loved and respected him."

"A local *caudillo*?"

"Of a sort. He was known as Don Isidoro. Your *abuelo* wielded tremendous clout in this region for years. Some said he was the eyes and ears of Trujillo. When the Depression destroyed the business, Don Isidoro became disheartened and ill just before World War II. He died in his bed as Europe fell to the Third Reich."

"Where you there?"

"Yes. I was fourteen. The whole family was by his bedside. We all kissed him just before he passed."

He spoke with considerable nostalgia for our family's fortunes and how far we had fallen. Dad seldom mentioned family history back in the States. Yet, as we sipped rum on a deserted beach in a village called Paradiso, he became sadder and pensive, resigned to a life that unfolded unlike he anticipated. I trembled, thinking my life might also end up somewhere unforeseen.

The idea that behavioral patterns in families repeated themselves intrigued me. Márquez's *Cien Años de Soledad*, one of the books Maria and I loved, exemplified this theme. My grandfather lived his dream only to see it dissipate from events beyond his control. My father grew up thinking he would be wealthy and respected as his father but became a struggling middle-class businessman. I planned for an academic career but now harbored doubts about whether I would succeed. Was it chance, or something in our character? Perhaps how we overcame these obstacles remained the actual transformative action of our nature.

The fact that I had earned a college degree filled Dad with pride. He bragged for days to everyone we met about how I had graduated from one of the top universities in *Los Estados Unidos*.

I described Maria to him, including the end.

"Her horse reared up suddenly, and she lost her grip, falling against the railing. Maria had been riding for seventeen years. A freak accident, really."

"Horse accidents are common in the Dominican Republic. When I was growing up, we often rode. I took quite a few tumbles myself."

"But you were never hurt seriously?"

"*Gracias a Dios*, the ground is soft, and my head is hard."

I showed him the only picture of Maria I still owned, the one in color Lila took of us standing in front of the fireplace. I always remembered her there, her Mona Lisa smile, hand on her hip seductively posed. Dad found Maria quite beautiful and complimented me on my good fortune to know such a woman.

"We were blessed to enjoy a little time together before the accident."

"You loved her deeply, I think."

"Yes. We were supposed to be married last June." The sadness in my voice was not lost on Dad.

"I'm sorry, son." He placed his hand on my shoulder with a pained look.

"It's not fair, Dad. Maria was so young and had so much life ahead of her. How did our lives get so screwed up?"

"Life is filled with incredible highs and, I'm afraid, lows so deep you believe you'll never climb out of them. We have to learn to live with disappointment."

"It's so hard."

We continued our father-son talks on his townhouse's patio once we returned to the capital. The sun had set earlier, and the oppressive heat let up a little. The overhead fan turned lazily above us. He spoke of his life since moving back to the DR and his struggle to earn a living. Readjustment to the chaos and disorganization of the Third World proved challenging after his comfortable years in the United States.

"People outside the States badmouth it, but the US is one of the greatest countries. Now that I don't live there, I miss how well-run it is compared to this place. I guess I lost my *mañana* attitude and my tolerance for chaos," Dad said.

"You could move back."

"I'm settled here now. My life with Adita wouldn't work anywhere else."

Still, his happy marriage to a younger woman, who supported his ego and mitigated his loneliness, helped. He loved Adita. I had never seen him calmer or more content despite his perceived setbacks. About to celebrate his 49th birthday, Dad had settled into middle age with fewer regrets than he let on.

"What are your plans once you return to California?" he asked.

"Two graduate programs accepted me for this academic term, but I decided to postpone for a year, so I guess I'll find a job."

"Why did you postpone?"

"Maria's condition. I postponed because of her. We had planned to go together."

"She's gone, son. You can't live your life rooted in the past. What about your future?"

"Maria's dad said he would find an accounting job for me where he works. My minor was business, so at least I have a real-world skill."

"Is that what you want to be, an accountant? For such a small job, you don't need four years of college."

"The position is temporary until I figure out what I want to do."

"You ought to know by now." Irritation fused his response.

"I thought I did. Maria's death threw me off the path I was on. Now, I'm recharting my way." I finished the rest of my drink. Dad tossed some ice cubes into our glasses and topped them off with Brugal, finishing the first bottle of rum.

"You have no ambition, Jim. You spent years in school and still have no vision of what you want. Have you learned nothing from my mistakes? I dropped out of college after the first semester, and look where I am and what I'm doing. I hoped you'd become a professional and acquire skills people will pay for."

"I *am* ambitious. I'm re-evaluating." The excuse sounded lame the moment I voiced it. Dad shook his head and sighed, unable to hide the flush of disapproval. My spirits sank. He did not want his son to lead the life of a *flâneur*.

"As long as you are soul searching, why not stay here and work with me? Adita can always use help in the office. We could split into two crews and double our profits."

"Thanks for the offer. Let me think about it."

The belief I would accomplish more than a business career still motivated me. Giving up academia was not a concession I was ready to make. I never had ambitions to make a lot of money—I wanted to teach and write, to contribute to the world of literature. Derailed, I second-guessed how to find my way and start moving in my previous trajectory. Without a set course before me, I scrambled to realign my future.

You will find your way, James. I have confidence in you.
I wish I shared your optimism, Maria.

Dad and I jetted to New York City to visit his compadre, Franco, and to call on a shipping company that expressed interest in buying Lignum Vitae.

While he worked, I wandered throughout Manhattan—a fantastic city—especially keen to explore the New York Public Library in midtown. Only the Library of Congress was more extensive. I browsed among its volumes for half a day, lost in the books and journals, and wished I could access the nonpublic stacks. Of all the things to do in the city, I sought the sanctuary of the libraries.

I rode the subway from north to south, checked out the Whitney Museum, the Met, and the Guggenheim, and toured the Twin Towers. From Battery Park, I admired the Statue of Liberty across the bay and imagined my great-grandparents landing at Ellis Island from Italy, ready to start their new life in the land of the free.

However, all my explorations did not relieve the emptiness that had become a part of me since Maria's death. Every morning I awoke without a plan, resolved to let the world happen to me. I was not too fond of this aimlessness but could not bring myself to do anything about it. I convinced myself I could do nothing but accept whatever came my way.

In the evenings, we gathered around, eating and, of course, drinking. Dad and Franco were excellent cooks. Traditionally, men cooked for holidays and special occasions; now, every day warranted a celebration. Every meal started with rice and beans, followed by potatoes, plátanos, yucca, chicken, chuletas, bacalao, or shrimp asopao, all cooked *à la Dominicana.*

Franco and Dad preferred blended spirits like Johnnie Walker Black. By the second bottle, I switched to beer. I learned not to try to keep up with them. After the whiskey ran out, we jumped into a cab to explore the local Dominican nightclubs if it was early enough. The old joke proved accurate: New York was the second-largest city in the Dominican Republic.

Parts of the Bronx reminded me of Santo Domingo. Not the architecture, but the people on the street and the *Merengue* at high volume on every corner. When Dominicans congregated, they slipped into an island dialect I had trouble following. I understood the context but missed the nuances. My dad or Franco sympathized with my bewilderment and shifted to English to bring me up to speed on the conversation, telling me I had to learn more Spanish.

The patois they spoke sounded like Spanish but not the language I'd learned in class or México. Its rapid, clipped sounds, and swallowed endings showed how much Spanish had drifted from its orthography to its real-world usage, not unlike French.

Countless hangovers and blurry mornings later, the day arrived to return to Los Angeles. Dad drove me to JFK, where I caught the 9 o'clock flight. He waited with me at the gate until my flight boarded.

"Think about my offer to join the company, Jim. Should you change your mind, spring is a good time to return. Adita and I have several customers lined up next year. Nothing will sharpen your focus on the future quicker than hard, physical labor under a blazing sun in 100% humidity."

"Gee, Dad, you sure know how to sell it. Sounds tempting. However, my sights are still on graduate school. I'll work until I return to school next fall."

"Whatever you do, son, I'm behind you, but please do *something*. Okay?"

"I will."

"Let's stay in touch. Drop me a line now and then, or I'll call you, collect."

The flight boarded; we embraced and promised to talk at Christmas.

Ten weeks of traveling finally caught up with me. Once I settled into my seat, I slept the entire way back.

Chapter 24

At midnight, my parents greeted me as I rolled off the plane. I gave them the Reader's Digest version of my travels through México and the Dominican Republic.

During the long ride back to Diamond Bar, I stared out the window at the endless metropolis that never slept: no joy, relief, or nostalgia, only desolation over facing my life without Maria. With nowhere to run, the return to Southern California signaled the long slide that began imperceptibly and increased momentum until the ultimate collapse several years later.

The following day, I drove to the cemetery. At the kiosk inside the gates, I bought a bouquet and candles. This visit was only the second since the burial. After strolling up and down the rows of neatly manicured grounds, I became disoriented but found her after getting directions from a groundskeeper. Already adorned with fresh-cut flowers, her gravestone appeared well-attended. I found out later that Mrs. Compagno visited every day.

Seeing how well-kept Maria's grave was, I recalled how abandoned Charlotte's site had appeared the last time I visited. I promised to gather some tools and cleaning supplies and give poor Charlotte the attention she deserved.

I added my offering to the metal vase and lit the tapers with my lighter. Seated on the gravestone, I traced the name etched into the stone with my fingers: *Maria Isabella Compagno, amada hija, 1954 - 1976.* Instead of the sharp pain of chiseled verges, the sun-heated granite elicited nothing but numbness. Only the tearless, dull ache of sorrow and heartache rooted me to the earth, her earth over which I kept vigil.

I miss you, Maria.
I miss you, too, mi amor.
How do I go on without you?
You must learn to live without my physical presence.
But it hurts so much!

Time will lessen the suffering, but scars will remain.
I am lost and blind.
You will find your way, eventually.
What if I cannot?
Through love, you will. Have faith.

The sun passed overhead until it slipped below the trees, which shaded the knoll and the Compagno plots. From somewhere, a cool breeze carried citrus and lilac. A gust blew out the candles, and I relit them before leaving.

Incognizant, I drove back to Diamond Bar, where I slept until my mother called me to supper. Unable to focus, I lounged on the couch after eating, staring at the TV, desensitized, questioning whether I would pull through and recover some essence of the life I had lived before.

Guided by Marc Compagno's influence, the accounting department at the Pomona Global Dynamics plant hired me after a short interview. After all, I was starting at the bottom. At least I was well dressed.

Instead of beginning the first term of my doctorate in comparative literature, I found myself wandering the men's department at Sears with my mother.

"You'll need at least two suits, a sports coat, several ties, dress shirts, and comfortable shoes."

"Mom, I don't have money for all that. Maybe after a couple of paychecks if I get the job."

"They'll hire you. Don't worry about the money now."

When we left the store, I owned a complete set of business attire to make my debut in the corporate world, a clubby microcosm I never thought I'd join.

I discovered right away that the theoretical knowledge of finance and accounting taught in undergraduate business classes did not prepare me for the aerospace industry's day-to-day corporate accounting grind.

For the first month, all I did was match debits and credits from ledgers spit out on miles of computer printout. I suspected reading glasses lingered in my future.

The life of the mind I envisioned as a member of the Academy remained as elusive as ever. The mind-numbing tedium of account reconciliation shattered any delusions that I was born for more extraordinary things. Still, as I gained experience, my duties became more tolerable, and I settled into a predictable white-collar routine I had heard about but never cared to experience.

On March 31, 1977, as I dressed for work, Adita called from Santo Domingo.

Mom handed me the phone. "Some Spanish lady for you."

"*Hola Jaime, soy Adita*," She had been crying. "Your father passed away this morning."

"What? How?"

"He collapsed in the mountains. After several hours, his men got him to Barahona in the back of a truck." I remembered those routes—potholed country roads; Dad called them *las careteras del diablo*.

"I chartered a small plane to pick him up and bring him to a hospital in the capital."

"So he made it to the hospital?"

"Yes. Your father arrived in critical condition but survived surgery and recovered in a private room. I don't know how to say it in English. He had *un infarto de miocardio*."

"A myocardial infarction."

"*Sí, sí, ese*."

Adita started to sob, and I waited for her to collect herself.

"That was Monday. The doctors said he would recover but he had another heart attack the day after. A little one."

"But they stabilized him?

"Yes."

Adita explained that he asked for a priest three hours before the final cardiac arrest that took his life. My father had not entered a church since his teens, yet, near death, he sought redemption from the religion he scorned as an adult.

"When I arrived this morning, he was already gone."

"Adita, I'm so sorry."

She had scheduled the funeral for next Thursday.

"I'll buy you a ticket, Jaime. Please fly down right away."

"I can't leave now on such short notice. At work, we have month-end closes to do. They won't give me the time off."

"For your father's funeral? No time off? *No puede ser.* Please come. I need you here. There's the funeral, and we have two pending shipments of *Guyancán.*"

"Adita, I can't quit my job to take over Dad's business."

Nothing I said would placate Adita. She begged and cajoled, but I said no. What prompted my obstinance that morning escaped me. I had no idea then, but my decision to blow off my father's funeral would torment me for years. I should have gone, but I couldn't face another gut-wrenching funeral.

"I promise I'll fly down soon. Please try to understand."

"I understand you do not love your father."

Adita hung up. Her tearful entreaties stabbed me in the heart as the dial tone droned in my ear. Apparently, she never forgave me, because we never spoke again. Every time I called, she refused to talk with me. No answer to any letter I wrote. I didn't just burn a bridge; I dynamited it.

Perhaps she was right: I didn't love him. Was the guilt I endured over my decision not to attend his funeral a sign of love? Years would pass before I recognized a glimmering of my answer.

After work, I went barhopping and drank much more than usual, brooding about the phone call with Adita and my unforgivable and callous response. How did I become so selfish? Had I ever loved him? Maria would never have let me get away with such behavior. How did I get to be number one on my own shit list?

Around midnight, the bartender cut me off.

"One more, please."

"Sorry, Bud. You've had enough. House rules."

"My father died today without warning, and I can't attend the funeral."

The bartender sighed. "That's rough." He poured me one last shot of cognac.

Outside, I wandered the street, looking for the parking lot where I had left my car. I threw up on my shoes and struggled to put the key in the lock. Too drunk to drive home, through the windshield, I watched the world spin out of control before I passed out. The last thing I remembered was I had not read a book since Christmas.

Three years lapsed at Global Dynamics, an indistinguishable, unremarkable epoch gone forever, years I'll never get back working for a soulless corporation. From accounting, I advanced into Information Systems Internal Audit, where I learned to verify and validate the financial data stored in our computer systems. The PC era had not yet arrived, so we relied on IBM mainframes and various networked minicomputers and terminals.

Hundreds of hours among external auditors, programmers, systems analysts, and administrators slipped by unnoticed as each day passed identically to the previous one. I absorbed what I needed to do my job but derived no satisfaction from my assigned tasks. Still, I received accolades in my performance reviews, raises, and bonuses, which meant nothing.

Every autumn, I requested applications for PhD programs. Helpless to overcome Newton's First Law of Motion, I blinked as the application dates lapsed without action, unable to muster the will to recapture the dreams of my youth. All I had to do was submit the forms, but I never found the time.

Sixty-hour weeks dampened my enthusiasm for activities other than sleep and the *de minimis* social life among the various bars and restaurants I haunted. There were lots of one-night stands until even those became routine and banal.

Twenty-five years old and still living with my folks. I banked much of my paycheck with little interest in material things, vacations, or frivolous expenditures. I managed to drop a hundred or two a week in restaurants, though, which did not strike me as profligate, considering my drive to fade away in an alcoholic haze.

I upped my monthly stipend to my parents, which covered the extended stay in their house and allowed my mom to stash a little money in their savings accounts.

At first, I acknowledged their consternation and incessant questions about whether I was okay as they witnessed me squander my talents and devolve into a working schlub without ambition, as my father had predicted, but I stopped caring what they thought.

I considered moving elsewhere, but my fractured imagination failed to conjure a motivating reason. I toyed with a return to the Bay Area, perhaps San Francisco. I'd always loved the City and thought the change might free me from the slump that became normal.

Perhaps next year, in San Francisco.

Someone left a day-old *New York Times* in the company lunchroom. In the arts section, a headline caught my eye: *Lila Perl Retrospective: Photos from the 1970s at the L'eau de Velle Gallery.*

After four years, I wondered what had become of Jim Hoffer and Lila Perl. Employing my sleuthing skills, I located Lila's phone number and called her one evening.

"Lila? This is James Montez from Russell Street."

"James! How are you?"

"I'm well. Working in LA for an aerospace firm. I saw the *Times* article about your show. Congratulations."

"Thanks. Any chance you'll be in New York? The show goes on to the end of the month."

"I'd love to, but can't."

"How's Maria doing?" Silence. "James? You there?"

"I guess you didn't hear. Maria died in June 1976 from a brain aneurysm. She never emerged from the coma."

"Oh, I'm so sorry to hear that. I left Berkeley in early May when Jim and I broke up. We thought the coma thing was temporary."

"All of us hoped for that." The seriousness of my voice transferred to Lila.

"I adored Maria. I thought you two were the perfect couple. You know, I have hundreds of negatives from the Salon. Would you mind if I put together a photo memorial in her honor?"

"You mean like a show? She would have loved that."

"Sure. Let me look through my stuff. If I can make it happen, I'll let you know."

"Thanks. So, you're not in contact with Jim anymore?"

"No. We didn't part on the best of terms. Jim's gay, you know."

"I thought he was bi."

"Maybe he was, but he came out at the end of law school and wanted to move to the City for his new job. Homesick for New York and my family, I moved back. I heard he's working for a law firm downtown."

Lila riffled through some papers and gave me the name of the firm.

"You should call him. I'm sure he'd be thrilled to hear from you. You and Maria were always his favorites."

"I'll do that."

Lila and I chatted about safe subjects, steering away from the last days of Berkeley. We exchanged contact info and promised to stay in touch, but we never spoke again. Sometimes the events and people of the past have no place in our present.

I drove to San Francisco three days later to spend a long weekend with Jim. Unfamiliar with the City, I parked my car in one of those $25-a-day lots. We agreed to meet for drinks at a chic club a block from his firm.

I arrived early, grabbed a seat, and ordered a bourbon and soda. The clientele, mostly men in business attire, swayed back and forth to a disco beat thumping around me, loud enough to strain conversation.

Jim strolled through the double glass doors a half-hour later, clean-shaven, dressed in a sharp thousand-dollar suit and sporting a corporate haircut, while I teetered on my barstool, staring, unsure I recognized him. He always wore jeans and distressed long-sleeved dress shirts in Berkeley, with sandals in the summer and sneakers in the winter.

He gave me a brotherly hug and stepped back to check me out. I wore a sports jacket and Levi's. Before he spoke, I said, "Prosperity and the big-time corporate lawyer thing suit you, Jim."

"It's a living. I'm up for a partnership in two years, so why not dress like one? You were a little fuzzy on the phone. So, what brings you back to the Bay Area? After what happened, I thought you left forever."

"I'm burned out as an internal auditor and need a change. Now might be the right time to move, to change my life."

"Have you been back to Berkeley?"

"No, and I don't think I will. Those days are gone."

"Understood. Some friends live in the old neighborhood, but I seldom visit. Don't miss Berkeley much. The atmosphere there mutates with time, but the languid disconnection from the outside world always persists."

"You got that right," I said.

"You mentioned you spoke with Lila?"

"She's got a show of her photographs at some midtown gallery."

"I'm happy for her. Lila's like Paul and Laura, a true artist. Did she tell you I'm *out* now?"

"Yes, she mentioned it. Congratulations."

Jim stirred his drink. "Thanks. You'll stay at my house, yes? My partner's looking forward to meeting you. At last, after the stories I told everyone about Russell Street, we can prove everything I said is true, with only a little exaggeration." He chuckled.

"I'm all yours. Tomorrow, I would like to look for a place to live. Once I move, I'll tackle the job hunt."

"I checked; my firm doesn't have any openings in accounting now, but word-processing jobs are often available. You listen to tapes, transcribe them, edit the results, et cetera. Not the greatest, but enough to keep you in perfume and occasionally paint the town livid pink until you find something more suitable."

"I may take you up on the idea."

"Listen, I'm waiting for Roberto to meet us here. After a drink or two, let's head back to our place. We can do the City tomorrow night. Roberto is a superb chef. You parked nearby?"

Jim and I finished our drinks. We ordered another round when Roberto Sanchez stepped up behind us, put his arms around Jim, and kissed him.

Jim introduced us. Roberto ordered a glass of chardonnay, and we moved to a table. Jim explained how he and Roberto met clubbing downtown soon after Jim started at his firm. Roberto, three years older, was a partner at a rival law firm.

Both practiced product liability law and insurance defense litigation, representing insurance companies that might be on the hook to pay claims when parties sued over alleged product failure. The topic sounded dry, but they relished their specialty once revved to talking business.

We retrieved my car and headed up Market Street to Noe Valley, where the couple lived together in a fabulous two-bedroom condo on Grand View Avenue above the Castro District. The living room window exposed a panoramic view of the city, illuminating Market Street from the Castro to the Bay like an iridescent string of pearls.

"Wow! What a view."

"Everybody who comes here says the same thing," Roberto said. "We decided to buy the unit within the first few minutes. This is what $300,000 will buy you these days."

My jaw slacked when he said three hundred grand, a massive sum out of my reach. "Law must pay pretty well. I missed my calling."

"What are you now, twenty-six? Not too late to go to law school," Jim suggested. "It's great having enough money to spend on cool stuff like toys and real estate."

"But with the long hours, do you have time to spend it?" I asked.

"Good point. However, look around. We're making the most of our dough." Jim pointed to the living room, looking over the city.

"Come on. We'll give you the *grandiose* tour."

Jim and Roberto gave me a quick turn around the apartment and dropped me off at the guest bedroom to change clothes.

They had furnished the place in a modernistic style, a white and black décor, not quite my preference, but upscale and expensive.

I told Jim, "You've come a long way since Russell Street."

"Yes, indeed. Almost a rags-to-riches story. Lila would be surprised but not shocked. Did you know her family is Long Island old money? She is or will be quite wealthy someday. Our Berkeley vows of poverty were a pose. We lived the way we did because she wanted to live independently without family help. She accepted the occasional cash gift from her mom, however."

"Money was a contention between you?"

"That, and because I'm a friend of Dorothy's." Jim laughed. "Lila wanted to go back east. She landed a photography gig for some magazine, but I prefer the Bay Area. And our sex life went south before you guys moved in upstairs." Roberto banged around in the kitchen, doubtless half-listening to us. "Roberto convinced me to come out. You don't know how stressful life is pretending to be something you're not. I was confused throughout high school and undergrad, but now I'm where I should be."

"I'm glad. Everything's working out as far as I can tell."

"I've never been happier."

The doorbell rang. Roberto yelled, "I'll go. It must be Jennifer."

"Jennifer?"

"She's Roberto's little sister. Jen lives the next block over and eats dinner with us whenever she's around."

I caught my breath and smiled when Jennifer Sanchez breezed through the door. I learned later she was the daughter of a Swedish mother and Puerto Rican father; her Nordic features, bronze skin, blue eyes, and light brown hair found me staring with my mouth open like some adolescent. Roberto looked more Hispanic and likely favored their father. I was helpless to look away.

Roberto introduced us as she shook my hand and kissed my cheek.

"So, you're Jim's friend from the Berkeley Salon days?"

"Oh, you know about those?" I asked, surprised.

"Every detail. Whenever Jim gets inebriated, he tends to reminisce." She laughed.

Jim went into the kitchen to help his partner prepare supper. We settled on the white sectional leather sofa and enjoyed the San Francisco lights.

"I never grow tired of this view," she offered. Jennifer was an electronics sales rep. A year older than me, she moved here with her brother from Miami when he accepted the law firm's associate position.

Jim opened a bottle of chardonnay and brought us each a glass. Jennifer politely listened as Jim reminisced about his favorite Berkeley highlights for the first, second, or third time.

We moved to the table to enjoy roasted chicken (reheated from earlier in the week) and a chef's salad made from ingredients Roberto bought from a farmers' market in Daley City. Jim, Roberto, and Jennifer chatted about their week. I enjoyed the company of people who were comfortable with each other.

Jennifer offered to drive me around to various neighborhoods to see where I wanted to live, while Roberto promised to inquire at his firm for any open accounting slots. I relaxed among my new friends, eager to leave LA for the last time and start anew.

After supper, Jim put on some jazz as Roberto poured us all cognac snifters.

"Hey, James, see if you can spot this one," Jim said. Three bars into the jazz piece, I recognized the style immediately.

"Paul!"

"Correct. This is Paul and Laura's newest album, one of their best."

I went quiet for a while, listening to the new songs. I loved the quartet's music, and to hear their latest on such an impressive stereo system took me back to those nostalgic days on Russell. The contrapuntal melodies, characteristic of the Paul Stern Quartet, showed greater sophistication than I remembered. The music seemed to meld spontaneous inspirations with an underlying intent. I pictured them in our living room years ago before our Salon audience, fully absorbed in the music.

Afraid melancholy might overwhelm me, Jennifer switched positions to sit beside me and placed her hand on my arm to say she understood. I suspected Jim told her about those final days and how some Berkeley reminders might be a downer.

She said to us, "Anyone up for some blow? I got this batch of Bolivian flake. I think you guys will appreciate quality for a change."

Before anyone responded, Jennifer pulled out a compact gilded mirror and an amber bottle, then tapped a generous amount on the reflective surface. Using the edge of a business card, she adroitly arranged the flaky powder with a slight yellowish tint into several lines and snorted a couple using a small copper straw.

Lady Heather, my favorite dominatrix. I wondered what happened to her.

She passed the kit around, and we all did two lines each. All my fatigue and melancholy vanished moments after the numbing sensation spread through my nasal cavity and brain. My heart rate shot up. I glanced at Jennifer to find her smiling at me with a mischievous grin, which sent tingling tremors into my groin and down my legs.

The music played on, and we enjoyed an entire bottle of an excellent Hennessy XO.

The following morning, the familiar aroma of bacon and eggs roused me from a deep sleep. For a second, I flashed back to Grandma Compagno's house, minus the roosters.

After breakfast, Jennifer dropped by in her car with a list of apartments to check. A guy about our age, tall, with short brown hair and wire-rimmed glasses, wearing a white dress shirt with rolled sleeves, sat in the passenger's seat.

"James, this is my boyfriend, Barry Marsden. He works for IBM in International Sales."

We shook hands once I settled in the backseat of Jennifer's blue BMW.

"I hope you don't mind, but Barry grew up in the City and knows it better than anyone."

"You're tired of all the fun and sun of Southern California," he said.

"Right. I've always loved the Bay Area. After four years in Berkeley, why not give this side of the bay a chance?"

I thanked them for giving up their Saturday to help me.

All morning we drove up and down Noe Valley and across the Mission to the Potrero District, which I favored because of its location south of downtown and east of Mount Sutro.

Potrero Hill, Barry assured me, was the first to get sun and last to get fog. He steered me away from the Sunset district because of the gloomy cloud cover from April through September. The cheaper rents didn't warrant the perpetual cold and dark overcast.

"So, is it true what they say about summers in the city?" I asked.

"The coldest winters are summers in San Francisco." Jennifer laughed. "I carry a sweater with me year-round."

On 19th Street and Carolina, we passed a complex called Victoria Mews. The moment I saw the development, I had found my place. Jennifer parked the car in front of the building.

"One thing I like about Potrero is street parking is available any time of the day or night, and no permit is required because the housing density is much less here than in other parts of town," Barry said.

We walked around to locate the manager's office. The Mews featured lush and exotic landscaped gardens interspersed with walking paths, small ponds, waterfalls, and palm trees surrounding the pool and tennis courts—an urban oasis. Some apartments offered stunning scenes of downtown San Francisco to the north. The thirty-minute bus ride to the financial district made the complex the perfect location for a downtown commuter.

I leased a junior one-bedroom with a stall for one car in the gated subterranean garage. My first-floor unit presented a beautiful view of the downtown skyline if I stepped out of the front door. I figured I would move to a better apartment at the end of the lease.

Although the rent came in a little above my budget, the Mews provided a pool, spa, gym, and off-street parking included in one price. As I wrote out the check for the move-in fee, the first and last month's rent, and a security deposit, the final amount caused a momentary arrhythmia.

Jennifer loved the place and congratulated me on the find. She mused about Barry and her moving there to live together when their leases expired. I fantasized about her sunbathing by the pool.

"You guys are invited to drop by for a swim or soak in the spa anytime."

"We will, thanks," she said.

The following week I gave a two-week notice to Global Dynamics and strolled over to Marc Compagno's office to give him the news personally. Although we worked in the same company we rarely spoke. He expressed support for my decision to make a change, though I couldn't tell if he were happy to be rid of a reminder of an unpleasant past.

"We'll be sorry to lose you, James. You've advanced nicely through the ranks here."

"I'm close to burn-out. The change will be good for me."

"Do you have anything lined up?"

"Not yet. I have an apartment and some job leads."

"Glad to hear it." Marc glanced at a flashing light on this phone but ignored it.

"How's the family?" I asked.

"Angelina's good; still at the hospital. Jon got into Stanford. He's studying computer science. Alicia was just promoted to managing director at her firm."

"Really? So young?"

"That girl works hard. Much harder than her old man." He chuckled.

"I don't doubt it."

"I wish she would find the time to settle down and get married. I hate the thought of her ending up as a spinster."

"And your folks?"

"Mom and Dad ranching as always. You'd think those two would slow down, but no, they are still going strong. The world needs fresh eggs."

"Smokie and Old Yeller?"

"Smokie's fine. Old Yeller passed last year. He was almost thirty."

Regret, mixed with sorrow, took me aback. "Yeller was my first horse. Well, my only horse."

"Yeah, I used to ride him when I was younger. He was my favorite. I miss him too."

I left Mr. Compagno's office with mixed feelings, happy to know the family was well but sad about Old Yeller. For the rest of the day, I reminisced about all the rides we had taken together. His death hit me hard, perhaps because my memories of him and Maria were so intertwined.

I headed north with an overnight bag in the trunk of my car, without furniture, appliances, or books with me. I wanted a clean start. I left most of my old clothes. My parents waved as I backed out of the driveway, not a see-you-later sort of wave but a definitive goodbye. A year would pass before I returned.

I landed a word-processor job at Jim's law firm. Before, I had never used the Wang 2200 VP Word Processing System, but I lied and said I'd worked with a similar setup at GD. Jim borrowed a manual, which I studied thoroughly before my first Monday.

Although monotonous, the work introduced me to legal and analytical thinking. Ensconced in a windowless room where I seldom interacted with my colleagues, I wore studio-quality headphones that blocked out the world. I transcribed cassette tapes on numerous subjects as arcane to me as medieval romance philology might be to an attorney. Careful listening helped me decipher summaries of depositions, interrogatories, medical records, court testimony, and a surplus of memo-to-the-file reflections where attorneys recapped factual and legal musings and opinions about the cases they managed.

Jim touted my language skills to his colleagues.

The firm represented Lloyds of London, Swiss Re, and other reinsurers in Europe and Latin America. Whenever a Spanish or French case came up, the original language materials went to me for translation into English.

My bosses split my time between word processing and foreign language paralegal, which soon earned me a $300 monthly raise, probably out of concern rival law firms might pay more for my transcription and translation skills.

Roberto once said over drinks, "If you get tired of word processing and want a full-time paralegal job, I could get you in at my firm with your language expertise and a nice salary increase and bonus."

"Hey," Jim said, "No poaching my guy."

"I'm cool where I am now, but thanks for the offer." I thought it best to keep peace in the family, though Roberto's suggestion proved tempting.

I never thought about work when I left the office at the day's end. Two or three nights a week, Jim, Roberto, I, and sometimes Jennifer and Barry would go for drinks or supper. Since the weekends began on Wednesday in the City, we enjoyed four good party nights until Sunday. Jim and Roberto liked to drink, reminding me of my Dominican cousins.

After a late-night bout of carousing, I treated myself to three espressos and 600 mg of Tylenol to sharpen my concentration to survive the rest of the day. Young and indestructible, I recovered and looked forward to the next round of alcohol-infused barhopping, usually through the downtown disco-punk-themed gay clubs that catered to ambitious white-collar types like Jim and Roberto.

All the gay men left the hopeful hetero women always looking for a straight man. My batting average improved, given the odds. More one- or two-night stands than I could count came my way, yet nothing blossomed into anything permanent. Perhaps I should have hidden my ambivalence better, but after my time with Maria, I lost the desire, or the ability, to form lasting relationships with women. In retrospect, this attitude was one of the many blunders that facilitated my eventual bottoming out. Drinking, drugs, and indifference preoccupied my life until the day of my arrest.

While HIV ravaged my adopted town, Barry and I attended a Department of Commerce Small Business Seminar about starting one's own business. We sat in the back row next to Bill Perry, a software project lead for a small, nondescript company in San Jose. Afterward, we went to lunch at the Zuni Café on Market.

The three of us hit it off. We enjoyed a fabulous meal of *duck à l'orange*, generous plates of *pomme frites*, and two bottles of a pricy award-winning chardonnay from Stag's Leap Wine Cellar.

Barry said, "Here I am in International Sales at IBM and hardly ever travel. All I do is paperwork for the guys who make the sales."

"Wouldn't it be great to see the world and get paid to travel?" I added.

"I'm tired of no control over my daily life at work," Bill said. "All the restrictions of an employee while management reaps the benefits."

Barry put it succinctly: *If you don't work on your own dream, you work on someone else's.*

By three that afternoon, we decided to create our export company specializing in high-technology products. We named the new venture MPM Exporters, using the first letter of our last names.

We grossed almost two million dollars in the first 18 months. At the end of the first year, we quit our jive jobs, as Barry called them, and worked full-time for MPM. I managed the finances and reinvested our business profits to spur growth and provide additional unearned income from bonds, CDs, and other securities.

The three of us traveled throughout Europe, Asia, and Latin America, making our dream happen. We bought a café-level espresso machine for our office. Jennifer kept the quality cocaine flowing.

In adrenaline-hyped euphoria, we concentrated on making money and believed the good times would roll forever. There's something about all that cash that entangled us. The more we made, the more we wanted to keep going. Our profits became our way of keeping score.

I didn't recognize myself. My life unraveled in a direction I never imagined. I only cared about the next transaction and booking my flight to Europe for a few weeks of business enmeshed with pleasure. I knew all the hip spots in Paris and Madrid. Our clients loved it when I arrived in town because I insisted on showing them a good time with my generous expense account.

By year three of our venture, the government changed the rules for exporters of high technology, and the rapid downward spiral gathered momentum.

Then came the knock.

PART IV

Chapter 25

The Department of Corrections transport dropped me off at the halfway house, where I reported to my new parole officer in his office next to the entryway. I handed him my release packet, and he glanced over the documents. Mr. Iskaz, middle-aged, balding, with a hook nose and enormous biceps, pulled out a notepad and started writing as he dug into my dossier.

"Let's go over some things. Have a seat."

"Sure," I muttered.

"While you're here, you will seek gainful and lawful employment. After three months, once you have a steady paycheck, you may hunt for a place to live, and we'll transition you out of here. Meanwhile, you'll follow all posted rules. I'll have access to your room, wallet, bank account, W2s, and pay stubs as long as you are under supervision. Clear?"

"Yes, sir."

"Any infractions and I'll violate your parole and send you back to prison. And that's non-negotiable once I say you're done here." Iskaz stared at me over his reading glasses, leaving me nowhere to hide.

"I understand, Mr. Iskaz."

"No cavorting with felons, except for the yokels you'll find here. Otherwise, I'll violate you."

"All right."

"Curfew is 6 p.m. if you have a job, then at 8 o'clock. Stay out beyond curfew without checking in, and I'll violate you."

"I don't want to be violated." The double entendre associated with the word *violate* occurred to me. I hadn't been out of prison for 90 minutes, and someone was already screwing me.

"Absolutely no drugs or alcohol. Otherwise, I'll violate you. Let's get started on the right foot. Here." Iskaz opened his drawer and pulled out a plastic bag with a UA cup. "Behind you is a head. Piss in the cup. I can ask you to piss anytime and anywhere. If you come up dirty, I'll violate you. *Capiche*?"

"*Capsico.*"

"Don't be a smartass. Fill the cup. And leave the door open."

I went into the small bathroom and peed in the cup.

"Here's your key. You're in room eight on the second floor."

Iskaz took me upstairs to my room, slightly larger than the cell I had just vacated, which I would share with someone who worked in the free world. Then, he left me to unpack.

Next to my bed was a small dresser. I put my prison-issued garb inside. Once I cashed my check, street clothes were a high priority for my upcoming (I hoped) interviews. Since I'd worn blue jeans every day for the last three years, I'd grown to hate them. Twenty years would elapse before I wore them again.

On my way downstairs to lunch, I examined myself in a full-length mirror at the end of the hall. Four years had passed since I'd gazed upon an undistorted reflection of myself. I looked like a concentration camp survivor: gaunt but tan and weathered; my clothes hung off me like rags. My face appeared angular, and the skin around my eyes was darker than I remembered. Streaks of gray ran through my closely cropped hair. For the first time, I realized my youth had passed, and middle age approached. Nevertheless, old age was sweeter outside the fences; it could be worse.

The halfway house was a utilitarian post–World War II concrete structure desperately needing paint inside and out. Of course, the ubiquitous DOC gray covered the exterior, while a faded brownish tan made the interior look like the inside of a paper bag.

Management provided one electric typewriter for everyone to share. I composed two one-page resumes and carefully typed them after buying a new ribbon at my expense. I preferred clear, crisp text in my documents.

Two versions suited me. One emphasized my hands-on skills, and the other shifted the focus to my supervisory experience. I added self-employment consulting and time off to travel through Europe to obscure my prison time. I kept the gaps small enough to be easily overlooked or explainable. With the money I borrowed from my roommate, who worked at a grocery store, I entered the local AlphaGraphics and printed twenty-five copies each on ivory high-quality linen bond.

The residence offered a small reading room with several phone books. I pored over the Yellow Pages and the newspapers for companies and jobs within a 30-minute bus ride from the halfway house. I identified 19 leads and mailed each a resume with a short cover letter typed on the same linen bond. With books I'd checked out at the local library to keep me company, I waited by the house phone for the calls I knew would come.

The library had alerted me to one last step in my job hunt. To receive a library card, I needed an ID. Since the police had confiscated all my identification, I asked my mom to mail a certified copy of my birth certificate, which I took to the DMV to apply for a state ID card. Once I got a car, I figured I would return and take the driver's test and exam if this DMV didn't recognize my expired California license.

No one made reestablishment into civilian life after prison easy to navigate. DOC had issued me an uncashable check because I didn't possess an ID or a bank account. Once I had identification, I visited three banks, but none would open an account without a 15-day hold on a government-issued check.

Frustrated, I endorsed the check, mailed it to my parents, who Western Unioned the money back to me, and added three hundred bucks to the total. I used $200 to open an account, but the bank still placed a hold on the cash before I could take any money out. My parents then mailed me another check for $150, which I took to the counter to add to my new account.

"I would like to deposit this check, please."

"One moment," said the winsome young bank teller, who had to be one or two years out of high school. "I'm sorry, sir, we must place a five-day hold on this out-of-state, personal check, with your account being just opened."

"Thanks." Frustrated, I retrieved the check, tore up the deposit slip, and left the bank. Outside, I spied the ATM and had an idea. I inserted my ATM card, put the check and a new deposit slip into an envelope, and fed it into the bank's maw. The next day I called the bank. The deposit cleared, and funds were available. Why? Afterward, I did all my banking via the automated tellers and never entered the lobby or stood in line unless necessary.

Ten days later, the responses trickled in: eight rejections, and four phone calls requesting interviews. The remaining seven were still pending. While I waited for answers to my interview requests, I visited Sears. More than ten years had passed since my last shopping spree at Sears with my mom. I bought a cheap gray suit, two white dress shirts, three ties, and a pair of black wingtips that didn't quite fit. I returned to Sears and purchased thicker gray and black socks, which helped. Down to my last 50 bucks, I kept whatever was left for the bus fare, which only cost 25 cents each way in those days.

The interviews went worse than expected. I arrived early, filled out the applications, and waited until Human Resources called me in. My spirits sagged for the first three applications when I spotted the question: "Have you ever been convicted of a felony? If yes, please explain." My PO had said, "Never lie on an application, or I'll violate you," so I checked the "Yes" box and wrote an abbreviated description of my felony convictions. All three HR interviews ended with a short conference and no job offer.

"You show a lot of relevant experience in accounting and finance." The interviewer reviewed my resume, then picked up my application. Alarmed, I gaped as their demeanor mutated from business friendliness to professional ice when they reached the bottom of the form where the dreaded question appeared.

"Let us review your application, and we'll contact you soon. Thank you for coming in."

A day or two later, I always received a form letter stating that the company would not continue with my employment request.

In the fourth interview, I neglected to check the fearsome *box that cannot be named*. While the HR interviewer scrutinized my form, I chattered to distract her. She returned the application to me.

"You forgot to mark this last box at the end."

"I did? Sorry." I placed a slight mark near the *No* box, between the two boxes. I hated the subterfuge, but minimum-wage jobs just wouldn't cut it.

"Fine. Please wait. The hiring manager will see you when she's done with another applicant."

The interview went exceedingly well. Ten days elapsed as I hung around the halfway house, clinging to a dwindling hope that something would break my way. I continued to apply for jobs, mostly whatever I saw in the local want ads. I gave myself a deadline of two more weeks before I would start looking at waiter or retail sales jobs, areas out of my comfort and salary zone.

On the eleventh day, the phone rang. Five days later, I started my new job as a medical financial analyst for Sanos Health.

Eighteen months after my release, the Department of Corrections granted me full discharge from supervision. I celebrated with a five-star meal at the Phoenician, which set me back almost $100. The food, the service, the ambiance, and the freedom made the experience worthwhile. I ordered soup, salad, *canard à l'orange*, tiramisu for dessert, and a drinkable bottle of a 1986 Bordeaux.

Between release from custody and deliverance from parole, I'd experienced some minor glitches along the way. I rode the bus between my job and the halfway house for several months before accumulating enough money to rent a small studio apartment within walking distance of the office. The apartment suited me because I could seal the door from the inside, a trivial matter for those who have never been locked away. I had shared a cell or room with someone for over four years and looked forward to genuine solitude.

Out of the group home, DOC assigned a different PO, a forty-year veteran close to retirement who showed little interest in my parole. In one of those surprise visits, Mrs. Wachsam dropped by my new apartment several days after I settled in.

"Nice place. What's the rent?"

"$120 a month, water included, but I must pay for electricity."

"Not too bad." She walked around the one-room unit and feigned a close examination of my living arrangement.

"Here's the deal. I don't need to meet with you more than once every three months, so drop by my office after New Year's. If your job or situation changes, give me a call. If you need to leave the state, come by to fill out some forms before you go. White-collar types usually don't ruin my day, so we'll get along fine."

"Thank you, Mrs. Wachsam. I promise not to give you any trouble."

"Good. I have plenty of scofflaws to chase around town."

My PO never revisited my residence.

I stopped into her office at the mandated intervals, and we chatted about how things were going.

"How's your transition back to civilian life, Mr. Montez?"

"Everything's fine. I go to work, come home, eat dinner, collapse, rinse, and repeat."

"Sounds good."

"On weekends, I haunt my favorite bookstores, drink coffee, and write in my journal. Sometimes I must work on weekends too, which is cool."

"You're adjusting well."

"I am."

Not one for small talk, Mrs. Wachsam shooed me out of her office after a minute or two. Vargas had told me horror stories about his paroles and why he would not accept them anymore. I expected supervision to be more onerous, but I was lucky to be one of those guys who learned from his mistakes. Having a PO who essentially left me alone helped a lot. I didn't mind those quick visits every 90 days.

In spring, I applied for permission to return to California to retrieve my car, which had been collecting dust in my parents' garage for the last four years. My stepfather drove it to keep the battery charged and spruced it up before I arrived.

On a Friday evening, I flew into Ontario. During my absence, the airport had undergone a facelift. I barely recognized the old terminal that had become familiar during college.

Mom cooked an excellent *pasta fazool,* as it's called in the New York Italian dialect.

"I'm glad you're out of that awful place, Jimbo. John and I went through all that security to get to the parole hearing. Not a nice place."

"Thanks for everything you did, Mom."

"You coming home for good, son?" John asked. "Your old room is the way you left it."

"Once I'm off parole, we'll see. I enjoy the anonymity of a new city. I like my job. It feels like a fresh start."

Mom said, "It's not too hot in the desert?"

"Everything's air-conditioned. Everywhere there're drive-up windows for banks, pharmacies, and liquor stores. I'm only outside, walking from the bus stop to the office and back."

"We could use a few drive-up windows here, too," Dad said.

"What's strange is I only saw the city from the backseat of a van for three and a half years. Now, it's a new place from the sidewalk level."

After dinner, we played penny-ante poker. John lugged out two coffee cans full of pennies and dumped a handful in front of each of us. While he rustled up some new cards fresh out of the package, I carefully stacked my coins.

In no time, Mom cleared the table. She claimed it was luck, but growing up in a bar, she knew something about cards. Dad and I called it a night after she swept the last of our money into her pile.

"Good game. You guys aren't too good at hiding your hands. I can read your tells from a mile away."

Something is comforting about sleeping in one's childhood room. I woke up once, unsure of where I was, glanced at my shelf full of books, and went back to sleep. I never thought it possible, but the memories and feelings I had dragged around since Maria's death finally started to fade.

After breakfast, I left for the long ride back. I promised to return soon for an extended visit once I accrued enough vacation time.

Several hours into my return trip, I realized I had missed the open road and the unencumbered blue skies that stretched hundreds of miles before me. Light traffic on the Interstate, paved as smooth as a baby's butt, left me to daydream and reflect on my life. For the first time in years, a spark of liberty arced in my neglected synapses and spread throughout my nervous system. I never wanted to be caged, ever.

I moved across town to a larger apartment in early summer, farther from work but still close. The twenty-minute drive each way gave me time to think. I developed a driving meditation where I focused on the highway ahead yet let my thoughts rest. I arrived at my destination, refreshed and calm, unperturbed by city traffic. After my first work anniversary, I received a raise and a modest bonus, which I splurged on furniture and books. The anxiety of imprisonment faded eighteen months out, like a nightmare that vanished at first light.

Dating women who worked in my office building provided a welcome distraction from my solitude. None of these liaisons went anywhere, but we stayed friends. A few thought I had some sugar in my shoes; they were too polite to ask outright, but hinted at how open-minded they were about gay people. I didn't disabuse them of the idea, though I wondered what made them think I might not be into women.

Perhaps my over-politeness or mentioning I lived in the San Francisco Bay area for years or that I was in my mid-thirties without children or marriage gave them the impression.

Across the street from the office sat a T.G.I. Friday's. After fifty-hour weeks, the restaurant lived up to its name. I met many women over cocktails, enjoyed pleasant conversations, and engaged in occasional flings. What I could not hide was my noncommittal ambivalence to any long-term relationships. I reverted to the introversion that Maria had worked so hard to attenuate.

Compared to the lost years of LA and San Francisco, I reduced my drinking drastically. I enjoyed a beer or glass of wine but no longer cared to dull my senses or escape into a fuzzy haze. Alcohol robbed me of time to read or write, so I minimized social drinking. Coffee remained my preferred beverage, though I cut back because my doctor said I was borderline hypertensive.

Release from supervision came and went. I filled out some forms, received a few words of encouragement, and exited the parole office for the last time as one of the few rehabilitated ex-offenders.

I wandered into the downtown Borders Bookstore one Saturday morning, tired of my usual scavenging among the secondhand shops around town. Browsing this massive store evoked those wistful days among the Berkeley stacks a lifetime ago. Huge bookshelves lined with attractively arranged volumes under bright lights made navigating the selections a joy. I missed my role as a librarian and flirted with the idea of taking a part-time weekend job in a proper bookshop.

I almost didn't recognize the familiar figure. Out of uniform, with her strawberry-blonde hair past her shoulders and contact lenses instead of glasses, she looked thinner than I remembered, and paler. I walked over and stood beside her, pretending to scan the shelves. She looked over and recognized me, followed by a flash of apprehension.

"Hi, Evans. Don't panic. I'm not on parole." The department forbade officers from fraternizing with parolees.

She relaxed and greeted me with a grin. "Good to see you again. How's life?"

"Everything's going well. Life's good." Evans held the novel *Daniel Deronda*. "I recommend the book you have, *Silas Marner*, and the famous *Middlemarch*, anything by Eliot."

"Always the librarian."

"If you have time, I was about to have a coffee. Please join me."

We stepped over to this new café built into the bookstore, called Starbucks. I offered to buy her a coffee, but she insisted on treating me. With two cappuccinos, we found a table in the corner. Evans carried the book she intended to purchase and set it before her.

"Where are you working these days?" she asked.

"I'm a financial analyst for Sanos Health Solutions. The job provides an intellectual challenge most of the time. No complaints there. I rented a place on the Northeast side, near the office." I sipped my coffee, admiring her brown eyes.

"I figured you'd rebound quickly. I'm still on the Santa Cruz Yard."

"All the prime suspects doing all the same things?"

"Something like that."

"How's my buddy Larsen?"

"He died last summer. A stroke."

"Sorry to hear it. I liked him."

"He collapsed one morning behind his desk. Everyone thought he had fallen asleep, as he often did."

"Well, he *was* ancient. How much time did he have left?"

"He'd caught a twenty-five-year sentence for child molestation that ended in his victim's death, since she committed suicide after the trauma he inflicted on her."

"Really? And no one outside the administration found out?"

"He transferred in from Vermont with a sealed jacket. None of the inmates knew of his circumstances. Otherwise, we would have been held in protective custody."

I shook my head. "You never know about people. He seemed laid back and level-headed. A little cynical, perhaps. Not that I'm defending him. He deserves condemnation."

"Larsen was a lousy clerk. A guy named Carlson took his place."

"Carlson, the jailhouse lawyer? He helped me sort out my detainer."

"I thought you knew him. He's lightyears beyond Larsen in efficiency. He actually gets work done."

Evans sighed, clearly not interested in talking about work. She stirred her cappuccino, tasted it, and scanned the café, distracted.

"You seemed ambivalent about your job last time we spoke. Are things better?" I asked.

"Yes and no. I finally finished my bachelor's degree in criminal justice and am waiting to sit for the lieutenant's exam. I want to become a warden someday. I need more responsibility, and honestly, I'm tired of working the Yard, being on my feet eight hours a day in this desert heat and wind."

"That sounds like a worthwhile goal. I recall you considered moving up. If things go well, I hope to be promoted to associate director in the next two or three years."

"I'm happy for you." Warming up to more personal matters, Evans opened up about her life and filled in some gaps I'd only guessed at before.

"My brother, uncle, and cousin are all local police officers."

"You mentioned you came from a law-enforcement family."

"Everyone except my dad. He's a successful financial advisor for Edward Jones. He builds and manages retirement portfolios for his clients."

"Sounds like my kind of guy."

"You two would like each other." *Was there a subtle hint there*? She paused and asked tentatively, "Are you seeing anyone?"

"Not really. A date now and then, nothing significant. I spend a lot of my free time alone."

"With no solitude on the Yard, I can see that. Don't you get lonely?"

"Yes, but I'm used to it by now. I have my books."

I noticed the white line around the base of her ring finger where her ring once was. "How long have you been divorced?"

She held out her left hand and stretched her fingers as though she had never examined them in detail. "I seldom wore my ring at work. It's off forever now."

"Sorry."

"Don't be. Before you arrived at the complex, I married a fellow officer. He worked over at the Women's Unit. We finalized our divorce last summer."

"The divorce was contentious?"

"My ex and I were best friends once. To lose both the love of my life and my best friend hit hard. I'm only 32, but my life feels over. Of course, it's not true. I'm at a crossroads, I suppose."

"Losing someone you care about is the hardest thing in life," I said.

"The voice of experience?"

"Indeed."

"I can't shake betrayal, the violation of trust. I caught the bastard *in flagrante* cheating on me with the warden from the Women's Unit. In our bed! I lost it. Thinking about him still makes me so angry." Tears formed as her cheeks flushed.

"Evans—" It seemed inappropriate to call her by her last name. "May I call you by your first name?"

"Mary Anne—Anne with an e."

"Really? Your name is Mary Anne Evans?"

"Yes. Why?

"Coincidence." She still held a copy of *Daniel Deronda*. "You see, the author of this book, George Eliot, was a woman who used a pen name. Her real name was Mary Anne Evans."

Mary Anne opened the book to the blurb about the author and verified what I told her.

"I think I'll buy this," Mary Anne smiled as she flipped through the pages. Her mood brightened after the intensity of moments before. "I don't mean to dump on you like this. Still, we barely know one another." Mary Anne caught herself as she said this. "That's not true, is it? We have known each other for years."

"We are like intimate strangers," I suggested.

"I like that. Intimate strangers. We know a lot and so little about each other. Why are you still here in the valley, James? I thought you'd want to go back to Cali."

"Nothing to go back to. Before my arrest, I lived in San Francisco, but it was never my home. My folks are in Los Angeles, but I'd rather not live there—too many memories. I figured I'd start over right here. No one knows me or my past."

"I've lived most of my life in this city except when I joined the department at twenty and worked throughout the state until I transferred back to be with my ex."

Mary Anne explained how her ex-husband was her high-school sweetheart and first love, making his adultery unforgivable.

"Have you ever been married, James?"

"I was engaged. The story's long and sad. We were very much in love, but . . . perhaps we can talk about it some other time."

"I didn't mean to pry."

"No, it's not that. What happened is not something I'm comfortable discussing in public, that's all. Crying in public is hard for me."

"Okay, perhaps another time in a more private place. I find your vulnerability attractive, something I usually don't find in men."

We shifted to more neutral topics. Mary Anne asked how I liked the city, whether I had traveled to some of the tourist attractions around the state, etc.

"Given my work schedule, I haven't gone anywhere. I work long hours and occasional weekends. The job distracts me, so I won't dwell too much on the present or the past."

"I know what you mean. Extra shifts kept me distracted. Sitting at home alone after so many years with someone depressed me. I spend more time with my dad. He lives alone, too."

As my old CO and I chatted, a wistfulness arose, inspiring me to let down my guard. For the first time in years, I longed for a true friendship. Time with her, no longer proscribed by rules or fences, appealed to me.

We'd finished drinking our coffees long ago.

"It's been lovely seeing you again, but I have some shopping before the New Year."

I waited for her to suggest we meet again, but she said nothing. I hid my disappointment and left her in the checkout line.

The good spirits of the last hour dissipated as I strolled to my car, in no hurry to reach it as though she might come running after me, having forgotten to exchange phone numbers. A fantasy, of course. I picked up that she wanted to focus on establishing her new life after a failed marriage, with no room for friendships with ex-cons. Still, I had hoped we'd meet again, but in a city of a million people, such a chance encounter was remote.

For weeks after our initial visit, I appeared at the bookstore every Saturday morning and hung around the café until noon, hoping Mary Anne would return. Thoughts of our conversations over the years, things said and unsaid, rolled around in my mind for weeks. I yearned to spend more time with her, to get to know her, and let her know me. No need to hide my sordid past. Intuition suggested she might share my sentiments and be open to my gestures, yet Mary Anne had taken flight on the desert wind. Perhaps I would find out someday.

One morning in late January, I camped in Starbucks, a cappuccino before me, as I read Hermann Broch's novel *The Death of Virgil.* I sensed someone behind me and turned around.

"May I join you?"

"Mary Anne. Of course, please." I don't know who showed more surprise by my enthusiasm, her or me.

"I'm glad I ran into you. I thought about our last chat and wanted to tell you how much I enjoyed seeing you again. Few men I meet bat around anything besides sports, hunting, or cars."

"Kind of you to say so. Those are three subjects I know nothing about." On a business card, I wrote down my home number.

"I'll tell you what. Should you wish to talk sometime, give me a call. No obligation whatsoever."

"Thank you. I'm nervous about what department regs say about social encounters with ex-residents. I should check first."

"Is that what I am, an ex-resident?" I said, amused.

"It's true, in a manner. Better than an ex-con or ex-inmate. The department hired some consultants to make us more non-biased."

"Anything in the consultants' advice to reduce the recidivism rate?"

"I'm afraid not. DOC takes its cues from the state capital. If I make warden someday, perhaps I can implement some changes. My years on the Yard give me a unique perspective."

With all the *hierarchical* barriers between us removed, I felt more comfortable broaching more personal subjects with Mary Anne. "You look more relaxed than last time. Things are improving, generally?"

"Yes. I was depressed over the holidays, but I have something to be optimistic about. I am taking my Lieutenant's exam next week."

"That's good news," I said as I reached over and touched her arm.

"Did you do anything on New Year's Eve?" she asked.

"I lead an ascetic life. I cooked pasta and vegetables and read a book before falling asleep around eleven, missing the turn."

"We all rendezvoused at my dad's place. I enjoyed spending time with my family. I don't get to see my brother enough these days."

"Your brother is younger?"

"By two years."

"I grew up an only child."

"Were you lonely?" She asked in a solemn way that surprised me.

"Sometimes. I spent much of my teenage years alone, probably contributing to my tendency to introversion."

"That's funny. I don't think of you as an introvert. You're always willing to talk."

"I feel comfortable around you. Even in prison, you were one of my favorite people, despite the barriers between CO and residents."

"Yeah. I stretched some rules back then."

I found her confession touching. "I know you did, and I appreciate you not treating me like a leper."

"You were always so interesting, so different from the people I knew. And you made me feel, how should I say it, intelligent. You never talked down to me the way so many men do."

"In college, I had two female roommates who trained me never to speak with condescension to anyone. "

"Those girls did a fine job. I'd like to meet them."

"My favorite memories are the times we chatted in my little library. In fact, on your days off, I wondered how you were doing and if you were bored too."

"At first, I wrestled with my feelings since they taught us never to become attached to inmates, but I'm human, and let's face it, you're a smart, good-looking guy. I'm so glad you never did anything to make me assert my authority as a corrections officer or as a woman. You were always a gentleman." Mary Anne flicked grains of sugar off the table.

"Any more plans to attend school? A master's degree?" I asked.

"No. I'm done. I accomplished my goal of getting a bachelor's degree. Now, I want to focus on my profession."

"I considered returning to earn a PhD but never did. Time flew by, and I missed my window." I chuckled. "Time lets us think there's plenty of it, then leaves us behind."

"You didn't go back because of your job?"

"Partly. I wanted to be an academic my entire life, but several years working in corporate America disabused me of the idea I could teach anything. Living as a starving student also lost its appeal after a few years of steady paychecks and the so-called good life."

"I'm sorry. I think you would have been a wonderful teacher. I learned so much from you."

I bought another cappuccino while Mary Anne nursed her grande something-or-other, one of those sweet, chocolatey coffee drinks.

We chatted, our conversation punctuated by small, comfortable silences until the time to depart. Not that we ran out of things to discuss, but we both had weekend errands.

Mary Anne slipped in next to me while I stood in the queue and handed me her business card with her home phone number in her small, precise lettering.

"Here. Let's get together soon."

I took the card and touched her wrist. She blushed and hurried away. Whatever DOC thought of her off-hours with an "ex-resident," she overcame her reluctance. I stood in line, pleased, daydreaming until the guy behind me said, "You're next, Sir."

Later in the evening, a little before ten, I fell asleep with a book in my lap. The traffic noise outside my window finally dissipated. I closed the novel and switched off the lamp. Light from the street created a flickering wedge across the ceiling.

The phone rang.

"Mary Anne? Miss me already?"

"I do. Thank you again for today. Talking to you always puts me in a good mood."

"I love spending time with you."

"I'm inviting you to dinner next Friday at my favorite Italian place over in the Avenues, say, 7 o'clock?"

"I would love to, thanks for asking."

"Perfect." She gave me the address, and we spoke briefly before saying goodnight. In bed, I listened to the occasional vehicle passing. With a spark of optimism, I slept through the night without waking.

CHAPTER 26

During the week before my first dinner with Mary Anne, I considered how fate had unraveled. We had seen each other almost daily for nearly three years. I'd barely allowed myself to indulge in any emotional bond while incarcerated. The one time I did with Consuelo, the result proved disastrous. And now, she'd asked me out to dinner where rules and regulations no longer constrained us, and we could relate to each other as kindred spirits, both alone after some severe personal setbacks.

The trattoria was a small hole-in-the-wall family eatery nestled between an insurance agency and a clothing store. Mary Anne waited at the entry in a dark red dress with thin straps and medium-heeled shoes.

"You're doing your best to erase my image of you in the brown uniform. You look *très chic*, mademoiselle."

"It's our first official date. Why not go all out? I'm not *all* business," she said, smiling.

The hostess, a young Italian-looking woman, perhaps a member of the owner's family, showed us to an intimate table in the back. Murals of grapes and harvest adorned the white walls of the restaurant. We ordered a generous carafe of the house chianti and examined the menu. We both got Caesar salad. I ordered the chicken saltimbocca, and Mary Anne chose the spicy chicken carbonara risotto.

I didn't expect too much, but the food surprised me. The cuisine wasn't quite Grandma Compagno's cooking, but I enjoyed the meal. Following my release, I had avoided such restaurants because of the memories Italian food elicited.

Sadness beset me as I recalled that Grandpa and Grandma Compagno had died several months apart last year. Marc Compagno called me at the office one morning, leaving me a voice message.

"Hi, James, Marc Compagno here. Your mom gave me your work number. It's a little late, but I wanted to let you know my folks died last summer.

Dad went first, and Mom, inconsolable, joined him a few months after. I retired from Global and took over the ranch. Next time you're in town, drop by if you want. It would be great to have you. We can ride; I'm boarding four horses, and Smokie would be thrilled to see you."

Mr. Compagno left his number. I called him back and promised to visit after offering my condolences.

My momentary distractedness did not go unnoticed by my companion.

"You seem sad, James. Is something bothering you? Where did you go?"

"Into old memories of lost places, of irretrievable people. Some people I loved passed unexpectedly last year. When I think of them, I realize how life moves on; we grow older, and things change." I sighed. "No worries. You make me happy, not dark. Here, let me refill your glass."

"Should you feel like talking, I'm a terrific listener. We could trade life stories sometime."

"I'd love that. I want to know all about you, and well, you know about my last few years, and the times before weren't so great either . . . " My voice trailed off into a whisper.

"Isn't that always the case? Don't we all live with past experiences we want to downplay or forget? Everyone harbors painful memories. I have seen you at your lowest. I hope this evening hasn't triggered a past you'd rather not revisit."

"Sometimes, sadness overwhelms me, but I try not to dwell on it. I acknowledge the feelings and let them go. That's the goal, anyway."

"I understand. I succumb to those feelings, too, hoping they don't lead to regret. I prefer to live well today and not regret tomorrow."

"I don't want to frighten you on the first date," I said.

She laughed. "Forget about it. What would top what I know already? If you could scare me, we wouldn't be here. I am resilient. You should know that by now."

"I do, indeed. Resilient on the surface, firm and fair, but soft and sweet underneath?" I added lightheartedly, trying to elevate the mood.

"Perhaps you'll find out," she said. "One-dimensional, I am not."

Enjoying our banter, I lifted my glass, "Here's to letting go of the past and a fearless embrace of our future in all its facets. *Salute!*"

"Amen, *Salute.*"

The personal struggles of the last few years had left me hollow, but now I sensed a readiness to share what I had suffered. What better person to confide in than Mary Anne, who, as she suggested, had witnessed me undergo an existential crisis and survive? She was still young, divorced, vulnerable, and perhaps open to expanding a relationship with an intimate acquaintance. Her self-assuredness encouraged me. With a deep breath and a newfound resolve, I opened myself to whatever came next.

We spent weekends together, eager to regain time lost through simple excursions like supper, a movie, or a concert. We bought tickets to Acoustic Alchemy, Neil Diamond, a so-so production of Andrew Lloyd Webber's *Cats*, and several classical concerts. Country music was her thing.

One Saturday night, we stayed home and listened to the Grand Ole Opry on the radio, something I had not done since early childhood with Gladys Harris. It surprised me that Gladys and my mom still exchanged Christmas cards every year.

I said, "I must have been three or four the first time I listened to the Grand Ole Opry. The lady caring for me loved the old country music."

"My mom loved the Grand Ole Opry too. She grew up listening to it, and I used to sit with her with a big bowl of popcorn and a soda. My dad and brother never cared for it."

"There's something honest and down-to-earth about that music, always about something real, about life, things anyone can relate to."

"That's right. Seldom are the lyrics frivolous or unrelatable." Mary Anne reached over and touched my shoulder. "I'm glad we're copacetic on that point."

Mary Anne invited me on our third date for her Mexican food specialty. She lived on a quiet residential street without sidewalks but with spacious yards surrounding the homes. French doors opened from the kitchen to a tiled patio covered by an awning with misters installed by her ex-husband.

"At least he was handy around the house," she said. "Not much good in other areas though," the bitterness not so subtly suppressed.

Refreshing moisture spritzed the area to replenish the air from the relentless heat and aridity. An afternoon shower left a pleasant petrichor lingering throughout the yard.

A wooden table and chairs provided comfortable seating, where we sat before supper. My hostess had prepared everything beforehand, and after a reheat, she served spicy chicken enchiladas, rice and beans, and a green salad generously trimmed with avocado, all made from scratch.

"I hope you like spicy food. I love it. Take a cold beer just in case," Mary Anne said as she pulled a Dos Equis out of a small cooler alongside the table.

"You're certainly set up for the outdoors here. My place doesn't even have a balcony."

"You might hunt for a more suitable spot. Lots of small houses are available for rent. Most have covered patios."

"Yes, perhaps, I will. Cheers." We touched our bottles of beer.

"I grew up in this town and hate to spend all my time inside. At least my job keeps me outside much of the time. I probably walk five miles a day around the yards. How do you think I keep my girlish figure?"

"I wondered about that."

"I know you were checking me out on the Yard. Feel free to check me out at any time."

"If you catch me staring, think of me as an awestruck admirer."

This playful banter continued throughout supper and into the evening. In the living room, Mary Anne played selections from her music collection. She favored modern jazz, the older rock from the sixties, and many country-western songs. She owned no music from the Paul Stern Quartet, which suggested a gift idea.

After the second beer, she brought out a bottle of tequila called *Partida Añejo*. I'd never tasted such a smooth tequila. Produced in Jalisco, México, from agave grown in volcanic soil, *Partida* evinced a fruity undertaste with sea salt, pepper, and a touch of oak. I swirled the silky liquid in my mouth. The liquor hinted at vanilla, with a soupçon of lemon and other herbs I couldn't identify. I realized all the tequila I'd drank in México was third-rate.

"Where did you find this tequila? Fantastic!"

"The brand is a little hard to locate and somewhat pricey, but a neighborhood Mexican liquor store imports it. I'm glad you like it. It's a favorite in our family."

In my enthusiasm and slightly inebriated state, I reached over and put my hand on Mary Anne's knee. She moved closer to me until both sides of our bodies touched.

"I hoped you'd get around to touching me. I thought I might have to throw myself at you. Four years is a long time to wait."

"I wanted to kiss you whenever you came into the library. Always forbidden to touch you, I'm a little intimidated."

"Those days are long gone, thank God. Make my fantasies come true and kiss me."

"What fantasies?"

We kissed long and slow and forgot our tequila glasses, absorbed in our urgent desire to experience what we yearned for. Mary Anne rose to her feet and pulled me up.

"I haven't been with anyone for a long time."

"I know what you mean."

"Bring your drink," she said as she led me to her bedroom with urgency and a gleam in her eyes, making my heart soar.

For seven months, Mary Anne and I lived an adult Goldilocks life. She invited me to supper every weekend. We liked to shop for groceries at AJ's, a gourmet grocery store, long before Whole Foods came to town. I introduced her to café culture, and soon our weekend mornings found us with cappuccinos and a book at one of the four or five cafés around town.

The mass migration of Californians with all their amenities had not yet begun. AJ's sold a stovetop espresso maker, which I slipped into our cart as a gift. She didn't realize how bored with drip coffee she was until I showed her how to make various espresso drinks.

Besides our outings to restaurants, concerts, and movies, sometimes we stayed home and viewed a rented video or read books like an old married couple. With soft ambient music, we often sat and talked about the latest advances in penology, my career in the fascinating world of medical finance, and life in general.

One Friday evening, I discovered a second toothbrush in the master bath. "A toothbrush is the camel's nose under the tent in Italian and Spanish society," I suggested. "And it's blue, my favorite color."

"Since you spend lots of time here, I got tired of you lugging your toiletries around like you're staying in a hotel. I might buy you a razor too. Anyway, it's important to me that you be comfortable. I love having you here, in case you hadn't noticed," she said with a wink.

I reached over and hugged her. "After years of unhappiness, I never thought I would dare to feel this way again. Life is much better now; I can hardly believe my good fortune."

"I'm reading *The Diary of Anaïs Nin,* where she says that life shrinks or expands in proportion to one's courage. We're both lucky and brave these days," she said as she kissed me.

"Anaïs Nin? I love her. She was a favorite read in college, especially the stories about Bijou."

Occasional midweek sleepovers supplemented the weekends until I received a drawer in her dresser *and* a spot in her closet.

"You know," Mary Anne said one evening after supper and a shot of *Partida,* "I would love to have you move in here. There's plenty of room."

"That's a big commitment," I answered, hesitating.

She blinked several times, tilting her head to one side to determine whether I was kidding.

"You're not sure?"

"I love the idea. Can fear and ecstatic joy coexist? I think that's what is pulsing through my tired brain. You're sure?"

"Yes, I've been thinking about it for a while. You spend so much time here. It just makes sense. The last several months have been the best." She set down her glass and wrapped her arms around me. "Besides, I've fallen in love with you and want you close."

Mary Anne had never explicitly said she loved me before. Her declaration was an unacknowledged truth between us. Holding each other, I said, "I love you too. I should have said it before, but I assumed you knew. I've wanted to be with you since that first day at the bookstore."

She shook her head. "James, for a man of letters, you don't always articulate what's going on with you. My mindreading skills are rusty."

"I know. Let's work on that together. It has been a long time since I've talked about my emotions. After being shut down for so long, it's hard."

Seven months after my introduction to *Partida Añejo,* and after Mary Anne had verified no explicit rules banning a DOC employee from living with an ex-inmate off parole, I moved into her house, our home for the next thirteen years.

John O'Donohue wrote: "We do not need to go out and find love; rather, we need to be still and let love discover us."

On occasion, we dined out with Mary Anne's father, Jerry. Mr. Evans stood over six feet, gray, slim, and solid, with an intelligent face that reminded me of Peter O'Toole. His firm handshake exuded confidence and friendliness. Both men of finance and literature, we liked each other immediately. She was relieved that her father and I got on so well. I told her I was an *expert* with parents, but she fretted anyway.

"What do your dad and your family think about my background?" I asked while we sipped coffee before work on the patio.

"Dad's totally cool with it. The rest were apprehensive, but I think they've come around."

"All right. That's good, then."

Mary Anne scanned the backyard, thinking.

"Since we're on this subject, this is how I see it."

"Go on."

"In my years as a corrections officer, I've seen two types of convicted felons: those who are essentially criminals and those who committed felonies but are not by nature criminals."

"I agree. That's what I've seen too."

"You are in the second category. You committed crimes, got caught, and were punished. You are remorseful. I see that. But, there's something in your character, some flaw, that compelled you to break the law even though you knew it was wrong."

Spinning my coffee cup, I said, "Yes. That has bothered me."

"I believe in redemption. Inasmuch as you need my forgiveness, I forgive your past. I only know the man after, not before the events and bone-headed decisions that brought us together in Santa Cruz."

"I admit to being a flawed human being."

"We are all." Mary Anne reached over and took my hand. "I have to be completely honest now."

"Yes?"

"If you ever lie to me, betray my trust, or commit another crime, we're done. I will always love you, but that doesn't mean I would share my life with you if you upended my faith in you or my values. Sorry, that's just how I am. I don't mean to sound harsh."

"I understand. You are the most forthright person I know, and I expect you to hold me accountable. I love you and swear on Maria's grave never to give you cause to question our life together."

She held my gaze for a long time, processing my oath of fidelity to her.

"Thank you. Come on. We're going to be late for work."

We stood and hugged each other for a full minute. The bond of love and commitment bound us so profoundly that we never felt the need to clarify our allegiance again.

Mary Anne insisted we attend a cookout at her dad's house to mark our official status as a couple. She prepped me to meet her inner circle of close relatives during the drive over.

"Now I know what a debutante goes through. After being shut away for so long, am I now ready for polite society? This reminds me of my parole hearing."

"I think you're ready for the Evans fraternity."

The entire family, including Mary Anne, considered themselves Reagan conservatives, which didn't bother me, except UC Berkeley grads carried the stigma of political radicalism, further colored by my run-in with the criminal justice system. My experience with government rules and regulations made me a financially conservative libertarian. She briefed everyone beforehand and clarified she didn't want any problems.

Still, my felony convictions and prison record made the upcoming back-yard barbecue a tense affair. I prepared myself for more than one kind of grilling. We packed Mary Anne's famous enchiladas into a cooler, then drove across town in her new Ford pickup, purchased after her recent promotion, which included a generous raise by government standards.

Jerry Evans greeted us at the door as I followed my rich girlfriend into the 4,000-square-foot ranch house with a four-car garage, circular driveway, and immaculate desert landscaping. The engines from three other vehicles still crackled from the heat.

We arrived last. After father and daughter embraced, Jerry and I shook hands.

"So great to see you again, son. I'm glad you've finally made it to my home." His enthusiastic welcome calmed me.

Mary Anne went to the kitchen as her dad herded me to the covered patio decked out with the fans and misters running on full.

On the way to the backyard, he stopped to show me a picture of Mary Anne's mother, Catherine. He said, "I took this photo two years before her cancer." I glimpsed how Mary Anne would appear in her late forties. Like her daughter, Catherine struck me as a pretty good-looking woman.

Outside, to one side, a built-in brick barbecue glowed with charcoal briquettes ready for the cookout. An impressive swimming pool and spa stretched out along the back, surrounded by an acre of open desert and a wire-mesh fence encircling the perimeter to deter snake encroachments. The household provided towels for guests in the cabana next to the pool.

The blue water beckoned me.

Mr. Evans introduced me. "This is Mary Anne's *beau*, James Montez."

Jerry's twin brother, Michael, stepped up to shake my hand. "I'm Mike, my son Bob, and his wife, Evie." I greeted everyone and repeated their names so I would remember them. Michael's wife did not attend because she was home nursing a head cold.

Mary Anne's brother, Larry, and his girlfriend, Peggy, stood by the grill and loaded corn cobs wrapped in foil on the top rack.

Bob and Larry, although cousins, looked like brothers. Evie and Peggy were cousins who also could be mistaken for sisters, suggesting a fascinating symmetry. I thought it odd that a pair of cousins dated another set of cousins, but why not?

I imagined their kids playing together someday in this fabulous back-yard, all looking alike and challenging for an outsider to tell apart. Adding the children Mary Anne and I might have eventually injected contrast as I was olive-skinned with dark brown hair, while everyone else was fair-skinned and blondish.

After the introductions, Jerry thrust an icy Heineken into my hand as I joined the Evans brood.

Brother Larry sidled up to me. "Mary Anne says you're into finance like my dad?"

"Medical finance. I work for a healthcare conglomerate."

"My uncle and cousin and I are cops." He let that revelation sink in.

"That's what I heard. For the city?"

"I'm a uniformed officer, Uncle Mike is a detective, and Bob is a deputy sheriff working at the downtown county jail."

I glanced over at Bob and decided I didn't recognize him. He behaved as though he didn't remember me either, thank God.

Mr. Evans grilled hotdogs and steak while his daughter served enchiladas. We gorged on meat, sweet corn, potatoes, and fruit salads.

"These enchiladas are the best, sis," Larry said as he loaded a second helping on his plate.

"I make them for James all the time now, so I'm getting lots of practice. Next time, I'll treat you to my new flan recipe."

"She makes the best flan," I said, patting my stomach.

Uncle Mike took a moment between bites to ask, "So, Mary Anne, I hear you made lieutenant. Congrats on the promotion. You going to stay at Santa Cruz?"

"For now. I lucked out. Our previous lieutenant transferred to Florence, and I got his spot."

"Good deal. You'll make warden one day."

"That's the plan. DOC has a program to help promote more women into management positions."

"What do you think about that?" Cousin Bob asked me.

"She's smart, hard-working, and determined. We're planning a huge party when she's promoted, and everyone's invited." We laughed.

After lunch, I selected another beer from the cooler and strolled to the pool's deep end. The desert sun blazed at a comfortable (for me) ninety degrees. A desert breeze from the north kept the temperature moderate, but I expected more heat later in the afternoon.

Mary Anne chatted with Peggy but glanced up to study me circling the pool. As I approached the shallow end, Peggy's cousin, Evie, walked over and stood beside me. We pretended to admire the shimmering water.

"Does all this law enforcement make you nervous?"

"Not at all. I'm around Mary Anne constantly."

"Oh, right. I can't imagine what life was like inside. You aren't what I expected."

"How's that?"

"I expected some rowdy guy, all buffed up, a skinhead type, but you are calm and soft-spoken. You also don't talk like most of the people in our circle. You speak in complete sentences and use words I learned in high school but forgot." Evie laughed.

"I went to college and majored in literature."

"I wanted to attend college, but I got married instead."

"What's stopping you now?"

"Nothing. I want to have a career like Mary Anne. She's my role model."

"She is impressive, yes."

"I can see why she likes you. You remind me of her dad. Jerry's brother teases him because he's a nerdy guy, but none of us can afford a house like this. Law enforcement is necessary, but the job doesn't pay."

"Police officers and sheriffs are underpaid, given the garbage they put up with. The work can be dangerous too."

Evie reached down and put her hand in the water. "The water's perfect. Do you feel bad about whatever you did?"

"Yes. It was stupid, and it cost me. The worst part was the shame and the neverending boredom and isolation."

"What's Mary Anne like in there?"

"All business, polite but firm. I think the staff and residents respect her."

"I could never break any laws that would get me arrested."

"Please don't. There are so many legitimate ways of being dishonest. Take Congress, for instance." I smiled.

Evie stared at me, her mouth parted slightly. "Oh, you're joking."

I was only half-joking.

Mary Anne's father and I shared many common interests. He attended the University of Texas at Austin with a major in economics and a minor in English literature. He surprised me one day with his conversational knowledge of Spanish and French. Jerry had wanted to learn both languages well enough to read the literature in the original, a goal I wholeheartedly agreed with.

He dedicated one of the bedrooms in his five-bedroom house to his library and study. Bookshelves running from floor to ceiling covered three walls, and perhaps two thousand books were collected over the years. Comfortable armchairs filled the center of the room, each with adjustable lamps for the best illumination. A large sliding glass door opened on the patio, letting in lots of natural light.

Jerry Evans became the first in his family to graduate college and the only financial professional. He shared almost no overlapping interests with his son or brother's family. A gentle, bookish man, he appeared out of place among a family dominated by public service.

Jerry and I sat in his library one Sunday afternoon sipping Coronas.

"Because I went away to the university, the paths my brother and I took diverged. He had wanted to join the force since he was ten. I loved numbers and reading."

"I hear you. I've loved books but never knew I had a knack for numbers."

"My mother was a school teacher. She taught high school English. My brother and I had her in the tenth grade. Mike never cared for reading."

"My parents live in LA but came from the east to California. Mom left school after the eighth grade in the middle of World War II, working in restaurants her entire life."

"My Catherine was also a teacher. She taught math and science, of all things, to middle schoolers until her diagnosis."

"I'm sorry for your loss."

"Thank you. Catherine's death was hardest on Mary Anne. They were very close. This library became her second home. Many years passed before she could talk about her mom without crying."

"I lost someone close to me at a young age too. Nothing prepared me for that."

"We are never ready for that kind of loss, James. We must face adversity, that's all. Loss is a test of our character, in my opinion."

"When my fiancée died, her passing messed me up for several years. I think I failed that test."

"Yet, here you are, stronger than before, I suspect, with a promising career and a woman who loves you. Propitious, don't you think?"

"You're right. Considering where I was five years ago, I have a lot going for me."

Jerry revealed aspects of Mary Anne I only guessed at. I wrongly assumed her interest in books and literature derived from politeness around others' enthusiasm rather than sincere engagement. Her parents instilled in her the love of learning and reading, qualities vital to me. The need to earn a living only distracted her from her appreciation of books, but did not diminish her passion.

My ego let me believe Mary Anne gravitated to the prison library because of me. However, after understanding her upbringing better, I decided our liaisons might be more nuanced.

She said, "I spent many hours in dad's library as a young girl, even more so after Mom died. Before her illness, I was outgoing and athletic. Afterward, I only wanted to be alone. My boyfriend, Roger, helped me through the rough patches."

"Roger, your ex?"

"Yes. After graduation, we married, completed community college, became corrections officers, and punched the clock at different facilities until we wrangled transfers to the same camp."

"From high school to full adulthood?"

"Exactly. Dad helped me buy the house you and I live in as a wedding gift. He put up the down payment and was wise to keep the house in my name."

Mr. Evans later admitted after a couple of glasses of *Partida*, he never cared for Roger.

"Roger was all right at first, but he got too possessive and controlling after the marriage. He thought he was too good for this family. Besides, I doubt he ever read a book from cover to cover."

"Sounds like a jerk," I said.

"Let's say we tolerated him for Mary Anne's sake. My brother was apathetic toward him at best."

"For selfish reasons, I'm glad Mary Anne moved on."

"You and me both. Listen, James," he began more seriously. "I think you're the best thing that's happened to my daughter. I'm glad you two found each other. The circumstances couldn't be more unusual, though."

"Pure chance, or destiny?" I said, smiling.

"Maybe both. One day, she sat where you are now and talked my ear off about some inmate professor running the prison library." Jerry topped off my glass.

"She used to call me 'professor' as a joke."

"The moniker suggests admiration. Renaissance men are rare these days. You certainly made a favorable impression. I'm so happy to have gotten to know you."

"Same here. I love talking to you. I love this room, and you serve the best libations."

"Cheers."

Later, I said to Mary Anne, "Your dad is a great guy."

"He's finally happy to meet someone to talk about investing and literature."

"He sounded lukewarm about Roger."

She laughed. "That's understating it a bit." Mary Anne leaned over and kissed me. "I really traded up, though."

"And the divorce?"

"I hardly think about it anymore. Everything worked in my favor. My family, of course, supported me all the way. Roger kept his vehicle, clothes, tools, and warden mistress, while I got the pickup, the house, and you."

"Very shrewd, Miss Evans."

"I got what I wanted and more." She leaned over to nibble on my ear. "Until we became acquainted, I had no idea what my marriage lacked." She paused.

"Go on."

"Passion. Roger was comfortable, like a pair of faded blue jeans. We married too young, perhaps. Our life was like an extension of high school, and I matured along a different path. Roger and I grew apart before we wed, but he wanted to marry me, and I agreed, but now I understand I was never fully committed. Looking back, the whole relationship was a mistake from the onset."

"You were young. We don't make the best, informed decisions in our youth. The world appears blissful to the Pollyannaish youngster."

"The voice of experience?" she said.

"Most of my youthful illusions evaporated soon after graduating from college. Losing Maria destroyed me."

"I'm glad we met in our thirties. Older, wiser, more certain of ourselves and our needs."

"I miss this kind of happiness, the way the desert misses the rain."

"You're a poet," she said as both a statement and a question.

"That metaphor might be a song lyric."

CHAPTER 27

The humid winter empowered the spring desert to explode with flowers. Mary Anne and I took the verdant yet ephemeral overflowing as a promising sign while we planned our marriage.

Thirty-nine months had passed since my release from prison. I turned 39, and she would celebrate her 34th birthday in October. We wanted children. No one learned of her pregnancy before our wedding day.

Despite my efforts to let go of the past, images of stillborn marriages haunted me as the planning advanced. Nevertheless, optimism and joy infused a quiet and permeable euphoria. My silent fear tried and failed to intrude on our exhilaration of love, marriage, and the new life we created. I carried on as though my history dimmed in anticipation of the journey I envisioned with Mary Anne.

She asked me what I was thinking during one of my more contemplative moods as we sat comfortably installed in her father's library while he was on a business trip to Dallas.

"The day after my parole hearing, I walked the track for hours, thinking I was ready to confront my inability to accept the past. I couldn't accept it because I blamed myself. I should have done more. What? I don't know. How could I forgive myself and the situation and move on? It's what she would have wanted."

"Maria?"

"Yes. She would have encouraged me to absorb my loss and live again, let go of the grief, and through love, find joy."

"She sounds wise beyond her years."

"She was, but I didn't quite understand how much. I never believed it would be possible, but I was wrong. Moving forward would always be difficult until I let go of all that came before."

"Do you mean letting go of Maria?" Mary Anne asked, her voice quivering.

"Yes. In a way. I imagined myself the guardian of her memory. Keeping her essence alive kept Maria alive. I didn't get that I could honor her memory and still move on with my life. Relationships with other women would not be a betrayal."

"Is that why you never formed any serious relationships in the years before we got together?"

"I think so. I had not yet accepted that Maria's role in my life had changed irrevocably. Who I am today is partly because of her. She helped me overcome my callowness, taught me to love, and always encouraged me to improve."

"She did a great job."

"Too bad I squandered years, forswearing what she gave me. The absolute bottom of my unhappiness could not be reached until I envisioned a realistic chance of happiness without her. On that day on the track, as I completed my final lap before release, I prayed I would love again. Perhaps not the head-over-heels, crazy kind of youthful love, but a quiet one, a love that germinated deep within and grew towards the surface. I wanted to tell you then."

"I wish you had, though I understand why you kept the realization to yourself given our positions. I was infatuated with you but could never show it."

"What would I say? I was leaving for parole and thought we would not meet again. The probability that my love for you would never go anywhere saddened me, but I was elated by the notion that I might love again. You remained on my mind during those eighteen months before we reconnected."

"I thought about you, too. I even called your PO to check on you."

"You did?"

"Yes. Mrs. Wachsam gave me a full report—both times I phoned. She suspected my interest to be less than professional, and I think she sympathized with me. She called you a model parolee, no trouble, always polite, conscientious, a calm young man, who, in her experience, would most likely not re-offend. I couldn't sleep for days after our chance encounter at the bookstore."

"Worried we might never run into each other again?"

"No. I knew you well enough to realize I would see you again wherever books and espresso were. Corrections links with DMV records. I could have looked you up in the database anytime."

"But you didn't?"

"No. I know myself. I knew it would not be only for coffee and conversation if I contacted you. My desire for you went way beyond a casual friendship between pals. After wrestling over whether I could commit to you, I returned to the bookstore, sure you'd show up eventually."

"My habits are rather predictable. I camped at the coffeehouse every Saturday morning, waiting for you. The attraction between us could not be ignored."

She placed my hand on her stomach.

"Wasn't I worth the wait?"

On September 26, 1993, I married Ms. Evans on what would have been my father's 66th birthday. I had sent Adita Christmas cards for several years, but she never acknowledged receiving them.

Mary Anne radiated luminous joy throughout that hot, dazzling, blue-skied Sunday. The ceremony was private—her family, my parents, and several close friends. Laura and Paul still had gigs in Asia and could not attend. Only once during the eventful day did thoughts of Maria flash through my mind. I believed she would be happy for us.

A month before the ceremony, Mary Anne asked me a straightforward question I found hard to answer.

"Sometimes I feel as though I'm the runner-up in your life. You were about to marry your childhood sweetheart and live the extraordinary life the two of you had planned. Do you ever look at me and see her or wish I were her?"

I remained silent, searching my feelings for the answer.

"No," I said finally. "I seldom think about Maria like before. Since we got together, she has faded more than I anticipated. Of course, I wished she had lived, but then we would not be talking. She will always be a part of me, but you are too. You are the most significant, most important part of my life now. I do not see or think of her when I look at you. I see you, Mary Anne Evans, my love and my life. I no longer have the need to cling to a past long gone, to what could have been or what should have been. You are the focus, the only focus. Never forget that."

Mary Anne wiped away her tears. "I'm sorry for bringing it up. I get scared when I realize how much I love you, our child, and how fleeting life can be."

"It's all right to be afraid. I'm here for you, always."

The next day at the doctor's office, Mary Anne reclined as the doctor prepared the ultrasound.

We watched the monitor, puzzled.

"Let's see. I'd say about fourteen weeks. Oh, what's this? Do you see these two shadows? Twins. Congratulations!"

My jaw dropped, and Mary Anne could not suppress her grin.

"Would you like to know the sex?" she asked.

Mary Anne looked at me, and I nodded.

"Girls. You have girls."

"Are they identical?" Mary Anne asked.

"Well, let me see."

The doctor moved the sensor around Mary Anne's belly to access different angles.

"Two placentas indicate most likely fraternal twin girls, Mrs. Montez, but we'll have a better idea when you're further along."

"Twins run in my family. My dad is a twin."

CHAPTER 28

We honeymooned in Paris, Madrid, and Barcelona, all cities I'd gotten to know well while traveling for MPM Exporters. Everywhere we went, a mixture of trepidation and nostalgia swirled inside me as the familiar sights and odors sparked memories of good and bad times and of people I met who I had not spoken to for many years. I marveled at how time accelerated while doing other things.

Without a schedule or list of tourist attractions, we roamed the streets and did whatever suited us. Mary Anne had never been to France or Spain, so I showed her the less-traveled neighborhoods most tourists overlooked.

"How do you know about all these places?" she asked one afternoon as we strolled through Paris.

"Insomnia accompanied me on many of my visits, so I wandered relentlessly through this street or that. Sometimes I got lost and stumbled on places few tourists go."

"How would you get back to your hotel?"

"I either kept walking in the general direction or hailed a cab. It's hard to stay lost in a city with good public transportation."

Of course we visited the Louvre, the Prado, and other lesser-known museums, but our biggest adventures happened in the small bistros and bars tucked away in hidden plazas, often only blocks from the tourist zones.

One cloudy afternoon near Montmartre, nestled among the pastel-painted buildings and stone walkways, we strolled past a faded bistro a half-block off the Rue Marx Dormoy that appeared closed from the outside. On my many business trips to Paris, I visited *La Cuillère Rouillée* every day.

"Let's try this place," I said.

"This looks a little rundown. Are you sure?"

"Yes. This is my favorite café in Europe. The food is superb, and the owner's a friend of mine."

"You know the owner?"

"Trust me. You'll see."

I pushed open the glass door and led Mary Anne inside. Several small tables clustered around the entry with a long, polished bar along one wall extending to the back, opening to an outside patio with several more tables and chairs. An old man behind the bar polished a tray of wine glasses.

He spoke in French, "We are closed for another hour."

"Jean-Pierre, you will not open a little early for some thirsty travelers?"

"*Qui est là?*" The proprietor squinted as he donned his glasses to see better in the subdued light. "Jaime, is that you, my friend? I should have recognized you from your Spanish accent."

"What accent? My French is near perfect." I laughed.

"Where have you been, my friend? So fantastic to have you here again. I thought you abandoned us." He came over and hugged me *et il m'a fait une bise.*

"I've been waylaid by life but would not come to Paris without several meals at the Rusty Spoon. Jean-Pierre, please meet my bride, Mary Anne. Sorry, but she doesn't speak French."

Mary Anne extended her hand; he kissed not only her hand but both cheeks after a fatherly hug.

"My English is not so good, but I try with you, Madame."

My friend opened a bottle of Bordeaux and carried three glasses to one of the tables on the shaded patio. Flowers bloomed on the trellis, and birds darted in and out of alcoves in the eaves high above us.

"Your husband was one of my best customers, Madame. I once offered to rent him a room upstairs, so much time he spent here."

"I was a lonely businessman in the City of Lights; I loved the food, drink, and conversation. Jean-Pierre treated me like family."

"So few Americans speak good French. Jaime was the first one since the war I got to know. I learn English from the British."

"Jean-Pierre was in the Resistance," I explained to Mary Anne.

"I did what I could. I fought for France." Jean-Pierre noticed Mary Anne barely sipped her wine while he and I had almost finished our first glass.

"Madame, you do not like the wine?"

"It's delicious, but I'm pregnant."

"*Mon Dieu. Félicitations.*" Jean-Pierre refilled my glass and offered a toast.

"I am so happy to see my friend married and about to be a father. Before, you were not so happy, but now I see life has returned to you. *Santé.*"

We finished the bottle, and Jean-Pierre brought another to hold us while he prepared to open his doors. The waiter and cook, who I did not recognize, arrived earlier to set up for the day. My friend introduced us in embarrassingly complimentary terms.

Mary Anne excused herself to visit *les toilettes*. Jean-Pierre reverted to French: "Tell me the truth, *mon ami*. Where have you been this, seven, no, eight years?"

"I was in prison for a white-collar crime. My business suffered financial problems, and things got away from me." I never meant to admit my crime and incarceration, but I would not lie to him when Jean-Pierre's blue, penetrating eyes searched my soul.

"Well, I am glad you returned to us. We all go through hard times and find our way to the end, *n'est-ce pas?*"

"The experience taught me a lot. You have no idea how thrilled I am to be here with you in this place again. For a while, I thought I would never revisit Paris."

"You carry the soul of a Parisian, born in the wrong country. I am not surprised you came back. What else could you do?"

"*Exactement.*"

My closeness to Jean-Pierre had developed over many visits. I traveled to Paris five or six times a year for a week to ten days for our export business. I read a story in *Rolling Stone* about how, in 1971, Jim Morrison often took long walks through the city. On one of his strolls, he stopped by *La Cuillère Rouillée*. Since I often explored Paris's streets, I wanted to find this bistro and see it myself. I discovered the café one rainy afternoon and kept returning.

For lunch, Jean-Pierre suggested the house's specialty, coq au vin with a hint of garlic, a traditional rustic dish bequeathed from the Romans. For dessert, we enjoyed an apple-pear tart, homemade by the chef's wife. Jean-Pierre refused to accept payment for the meal as a wedding gift. I didn't argue, but I stood firm on tips to the staff. He acquiesced.

Unable to eat or drink further, Mary Anne declined the snifter of cognac our host insisted he and I enjoy for old time's sake. The sun had finally set when we left the bistro, already crowded with hungry patrons. We promised to return before we moved on to Spain.

Throughout our visit, Marry Anne sipped some wine but did not drink. "The next time we tour Europe, I won't be pregnant. I feel like I'm missing out."

"Wine is part of Latin culture. I promise we'll return when you can taste everything Europe offers."

"Good. I prefer the full immersive experience when I travel," she chuckled.

Along the way, a splash of rain blessed our stroll among the mix of old and new buildings, sidewalk cafés, and the throngs of people gathered on a Tuesday evening. The scent of fresh soil from small gardens lining our route, laced with rainwater, infused the chilly air. The bouquet of greenery suffused our lungs and lifted our spirits.

"I never realized how much I would miss Paris after so many years away," I said as we waited for the traffic light to change. "The art, the literature, the history, the incredible artists who found fame, and fortune, and often misery amidst its streets inspired me in a way no other place could. What city would anoint a baguette a fashion item as one strolled home, or a visit to a farmer's market as *de rigeur*, and where a glass of wine with meals was as natural as breathing?"

"It's beautiful. Thank you so much for bringing me. The only large city I've visited is New York, but Paris feels different. I don't know, more human, less impersonal."

"Whenever I flew over France, I loved seeing thousands of farms carving up the French countryside. France is a country of farmers who raised cuisine into an art form. Jean-Pierre embodies all of it for me."

"Jean-Pierre is a lovely person. Thank you for introducing us," Mary Anne said.

"I love that man. He and I clicked from the beginning. Our upbringing differed, but we shared some life-changing tragedies."

"He was in the Resistance?"

"Yes. It's a tragic story."

"Tell me."

"When the Nazis rolled into Paris in 1940, they arrested his Jewish wife and six-month-old. He never saw them again. Once he confirmed they were murdered, he joined the Resistance and fought in the shadows. He looks like a gentle old man now, but during the war he punished quite a few Nazis and their collaborators. After the war, he worked at various restaurants until he opened his place."

"How awful."

"Talking about his family brings tears to his eyes. The memories are still raw. On several occasions, we exchanged life stories over copious amounts of wine and cognac. He understood exactly what I went through with Maria's death."

Mary Anne pulled me tighter towards her. When I mentioned Maria, she knew my sadness resurfaced and became so palpable she could sense it as I reacted viscerally.

"When I lost my mother, I thought the world would end, that I would never be happy again. Dad's love pulled me through it. He used to hold my arm like I'm holding yours until the wave of pain and anxiety subsided. I'm with you, James."

We continued in silence until we reached the hotel and took the lift to our fifth-floor room, not much larger than a closet. I adored Paris, but I loved Mary Anne more and shook off the ghosts, plaintive and romanticized thoughts that deserved no footing in our honeymoon.

Mary Anne adored Spain and the Spanish people. The austere landscapes and aridity of Madrid reminded her of home. Years of high-school Spanish and practice speaking to Hispanic inmates proved helpful as she felt less linguistically isolated.

On our last day in Madrid, we took a cab to the Museo Reina Sophia to view Picasso's *Guernica* up close. When we entered the hall where the gray, black, and white masterpiece stood, we paused twenty feet away, awestruck at the magnificence of this moving anti-war painting. Photographs do not convey the size and scope: 11½ by 25½ feet, occupying the entire wall.

"The painting is breathtaking," Mary Anne gasped. "I had no idea how much more imposing and detailed it is in person."

"*Guernica* is truly an inspired work."

"I feel so small in front of it. The event it portrays must have been horrific. The suffering, violence, and chaos jump off the canvas and through my bones." Mary Anne shook slightly.

"Few paintings evoke such a visceral reaction."

"Even though it's cubist or surrealistic, the terror and nightmare of those awful days come through."

"You're quite the art history scholar," I said.

"Dad has tons of art books in his library. I used to pore over them with a magnifying glass. I love art."

"Good to know. Perhaps we could buy a few pieces for the house."

Mary Anne laughed, "There's a Klimt and a Jackson Pollock I'm fond of."

"Sure. Let's talk to Jerry. Maybe he's got a few million we can allocate to fine art to diversify our portfolio."

We spent only three days in Madrid because I wanted to return to Barcelona, where my great-grandfather had hailed from.

After landing at El Prat, the Barcelona Airport, we rented a Peugeot. Rather than drive to our hotel, we detoured along the coast from Mataró to Tarragona on one of those distinctly blue early October afternoons. We opened the sunroof of our rental, rolled down the windows, and let the Mediterranean saturate our skin and hair. The salty air reminded me of those carefree times in Del Mar.

As we toured the coastline, I reveled in the freedom and contentment of the sea and open road. I held Mary Anne's hand as we went sightseeing along the highway, the sun warming our faces. After so many years in the desert, I missed the openness of the Mediterranean Sea with its white crescent beaches and emerald-tinted coves, along with its history, unique cultures, and ancient shipping trade routes.

After checking into our hotel several blocks off the Passeig de Gràcia, we changed clothes and explored the town. We rambled up and down the avenues and wandered into the Barri Gòtic, or Gothic Quarter, where we enjoyed a late lunch at a sideway café.

"What is that language the waiter spoke?"

"Catalan. A romance language evolved from the Vulgar Latin of the Middle Ages; it's spoken everywhere in Catalonia. It sounds like a synthesis of Spanish and French."

"You speak it?"

"A little. I can read and understand quite a bit. Whenever I visited before, I watched several television broadcasts in Catalan. I owned a Catalan grammar book, now lost in all the moves."

The next day we escaped from the touristy Las Ramblas and Old Quarter and made our way to the Gràcia district. We strolled through Antoni Gaudi's famous gardens, shopped for souvenirs, and lunched at one of the many sidewalk bistros.

I found Barcelona, Paris, and Madrid to be quite livable cities, places where cars were unnecessary and every street offered something new. Mary Anne adapted to walking, buses, and cabs without much effort. We returned the car to a local rental return and relied on our legs and public transportation for the rest of the visit.

"Everything is so green here. Trees line every block. Unlike what I'm used to, flower boxes and patios adorn the buildings everywhere."

"In the desert, we forget what a little extra water can do," I said.

"I love this climate."

"I've been thinking. Would you be open to buying some land, some farmland perhaps, and living in a place with more than ten inches of rain annually?"

"In Europe?"

"No. The US. Why not in a rural area with a major city, say, an hour or two away? I imagine a farmhouse with a few acres to grow crops."

"Like corn or wheat," Mary Anne said in jest.

"No. More like Christmas trees or grapes."

"A Christmas tree farm? Hmmm. Table grapes?"

"Wine grapes. Let's sell them to the local wineries in exchange for cash or cases of the finished product."

"What about our jobs?"

"We don't need jobs, just money," I said, grinning.

"I like the idea. Let's add this to the list of things to consider for the future."

"Fair enough."

On the last day of our three-week honeymoon, we decided to take a taxi to the airport for one last ride through Barcelona before returning to the mundane world of jobs, commuting, and routine. And our babies had begun to show.

The trip was the first time Mary Anne and I had been truly alone, away from familiar places and the people we knew.

"Thank you for the whirlwind tour of your favorite European cities," she told me as we finished our continental breakfast before leaving for the airport. "I have never spent this much time away from home, with time to do whatever."

"It's a good feeling, isn't it? Some call it a *vacation*."

"Very funny. I've taken vacations, but not for 22 days in foreign countries. When I was fifteen, our family went to Puerta Vallarta for five days. Because of Dad's work, we never left town for more than a week."

"A two- or three-week jaunt worldwide wasn't unusual for me."

"You've been more relaxed and confident than I've ever seen you. Jet-setting suits you."

"I'd say the same about you. You're always glowing, but maybe because of our daughters. Traveling can be a real education, though living three years in the same place taught me a lot too."

"Do you ever think about Yard D?"

"Now and then, something reminds me of it. Whenever I see a quarter-mile oval track or a Motel 6, flashes of my time there stab me in the heart."

"Hmm. For you, that place is a memory best forgotten, yet I'm there five days a week. Honestly, the Yard hasn't been the same since you left. I used to look forward to getting to work because you were there."

"I suppose we helped make it a better experience for both of us."

"Yes. I always feel like I'm learning new things and growing around you."

"I love to share what I know and love with those around me, especially with you."

"Have I told you I love you today?"

"You just did."

While looking forward to home, we shared the perception that we had left some of ourselves behind. Paris, Madrid, and Barcelona meant something to us as a couple. Yes, we had our memories, but we glimpsed the world with fresh eyes. New insights and unconsidered possibilities informed our thinking in ways yet unclear as we boarded the flight home. Our trip changed us subtly but irrevocably.

CHAPTER 29

The twins were born in spring, fraternal girls christened Charlotte and Emily, old-fashioned first names Mary Anne and I favored because of our fondness for works by the Brontë sisters. Days shy of my fortieth birthday, I held them for the first time, convinced it was impossible to love anyone as much as I loved our daughters. The love of children and family Maria imparted to me finally took root.

Still flushed after giving birth, Mary Anne's joy filled the hospital room as we gathered around her, snapping photos and spoiling the new arrivals.

In a reflective moment, I promised myself I would never allow my children to grow up without a father who loved them unequivocally, nor subject them to the fear of abandonment or indifference. I didn't know if I would become a good parent, but I had plenty of worthy models. My mother, the Harrises, and the Compagnos had showed by example what love and devotion could achieve.

Mary Anne returned to administrative duties at the prison complex after her maternity leave. Excellent in her new role, she never rejoined her old duties on the yards. My relief was tangible that she avoided the hazards of dealing with the prison population directly in the housing units, where most of the danger lurked.

Because I believed in a balanced universe, opposite but interconnected forces visited my professional career. I'd never envisioned that medical financial analysis would be my dream job, and it wasn't, but my management and analytical skills did not go unnoticed.

My director, Lisa Pardonner, called me into her office late one Friday afternoon. She was a spry woman in her sixties, an avid physical fitness enthusiast who had worked for the company for over thirty years. Originally from Newport Beach, she had the aging surfer-girl look.

"Are you aware Eric will retire next month? Assuming you're interested, I want you to move into his position."

"Yes, I'm very interested. Thanks for considering me, Lisa." I had already assumed many of Eric's duties anyway.

"Excellent. I'll put through the promotion. You'll have to attend a three-day management training seminar for associate directors and undergo a routine background check. It's a new policy for director-level employees. Afterward, the position is yours."

Until she uttered the *background check*, I had not considered whether my felony status would impact my job.

"There's something I need to tell you first . . ." Lisa studied me over her reading glasses.

"Yes?"

"I have a felony conviction."

Without expressing surprise or judgment, she removed her glasses. "Did you disclose this on your original application?"

"I left the box unchecked." Lisa stared out the window at the Interstate traffic.

"May I know the nature of this conviction?"

While I explained the circumstances and the outcome, Lisa listened carefully and took some notes. At the end of my recitation, she said, "I must review this with HR, but I will do what I can to help you. We value your work here and don't want to lose you."

"I appreciate that and everything you have done for me. I love working here and hope to continue.

"I believe in second chances. In the years we've known each other, I've never had any reason to question your honesty and integrity." While Lisa's voice indicated support, I detected a "but."

"The final decision is HR's. I think I can sway them, though."

"Thank you. I should have come clean sooner, but I'm ashamed of what happened."

"Understood. I can't blame you there."

We finished our meeting by reviewing some outstanding issues related to our workload.

That weekend called to mind the Joint, where every hour ticked by in slow motion. Fortunately, the twins diverted my attention from my problems to their well-being. I volunteered to change their diapers, not because I relished the task, but because the fidgeting kept my mind off work and the possibility of losing my job.

Mary Anne said, "Don't stress over it. You've proven yourself, and Lisa will convince them." Lisa and Mary Anne had met at several Christmas parties and found each other amiable.

"I'm trying to let it go; accept the things I cannot change."

"My salary is enough to get us through while you search for a new job. We have savings, and Dad has lots of connections. He can help get you interviews. Besides, isn't that portfolio you guys have been building making some money?"

"Yes. The dividends alone are over half my salary."

"You see? We'll be fine."

"I'm sorry. I wish we could finally put the past behind us, but there's no real forgiveness. Perhaps I should sew a big letter F on my sleeve or tattoo a red F on my forehead."

"There's always self-employment," she suggested solemnly.

"What's that smell?"

"Diaper time. How those two girls synchronize their bowel moments is beyond me."

"That's twins for you."

No one phoned over the weekend. I expected a call terminating my employment, but the phone remained silent. I showed up Monday morning and worked through the day. My boss gave no signal one way or the other.

On Monday evening, I revamped my CV, just in case. Doing something helped me cope better than fretting. Mary Anne poured me a small tequila, and I climbed into bed with Malraux's *La Voix du Silence*, but I couldn't wrap my mind around reading.

On Tuesday, Lisa called me back to her office. She began her long preamble in a measured tone. I braced myself. "Human Resources informs me if you had checked the box, they would have most likely shelved your application. Because no one caught the oversight, the hiring went through. You were right to raise the issue now because HR would uncover the discrepancy this time. I have always found you to be forthright. Everyone here is more than satisfied with your performance. However, Resources recommended I let you go."

She paused for a moment as my body tensed.

"However, they left the decision to me. Because we do not handle cash or access monied accounts, I want to keep you on and proceed with the promotion. Congratulations." She smiled and reached over to shake my hand.

"I'm relieved. The last few days have been, let's say, unsettling."

"I can imagine."

I allowed myself to breathe again, thanked her, and returned to my office, freed from the potential shame and disgrace of being fired and ignominiously escorted from the building.

While the stigma of incarceration might remain forever, I had learned to live with it. I still couldn't vote or own a firearm. Mary Anne's garage held a gun safe for as long as I knew her. When I moved in, she relocated them to her dad's but decided to bring them back. I never learned the combination. We consulted an attorney, who told us we would be all right if I could not open the safe. She only retrieved the weapons to maintain her certification and concealed-carry permit.

I suppose shooting was fine, but I preferred horseback riding, a calmer pastime. Mary Anne and I rented horses during the cooler months and took long rides in the desert. When they were older, Charlotte and Emily accompanied us. The girls took to horses early and became accomplished equestriennes as teenagers. Of course, weekly riding lessons accelerated their skills.

When I saw them riding bareback one afternoon, memories of the Compagno ranch came flooding back. Amazonian young girls galloping out of the wilderness, their long hair flowing behind them; I imagined them armed with spears like Valkyries, ready to guide our spirits to Valhalla. Nature loved symmetry as I flashed back to Maria's and Laura's childhood.

In a city of slightly less than a million people, running into someone I knew, though not impossible, was unlikely. One Saturday morning, as I pushed my cart through AJ's, I stopped in the dairy section to carefully review the yogurts when a man stepped up next to me. I glanced over. Luis Vargas stood there, older and grayer than I remembered, dressed in an expensive autumn-weight leather jacket, slacks, and pricey shoes.

"Luis? *¿Eres tu?*"

He looked over at me. *"¿Jaime? ¿También estás aquí?"*

Luis shook my hand and gave me an *abrazo*, something he would never have done in the Joint.

"It has been too long, my friend."

"Yes. I've been out two years."

"You're looking prosperous," I said.

"Everything is going well. I didn't realize you shop here."

"Sure. We've shopped here for a while. I'm surprised to run into you."

"My doctor scolded me and said if I didn't eat better, my heart would not last, so my wife buys all her organic groceries here."

"Is she here with you? I would love to meet her." I recalled Mrs. Vargas from the prison visits, but we were never introduced.

"No. My Amalia's ill, so I volunteered to do the grocery shopping this week. Not something I'm comfortable with, but I'm trying to make life easier." He held a handwritten shopping list written in a woman's hand.

Luis and I agreed to grab a coffee at the Starbucks next door. We stashed the groceries in our cars. With two cappuccinos, we settled at a table in the back, where we could sit with our backs to the wall.

"How's life in the Big City?" I asked.

"Business is going well. I avoid day-to-day activities and let my crew handle things. I never thought it possible, but I'm thinking of semi-retiring. You know I have six grandchildren now."

"Glad to hear it. I have twin girls. I'm working for a healthcare company, in finance of all places."

"They let you near the money? *Carajo.*"

"Well, I only count money. I never touch any." We laughed.

"How's Consuelo?"

Vargas stared out the window into the parking lot and sighed.

"She's better now, but went through some rough times."

"I'm sorry."

"Yeah. Consuelo married a *tipo* from her American Express job about a year after you left the Yard. I told her not to involve herself with a *güero*, but she wouldn't listen."

"I'm a white guy."

"I know, but I think of you as one of us. I don't know how you manage, but sometimes your accent sounds more Mexican than ours."

"I had excellent teachers, plus lots of time in México."

"Anyway, they had a son, a fine little boy named Luis Antonio. He's four now." He paused as though trying to decide to keep going.

"Sounds wonderful. And the trouble is over now?"

Vargas scanned the café to ensure no one was in earshot and switched to Spanish: "Consuelo's *cabrón* husband embezzled some funds and implicated her in the crime as an accessory: lies, all of it. The FBI got involved. *¡Qué carajo!* They found out she was my cousin. Of course, I also received a courtesy visit from the local cops and the Feds. I had insulated myself better from day-to-day things, so they had nothing on me. Still, they wanted to charge Consuelo with embezzlement, a felony."

"My God. Consuelo is such an innocent. She must have been devastated."

"She was. The *pendejos* threatened to take Luis Antonio away and throw her and her *marido* in prison if she didn't cooperate."

"Snitch?"

"Yes. At first, Consuelo wouldn't talk: a real Vargas, that girl, but once her husband tried to make a deal for himself by sacrificing her and their son, she gave them what they needed to convict him in exchange for her freedom. She had to do it. He got a nickel in a federal joint near Santa Barbara called Lonpick."

"You mean Lompoc?"

"That's right."

"Where is Consuelo now?"

"She and little Luis live with her sister in Flagstaff, working for an auto dealership."

"Please tell Consuelo I think of her and hope she's doing better."

"I will. Consuelo will be happy to hear you are well too."

I showed him pictures of Mary Anne holding the twins.

"Your wife, I think I recognize her."

"Officer Evans from Santa Cruz."

"You married your CO? *¡Ay, caray!* You are full of surprises, *amigo*."

"Not my original plan, exactly. One thing led to another. You understand how things go. Plus, I never had to hide my sordid past with her."

"Yes, life happens in mysterious ways, often when we are busy doing other things."

"*Eso, sí, carnal.*"

We finished our coffee.

"Terrific to see you again, Luis, but I still owe you money for the lawyer."

"Forget about it. It was my gift to you and Consuelo. She cared for you. It tore her up to tell you she had found someone else. I'm sorry you two didn't work out, but I see you landed like a cat."

"Well, thank you. I'll always appreciate your assistance and Consuelo's."

We walked to our cars and shook hands, but neither volunteered to meet again.

"I love your Mercedes, Luis. Beautiful car."

"My wife's car. I drive a Ford pickup. More practical, less flash."

I told Mary Anne in the evening, "I ran into Luis Vargas at the grocery store."

"Inmate Vargas, from your unit, the barber?"

"The same one. We had coffee and talked for a half-hour or so."

"Jesus. I hope there was no surveillance. The Feds are all I need." Mary Anne rubbed her hands together.

"I didn't spot any suspicious cars or guys in the parking lot. You're over-reacting."

"This isn't funny. Law enforcement has been after him for years. Promise me you won't hang out with him again."

"Except for the off-chance of running into him and his wife at AJ's, we made no plans to connect."

"Good. The man is bad news. He's the local contractor for organized crime out of New York and New Jersey. The Feds tried to build a RICO case against him, but he's too careful."

"But Vargas isn't Italian."

"No, but since the Mob doesn't maintain a real presence in this city, they use him."

"You're just an assistant warden. How do you know about organized crime?"

"We get monthly briefings from the Feds about their people in the state system."

"Don't worry. I don't know any specifics about his business. I doubt I'll see him again."

"Please don't. People around him find themselves in legal jeopardy or worse."

Two years after my promotion, my boss, Lisa, announced her retirement, and who better to take her place? The workload didn't change, except I got a slightly bigger office and had to attend more meetings with the uppity-ups. I accepted my rise into upper-middle management with the equanimity of someone who had meditated daily for almost a decade.

"Congrats on the promotion, James. Good job," my co-workers said. I thanked them with subdued enthusiasm as though it were no big deal. The salary increase of twenty percent thrilled Mary Anne.

"Wow. In my entire life, I never believed we'd reach my dad's income level," she said once during supper.

"We're securely in a much higher income tax bracket, that's for sure."

"Dad's a wizard at tax planning. You two will figure something out."

Before I banked my first paycheck as Director of Medical Finance, I received a frantic phone call from my mother. Whenever she called me at the office instead of at home, I knew something serious was up.

"John's in the hospital. I took him there this morning."

"What happened?"

"His back. The pain hurt so bad that he couldn't leave the bed without help."

"He's complained of back pain for years. What is different now?"

"I'm not sure. The clinic is doing tests. I'll go back this afternoon and find out."

Although concerned, I didn't give the news much attention. I assumed my stepfather would receive cortisone and painkillers and be sent home.

The following day, I called, but no one answered. On my way to work, I started to worry.

Just before noon, my mother called.

"I think you should come home."

"You have bad news."

"John has stage four kidney cancer. The tumor has spread throughout his body."

My administrative assistant cleared my calendar for the rest of the week, and I flew to Ontario, twenty years since I had haunted the hospital after Maria's injury.

Dad had endured back pain without complaint but refused to visit a doctor. The oncologist, a young man fresh out of residency, verified that the cancer had metastasized.

While my mother sat with John in his hospital room, the doctor took me aside to explain the diagnosis.

"I've already discussed this with your parents, but the prognosis is *less than optimal*," which is med-speak for *terminal*. "Had he come in sooner, perhaps the outcome would have been better, but he waited too long, which limited his options."

"Is there any chance?" I asked.

"A small one. I'm recommending chemotherapy. Your folks agreed to proceed."

The treatment began, which only worsened his condition.

Mary Anne and I jetted out each weekend as John grew sicker and sicker, weakened by the chemo. All of his hair fell out, and he lost weight quickly.

At first, his spirits were high.

"I know it's a gamble, son, but I can beat this."

"We're with you all the way," Mary Anne said as she hugged him.

"And I'm glad you guys are visiting every weekend. Mama needs the support."

"Mary Anne and I are here for both of you, Dad."

He camped in the den in his favorite chair and stared at the TV, interrupted by periodic trips to the bathroom and the outpatient clinic. He ambled painfully around with a cane and a walker for support.

My dad's fight for life affected Mary Anne. This was the second time she stood by as a parent struggled with cancer.

"When my mom was sick, I had just turned seventeen. I rushed home from school every day to be with her. She suffered, but hid behind her optimism to cushion my brother and me. Dad knew the score and kept the charade going that she would recover."

We lay in bed. Mary Anne rested her head against my shoulder. "After caring for Mom, I went into my room and cried. This went on for five months."

"I wish you didn't have to relive the past."

"I'm glad to help you through this." I kissed Mary Anne on the head.

"Thank you, but let me know if it gets too much to bear," I said.

"We'll see it to the end as a family."

Throughout my stepfather's final journey, I relived those long, somber days while Maria languished. The memories became so oppressive I awoke from a nightmare and sobbed in the sanctuary of our bed just before dawn. It was Mary Anne's turn to hold me.

"Every day, I prayed for Maria to recover, to wake up, and smile at me, with that *coffee always tastes better when you make it* look."

"I know the feeling."

"For three months, I walked around like a zombie, going through the motions, never forgetting that Maria struggled for life, to return to the light, her family, Smokie, and me. And I could do nothing. It's that helplessness that I'm reliving now."

Mary Anne pulled me tighter toward her, and I hung on, knowing I would fall without hitting the bottom if she lost her grip.

"So many things unsaid. First Maria, then my real father, Bill Harris, and now John. So many memories that link us through time. The little things I remember, the small moments, a distinctive turn of phrase that stays with me through time and space. I miss all of them."

Knowing John had little time left, Mary Anne and I did what we could by making John as comfortable as possible. He struggled to keep food down. Mom maneuvered him into a weekly bath and sponged him down. About to turn 67, Mom was too frail to act as his nurse.

Dad's condition deteriorated beyond our ability to care for him. Circumstances forced Mom to call an ambulance one morning to return him to the hospital for one last examination, which resulted in his admission to a hospice.

Before the complete regimen of morphine began, I sat next to Dad as he lay dying. The room, small and spartan, reminded me of a cheap motel. The hospice itself occupied the corner of two busy streets. Constant traffic noise made rest impossible for someone without sedatives, and I hated the thought of Dad stupefied alone in that pitiful room.

Mom and I discussed John passing at home. I spoke to the hospice physician, who told me he needed too much support to die at home unless we hired a full-time nurse and the necessary medical support equipment. The doctor invited me into her office to explain.

"Please sit down, Mr. Montez. Your dad doesn't have much time. We can manage the pain, but he will pass in a week or two. I'm sorry."

"Thank you, doctor. I appreciate your candor." Her sober demeanor suggested these conversations exacted a cost. What drove people to face the reality of death every day and to work where patients died without hope of recovery?

"Doctor, how do you cope with . . . with everything?"

She looked at me, puzzled. "No one's ever asked me that."

"I don't mean to intrude."

"No, it's not that. But since you asked, I'll tell you. Most of my patients know their life is ending when they arrive here, and each, in their way, to whatever degree possible, accepts the end of life. I try to make the last days as comfortable as possible. What keeps me going, though, is my renewed faith in people."

She saw my mystified look. "I see the friends and family of my patients at their best. They put aside their differences and unite to support the people they love. Their effort and sacrifice to be with their loved ones at the end moves and inspires me."

The doctor's explanation gave me insight into a new dimension of compassion and empathy.

"Thank you, doctor. You've given me something to think about."

In his last lucid moments, Dad said, "I'm not going to make it, Jim. I know that. I'm too tired and want to sleep. Please take care of Mama when I'm gone."

"Don't worry. I will make sure she's all right." He closed his eyes for a moment. I continued: "I'm sorry this happened, Dad."

"When our time is finished . . . the important thing is to make the most of your life. Do what you want to do while you can, and say what you need to say."

I nodded.

"I have few regrets about my life. Only I wish I would have been a better father to you. If I had done more, perhaps you might have avoided those lost years and prison."

"You were the best, Dad. You were always around for us."

"I was never one to show my feelings, but that doesn't mean I didn't care about you and Mama."

"I know you do. I love you too, Dad."

He nodded and fell asleep, the intravenous morphine finally taking effect.

The next time I visited Dad, the continuous morphine drip had destroyed his mind. He didn't recognize his wife, who sat with him for hours, nor me. I spoke to the staff about the mustiness in his room, but they said they cleaned every day.

Then the call I dreaded came.

"Dad died in this sleep this afternoon. I went home around four to change and get a bite to eat. When I returned to the hospice at about seven, he was gone."

"I'll fly out tonight, Mom. There's a 10 o'clock flight."

"No hurry, Jim. Tomorrow is soon enough. We can make funeral arrangements when you arrive." Mom's voice, full of emotion, sounded steady and quiet, with a timbre of resignation after a long ordeal. Realizing that their struggle had ended had left her calmer than I expected.

I rang off. I closed my office door after asking my assistant to hold all calls and visits for an hour while I sobbed at my desk. I didn't cry for my father for ten years after his death, but for my stepfather, the grief overwhelmed me even though I'd had months to prepare.

Don't worry. He's here with me. I'll safeguard him.
Where is here? Where are you?
I'm where I've always been—inside you.

Mary Anne and I dropped the twins off with their grandfather and flew to LA for the funeral, a simple, closed-casket affair to allow one last goodbye before his cremation. Only the three of us attended. John never made friends; almost all of his Pennsylvania family had already died. The somber, final send-off underscored how alone he was except for Mom and me. I hope he carried our love as he transitioned to what came after.

We divided his ashes into two faux Roman urns, one of which sat on a shelf in my studio. I promised to scatter his remains to the winds but always managed to put it off, unwilling to let go of a physical reminder of him.

The loss of parents continued. Soon after John died, Paul's dad suffered a fatal stroke. His mom beseeched Paul to move her to a retirement community she and her late husband had picked out in Jupiter, Florida. Paul sold the homes in Diamond Bar and Del Mar and set his mom up for the rest of her life.

The following year, I sold my mother's house, and she moved to the same Jupiter community, which made for an ideal arrangement for Paul and me to rendezvous and visit our moms together. Since neither Paul nor I had siblings, our lifelong friendship comforted them. Paul and I were brothers in all the ways that matter.

Chapter 30

Months later, after the raw emotion of John's death subsided, I gained a clearer insight into my feelings about him.

One evening as Mary Anne and I sat on the patio enjoying some wine, I said, "I loved John; he was a real father to me; he defended and never scolded me for my harebrained actions as a kid or an adult."

"That's an accomplishment."

"Not once did he admonish me for my arrest or incarceration. He accepted and loved me like his own."

"Only a great man would marry a woman with a kid and recognize him like his son."

"Yes. Despite the rough spots in their marriage, Dad loved my mother and me. You know he tried to adopt me several times."

"Your biological father said no?"

"It's complicated. When my mom was pregnant with me, they weren't married. My real father wanted my mother to get an abortion, but she refused. My father's sisters shamed him into marrying my mother to give me a name and to accept his responsibilities, which eventually he did. Once he got to know me, he wouldn't give me up."

"I didn't know any of this," Mary Anne said.

"Neither did I. My mom told me after the funeral. Why she waited so long, I don't know. Perhaps we all need a little more truth in our old age."

I divided the rest of the wine between us.

"John provided an excellent model," Mary Anne said, "and you're doing an incredible job caring for the twins and me. You're worthy of the legacy he left you. It's why we love you and know you will always be here for us."

"Always."

I watched my daughters grow up, start school, and become young girls. Tall for their age, Charlotte favored me, while Emily resembled her mother. We did not expect fraternal twins to be much alike, but their distinct personalities shared similar traits. Both loved reading, writing, and talking. They seldom fought, shared their toys, and played together the way one hoped siblings would.

The twins' love of horses gave Mary Anne and me an idea for the perfect gift. We surprised them with two fillies for their twelve birthday, which they named Franny and Zooey from J.D. Salinger's novel. The need to board across town for $300 a month got us thinking of moving somewhere with enough room for our own stable.

The strangest thing was that I saw so much of Maria in Charlotte and Emily. Strong-willed and fiercely loyal to each other, their love of animals and their compassion for others reminded me that Maria would be proud of how Mary Anne and I raised our daughters.

What also struck me as odd was, after more than two decades, I still sought and valued Maria's approval as though she were still with us. While I no longer thought of her every day, on the anniversaries of her birth and death, I set aside time to reflect on her passing and let myself reexperience the loss that had acutely wounded me for so many years.

One afternoon, a massive headache struck me, and I went home early from work. Rummaging through my collection of albums by the Paul Stern Quartet, I found one of their earlier ones and set it to play as I lay on the couch with a damp rag over my eyes.

The third track was one of their most melancholy songs. I remember them rehearsing it for weeks in the Russell flat. Maria and I would lie in bed while Laura and Paul practiced in the living room.

"I love that piece, but it's so sad," Maria said. "Where did it come from?"

"Paul was poking around one afternoon and came up with the melody."

"Music that reaches inside and compels us to feel is always the best."

"Yes. I think it's inspired, melodic, haunting, and heartfelt."

"Paul and Laura have already been able to touch their core and express themselves in music. I remember when we were kids how Laura always played with a depth of feeling that made me cry."

Maria laid her head on my shoulder, snuggling close to me, while I wrapped my arm around her, protecting her. I sobbed as these memories came flooding back.

"Daddy! What's wrong? Why are you crying?" Charlotte and Emily burst into the room, back from their riding lessons.

"I'm all right. The music made me sad thinking about someone I knew who died."

"You mean Maria?" Emily asked as she and her sister dropped beside me on the sofa.

"You know about Maria?"

"Mommy told us your best friend died when you were young and that it hurt you."

"That was a long time ago, long before I met your mother."

"Can we see the picture again?"

"What picture?"

"The one mommy showed us of you and the girl in front of the fireplace," Charlotte said.

"You've seen it?" I went over the bookshelf, thumbed through my copy of Proust's great novel, and removed the photograph from where it marked the volume of *The Fugitive*. In this part, Albertine falls from her horse, and Proust begins a hundred-page meditation on the metaphysics of grief.

Taking my place between the twins, we examined the picture together.

"You look so young, Daddy. I don't like the beard too much." Charlotte stated.

"Neither did I. I shaved it not long after my friend Lila took this photo."

"Maria is so pretty."

"Yes. Everyone thought so. Inside was where Maria's true beauty lay. She was full of love and kindness. She loved animals. Did you know she taught me how to ride horses?"

"She did? That's cool, Dad," Emily declared. "She did a good job."

"Yes, she did. Most of the things I know that are good came from her."

We heard the door to the garage open, and Mary Anne entered the living room to find us sitting together.

"Is this daughter-father bonding time, or can anyone join in?"

We made room for Mary Anne to sit with us.

Charlotte and Emily loved Aunt Laura and Uncle Paul, particularly their son, Paul Jr., who, although quite a bit older, did not demonstrate the same enthusiasm for them as they did for him. Paul and Laura's younger children, James and Maria, were similar ages. I loved to watch them play together and swim in Jerry Evans's massive pool on the infrequent occasions when the Paul Stern Quartet took time off to decompress and enjoy a few weeks of vacation. Although we did not spend as much time with the Sterns as I'd have preferred, the bond we'd forged long ago grew stronger as the years rolled on.

"How long will you guys be around before the next tour?" I asked the couple as we sipped beers on the patio by the pool, watching our children swim.

They looked at each other, deciding who should break the news.

Laura spoke first, "Throughout the years, we made several close friendships with some Nashville musicians. Have you been there?"

"No, but I hear it's beautiful."

"Well, Paul and I fell in love with Tennessee. Nashville is a medium-sized town that offers something for everyone, especially plenty of music venues. I love all the green hills covered with trees and the small farms and ranches. We also find Southern manners and camaraderie refreshing. After the rudeness of the East and West Coast, finding polite and hospitable people is fantastic"

Paul jumped in, "We decided to buy a farmhouse on 22 acres in an artists' community called Leiper's Fork, about 30 miles southwest of Nashville."

"We're not exactly breaking up the Quartet, but we're scaling back big time," Laura continued. "All of us are tired of touring. Though not as preeminent as country and rock, jazz has a devout and growing following in Nashville that we'd like to be a part of."

"The best part," Paul interrupted, "is we can sleep in our own bed after a gig."

"I didn't realize that," I said. " Nashville isn't called Music City for nothing,"

"There's even more good news," Paul added. "Will and Manny also bought some nice spreads nearby. Before he found a place, Will half-joked about wide lawns and narrow minds. Now, he's got one of those gigantic front yards, and his mind is expanding."

Laura said, "The people are practical and filled with common sense, something hard to find in New York, LA, or San Francisco."

"Common sense ain't so common," I said, paraphrasing Mark Twain.

"We're moving next month," Paul said. "Our booking agent already has some local gigs lined up. It's great having everyone in the same vicinity. Only one more piece we need to put in place, and we're set."

"What's that?"

"If you and Mary Anne moved to Tennessee too."

I laughed. "Now you're talking," I called out to Mary Anne, preparing lunch in the kitchen. "Hey, Mary Anne, you wanna buy a little farm and move to Nashville?"

"Let's visit first," she yelled back, apparently not opposed to the idea.

And that's precisely what we did. After the Sterns settled into their new digs, we borrowed Jerry Evans's seldom-driven Mercedes, loaded up the kids, and made a road trip east on I-40, 1,700 miles door to door.

After fifty trips or so trips between LA and the Bay Area, parts of Texas and Oklahoma reminded me of the countless drives up and down California as the nostalgic Interstate cut through the endless and monotonous miles of farmland and rolling hills.

With the three people I loved the most in the car, I ruminated on the people and events that had shaped me as the eastward miles counted down. Somehow, I survived over a decade of drugs and alcohol. So many lost opportunities, followed by years of prison before I woke up and focused on what was essential, not myself but the people around me who chose to share a common path and explore a future filled with what was important: love, family, and duty, old-fashioned ideas of diminished cachet in this modern era, but still valuable, carrying more significance now than ever.

Whatever came on the market in Leiper's Fork sold almost immediately, but the Stern's realtor had a beautiful property she was about to list in our price range. The sellers agreed to let us take a look-see, pre-listing.

A mile beyond the historic downtown, through a small valley, on a winding country road, we drove up on a two-story, custom-built home, barely visible from the road and immaculately landscaped. Nestled below a hillock among mature oak, sycamore, and magnolia trees, the property stretched eighteen acres, bordered by a lazy creek that fed the Harpeth River.

We pulled into a long driveway and parked in front of the four-car garage.

"I love it," Mary Anne gasped as we entered the grand foyer. Charlotte and Emily ran upstairs to select their bedrooms.

The well-appointed home had everything we might ever want: a sizable kitchen built for cooking and entertainment, a great room, separate living and dining rooms, a library, four bedrooms, four baths, and a stable large enough for four horses.

"Isn't it more house than we need?" I asked facetiously.

"Probably, but it's so inexpensive, considering. There's enough room for entertaining and for house guests."

"This property won't stay on the market long," the realtor added as she let us talk ourselves into buying it.

We opened the French doors from the kitchen and stepped out on an enormous covered patio with a built-in barbeque and outdoor kitchen and a large firepit to fit ten people around it.

"And what about our jobs? A little too far to commute. Are you ready to retire and renounce successful careers?" I asked.

"I've got over twenty-five years in at the state. There are plenty of people itching to move into my position. Are you willing to give it all up to live in the boondocks?"

"As long as we get the internet, I can manage our portfolios."

Some squirrels chased each other through the trees at the edge of the manicured backyard. Since it was late summer, some leaves had already changed colors.

We lowered ourselves into two cushioned chairs near the fire pit and scanned the woods at the edge of the lawn.

"Do you hear that, Mary Anne?"

"Hear what?"

"Listen."

"I don't hear anything," she said.

"Exactly. No street noise, no sirens, no city at all. And yes, I was ready to retire five years ago."

"With my pension and the income from all the investments you and Dad have made, I think we could swing it."

Before we submitted the offer, Mary Anne and I hashed through the pros and cons of buying a property that meant leaving our jobs.

"Are you ready to be put out to pasture, so to speak? We're only fifty-ish. Isn't that too young to retire?" Mary Anne said.

"Think of it as changing professions."

"And what are you changing into?"

"I decided to write novels. Without the 9-to-5 every day, I'll have plenty of time to destress and write."

"All right, but what am I going to do?" she asked.

"Whatever you what. What would you do if you could do anything, and money was no barrier?"

Mary Anne thought for a moment. "Remember when we were in Spain, and we talked about having a small farm, growing Christmas trees or grapes?"

"You still remember that?"

"Sure, I do. I did some research. We're buying eighteen acres. If we allocated three acres, we could plant about 300 trees. That's enough to satisfy the local market. If things really took off, we could expand."

"Sounds like an idea worth pursuing. There—you just found your next career."

"Oh, I'm not done. There are four shooting ranges within spitting distance of Leiper's Fork. I could become an instructor and teach firearm usage and safety."

"Really? So, what's the problem?"

"I don't know. Let's make the deal."

The realtor wrote up our asking-price offer and submitted it. The sellers accepted. Because we paid cash, we closed in nineteen days.

We submitted our resignations, endured the retirement parties, and gave up our steady jobs in the big city without remorse.

Saying goodbye to Phoenix didn't bother me, but Mary Anne wavered when the time to move arrived.

"I've lived my whole life here. Everyone I know lives no more than twenty minutes away."

"We have a huge house. It's only a three-hour plane ride. Everyone can visit us, and we can come back anytime."

"I know. Just cold feet. The fear of the unknown and all that." Mary Anne uncrossed her arms as I hugged her.

"Come on. We got a bunch of packing to do before the movers show up tomorrow."

After some tearful goodbyes, we transitioned to our new life as young retirees in a greener and more luxurious place than we ever imagined.

In no hurry to part with our two-bedroom house, we converted the property into a rental, earning us $800 monthly after expenses.

In late October, Laura and Mary Anne organized a housewarming party. The forecast called for blue skies, warm days, and cool nights. We invited our new neighbors, and the Sterns asked their musician friends to join us.

Tennesseans were a friendly bunch. Never great with names, I only remembered a few people who stuck around after the majority went home.

Forty people showed up, many of whom brought potluck since we would otherwise have run out of food and drink. We spread the meal over picnic tables on the patio, from salads and casseroles to hot dogs, hamburgers, steaks, and Nashville hot chicken, a fried chicken marinated in cayenne pepper. Only the Nashvillians and Mary Anne thought it could have been spicier.

"Man, this chicken is super spicy. How do you guys eat this?" I asked after biting into a piece that seared my mouth.

"Don't worry, James. I put some toilet paper in the freezer for tomorrow, just in case," Mary Anne said with a straight face.

Charlotte and Emily wrangled all the children and led them on safari, armed with cameras, to a spot at the edge of the property near the creek where wild turkeys congregated.

After everyone ate their fill and Paul tapped the second keg of beer, the Quartet played a set of some upbeat tunes from their latest album. After many years, Paul revisited his twelve-bar blues days, much to the satisfaction of our audience.

Once the wild applause tapered off, Paul called out from behind his electric piano, "Leon, Rob, Miranda, come on up."

Leon sported long white hair and a beard and was an established musician known for rock, country, and R&B.

Miranda was in her early twenties, blonde and pretty in a girl-next-door kind of way, and already showing promise as a vocalist and guitarist. Her demos had created some buzz. Paul expected her to break out soon.

 Rob was a rocker from the Midwest who loved the Nashville music scene and already had several albums to his name.

"Can we bring a few friends?" Leon asked.

"Absolutely. Hey everyone. If you wanna jam, get up here."

Several ran back to their vehicles to retrieve an array of guitars, fiddles, tambourines, and hand drums. One guy brought some bongos, and another an alto sax.

After an extended tuning session and a hushed discussion of keys and tempos, the entourage broke into improvised country music for over an hour. Everyone took their turn playing a solo. Participants offered variations that often steered the melodies in surprising new directions. The musicians found their Swing.

The audience clapped and stomped their feet. Beaming smiles lit up the woods. The music was loud, but nobody complained since we'd invited all the neighbors.

One of our guests had set up a recorder to capture the jam, which Leon's record label released six months later, with all the proceeds going to local charities.

Several hours passed. After the sun had dipped below the tree line, the few of us still left gathered around the firepit drinking Tennessee bourbon, something Leon swore by called *Heaven's Door*. Yesterday, Paul and I bought four bottles at Frugal MacDoogal. And Leon was right. The first wee dram opened in the nose with a mix of overripe pear, wintry spices, toffee, vanilla, and woody maple syrup. Delicious.

Once we settled in and the crooning over *Heaven's Door* subsided, I told Paul and Laura, "That was something. You guys have really branched out musically."

"That jam was a blast. We didn't know what we were missing all these years," Paul said.

"When in Rome," Laura added.

"The best part," Paul continued," is that some of our friends are coming around. I think jazz will be huge in Nashville someday. I'm working on ways to countrify it a bit. You heard some of it today."

"That was some tight jam," Leon said as he sipped his drink and let the amber liquor roll around his mouth. He turned to me. "You and Paul went to high school together? That's far out."

"That's right. We were roommates in college too. Laura, Paul, and I lived in Berkeley for almost four years. Seems like a lifetime ago."

"Y'all were tight, sounds like."

"Laura and Paul are my closest friends; I love them like family. They are my family, not by blood, but by choice."

Paul grabbed Laura's hand; both beamed love my way.

"It's cool having people you came up with still around after so many years and all that life brings," Leon mused. "I got a few like that."

Laura said, "We made each other a promise to stay in touch no matter what. Even though there were periods we didn't see each other, whenever we reunited, it was like no time had passed."

"Y'all must have seen some changes in the music since y'all came up," Miranda said.

Laura poured the last of the bourbon into her glass. "We loved rock, jazz, and classical and found ways to combine them."

"Paul was always a child prodigy in my book. He just kept getting better, especially after he met Laura," I said.

"Couldn't have done it without her." Paul put his arm around her.

"The Paul Stern Quartet made some breakthroughs in music," I continued. "Jazz-rock-classical fusion wasn't a thing back in the day, but lots of bands after made it mainstream."

"We used to host parties in college where we tried out all of the new stuff to see what people liked," Paul said.

Paul, Laura, and I looked at each other, reflecting on the girl we loved.

Mary Anne, Will, and Manny joined us, bringing an unopened bottle of bourbon. Manny refreshed everyone's drinks.

Mary Anne settled beside me. "What did we miss?"

"We've been reminiscing about the days of our frivolous youth," I replied. "And the importance of friendship and family."

"Let's drink to that," Leon and Miranda touched glasses.

Laura proposed a toast, "To good friends and family here and beyond. And to you, Maria, who brought us together."

"Amen."

ABOUT THE AUTHOR

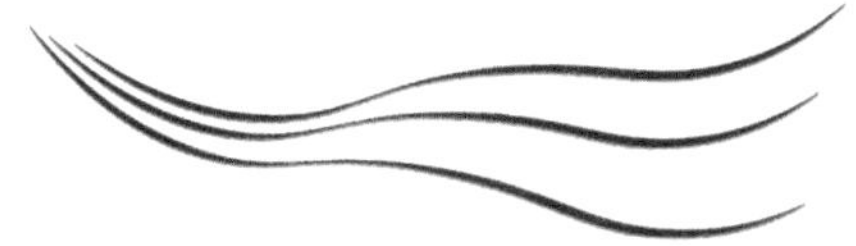

Jaime Gràcia grew up in Southern California and received degrees in biochemistry, comparative literature, and business administration from UC Berkeley. He splits his time between Nashville, Tennessee and Geneva, Switzerland, far from any deserts.